HOW
TO
DANCE

HOW
TO
DANCE

HOW
TO
DANCE

A Novel

JASON B. DUTTON

alcove
press

Copyright © 2024 by Jason B. Dutton

All rights reserved.

Published in the United States by Alcove Press, an imprint of The Quick Brown Fox & Company LLC.

Alcove Press and its logo are trademarks of The Quick Brown Fox & Company LLC.

Library of Congress Catalog-in-Publication data available upon request.

ISBN (paperback): 978-1-63910-637-0
ISBN (ebook): 978-1-63910-638-7

Cover design by Ana Hard

Printed in the United States.

www.alcovepress.com

Alcove Press
34 West 27th St., 10th Floor
New York, NY 10001

First Edition: February 2024

10 9 8 7 6 5 4 3 2 1

To Mom, Dad, and Uncle Philip.
You always knew I would dance.

1

It had taken Nick Freeman all of two seconds to decide to play the victim of a tragic garbage truck accident, so he wasn't surprised the woman sitting across from him was having trouble buying it.

"A garbage truck." She repeated it back to him slowly, watching his face as she poked at the ice in her drink with a swizzle stick.

"Yep," he said. "A big one."

Her eyes narrowed a bit. "So, like, what happened?"

He thought about it as he took a sip of his beer. Hopefully she would assume he was hesitating because of some traumatic memory. It was too boring to say the truck had simply hit him. A routine pickup could've gone bad, a trash can could've gone flying . . .

"I had to save some kids," he decided. "They'd climbed into the compactor."

She winced. "Sorry."

"Not your fault."

Not anyone's fault, in fact, and not one of the better tales he'd spun in this bar, but he knew she wouldn't call bullshit. He did have to give her points for being direct, though. Most people weren't brave enough to ask about his legs.

Her name was Kacey, with a K, and she'd introduced herself that way, as if that first letter was a source of pride. Tight jeans on this hot and humid May night in Columbus, Ohio, meant she cared more about looking good than feeling good, and she looked good enough for Nick to give her his full attention when she'd complimented his karaoke performance minutes ago.

After they'd settled into their seats, Kacey had watched closely as their server, Alexa, expertly lifted Nick's four-wheeled metal walker and placed it behind their booth, where it wouldn't impede Friday-night foot traffic.

Kacey had looked at the walker, looked back at him, and said, "So what's with the, um . . ."

"Walker," he'd said, cutting her off before she could say *stroller* or *buggy*. Then, after two seconds of deliberation: "There was an accident with a garbage truck."

And so here they were, very much not talking about his cerebral palsy.

"If it makes you feel any better," he said, "the rest of me works just fine."

She giggled, looking him up and down. "All of you?"

"Yep."

It had been fun once upon a time, this habit of finding exciting reasons to be crippled, but he couldn't remember the fun tonight. Tonight just felt like heavy lifting, like he had to physically exert himself to shift her focus from his damaged muscles to the ones that worked. It would get better from here, now that the walker had been dealt with.

Kacey glanced at the cocktail napkin on which her glass had been placed. "What is that?" she asked. "A dog?"

Nick rested his hand on her arm as he leaned forward to look at the napkin's logo. "That'd be a lion."

"Oh!" She rolled her eyes. "Should've figured."

"Nah, it does kind of look like a dog." Except they were sitting in a bar called the Squeaky Lion, and the dog had a mane, and yes, she should have figured. "The bar owner's dog has a favorite chew toy," he explained. "A squeaky lion."

Kacey grinned. "Look at you, Mr. Expert."

He smiled back, keeping his eyes on hers. "I know about all sorts of things."

As it happened, he actually was an expert when it came to this bar. After attending every karaoke Friday for the last three years, Nick knew that the owner's dog was named Scotty, and their server's stylishly spiked hair was cut by her sister, and the bar food was better earlier in the evening because the kitchen cared less the later it got. He doubted Kacey would find any of this impressive.

She was keeping his gaze, which was good, and she was letting him keep his hand on her arm, which was better. If he had a shot with her tonight, their words and glances and pauses would have to build on each other until leaving the bar together felt natural. He'd rely on his smile until he thought of the next subtle indication to Kacey with a K that going to bed with a cripple (with a C) would be worth her while.

"Kev, we've gotta dance!" A woman's voice shattered the moment, startling him.

At the sudden interruption, Nick's hand involuntarily left Kacey's arm and swept the table, knocking over his beer. The bottle was empty, but he still felt broken every time he reacted to an unexpected noise as if he'd been jolted with a cattle prod.

"Come *on*, Kevin," the woman pleaded playfully. "Please?"

Nick tried to smile an apology to Kacey as he righted his bottle, but Kacey wasn't looking at him anymore. Nick followed

3

her gaze, and then he couldn't look away. A guy and a woman in their twenties were dancing together a few feet in front of him.

It was a swing dance, and these two had to be professionals. They were moving with the sort of control Nick could only dream of, navigating the space around each other so well that each leap, each spin, each step to the right or the left became another word in the story they were telling. The guy was into it, acting and reacting, advancing and responding, but the woman— Nick kept glancing at her feet to make sure she hadn't left the ground. Her olive skin was glowing, her mouth was open in a delighted laugh, and her eyes were shining as she watched her partner. Nick wasn't sure he'd ever felt the kind of joy that was radiating from her as she danced.

A few onlookers were impressed enough to applaud when the song ended, and Nick found himself clapping too, wishing he had a better response to give. The woman's eyes caught Nick's as she brushed back the dark hair that had fallen in her face, and she grinned. Nick felt as if the sun had come out.

"Wow," Kacey said. Nick remained frozen in place, watching the dancers get in line at the bar. He vaguely realized Kacey was speaking to him, but couldn't bring himself to care about what she was saying. "Does that happen a lot?" she asked him. "I mean, I know this isn't one of those dancing restaurants, but do they get a lot of dancers in here?"

Nick looked at her distractedly. "Dancing restaurants?"

"Yeah, you know, like those diners where the servers have dance breaks."

"Oh." He glanced back at the dancers. "No. I've never seen her before."

"But other dancers, though?"

Nick almost started laughing. No, people didn't usually dance in the middle of the Squeaky Lion, and certainly never like that, and what the hell did it matter? He was sitting amid a noisy, sweaty swamp of people, trying to seduce someone a decade younger than he was so he could forget he was defective. Even if Kacey went home with him, he knew he'd be lucky to feel even a twinge of what had been shining in that dancing woman's eyes.

"Do you want to get out of here?" he asked.

Kacey paused with her glass in hand and swallowed. "What?"

"We could get in my car and leave. Right now."

Kacey's eyes were scanning the tabletop, like he had switched scripts on her and she was searching for the new one. "Can you drive a car?"

Nick sighed. "We could talk about the napkins, and we could talk about dancing restaurants, and you could spend the next hour figuring out if I'm worth it. Or you can leave with me right now, and we can go back to my place."

He saw the answer in her eyes as clearly as if a switch had been flipped. She couldn't figure out how to run away and be nice to him at the same time.

"Um." She reached for her purse. "I've got to use the bathroom."

He laughed. "Should I pretend you're coming back?"

"No." Kacey with a K disappeared into the crowd as quickly as possible.

Nick put his head in his hand, massaging his temples with his fingers. One woman didn't have to ruin the night. He could get a beer. He could sing more karaoke. He could step outside and slam his head into the brick wall.

Someone dropped into the seat across from him; he glanced up, then stared. The dancer had joined him, and her boyfriend was nowhere to be seen.

"Why'd you do that?" she asked cheerfully.

Nick squinted at her. "What?"

She took a sip of something purple out of a glass. "Why'd you do that?" she repeated. "You could've just left that girl alone."

Nick rubbed his eyes. Apparently he was an asshole for giving Kacey an ultimatum, which he'd only done because *this* woman had made his calculated flirting seem like a waste of time. Beautiful.

"Do you know her?" he tried.

"No."

"So don't worry about it."

She shook her head impatiently, her glossy brown hair sliding across her shoulders. "I mean why'd you sit down with her when you obviously didn't want to?"

"Of course I did."

She sat back and watched him, a smile playing at the corners of pink-lipsticked lips. "You're clearly miserable," she said. "What're you doing here?"

He was here to show off his singing skills. He was here to charm the regulars and maybe take a pretty woman home. He was here because he liked it here, goddamn it, and that certainly wasn't going to be ruined by some random, exuberant woman in a gray tank top and cutoff jean shorts just because she didn't have anyone else to talk to. Especially when she was the reason he felt miserable in the first place.

Except none of those thoughts made it into words. He sat in silence, locked on to her chocolate-brown eyes.

"Nick!" He heard his name called from the crowd by the bar. "You've got to help us."

Nick flashed a wide, automatic smile at the couple walking up to the booth. "Rory!" he exclaimed. "Max! You know I live to serve."

"Okay." Rory, who had gotten his attention, obviously had a story she very much wanted to tell—until she got a proper look at who was sitting across from Nick. "You were incredible," she told the dancer. "Who are you?"

The dancer laughed. "I'm Hayley."

Rory introduced herself and her boyfriend. "Do you do that for a living?" she asked. "Can we come see you somewhere?"

"I'm kind of in between jobs," Hayley told her. "But you might want to check out Vivez Dance soon."

"Oh, we will." Rory glanced at Nick. "Can we borrow him?"

Hayley waved a hand. "Of course."

"So, Nick." Rory had fully locked on to him now. "Max and I were flipping channels the other night—"

"It was Sunday," Max explained. "Free preview weekend."

"And we caught the end of this movie. Near the end, anyway, because there was this big kiss scene on a roof."

"It was Liv Tyler and this guy."

"We weren't really watching because Bowie was in a bad mood."

"He shoved his favorite toy under the fridge, and I wasn't going to go get it."

Nick was trying to look back and forth between Max and Rory in a way that conveyed his deep and undivided interest as their tag-team story unfolded. This would normally be second nature, but he could feel Hayley watching him, and it was throwing him off his stride.

"But just as they kissed," Rory was saying, "this song came on."

"Kind of sounded familiar, but not." Max's contribution was earnest and pointless. "But really good," he added. "Older, I think."

"And we thought if anybody knew the name of the song, it'd be you." Rory waited. "Do you?"

"Hmm," said Nick. He pretended to think as he reviewed questions of his own. Cable TV had a channel guide that would have told them the name of the movie, didn't it? If not that, couldn't they have waited and seen what songs were listed in the closing credits? Even Google would have been a better option

7

than some guy at the bar . . . but finding the song wasn't the point, he realized. Rory and Max wanted to see if he knew the song. Nick would have been flattered if he weren't busy wishing Hayley would leave.

"The movie is *Empire Records*," he said finally. "The song is 'Til I Hear It From You,' by the Gin Blossoms."

"Wow," Max said. "That's amazing."

Nick tipped an imaginary cap. "You flatter me, my friend."

"So you know the song, then," Rory said. "Well enough to sing."

Nick grinned. "Go put in the song slip for me."

"You're the best, Nick!" Rory looked excited enough to start jumping up and down.

"You know I can't compare with you, Rory." Nick kept his tone good-natured and his smile gracious. "Tell Bowie to behave himself, okay?"

Nick dropped his grin to glare at Hayley as soon as Max and Rory were a safe distance away. He couldn't tell if she was shocked or impressed.

"What?" he asked her. "What is it now?"

"That was amazing," she said. "Turning it on and off like that. I work on stage, and I'm not sure I've seen anyone that good."

"I like them," he said. "I don't like you."

"Sure you do." She picked up a cocktail napkin, tracing lines into that damn lion with her fingernail. "So. Your name is Nick, and you sing."

"Yes."

"Professionally?"

"No."

I could get up and leave, he thought. The walker was behind Hayley's side of the booth, which meant he'd have to carefully navigate his way past her to get to it, using the booth and the table as questionable handholds along the way. But he wasn't going to let Hayley see that process. He wasn't going to let her help him with it. And he sure as hell wasn't going to risk falling into her.

"And you know a lot about music," Hayley continued. "Or maybe Liv Tyler."

"Both," he said. "Where's your boyfriend?"

Hayley glanced over her shoulder. "Still out smoking, looks like." She laughed. "He told me he had to take a call. We play this game where we pretend he actually quit when I told him to."

Hilarious. "So what's he going to think when he comes back from his secret smoke to find you talking to me?"

"He'll be fine."

"I don't want to start a fight."

Her amused smile said a fight was unlikely. "He won't hurt you or anything."

"No," Nick said wearily. "I don't want you and your boyfriend to fight because you got drunk and thought you'd teach him a lesson."

"I am *tipsy*," she said triumphantly. "Drunk is a few drinks away. And I'm teaching *you* a lesson. You liked our dance."

"I . . ." He was embarrassed. "I was watching. Everybody was watching."

Hayley shook her head. "It didn't speak to everybody. It spoke to you." She watched him patiently.

"You're right," he said finally.

They sat with that for a while.

"You know how the universe comes together?" Hayley asked.

Nick considered this. "Not sure I do."

"Like, there are good times, right? And there are bad times, and there are times when the universe *comes together*. Like everything up until now has just been puzzle pieces creeping closer and closer, and then everything fits."

"And you're having one of those moments."

"Yes!" She leaned forward so fast she sloshed her drink. "Things were bad. Like, really bad. And now here we are, dancing in a bar in Ohio, and the universe fits, finally. And when I get to be this happy, I've gotta help other people get there, too."

Nick's neck tingled with approaching dread. "Hayley, I'm not the sort of—"

"I saw it on your face," she pressed on. "Your heart was there in your eyes, and then you turned back to that poor girl, and you just shut down. You're looking for your joy in the wrong place."

"Okay," he allowed. "Kacey wasn't a good idea. But I don't—"

"You should dance!" she blurted.

Nick felt sick. "Dance."

"I know you've got the whole macho thing of not wanting to look like an idiot." She took a quick sip of her drink and barely swallowed before she went on. "But you saw Kevin! There's nothing sexier than when my man gets on the floor."

"I'm sure," he said weakly.

"And this place where we'll be working—I don't know if they give lessons or not, but I'll check. I'll teach you, even. You've got to get up and move, Nick."

"No."

"Nick." He looked up from his bottle to see her staring at him intently. "Too many people sit in chairs their whole life," she said. "Because they're scared, or they're lazy, or they're comfortable, or whatever."

"Hayley . . ."

"And just think about the people who don't have the chance!" She gestured toward their laps with a sweep of her hand. "At least we *have* our legs, you know? At least we can move." She sighed. "God, I don't know what I'd do if I couldn't dance."

"Stop."

She looked at him in surprise. Nick's voice was low, but the one word had a dangerous edge to it.

"I know you think you can help me," he said. "But this happiness you have, it's not . . ." He gave a smile that looked more like a grimace, like his clenched jaw was barely keeping something contained within him. "It's one of many things that aren't accessible to me. Your universe fits because of those eyes of yours. Because you have Kevin. Because you can move like gravity's just an option for you. And trust me, you'd be better off getting the hell out of this booth and holding on to those things as hard as you can. Because your universe is only going to stay together until one of those pieces gets taken away from you."

He had expected to shock her, but Hayley didn't seem upset or even all that surprised. She leaned back in the booth, crossed her arms, and narrowed her eyes, peering at him as if she were about to take another crack at repairing a watch with broken gears.

He felt a hand on his shoulder. "You're up next," Alexa said.

Hayley seized the moment. "Tell Nick he should dance."

Oh, God, he thought. *She's doubling down.*

Alexa looked from Hayley to Nick. "If she's asking," she told Nick, "something tells me you'd find some moves in you."

Hayley pointed at him. "See?"

He sighed. "Could you just . . ."

"Yep." Alexa reached behind their booth and placed Nick's walker squarely in front of him. As he climbed out of the booth and into the three-sided square, Nick chanced a glance at Hayley. The wide, expressive eyes that had so readily shown him joy and passion now held confusion, surprise, uncertainty bordering on panic.

Nick gave a tight smile and winked at her. "Sorry to disappoint," he said.

2

"So," Linda Brandazzio said. "Why do you belong at Vivez Dance?"

"Dancing is all I've ever wanted to do," Hayley Burke replied.

Linda nodded from a red armchair, one leg crossed over the other, her foot absently tapping in the air as she glanced at a clipboard. Hayley sat in a matching chair across from her. She decided she liked the armchairs. The office wasn't large, and Linda would easily have more space if she sat behind her desk and forced her guests into folding chairs or made them stand. The armchairs said Linda Brandazzio cared about the comfort of the people around her.

Linda looked up from her notes and gave Hayley an easy smile. "Tell me about dancing."

Hayley thought back to her time at the Icarus Showcase. "Well," she said, "at Icarus we were doing at least four shows a week . . ."

She trailed off when Linda shook her head. "Not the nuts and bolts. Tell me about your love affair with dancing."

Hayley brightened. "I feel . . . *connected* when I dance," she said. "With the audience, with a partner, with myself. There's always some sort of connection in the movement."

Suddenly, that guy was in her head, the guy from the bar the night before. Nick. He'd connected with her when she hadn't even known he was watching. Then again after, when their eyes had met, his a pale, electric blue, flashing with recognition, with sadness. *"This happiness you have . . . it's one of many things that aren't accessible to me."*

She got the joke now. Accessible. So many things he couldn't do, and she had . . . God, what had she even said to him?

Nice going, Hayley Michelle. Get a few drinks in you, and you think you can change the world.

But his eyes . . . there had been something else there, along-side the sadness.

"A dancer can get pretty far on technical ability," Linda was saying. "But everyone I've ever seen light up a stage has one thing in common."

Hayley realized it was her turn. "They were connecting?"

"They all saw dance as *giving* something." Linda stressed the verb. "It's a two-way street, of course. The audience feeds you too. But the divas, the ones who need the spotlight or need to be great, they never have the luminescence of the dancers who can't wait to *give* of themselves."

"You've felt that way." Hayley could hear it in the other woman's voice. "Like you had to move, or something inside of you wouldn't be able to get out."

Linda nodded, chuckling. "My hubby would tell you I dance like others howl at the moon."

"I like that." Hayley said, and she did, very much so.

You can move like gravity's just an option for you.

What had Nick seen when he'd watched her? How had he felt?

"You didn't go to school for dance?" Linda asked.

Focus, girl. "I've been taking lessons since I was three," she said.

"But your degree is in early childhood education."

Hayley shrugged. "My mom is a professor, so tuition was free."

"So you could have ended up teaching kids somewhere."

"I could've, yeah."

Linda leaned back in her chair. "I couldn't do it," she admitted. "I had dreams of homeschooling my kid when he was younger." She looked over at the framed photo of a teenager on her desk. "Somehow I thought keeping him at home would keep him away from every mean kid in existence." She laughed. "Thank God I knew I could never be here and do that at the same time. Ben's got a scholarship to Ohio State in the fall."

"Congratulations!"

"He put in the work, I did the worrying. So." Linda got back on topic. "Why spend four years learning to teach kids, only to run off to Icarus after graduation?"

Hayley looked away for a moment, absently digging the nail of her index finger into the fabric of the chair. She'd found the Icarus Showcase when she was in junior high, and she still remembered every detail of that Saturday night: carpooling up to Indianapolis with her dance class for the show, discovering an entire building of people living her dream, then riding back home, knowing she needed to join them.

"I had to," she said simply.

She'd given the same answer when Mom had asked that question. Hayley had agreed to college as a backup plan, living at home to save money, finding comfort in doing the responsible thing, fighting the urge to be reckless and the certainty that she was smothering something important within her.

But two days after graduation, she'd arrived at Icarus, nearly begging for a chance to finally give in to who she was.

Linda was watching her, waiting. Hayley looked for a better answer.

"The degree . . . well, it seemed like a good idea."

"You still think so?" Linda surprised her with that one. "Four years at school is four years you can't give to the stage. This job only gets harder as you get older."

Hayley took her time. "I think everything worked out the way it was supposed to."

Linda's eyebrows went up as Hayley's heart sank. Her answer had been supposed to get them to move on, not dig deeper.

"How so?" Linda asked.

Hayley sighed, looked Linda in the eye. "I don't think I was ready for Icarus at eighteen."

"The work?"

Hayley shook her head. "I've always been a hard worker. And Icarus was very good at developing talent. But there was no interest in you as a person."

Linda jotted something down. "Would you expect some kind of personal development program here at Vivez?"

"No," Hayley said quickly. "This is a dance company. I'd be here to dance."

I'd just want you to care, she added silently.

"Well, it looks as if Cyd was letting you do more than enough of that." Linda said the name of Hayley's old boss with weary familiarity. "Why did you leave?"

Because she'd had to, as surely as she'd had to join Icarus in the first place. She'd been sitting at the kitchen table on a Tuesday afternoon, staring blankly into a tepid bowl of canned chicken noodle soup, because driving home for lunch was better than spending one extra second at the theater. The rest of her day was looming in front of her, a series of tasks steadily becoming insurmountable obstacles—and then Kevin had stormed into their house, all worked up about how unappreciated he was, so certain Cyd would regret taking him for granted once they joined a theater he knew about in Columbus. Just like that, escape became a reality—and because it was Kevin's plan, they'd never had to talk about how supporting him was a convenient way of saving herself.

"Kevin and I needed a change," Hayley said. "We were getting burnt out."

Linda nodded. "I don't think the work is any easier around here."

"I wouldn't want it to be. But I think the culture would be better."

"What makes you think so?"

For starters, she'd been treated with more consideration in the last three hours than she had in the last three years. Cyd Garland didn't have armchairs in her office. She preferred to conduct meetings in the theater, even one on one, so she could look down on you from the stage.

"I think you care about people," Hayley said.

Linda smiled. "And Cyd doesn't?"

Hayley winced, backpedaling. "The thing about Cyd . . ."

Linda waved away the reply. "Don't worry about it," she said. "I know Cyd. I even saw you and Kevin dance together a couple of times."

Hayley sat back, surprised. "At Icarus?"

"Yep. I try to steal as many good ideas as possible."

Hayley laughed. "What'd you bring back with you?"

"The café, for one thing," Linda said. "What'd you call it?"

"The Menagerie." Hayley felt embarrassed just saying the name.

"The Menagerie, right. Why'd she call it that, do you think?"

Hayley had wondered that herself, with every shift she'd spent bartending at the café that also served as a waiting area for

Icarus patrons. Had Cyd meant to evoke thoughts of caged animals?

"I wouldn't be surprised if she just liked the sound of it," Hayley said.

Linda laughed. "I'll bet you're right. At any rate, having a place where people can get food and drink before the show is a stroke of genius. We get paying customers who come in for a drink and never see the show."

"How'd you name your café?" Hayley asked.

"Adagio?" Linda winked. "I liked the sound of it." They laughed. "And a slow tempo is appropriate, you know, for a place where people are supposed to relax." Linda walked the clipboard over to her desk. "I've just got one more question for you."

Hayley smiled. "I'm ready."

"What do you hope to find here that you didn't find at Icarus?"

Peace, she thought immediately. "I'm hoping that giving my best to Vivez doesn't mean giving everything."

Linda perched on the edge of her desk. "Then I don't think you'll be disappointed."

Hayley grinned. "So what's next?"

"Well, Ms. Burke, your name goes to the top of my list, and I'll see if we can't get you dancing here by September."

Her smile faltered. "September?" That was four months away.

"After Labor Day would be my guess." Linda saw the look on her face. "I don't have room for you right now," she said gently. "I told you that when you guys walked through the front door."

Hayley tried to recover. "I guess I thought . . ."

"You thought that was something I said to everybody?"

She'd thought she was good enough to make room for herself at Vivez Dance. The universe had come together so beautifully that she had dared to think it would be permanent this time.

What had Nick said? *"Your universe is only going to stay together until one of those pieces gets taken away from you."*

Damn that guy.

"Hayley." Linda's tone was sympathetic. "I like to let a lot of my kids come back for seasonal work in the summer. Normally I wouldn't even be holding auditions right now, except I toured with Kevin's mom back in the day, and . . ." She sighed. "I'm saying *he* wouldn't even have a job here, except I'm short on guys at the moment, and he can tap better than anyone I've got." She dropped her voice conspiratorially. "I wish he didn't know it."

Hayley laughed weakly. "I know what you mean."

"I'd suggest some sort of internship, just to have you around, but since I can't pay you, and I can't put you in a show . . ." Linda shrugged. "You're welcome to hang out, get a feel for how we do things. Might get old pretty fast, though."

Hayley barely heard her. Kevin didn't have enough money to support both of them, not even for a month, not even with her meager savings. She'd have to get a job, fast—but this could work. She'd just come here when she wasn't working.

And how pathetic would she look, hanging around her boyfriend's rehearsals like a groupie who wasn't good enough to join in?

"Thanks." She tried to sound enthusiastic. "I'm sure I'll drop by."

Linda snapped her fingers as an idea hit. "You know what I can offer you?"

"Really, you don't—"

"I can give you dance space. For when you have to move."

Hayley hadn't even considered that no theater job meant no rehearsal space. She needed to dance, professionally or not—and if she was going to be spending the next three months waiting tables, she was really going to need to dance.

"That'd be really great," she said. "I wouldn't want to get in anyone's way, though."

Linda waved a hand. "I'll get you a copy of our schedule. Show you where the rooms and lights are and so on. As long as the building's open and you don't leave a mess, you're fine."

Linda was opening the office door; Hayley nearly leaped out of the armchair so she wouldn't lag behind. "I really appreciate it," she said, shaking Linda's hand. "The audition, and the offer. You didn't need to be so generous."

"If I *needed* to do it, I wouldn't be generous, would I?" Linda led the way out the door. "Happy to help, Hayley. I'm really excited about you joining us."

Then they were nearly jogging down the hallway, passing costume racks and offices. "Sorry to hurry you along," Linda said, pushing open the door into the café, "but I've got another appointment, and I'm already late."

Hayley opened her mouth to reassure Linda she had nothing to be sorry for, that of course she loved speeding through narrow hallways while reeling from rejection, but the words never came out. She was looking past Linda at the man standing by the front door. Caramel-brown hair, pale blue eyes, both hands grasping the red handles of his walker.

Holy shit. Mr. Inaccessible himself.

3

He'd thought something like this was going to happen.

Nick hadn't *known* it, of course. He was here because Ben Brandazzio's mother wanted to talk to him about a summer job. Hayley had mentioned Vivez Dance last night, but that didn't mean he'd have to see her today. It wasn't like he'd be dancing.

Except Nick's world didn't work that way. The pieces of Hayley's universe might be coming together perfectly, and good for her. But the pieces of his universe tended to have jagged edges, and if there was one person he was hoping not to see, Nick had a feeling he was going to see her.

Which was why he had to bite back laughter when it actually happened.

He'd been waiting in some sort of restaurant area when Linda hurried into the room, all energy and smiles, telling the dancing star of the Squeaky Lion bar how much she was looking forward to September. Hayley seemed muted by sadness today, even before she spotted him, and Nick wondered what could've happened to bring her down from the night before. Hayley couldn't still be dwelling on him, could she?

You'd like that, wouldn't you, he thought. *Doesn't matter how much of an asshole you are, as long as the pretty girl keeps you in mind.*

"Mr. Freeman!" Hayley slipped past him before he could speak to her, and now Linda had him in a firm handshake, which meant he had to be mindful of his balance as he kept one hand on the walker. "Can I call you Nick, outside of school?"

"I'd actually *prefer* Nick." He gave his best "Mr. Freeman is my father" sort of smile. "What happens in September?"

"September is when you'll want to be sure to come back and catch a show."

Nick remembered Hayley's words to Rory in the bar: *"You might want to check out Vivez Dance soon."* Sooner than September? Maybe September was an unwelcome change of plans.

He cleared his throat. "So, how can I help, Mrs. Brandazzio?"

"Linda, please!" she said, and he nodded. Then, to his confusion, Linda's gaze went skyward, her head tilting back and forth as if debating something before she met his eyes apologetically.

"Here's the thing," she said. "I feel like I shouldn't ask you to commit until you actually see what you'll be doing. But I also don't want to make you walk through the theater just to tell me no."

Nick preferred not to have this conversation at all; it would have been worth sore legs and sweaty clothes to have Linda treat him just like anyone else. "How about this," he said. "You give me the headline, and we'll take a walk if I'm still interested."

Linda grinned, visibly relaxing. "I need you to put footage from a mountain of VHS tapes on the computer and organize it."

Nick tried to hide his surprise. "Do you have all of the equipment you need?"

"Oh yes," she said dismissively. "Ben helped me find the software and everything."

"I'm sure Ben could do the conversion easily enough."

She laughed. "Ben and I would both be better off with him working for someone else. *Anyone* else."

Nick laughed along, buying time to think. He didn't need a summer job, but Ben had said his mother very much wanted to work with *him*, specifically. The Brandazzios knew Nick taught computer electives, so he was qualified for the job, but what made him so essential here? Nick decided he wanted to find out.

"Let's go for a walk," he said.

Before long, they were standing in the doorway of a small room packed with shelves. A table with a monitor and a VCR on it was against the left wall; Nick spotted the computer under the table, though his view was partially obscured by a cheap office chair. His walker was about two feet wide and three feet deep, and there was space enough to get it into the room, but not to turn it around. He'd have to walk out backward.

"So," Linda said. "We've got years and years of VHS tapes in here, shows we did and rehearsal stuff. They may or may not be labeled correctly. There are binders . . ." She went to the shelf at the back of the room and indicated a row of dusty binders with a sweeping hand, game-show style. "These have programs from our shows in them, so that may help you figure out what you're watching."

Nick took in the scene in front of him. "So you want me to digitize all of this and organize it somehow?"

Linda nodded. "First priority would be just to get it on the computer with some sort of label on it. But yeah, the easier it is to sift through all this stuff, the better."

"Okay."

"It's too much," Linda guessed. "Too boring."

"No . . ." Although it would be boring, and he was under no obligation to help this woman. "When you transfer from

VHS, the computer captures the footage as it plays," he said. "So if I'm capturing a two-hour video tape, it's going to take two hours."

"Uh-huh," she said. "I read about it online."

"I'm saying a lot of this job is just going to be pushing a couple of buttons and sitting there while the tape rolls. You'd be paying me to wait."

Linda's eyes widened as she remembered something. "Oh! Right. I want to pay you ten thousand dollars for the summer." Nick stared at her. "Whether it takes two weeks or three months," she said. "It'll be simpler than keeping track of the hours."

Nick's eyebrows rose in disbelief. "You'd be paying me this to . . ."

"I'd want you to be done by Labor Day, but you can make your own hours."

"Well, sure." He was still in shock. "The school year will have started by then anyway. But are you sure you—"

"I know it's not an exciting way to spend the summer," she went on, "but you'd have the run of the place. There's no reason you can't start a tape, grab some lunch, and come back, right? We've even got a kitchen here."

"I guess I could do that."

"You could bring books, music, whatever. Just so long as I can throw all those tapes in the trash by September."

Nick took a breath. "Linda, you know Ben and his buddies took my computer science class last semester, right?"

"Of course. He wanted to take whatever you were teaching."

"If you don't want to hire Ben, there were plenty of his friends in that class who would do this job for a quarter of the money."

Linda looked delighted with herself, and he had no idea why. "Are you saying they'd do a better job?" she asked.

"Not at all, but I feel like I'm ripping you off."

She chuckled. "Nick, there's something you ought to know about me."

"Which is?"

She leaned in a little. "I take great pleasure in rewarding inspirational people."

Inspirational. Nick got it now. He had computer experience, but he also had a walker—and he'd long ago learned the disabled got extra points just for showing up. Ben had probably told his mother all about how *inspirational* Mr. Freeman had been to show up every day and teach so many kids in spite of his condition. Or maybe Linda saw the walker at Ben's senior awards ceremony. This was her way of spreading some good in the world—and making him feel like a charity case.

"I really appreciate that," he began, "but . . ."

"Come on, join us for the summer." The woman was playful, cajoling, and relentless. "Are you a dance fan?"

Not until last night. "Sure."

"Well, there ya go!" Linda Brandazzio exclaimed. "And you've never seen one of our shows before?"

"No," he admitted.

"We've got a great crew around here for the next few months," she said. "Really great kids, all sorts of talent—you get a backstage pass, and they get an audience. Maybe you'll get some material for your classroom. There's math to be found in dancing."

"There will be shows this summer, then?" Nick asked innocently. "I thought you said I'd want to come back in September."

Linda got a gleam in her eye. "There will absolutely be shows. And if you like what's on the stage this summer, you'll love what's coming in September."

He was impressed. Linda had managed to answer his question, promote her shows, and keep him out of Hayley's business without breaking a sweat. The proprietor of Vivez Dance seemed smart, generous, and kind, and was it really worth turning down easy money from a good boss because he didn't like her motivations?

"Can I make one request?" he asked.

Linda spread her hands. "Please."

He nodded at the shelves of video tapes. "There's not a lot of room to move around in there."

She beamed. "Let's give you an office with a view."

4

Hayley pushed through the swinging door of the Squeaky Lion's kitchen. Tonight would be her fourth shift as the bar's newest server and bartender, and tonight was the first time she was nervous. It was karaoke Friday.

Alexa was loading plates of appetizers onto her tray. "Right on time," she said. "We're going to keep you hopping."

"I don't mind." Hayley tried for casual. "Hey, how well do you know Nick?"

Alexa smiled. "I saw the way he looked at you."

"What?"

Alexa shifted her weight under her tray. "What do you want to know?"

"He . . . well, I noticed everybody helping him," she said. "Do I need to help him too?"

"No." Alexa started for the kitchen door. "Just treat him like anyone else. Nick pretty much runs this place on Fridays."

Now she felt worse. Inconsequential. "I want him to know I'm willing to help. I'm just worried he'll get offended if I offer."

Alexa laughed. "Honey, I'll win the lottery before Nick Freeman gets offended by a pretty woman."

He seemed pretty offended by me, Hayley thought.

"Don't worry." Alexa swept through the kitchen door, Hayley following her. "If he wants you to be part of the fun, he'll ask you."

It wasn't just that Nick had a good voice. Nick actually had a great voice—better than a lot of the singers she'd worked with—but that wasn't what had impressed Hayley the week before. It was the way he'd commanded the stage, the spotlight—the whole bar, really. He'd stepped out of the booth into that walker, and she had expected him to start clumping away from her, facing the metal bar in front of him the same way she'd seen in nursing homes. But he'd actually turned around within the square—the word *cage* had come to her mind unbidden—until he was facing her, butt against the metal bar, fingers closed around the handles, shoulders squared. She knew when he winked at her that he saw exactly how overwhelmed she was, as all she'd just said to him got jammed into a new context. Even so, he'd added those three words, like a slap in the face: *"Sorry to disappoint."*

Then the place went nuts.

She'd really never seen anything like it. The guy running the karaoke actually gave him a full-fledged intro, like he was bringing the main attraction to the stage after the openers: *"And now, ladies and gentlemen, the one, the only Nick Freeman!"* The bar erupted in applause. Nick turned away from her and started making his way to the stage, nodding and smiling, laughing and chatting as a path cleared in front of him like a red carpet for a movie star. Hayley was sure walking had to require significant effort for Nick, even though she could only see him from the back—each foot dragged forward before leaving the ground, his hips swung back and forth awkwardly, his shoulders lurched. Yet

Nick seemed not to notice any of this. His gait wasn't pretty, but it was effective, and without anyone in his way, he made it to the stage faster than some other able-bodied performers had.

The Squeaky Lion staff had stepped in; Hayley knew all of their names now. Alexa and Stephanie stood on either side of Nick, perpendicular to him, each extending an arm across the small of his back for support as he put his arms across their shoulders. They moved upward as a single unit, the singer mounting the two steps to the stage head-on as his friends climbed them sideways. Theo, the bar's bouncer, easily hefted Nick's wheels from the floor to the stage, and Stephanie smacked Nick's ass as he transferred his weight to the walker. Nick laughed, blew her a kiss, and made his way to the microphone like a rock star. When the karaoke track started, Hayley couldn't spot a trace of the weariness she'd seen in him moments before.

Nick didn't glance at the words on the screen, not once; he sang with an energy that seemed to physically fill the room. She knew how hard it was to capture and keep an audience, and so it startled her to realize Nick wasn't actually moving, beyond an occasional nod or turn of the head. She had assumed Nick didn't know joy, but it was right there in front of her, burning in his eyes, filling his voice. Was so much passion flowing from him now because it had no other way of getting out?

Hayley had slipped outside and joined Kevin in the parking lot while Nick was still singing. She was terrified their eyes would meet, and she would connect with him like they had before, except this time he'd be the one in the glow of his element, and she'd be peering in from the dark. It was only now, in the middle of her shift a week later, that Hayley realized why that connection scared her so much. There had been sadness in his eyes when he'd seen her dance, but there'd also been raw need. He'd seen something in her that was missing from him. Hayley was afraid

Nick would find her while he was on that stage, and his gaze would reveal something missing in her too.

She didn't want to talk to him tonight, didn't want to even see him now that Vivez Dance hadn't worked out as planned, but she wasn't about to let one guy keep her from a good job at a nice bar. Truth be told, she liked the work—she'd even liked bartending and serving at Icarus, especially on a packed Friday night. The faster she had to move, the easier it was to find her rhythm. Take this order, carry this plate, deliver this drink—no matter what, she always knew her next step. While Hayley worked, it didn't take long for doubt and guilt and fear to fade into the rest of the room's background noise as her focus narrowed to each task at hand. She actually had a spring in her step and a smile on her face by the time Elliot, the bartender, waved her over.

"What's up?" she asked.

He had two bottles of beer in his hands. "Gavin," he said, lifting the left one slightly, "and Nick. They're in the booth behind you. Gavin's the one with the cap."

Her smile disappeared as she recognized Nick Freeman. "Do they need to pay?"

"Nah," Elliot said. "They opened a tab up here. Nick can't carry the bottles, so we bring 'em over after he sits down."

Of course they did. Nick really did run this place.

Come on, girl. Go talk to him. Do your job.

She nodded at Elliot, put the beers on her tray, and started what suddenly seemed like a very long walk to Nick's booth.

Nick was wearing a steel-gray shirt, sleeves rolled up past the elbows, and as he gestured at Gavin, Hayley noticed how big and toned his forearms were. *Well, sure,* she thought. *He's got to drag those legs around all the time.* Which immediately made her feel like a bitch.

Gavin's cap was a darker gray than Nick's shirt, and he was thin, with a gray vest over a light blue shirt, and an impeccably trimmed blond beard. The pair was obviously very entertained by their conversation, and Hayley was glad—it meant neither of them noticed her coming.

"I can't be a Navy SEAL," Nick was saying.

Gavin wasn't giving in. "Why not?"

"Because one day there's going to be a Navy SEAL in this bar, and when I say I got my ass kicked rescuing kittens from a desert fortress or whatever, he's going to figure out I learned about the SEALs from that Demi Moore movie, and then I'm *actually* going to get my ass kicked."

"No one would ever kick your ass," Gavin said. "You saw *G.I. Jane?*"

"*We* saw *G.I. Jane.*"

"What? When?"

Nick took a breath to reply and glanced to his left. Then came what Hayley had expected and dreaded: the double take. She watched him notice the beers, then the black T-shirt, matching leggings, and apron that all said she was on duty. She forced a smile.

"These are for you?" she asked him.

"Oh. Yes. Thanks." Nick actually scooted closer to the wall, like she needed more room to work. "Gavin, this is Hayley. Hayley, this is Gavin Beckett."

Hayley turned to Gavin. "Did he run out of girls to invite?"

She tried not to cringe. She'd meant it as a joke, but it didn't sound like one.

Gavin, God bless him, didn't seem bothered in the least. "We have a deal," he told her. "He gets me out of the house once a month, I pay for the drinks."

"Sounds fair."

"Hey," Nick said, "I think you really impressed Linda."

She felt her face grow warm. She wished he'd welcomed her to the Squeaky Lion team or lied and said it was good to see her.

Ignoring her would have been better than bringing up Vivez Dance.

She said, "I didn't realize you knew Linda."

"I don't," he said. "Not really. She's got me on a project for the summer."

"How'd you get that job?"

His eyes cooled. She'd heard the anger in her voice, but she hadn't intended to hit whatever nerve she'd just found. A rush of satisfaction unsettled her, like she'd scored a point. Like fencing. Like she'd stabbed him.

"I guess she knows there's more to life than dancing," he said.

More to life? She hadn't been good enough to get the job she'd thought she was made for, but hey, there was more to life, so apparently she was just shallow. This from the guy who built his life around picking up women on karaoke night.

She shot back her best frosty smile. "Don't worry. My boyfriend will do all the dancing for you."

5

Nick woke up the next morning to a knee in his ribs and a hand grabbing his T-shirt; he gaped comically at a little girl in fuzzy footie pajamas, her blond hair sticking up in all directions. "Hey!" he exclaimed. "It's my Rosie Bear!"

"Mommy's makin' pancakes!" She delivered the message with a triumphant smile.

"I love pancakes!" Nick reached out and hugged her to his chest, rocking back and forth as she squealed with delight. "Let's go find Mommy, huh?"

She waited until he'd climbed off the couch and stepped inside the walker before she placed her hand on top of his. Nick would let her lead him anywhere.

It was a short journey out of the den, down the front hallway of the Beckett house, and into the kitchen. Rosie's mother was standing over a griddle on the stove.

"Hello, Rose Beckett!" she said. "What did you find on the couch?"

Rosie grinned from ear to ear, pointing up at her companion. "I found Uncle Nick!"

"Yay! Let's see if Uncle Nick can get you into your high chair, and I'll bring you your pancakes."

"Hang on just a second, Rosie." Nick gave the cook a quick kiss on the cheek. "Morning, Mel."

"Good morning, Nicky," she said. "Did you boys have a good time last night?"

"Of course! You know we bring the good time with us."

"Uh-huh. I'm sure your audience was grateful."

"Some more than others." Nick sat down at the kitchen table. "C'mere, Rosie girl."

Mel deftly flipped a pancake before throwing him a look. "I didn't name her after a riveter, Nicky. You'll have to start calling her Rose when she stops being adorable."

"That'll never happen." Nick lifted Rosie into her seat and started fiddling with straps. "Besides, we have a song!"

"Yeah!" Rosie declared. "Sing the Rosie song!"

"Are you gonna sing your part?" Rosie nodded vigorously, and Nick started singing. "I'm gonna eat some pancakes with Rosie, how many will we eat, who knowsie? We'll fill up from our heads to our toesies, 'cause we need breakfast to help us growsie!" Rosie and Nick took a wide-eyed deep breath and sang in unison: "No matter what, it's plain to see . . .

"I love Uncle Nick, and Uncle Nick loves me!"

Rosie loved the Rosie song because Nick always made up new words on the spot, and because her part, and the part they sang together, never changed. At nearly three years old, Rosie still announced her special last line more than she sang it, but Nick loved hearing the end of the Rosie song more than anything else in the world.

Gavin came in from the hallway as Nick and Rosie clapped for each other, his eyes on the watch he was fastening on his wrist. "You were right, hon," he said to Mel. "It was in the laundry basket."

"Of course I was right." Mel effortlessly kissed her husband on her way to the table with a plate full of pancakes. "Okay, Nicky, tell me everything."

Nick looked at her. "What?"

"Gavin said you needed my help with Hayley," Mel said.

Nick rolled his eyes. "Really?" he asked Gavin.

Gavin dropped into the chair across from him while Mel took a seat between her husband and her daughter. "You told me you wanted to know what she thought."

"Sure, but tell her I *need* her, and she'll start getting cocky."

Mel said, "You know you're only an honorary uncle, right?" She apportioned the pancakes among their plates. "Keep talking like that and you'll just be the guy who used to stay on our couch."

"You know you can't get rid of me." Nick grabbed his knife and fork and got to work. "But I do need you to tell me how to fix things."

Mel sighed. "What did you do to that nice girl?"

He was surprised how much the question hurt; he hated that he'd done anything to Hayley. "Why do you assume it's my fault?"

Mel merely raised an eyebrow. Gavin and Nick were both very familiar with that look—it was Mel's infallible way of calling bullshit.

"Okay." Nick surrendered. "I may have been a bit short with her last week." He took a bite of pancake. "She pretty much told me I was miserable, and dancing was the solution to all my problems."

"Great." Mel cut up a pancake for Rosie. "What did you do?"

Nick hesitated. "You need to understand that she started it."

"Like that matters."

"They both looked pretty rankled to me," Gavin offered.

"Rankled?" Nick said. "What does that even mean?"

"Irritated," Mel explained. "Like you're rankling me now."

"Being an English teacher doesn't mean you can trot out words nobody uses anymore," Nick told him. "You don't see me dropping theorems all over the place, do you?"

"No," Gavin pointed out calmly, "because unlike a robust vocabulary, they wouldn't be of use to anybody."

"You do this in front of the kid so I can't swear at you."

"Nicky." Mel got them back on track. "If you really thought this was her fault, you wouldn't be talking to me about it."

Nick didn't want to relive it, but he'd shared far too much of his life with the Becketts to hide something like this. "She literally danced through the place with her boyfriend, and then she was just so flippin' *happy* that she couldn't help but share with me how miserable I looked and how that could all change if I could *find my joy* in dancing. Like I could just stand up, cut a rug, and be on cloud nine. So I told her it wasn't so easy for all of us, and maybe if she didn't have the boyfriend and the talent and those big brown eyes of hers, the world wouldn't be all candy and roses for her either."

Nick saw sympathy on Mel's face, and he didn't like it. Sympathy meant she probably understood the situation better than he did. Melanie Beckett had an unnerving knack for seeing what Nick didn't mean to show—or didn't want to admit to himself.

"Did Hayley know about the walker?" she asked.

Nick shook his head. "Not until afterward."

He could feel Mel's amber eyes on him—not judging, but not letting him hide either.

"And were you miserable?" she asked gently.

Nick focused on stabbing at a blueberry. "It was not a good night," he said. "But nothing compared to yesterday's humiliation of helping your husband pretend he's a Jamaican rapper."

"Aw, come on," Gavin protested. "Who doesn't like that song?"

"Honey, we talked about this," Mel said wearily. "Stop embarrassing yourself."

"Too late. He actually made me go up there and sing about getting caught . . ." Nick glanced at Rosie, who was engrossed in trying to pick up a slippery chunk of strawberry. *"Playing Legos* with the girl next door. I had to sing this. I had to sell it."

"Down, Daddy?" Rosie had lost interest in her food and wanted out of the chair.

"Sure, sweetie." Gavin started to move, but Mel stopped him with a glance. "She asked you because she knew what I'd say."

"Which means we're raising a very smart child." Gavin smiled at his wife. "It's Saturday, honey. Uncle Nick is here. Let her eat in stages."

Mel gave in. "Wash her hands, and keep her in the kitchen."

"Yep." Gavin lifted his daughter into the air. "And I will have you know that the bar loved that song."

"Only because I made it work," Nick said. He turned to Mel. "Even though he was wearing his Irish gangster hat."

"Stop it," Mel scolded. "He looks like a poet in that cap. And it's not like he *made* you get on stage."

"Oh, he totally did." Nick was chewing as Mel looked at him skeptically, so he tilted his head toward Gavin.

"Those are the rules," her husband said, wiping Rosie's hands at the sink. "If I go with him, I get to pick a duet and his backstory."

Mel tried to squeeze the last of the syrup from a nearly empty bottle. "You should tell people the truth." She pushed back her chair. "Gav, do you know if we—"

"Stay there," her husband said firmly.

Mel rolled her eyes. "I can get the syrup, babe."

"But you won't." He swept Rosie off the counter and high into the air. "Ready to fly to the syrup, young one?"

"Yeah!" Rosie laughed. "Let's go, Daddy!"

Nick watched Gavin pilot his daughter through the kitchen, her arms outstretched like she was a human airplane. "What just happened?"

"Gavin thinks I never sit long enough to enjoy a meal," Mel told him.

Gavin flew Rosie over the table, Rosie strafed her mother's hair with tiny fingers, and Mel leaned her head back and kissed her daughter's cheek. Nick grinned, even as the scene sent wistfulness flitting through him. Rosie put out her hand, and he gave her a high five before Gavin swung her back toward the pantry.

"So," Mel said. "You feel bad about starting off on the wrong foot with the new waitress, and you want to make her feel better."

He nodded. "She's nice. Naive maybe, but nice." He wiped his mouth. "And I don't want her thinking I'm a jerk if we're going to see each other at the bar every week. Just because I told her things were going to go wrong doesn't mean I wanted it to happen."

"What went wrong?"

"I think she and her boyfriend were both counting on getting a job at the same place, and I'm pretty sure they won't take her until September."

"That can't be your fault."

"And it's not her fault I'm disabled."

Mel looked puzzled.

"That whole dancing thing . . . she was talking about something she really believed in," he explained. "It's not her fault she chose the one guy in the bar who literally can't dance."

Gavin glanced over while he guided Rosie toward the shelf with the syrup bottle. "I know that's not true."

"Sure it is," Nick said.

"I've seen you dance."

"You've seen me sway or—I don't know—move my shoulders a few times. She's in a completely different league, trust me."

Mel smiled then, though he wasn't sure why. Nick watched Rosie fly back to the table and put the syrup bottle in Mel's hand.

"I tried to be nice and move on," he said, "but it's like every word that comes out of my mouth makes things worse."

"Wow," Mel said. She hugged her daughter tight and gave her a kiss on the forehead before lowering her to the floor. "Are you telling me Hayley is immune to the full-on, double-barreled Nick Freeman charm?"

"She's taken, babe," Gavin pointed out. "It'd be irresponsible of him to hit her with *all* the charm."

"They can be friends," Mel said. "Better Nicky put his energy into someone who needs it instead of those poor college girls he runs after."

"You joke about the charm," Nick said, "but people actually like me."

"You should probably cross a few names off your list," she retorted.

He rolled his eyes. "You're making it sound like I'm a predator or something."

"I did not say that," Mel insisted calmly. "But you do go after women who aren't worth your time. You just said you were miserable."

"I did not."

"Well, some woman you'd never met saw it all over your face."

Nick watched Gavin slide back into his chair, looked at Mel studying him, tracked Rosie running joyfully back and forth across the kitchen just because she could. The little girl grinned at him, and he couldn't help but grin back.

"I tell ya, Rosie girl, if everyone looked at me like you do . . ." he said softly.

"You rock, Uncle Nick."

Hayley had grinned at him the first time he saw her. She'd been breathless and glowing, and even though she'd had no idea who he was, she'd grinned at him like she was happy to see him.

"Look," Nick said. "Cerebral palsy isn't hot."

Mel scoffed. "They don't have to be attracted to the walker, Nicky."

"And you've . . ." Gavin cleared his throat. "You've played Legos a few times."

"Sure," Nick said. "A few girls get past it. But a lot of girls like to flirt with me because they think it's funny. Like they can hang all over me because the joke is they'd never actually go there. And then I ask if they want to come back to my place, and the joke's over." He thought of Kacey. "They don't want to be mean, but they don't want me either."

They were all silent save for Rosie, who ended each lap across the kitchen with a triumphant "Ta-da!"

"Nicky," said Mel, "any woman worth having wouldn't think like that."

"Yeah, well, Hayley does," he said.

She squeezed his hand. "If she really does, then maybe you don't need to fix anything. But I think you know better." She turned to her daughter. "Ready for clean clothes, Rose?"

Rosie came to an abrupt halt. "Upstairs?"

"Yep. Your clothes are upstairs."

Rosie looked toward Nick, and he smiled at her. "I'm not going anywhere, sweetie," he said. "Go get changed, and then you can come sit in the big girl seat in my car if you want."

"And play the radio?" she asked.

He nodded. "You bet."

Mel hefted Rosie onto her hip. "Here we go, baby."

"I'll be back, Uncle Nick!" she declared.

"I'll be here, honey."

Mel looked at Nick. "Don't think about what Hayley wants or doesn't want from you. She has a boyfriend, and it's not your job to make her happy. But do be honest with yourself about what you're sorry for, and be honest with her when you apologize. Then the charm will work."

Gavin and Nick went to the den to retrieve Nick's overnight bag after the ladies had gone. Nick glanced at Mel's piano keyboard across from the old couch. "Has Mel been writing anything new?"

"She said she's working on something, but a lot of the time she just plays to unwind."

"I get that." Mel had been a music professor and a vibrant part of the local music scene before having Rose, and as much as she now claimed to be content teaching a few piano or voice students from her home and devoting most of her time to motherhood, Nick missed seeing her perform on a stage. "Maybe if you gave her some lyrics to work with," he said.

"My best stuff is about smacking around underachieving students."

"Well, hey, dark songs are in right now."

Gavin stepped ahead of Nick when they reached the front door, then held out an arm for Nick to grasp as he made his way down the porch steps, dragging the walker behind him until his four wheels and two feet were all on level ground.

"Hey," Nick said, "it's really annoying the way your wife's always right."

"I wouldn't know," Gavin said. "We're always in perfect agreement." They laughed as they started down the driveway. "That thing you said about women not wanting you?"

"Yeah?" Nick glanced back toward the house; Rosie would soon be dashing out to scramble into the passenger seat of his SUV and listen to music.

"Hayley was pissed at you, but it didn't look to me like she was pissed because of the walker."

Nick thought about it and laughed. "You're saying it's not that she doesn't like disabled people. She just doesn't like me."

"Pretty much, yeah."

"And I should be happy about that."

"I would be," Gavin said. "It means you can change things."

6

Friday afternoon, Hayley strolled into the living room and plopped down next to Kevin on the couch. He put his arm around her while Patrick Swayze defended a bar from hooligans on the television screen.

"I will never understand," she said, "how he could be in both this and *Dirty Dancing*."

"It's just different choreography," Kevin said. "Look at how clean that spin is. He might as well be doing ballet."

"Except he kicks that guy in the face."

"Which is why this is better than *Dirty Dancing*."

She made a face at him, and he laughed and gave her a kiss. This was good. This was comfortable and familiar, and a perfect beginning to their fresh start.

But something was missing.

"When're you going in?" she asked him.

"I should leave soon." He paused, reading the silence. "But you don't want me to."

"I never said that."

She did want him to go, actually—this odd distance between them was much easier to handle when he was actually distant, but she sure as hell wasn't going to say that either.

"I know they don't need me for anything today, but if I want to make a mark at this place, I have to show up when they don't ask for me."

"I get it, really." She sat up straighter. "I just hate that I'm not making that mark with you."

"So come with me."

"What?" She looked at him. "We can't just pretend I work there, babe."

"We can see the show. Have some drinks." His cocky grin came out, the one that always made her melt. "I want to show you off."

It was tempting, and an evening at Vivez would get them out of this house, off the couch. But she couldn't go to Vivez yet. She didn't want to be introduced to all of her talented future coworkers as merely an extension of Kevin.

"Next time I walk into that place, I want to belong there," she said. "Talk me up in the meantime. Get them ready for me."

He winked. "I don't think they'll ever be ready for you."

She told herself she was imagining the disappointment that flickered through his smile.

As Kevin got up from the couch, Hayley said, "I was thinking I might go to the bar tonight."

"The Squeaky Lion?" He frowned, confused. "Why? You're not on shift tonight."

"I need to apologize to that guy. Nick."

He relaxed. "The one with the wheels?"

"The walker, yeah."

Kevin chuckled. "That's sweet, Hal, but you don't need to go out of your way just because he can't walk."

"It's not that," she insisted, standing up. "It's not just that."

43

"I know, I know." He held up a hand. "Sometimes I forget I live with the nicest woman on earth."

"You say that like it's a bad thing."

Kevin shook his head gently. "It's why I love you," he said. "I just don't want you thinking you have to go. Don't chain yourself to other people's expectations."

"I'm not," she said firmly. "I just want to fix this."

"Then you go make that guy's night, babe." He kissed her forehead. "Have fun."

A minute later, she heard him scoop up his keys from the table in the hall as he headed out the front door, to the new family that didn't include her. She took her phone from her pocket, hesitated, then called the number at the top of her favorites.

Denise Vincennes answered immediately. "How are things in sunny Columbus?"

"Things are hot and humid." Hayley smiled. "Got some time before the show?"

"Oh, absolutely. Andrew and Cyd just got into some big thing about the lighting, so the show might not even go on."

Hayley scoffed. "That'll never happen."

"A girl can dream, can't she?"

Hayley felt herself relax as Denise told her the latest gossip about all their friends and foes at the Icarus Showcase. She almost wanted to go back, to tell her friend she hadn't really abandoned her after four years of dancing together—but even Denise's stories of the place caused a faint tightening in her chest.

She headed upstairs. "I'm going to talk to him."

Denise didn't miss a beat despite having been interrupted mid-sentence. "The karaoke guy?"

"Nick, yeah." Hayley paused outside her bedroom door. "I should talk to him, right?"

"What'd Kevin say?"

She rolled her eyes. "You don't care what Kevin said."

"I do not," Denise agreed cheerfully. "But now I know you told him."

Hayley dropped down on her bed. "Of course I told him."

She heard movement and a muffled curse, and pictured Denise sidestepping props and costume racks. "You two weren't exactly communicating well the last time I saw you."

"We're getting better," Hayley insisted.

A pause. "Is *everything* getting better?"

Denise meant the panic attacks. The ringing in her ears, her jackhammer heartbeat—the certainty that the body she knew so well when she danced was suddenly and completely out of her control and would destroy itself.

Hayley swallowed. "Nothing's happened since I've been here."

"Good."

It was just one word, said kindly, but Hayley felt guilty anyway. She'd left Indianapolis for her boyfriend. She'd left to get better. She'd left her best friend alone.

"Anyway." She jumped up. "What should I wear for an apology?"

"Apology?" Denise snorted. "You wear what you want, honey. He'll just have to deal with it."

7

There was a back door to the Squeaky Lion, near the bar's two handicapped spaces, but Nick was pretty sure it opened into the kitchen, and he couldn't bring himself to ask for special access. Besides, this was downtown Columbus, and he was lucky there was a parking lot anywhere near the bar. His walk around the building was always a slow one—anything faster would get him winded and sweating by the time he stepped inside—but tonight he barely minded. Tonight he practiced his apology.

There was one step at the bar's entrance, and it wasn't a very high one, but it had nowhere near enough surface area for all four wheels of the walker. Nick had to stand on the ground, reach over the step to grasp the handle of the door, then pull backward and hope he could hold that door steady while he moved his feet and wheels up and forward. It was a risky process, but this time, as always, Theo the bouncer came to the rescue within ten seconds.

"Hey, Nick." Theo leaned against the door and offered Nick his arm. "How're things?"

"Theo, we're going to make tonight a good one." Nick stepped through the entrance and pulled the walker in after him. "Anything to report so far?"

Theo shrugged. "Haven't had to throw anybody out yet."

"Aw, I'm sorry, man." Nick grinned at him. "I know how much you like to do that."

"Hey. You." Nick felt a tap on his shoulder and heard the familiar voice behind him. "Rock star."

Nick turned around to face Hayley. "Um, hi," he said.

She tilted her head with a knowing smile. "What?"

"Just surprised me, is all."

"Uh-huh."

Hayley was wearing faded jeans with huge holes in the knees, and her blue-and-white-checkered shirt was rolled up at the sleeves; she wore it unbuttoned over a white tank top. There was something in the way she carried herself, something about the touch of eyeliner he hadn't noticed before—she knew she looked good, but she hadn't dressed for anybody's approval. Nick had focused so much on protecting himself around her that he was just now realizing how utterly comfortable Hayley was in her own skin. He was still recovering from his walk from the car, aware of his balance and his grip on the walker, hoping fervently he'd stop sweating now that he was standing still, but none of those things would ever be worries for Hayley. She simply stood there, eyes boring into him. He couldn't gauge her mood, or what she wanted from him, but he liked the way she was making his pulse speed up.

"Hey," he started brilliantly. "We need to—"

"We need to do pickleback shots," Hayley told him. "You're buying."

He blinked, his mouth stuck in mid-sentence. "I don't know what those are."

To his astonishment, she grabbed his forearm to pull him forward. "Now."

Nick let himself be towed to the bar, where Hayley flagged down Elliot. "Two pickleback shots," she said. "On the rock star's tab."

He went for his credit card. "You're not working tonight?"

"Nope." Hayley shook her head. "I am off duty."

"Here for the karaoke?"

"No."

When she didn't elaborate, Nick went with, "Ah."

"Kevin," she pronounced, "is at Vivez."

"Ah," he said again. "And how do we feel about that?"

"Great. Peachy keen." Hayley thanked Elliot as he delivered four shot glasses, two of which she shoved toward Nick. "Go for it, rock star."

Nick refused to go for it. He had prepared an apology, and he realized now that he had put an absurd amount of time into that preparation, but he was not about to let Hayley demolish all his careful planning without knowing what the hell was going on.

Which was why he asked, because he had to start somewhere: "What's with this rock star stuff?"

Her stare said he didn't want to cross her. "Drink."

"Which?"

"Shot of Jameson first, then you drink the pickle juice."

Pickle juice? "Why would you—"

"Damn it, Freeman, raise your glass." He surrendered. "To dancing with your heart," she said.

"Um, to dancing with your heart." He grimaced a bit at the whiskey's burn. "Pickle juice!" she commanded. He braced himself, tossed it back, then looked at the empty glass, surprised. It actually wasn't bad.

"See?" she said. "It washes down the whiskey."

"It really does."

"Want another one?"

"No, thank you."

"So *polite*." She drew out the word. "Go to your booth."

He squinted at her. "I'm sorry?"

"Go. To. Your. Booth."

Nick did as he was told, even though he was quickly becoming more irritated than confused as he climbed into his seat.

After a minute, he spotted Hayley heading his way from the bar.

Whereas Nick was resigned to deliberately dragging one foot after the other, moving forward through brute force and reflexive apologies and a healthy dose of endurance, this woman commanded the space around her without even trying. He felt like every movement she made, every step and flexed muscle and every shift of weight, were all evidence of her body perfectly doing exactly what it was designed to do. She wasn't walking, Nick thought. She was gliding, like every step was skimming across the placid surface of a lake. And she was doing it with both hands full of fresh drinks, keeping her eyes on him.

Nick saw all she could do and all he would never do, and he felt deeply sad.

"Jack and ginger." She handed the glass to him. "And whiskey sour for me."

He was surprised. "How'd you know I like Jack and ginger?"

"I'm a bartender. It's a gift."

Hayley hopped up onto the seat across from him in one fluid movement. Witnessing that sort of casual grace was almost more amazing than seeing her dance.

She said, very deliberately, "Mr. Freeman."

"Ms. . . ." Nick was at a loss. "I actually have no idea."

"Burke," she said. "Hayley Michelle Burke. You and I need to work out our shit."

He spread his hands. "I'm sorry."

"Because I know you don't . . . like, I know I shouldn't have said all that stuff about people's legs, but what you said was really shitty too. You acted like I was five years old, like I'd only be okay until I broke one of my toys." She stopped, cocked her head. "What?"

"I'm sorry," he repeated. "You were really happy, and it wasn't right to act like you don't deserve to be. That's not who I am. I'm sorry."

She watched him, intrigued. "How long've you been rehearsing that one?"

"About a week."

"Most people'd just say, 'Sorry, I was a dick.'"

Nick laughed without intending to, and liked that she'd made him do it. "Was my version better or worse?"

"It was very *deliberate*." She tilted her glass back and forth and watched her drink swirl. "You thought about that a *lot*."

Nick caught something in the lazy cadence of her speech and realized he had no idea how many pickleback shots had shown up before him. He guessed Hayley would say drunk was still a few drinks away, but judging by the way she was downing her latest one, she was headed for drunk pretty quickly.

"So we're good?" he asked.

Hayley blinked at him, jarred out of her thoughts. "What?"

"We're good?" he repeated. "All's forgiven?"

She let out a long breath. "Yeah. All's forgiven."

Nick wasn't sure how to respond; his apology seemed to have depressed her. "Um, okay." He started sliding out of the booth. "Have a good night."

"You like them better than me, don't you?"

He stopped. "Who?"

"Everybody," she said. "You like everybody better than me."

"*Everybody?*" He waited for a retraction. "Hayley, there are people in this room I don't even know."

"And you will be nicer to them tonight," she said, "than you have ever been to me."

Nick felt the back of his neck heat up, like he'd just been caught cheating on a test. He slid back into his seat. "Look," he said, "I said I was sorry."

"Yeah," she said. "And now that you've fixed this problem, you're off to be the king of the bar and greet your adoring public."

Nick was stunned. She had seen right through him: He had done what he needed to do, and he was escaping. But he would be damned if Hayley Michelle Burke left this bar tonight thinking of herself as a problem.

"I know I said I didn't like you," he said quietly. "I didn't mean it."

"Sure you did." She didn't meet his eyes as she said it, and there was tired acceptance in her voice, as if not liking her would be completely understandable. He was horrified—did she really think of herself that way?

"Really," he insisted. "I didn't mean it."

"Then where's that smile?" she asked. "I watched you last week. Everyone gets blinded by that smile of yours except for me."

He was confused. "You want me to try and impress you?"

"You don't want to impress me?"

"No. I mean, of course, but . . ." He gulped the drink she'd brought over. "There's more to it than that."

"I know it's because you're putting on a show," she said lazily. "I put on shows for a living. But yours is a really good show."

If Hayley knew that she was casually ripping apart his armor with every word, she showed no sign of it. She wasn't even looking at him, and still Nick felt panicky and wounded. Hayley knew he was putting on an act, and yet that act seemed to be exactly what she wanted from him. Why wasn't that great news?

He'd been charming women from this very booth for years; why couldn't he do it one more time?

Because as annoying as Hayley had been when they'd met, she had been passionately trying to save him from his own misery. She had seen joy in him and tried as hard as she could to bring it out. He wasn't going to repay such a genuine act of kindness with his pathetic karaoke-night charm, even if she wanted him to. Hayley deserved better, and she didn't seem to know it.

"Okay." He caught Alexa's eye and waved her over. "More drinks."

After they'd done two more pickleback shots, Hayley said, "Aren't you gonna sing?"

"Eventually," Nick said.

"You can't not sing."

"I will, but now I'm talking to you," he said. "You're more important than the songs tonight."

She watched him take a tiny sip of his drink. "You've gotta do better than that if you want to catch up with me, rock star."

"Yeah, but I have enough trouble trying not to fall over as it is."

She guffawed at that one. "Shit, sorry," she said, still laughing. "Not funny."

"It's a little funny," he said, and drank more. He hadn't meant it as a joke, but he really liked her laugh.

"Hey, did you really hurt your legs in a manicure accident?"

He tried to keep a straight face. "Who told you that? Alexa?"

"Because manicures are for your hands, so I don't see how the hell that was true."

He started laughing and had trouble stopping. "I'd had a lot to drink that day," he said. "Could never keep manicure and pedicure straight anyway."

She grinned. "So what happened, rock star?"

He changed the subject. "I like it when you call me that. It's growing on me."

"What happened to those legs of yours?"

He took a sip of his drink. "Next question."

She suddenly looked wounded. "After all we've been through?"

He would have fallen for it completely, but he was enjoying her eyes far too much to miss the twinkle in them. "Oh, *wow*," he said. He sat back and started to laugh. "You're good."

Her grin was back. "More than good enough for an honest answer."

"I won't lie to you," he said solemnly. "But I refuse to tell you everything."

"Aaaand now!" The booming voice belonged to Dynamite Don, of Dynamite Don's Karaoke. "It's time for Nick Freeman to come up to the stage for a little million-dollar magic!"

Nick looked over his shoulder at the stage. "I didn't put that one in," he explained to Hayley. "Sometimes he calls me up to do this one with him."

"Then get the hell up there," she said.

He slid toward the end of the booth, and the better part of four drinks made the world start tilting as he stood to climb out. "Oh," he said. "Okay. Slow and steady."

Hayley hopped out of the booth—how the hell did she make everything look so easy?—and stood next to him as he slowly backed out. "You ready to rock?"

Nick was hanging on to the table with a viselike grip. "Well . . ."

"Here." He felt her hand on top of his, saw fingers expertly tipped with lilac nail polish. "Put your arm 'round me."

He kept a hold of the booth with his right hand and let her guide his left hand off the table and around her shoulders. He stepped back cautiously, but his feet still found the ground a little more abruptly than he would have liked. Hayley's arm shot around his waist to steady him as he stumbled, pivoting him in the process, and suddenly their faces were inches apart. Nick was close enough to see the light freckles on the bridge of her nose, and a tiny scar under the corner of her eye, a thin line no longer than the width of his fingertip. He felt his pulse drumming in his ears, and then she smiled—real, spontaneous, and warm. For the first time since he'd seen her dance, he felt like he was basking in the sun.

"Easy does it," she said. "We've got this, rock star."

He was being pulled into her gravity. Hayley's gaze flitted from his eyes to his lips and back again. His mouth went dry.

"Why do you keep calling me that?" he asked.

"You own that stage when you sing," she said. "And you own this bar the rest of the time. You *are* a rock star, Nick."

He told himself his body was tingling because of the whiskey.

"You're right," he said, backing into the walker. "We've got this."

Hayley let him go, and she joined in the applause and even gave an enthusiastic whoop as he turned toward the stage.

This was not good.

She has a boyfriend. The thought played on a loop in his head; he recited it with so much determination that he was afraid he'd sing the words when the karaoke track started. Mel Beckett could scold him all she wanted about the type of woman he was liable to take home, but Nick had never—would never—move in on someone's girlfriend.

He walked through the crowded bar and thought of his ex, Vicki, of feeling physically ill at the thought of her being with anybody else—and if he'd had that reaction when it was over, when she had every right to move on, he couldn't fathom what it would have been like to find her cheating.

Nick shook his head to clear it of Vicki, of Hayley, of anything but the song he was about to sing. He wouldn't let himself hurt Hayley Burke anymore, not even if she kissed him.

Not even if he wanted her to kiss him.

He was at the steps of the stage, and Stephanie and Alexa were helping him.

"Doing okay, champ?" This from Steph. "You look a little shaky."

He nodded. "Maybe some ice water after?"

"I'll leave it at your booth," Alexa said. She and Steph waited to back away until he had both hands firmly on the walker. "Knock 'em dead."

Nick gave another nod, and then he and Don were singing about what they'd do if they had a million dollars.

It was good that the song was easy and familiar, because his mind was having about as much trouble dealing with thoughts of Hayley and Kevin as his stomach was dealing with all the alcohol.

He *would not kiss* Hayley Burke. Not if they had a dozen more pickleback shots, not if she begged him—

If she *begged* him?

Hayley hadn't come on to him.

How arrogant was it to think this woman, who was obviously in a relationship with somebody she loved, an able-bodied somebody—how deluded did Nick have to be to believe Hayley was going to jump a cripple after a few drinks? Really, the jury was still out on whether she even liked him. Worrying about her advances was about as ridiculous as getting a restraining order against her.

The much bigger problem was how he'd felt when she'd kept him from falling. She'd smiled at him. It was laughable to think Hayley wanted the artificial warmth of his game-show grin after the smile she'd just given him. She knew he was a miserable jerk; she could tell when he was putting on an act, and still she'd found it in her to lend him a hand, to link herself with him, to smile like that.

"We've got this, rock star." We. She could've said *you've* got this, or told him to get the hell away from her. But Hayley Burke, the woman who moved with such grace, the woman whose smiles seemed to be fueled by something wonderful and pure deep inside her—Hayley Burke had chosen to be a part of something with him, and he was afraid of how much he wanted that.

Nick looked at the booth, hoping to catch another smile, but Hayley was looking at her phone. Probably texting Kevin. Because Kevin was the guy she was actually with, instead of the drunk guy she'd been decent enough to help down a step or two, the guy who was overthinking the hell out of what had probably been just a simple act of kindness. Because keeping a cripple from hurting himself was the kind of thing people like Hayley did.

He needed a new plan.

Nick finished the song, put in a food order with Steph while she and Alexa helped him down the steps, then told Hayley he was headed to the bathroom as he hurried past the booth. After relieving himself, he found the sink and splashed some water on his face. He glanced in the mirror and made a halfhearted attempt to improve the look of his hair. He felt the tension in his shoulders, the frustration hijacking his nerves until everything in him demanded he get the hell out of this bar.

He closed his eyes, pictured the beach, the color of the ocean, the sky.

"It's up to you, man," he said to his reflection. "You're the only one freaking out."

He could leave. For the first time in the history of his Squeaky Lion karaoke career, Nick could go home before the place shut down. But what if leaving now made Hayley more certain he didn't like her? What if she spent the rest of the evening drunk off her ass, with no one to make sure she got home safely?

Come on, he thought. *You already know what you're going to do. Otherwise you wouldn't have ordered the food.*

He would go back to the booth. He would let the food soak up the alcohol, and he would talk to Hayley Burke. He wouldn't touch her, he wouldn't get close to her, and he wouldn't flirt. He'd just have a harmless, careful conversation with her while he sobered up, and then he'd figure out when to leave. She probably wouldn't remember any of this tomorrow.

"That was really good," she said when he arrived back at his seat.

"What?" Nick watched her put the walker behind their booth. She had asked permission, but he still felt locked in place with his wheels out of easy reach.

"Your song," Hayley said. "Really good."

"Thanks." He bought a little time with a sip or two of ice water. "So Kevin's at Vivez tonight, huh?"

Hayley let her head fall back dramatically against the cushion of the booth so she was staring at the ceiling. "Yes," she said. "Kevin is at Vivez."

Oops. Nick had figured talking about Kevin would make it a lot harder for either of them to forget about Kevin, but clearly things with Hayley's boyfriend were not, in fact, peachy keen.

"I'm sure you'll be working there soon," he said.

She laughed. "You know the worst part? I *wanted* him to go in tonight. It's easier to miss him than to figure the rest of it out."

Three steaming plates of bar snacks were placed in front of Nick, and he thanked Steph and dug in. Hayley ordered another drink, then watched him eat, amused. All the plates held the same thing.

"You really like fried mushrooms," she said.

"You bet your ass," he said, chewing. "Have some."

She did. "He asked me to go with him," she said through a mouthful of mushroom.

"Kevin?" he said. "To Vivez tonight?"

"Yep." She licked dip off her fingers. "I said no."

Nick's pulse picked up. "So you could be here with me?"

She rolled her eyes. "Don't say it like *that*."

"Well, I mean, how do you want—"

"Look, I just thought I'd feel better once I worked things out with you."

Nick sipped his water and remembered the dejection on her face once they'd "worked out their shit." He'd apologized for what he'd said about her happiness, and she'd looked disappointed. He realized now that Hayley hadn't been looking forward to spending time with him tonight. She wanted to blame him for whatever was going wrong in her life.

"Damn," she said. "These mushrooms are good."

"Uh-huh."

She saw the look on his face and turned apologetic. "That's not the only reason I wanted to talk to you."

"I get it," he said. "We both wanted to feel better."

Hayley sat back against the booth and stared at the table for a long time. "You were right," she said. "The universe only stays together until . . ." Her shoulders slumped. "Actually, it never stays together."

Nick felt sick. "It can," he offered.

Hayley shook her head with a rueful smile. "For a couple days, maybe. A week, tops."

"Forget it," he said weakly, almost begging her. "Just forget everything I said that night, okay? I promise you that was—"

"Not who you are," she cut in. "You said." She leaned forward. "But you can't not be you."

She was absolutely right. The most joyful woman he'd ever seen was getting drunk on whiskey sours because he'd wanted to believe that happiness was something that didn't exist as opposed to something he couldn't have. It didn't matter how much he hated himself for it. He'd wanted to take joy from Hayley Burke the night they'd met, and now he would do anything in the world to give it back.

He tried again. "Just because I'm a jerk doesn't mean I was right."

Hayley batted away his words. "Just stop it."

"I need to—"

"You *think* you need to fix it by making everything your fault," she said, irritated. "I'm the one who decided the world was all sunshine and rainbows just because Icarus was in the rearview mirror. I'm the one who just *had* to get some cute guy to smile. God."

"You thought . . ." Nick closed his eyes and pinched the bridge of his nose, hard. "Great. That's just great."

"What?" she demanded. "What did you think I was doing?"

"You said I was miserable," he said, head in palm. "Not cute."

"Congratulations. You're both."

"What is it about the walker?" he asked her wearily. "Seriously, do the wheels make me look like a five-year-old? I mean, my God, the number of women who've looked at me like I'm a preschooler handing them a Valentine's Day card . . ."

She squinted at him. "That's not what I meant!"

"Oh, really?" He laughed. "How did you mean it, then?"

"Kissable!" she snapped. "I'd have fun kissing you!"

Nick very slowly brought his head up to stare at her, and the anger on Hayley's face faded as her words sank in. She'd have fun kissing him. He hadn't imagined it; she'd glanced at his lips as if she wanted to taste them. But she was obviously embarrassed to have admitted it.

Because she could do better than him.

"I wouldn't. I won't." The words dropped out of her mouth as she tried to get her bearings. "I'm with Kevin."

"I get it," he said.

They both went for the mushrooms and chewed slowly.

"You're saying when you ask girls out," Hayley said. "In this bar, where you're the king of the world, you ask a girl to leave with you, and she says, 'Oh, you're cute'? Like she's talking to a kid?"

He shrugged, staring into his drink. "Not all the time."

"Well, that's just ridiculous."

He met her gaze with a silent *thank you*, and the warmth in her eyes said *you're welcome*.

"I don't know if anything stays together forever," he said quietly. "But I really do think you can find what you're looking for."

As he kept his eyes on hers, something strengthened between them. Nick had never felt this before, and he couldn't explain it now, but he knew they were linked—maybe they'd been linked since the first time she'd met his gaze. It was easy to tell her the truth—terrifyingly, mystifyingly easy—and he didn't want to do anything else. She would spot anything else, and she would look away.

She held his gaze a beat longer and then wiped her hands on a napkin. "I couldn't make it work before," she said. "And that was when I had a job."

"Icarus?"

"Yep." She reached for her drink. "We used to dance at the Icarus Showcase in Indianapolis."

"And that's the piece of your universe that needed to change," he guessed. "You came here for a better job at Vivez?"

"That was the plan," she said. "But of course I screwed up the job, and things are still weird with Kevin . . ."

"But you didn't screw up," Nick said gently. "You'll dance in September, won't you? That's what Linda meant the other day?"

Hayley perked up. "Sure," she said slowly. "But Kevin and I have never not been dancing at the same time before."

"Sounds like a pretty big adjustment," Nick said, hoping he sounded supportive.

"It is." She was smiling now. "It is! God, I was *freaking out*, but that's it. We just have to *adjust* to our new rhythm, is all. We're not used to being this happy."

Nick tried to follow her logic. "A good problem to have," he offered.

Her eyes widened. "But what if I don't dance?"

He scoffed. "You'll dance."

"Seriously," Hayley said. "What if she changes her mind? If I'd really been good enough, Linda Branflakesinwhatsit would've given me a job, right along with Kevin. She would've said, 'Hayley, I don't give a good goddamn who I've got already. You've gotta be up there.'"

"She'll put you on stage."

"You can't just say that."

"I know it."

"How?"

"Because you're beautiful," he said.

Silence.

He'd gotten too comfortable. Nick had cheered her up, and so he'd been riding the high of his success, busy shoveling mushrooms into his mouth and washing them down with ice water while he half listened to Hayley worry about a problem he knew for a fact wasn't a problem, because there was no way in hell anyone would deny this woman a spot on stage. While his guard was down, the truth came out of his mouth, and then panic hit so hard and fast he thought he might throw up. When he finally found the courage to look at her, he saw pure joyful surprise on Hayley's face.

"You really think I'm beautiful?" she asked.

He was a little taken aback. Surely Kevin had told her, if no one else. How could she not know she was special?

"I think you're full of beauty," he said. "Yes."

Her smile was small then—shy, even—but Nick thought she glowed a little.

She said, "Thank you, Nick."

"You're welcome."

Well, at least she didn't think she was a problem anymore. Maybe his work here was finally done.

"How d'you get an Uber?" she asked him out of nowhere.

Excellent—this meant she was leaving. "I think you have to download the app and get an account," he told her.

"You mean you don't know? Didn't you have to call one to get here?" He shook his head gently, and she put her face in her hands. "Shit," she said through her fingers. "You can drive. I'm so sorry."

Nick could've explained how much he hated struggling to climb into an unfamiliar car, or how excruciating it was to watch someone he'd never met try to manhandle the walker into the trunk, but he and Hayley had both been through enough for one night.

"It's okay," he said. "How about a taxi?"

Two minutes later, Hayley was on the phone with a taxi service, and he gave her the address of the bar. "Okay," she said. "Now where'm I going?"

He looked at her quizzically. "How should I know?"

"Oh!" She started laughing. "My place. Right."

Nick was more confused when Hayley put down her phone and started rummaging in her purse. "Are they still on the line?" he asked.

"I wrote it down here somewhere," she said.

Nick picked up the phone. As it became increasingly clear that Hayley wasn't finding her address, a bored man on the other end of the line told him the cab company did not pick up drunk people from bars without first knowing where they would be dropping those drunk people off. Nick thanked him, hung up the phone, and watched Hayley search.

"How about you call Kevin?" he suggested.

She shook her head emphatically. "No. He might be doing something important."

"Come on. He'll understand."

Hayley wordlessly took the phone from him, put it to her ear, then hung up after less than a minute. "No answer," she said.

"Maybe if you call again, he'll know it's important."

"I'm not going to be a problem anyone has to fix."

She wasn't—not technically—but he knew that ship had sailed a while ago. He couldn't just leave her here. He didn't love the idea of staying either; he was sober now, but he felt depleted enough that the drive home was likely to get harder the longer he stayed in this booth. If he couldn't leave her to fend for herself, and he couldn't wait here until she figured things out; if a taxi and an Uber were not going to work, and Kevin wasn't answering the phone, then Nick saw only one more option.

He didn't like it.

8

Hayley was alone in a strange bed, clad only in her panties.

She sat up slowly, getting used to the pain in her head and the light slipping into the room through a crack in drawn curtains. She saw a dresser, an overstuffed armchair, a bedside table with a lamp. An alarm clock read nine. There was a photo of a beach on the far wall.

Her bra was on the floor next to the bed, and the rest of her clothing had disappeared.

She glimpsed a sink and mirror through the open bathroom door, and a hazy memory found her: She'd decided it was too hot, thrown her shirt, and shucked her tank top over her head as she walked down the hallway. She'd stepped out of her shoes, peeled off her socks, slipped out of her jeans. They'd both come into the bedroom, but he'd ducked into the bathroom while she'd climbed into bed. Hayley remembered him standing in the doorway, light streaming into the dark room from the hallway behind him. *"Goodnight,"* he'd said, and she couldn't see his face.

Shit. She was in Nick's bed.

Hayley put on her bra and walked gingerly toward the bathroom, trying to replay the evening in her head. Feelings arrived before the memories: She was supposed to be upset about something, maybe embarrassed . . .

She'd told Nick things weren't okay with Kevin.

That one hit her in the gut. Her boyfriend had been at Vivez, taking his job seriously, and she'd been complaining to a total stranger about a feeling she didn't even understand. Hayley looked around for her phone but wasn't in a hurry to find it. She'd have to explain to Kevin how she'd ended up in Nick's bed. Which sounded worse than it was, because she hadn't actually done anything.

Even when his lips had been so close, and leaning in felt like the most natural thing in the world.

Except for some reason it *felt* like she'd . . .

Oh no. She'd told him so. She'd said she would have fun kissing him.

Damn it, girl . . .

Hayley flipped on the bathroom light. There she was, every flaw reflected in the bathroom mirror. She saw something else in the reflection and turned around to face the walk-in shower. There were grab bars mounted on the shower walls and the wall next to the toilet.

Well, sure. Why wouldn't Nick have those in his bathroom?

Why did every reminder of his condition throw her for a loop?

Hayley took a breath. This was no big deal. Just a surprise, like the walker had been a surprise, and there were going to be more surprises because she knew absolutely nothing about what was wrong with him. At least she hadn't treated him like a five-year-old. Called him *cute* in the worst way.

Come on, Hayley Michelle. You're not enlightened. You're scared. Ever since you freaked out over the walker, you're terrified you'll do something worse.

What would've happened if the walker had shown up right away?

Hayley imagined Nick approaching her that first night, instead of the other way around. He would have tapped her arm at the bar, given an easy hello, found a clever way to tell her how great a dancer she was. He'd have leaned close to do it too, using the noise around them as an excuse to close the distance, his mouth next to her ear. He would've smiled.

The thought gave her goose bumps.

She would've told him thanks, but no thanks, of course. She would've said she had a boyfriend. But there was no way in hell any woman could look at that jawline and those ice-blue eyes and not at least consider what it would be like to go to bed with him.

She turned back to the sink, paused. A toothbrush in a plastic wrapper sat in a glass next to a tube of toothpaste, a bottle of headache medicine, and a folded washcloth.

He'd set all of this out before saying goodnight, she realized. Nick had quietly taken care of her as she'd stumbled through the evening, watching from a distance as she fell apart. She'd gone to the bar to confront him, to get rid of whatever was keeping her off balance and look damn good doing it. Instead, she'd gotten sloppy, life-before-Columbus drunk, and he'd calmly driven her to his apartment, where she'd pretty much stripped for him. She'd made herself his problem.

Hayley chased a couple of pills with two glasses of water, then vigorously brushed her teeth, literally frothing at the mouth.

She was *too* nice. That's what it was. She was wasting time worrying about how to treat him, and he was probably counting the seconds until he could very politely kick her ass out the front door. Nobody had forced him to bring her here. She hadn't asked; she was sure of that. Nick Freeman could have left her alone in the bar, and instead he'd slept on his own couch, like a martyr, for the sympathy points. For the story. So he could go back to the bar next week and tell some coed how he'd suffered for a damsel in distress. And she'd been stupid enough to think he didn't know he was kissable! That man damn well knew his legs wouldn't matter in bed anyway, not when he had the rest of him to offer. Who knew how many women had left fingernail tracks across those broad shoulders of his? Even standing up, even with the walker, he'd have no trouble using the strength in his arms to press her up against a wall. Or she'd hop up on a counter, wrap her legs around his waist . . .

What the hell?

Hayley gaped at her flushed reflection in the mirror, grabbed the washcloth, and scrubbed at her face with a vengeance. She wasn't his problem, he goddamn knew it, and she needed to get the hell out of this apartment.

After she got out of the bedroom.

The very cold bedroom.

God, Hayley Michelle—you just had to strip in the hallway, didn't you? Great idea to leave your clothes out there with him. Fucking brilliant.

Hayley opened the door nearest the bed, and found a walk-in closet and a red silk robe hanging from a hook on the wall.

It was either this or one of his dress shirts.

She left the bedroom and padded down the hallway, wishing she had socks to guard against the chill of the hardwood floor. She passed a bathroom and what looked like a small office; he wasn't in either. The hallway opened into a living room in front of her and a kitchen area to her right.

And there was Nick Freeman, standing at the kitchen counter, slicing a grapefruit in half.

Gone was the blue button-down that had brought out his eyes the night before, but he was still wearing the same gray T-shirt and jeans and sneakers. Hayley realized she was used to seeing him look polished, put together, and now the light, caramel-brown hair he so deliberately styled to look casually mussed was damp and falling into his face. His eyes were narrowed as he held the fruit steady, and his frown of concentration seemed to sharpen the features of his already angular face. Everything was a little rumpled, and she found she liked him better this way.

Nick must have caught sight of her in his peripheral vision, because he suddenly did a double take and put down his knife. He tried to recover, but she saw his eyes widen.

"That bad, huh?" she said.

"Huh? Oh no," he said. "You look great."

"I don't believe you."

"It's the robe," he said sheepishly.

"Then give me my clothes, and I'll give this back."

"They're in the dryer." It sounded like an apology. "They were . . . I figured you'd want them clean, and I was going to leave them outside the door, but I overslept."

Hayley spotted her purse on the nearby table and walked over to find her phone. She had no new messages, no voicemails, no missed calls.

If Kevin didn't care that she was gone, she didn't care about calling him back.

"You want some coffee?" Nick asked her. "Or I can make some tea."

"Water's fine." She sat at the table, angling her chair to face him.

He reached into a cabinet and brought out a glass. "How about breakfast? Bacon and eggs."

She really wanted to see how he was going to make that happen, but the thought of bacon and eggs was nauseating at the moment. "Do you have chocolate?"

He blinked. "Chocolate?"

"Chocolate," she said, irritated. "Candy bars. M&Ms. Chocolate."

"No."

"How can you not have chocolate?"

"It's not good for you."

"That's not the point."

"Chocolate would honestly make you feel better right now?"

"Chocolate always makes me feel better."

They stared at each other, Nick leaning forward on the counter, Hayley looking stonily back at him.

"What would be your second choice?" he said evenly.

Hayley took her time. "Toast would be okay."

He nodded once. "You want grape jelly on that?"

"Yes. Thank you."

Hayley watched as Nick silently filled her order. There was only a space of a few feet between the stove behind him and the sink in front of him, wide enough for the walker but narrow enough for his arms to easily span the distance between the two counters he was using. Sometimes he'd hold on to the walker, but more often he used the surfaces around him for support. One hand gripped the counter as he opened the fridge with the other hand and grabbed the jelly; he used the same technique as he opened a drawer for a knife or filled her glass of water. Sometimes he could use both hands, like when he was opening a bag of bread, so long as he could lean slightly on the walker for balance.

Hayley was fascinated by the efficiency of it; Nick looked like an ordinary guy making breakfast until she made a point of watching for the small allowances he made to keep his balance, or the way he transferred one item at a time from counter to counter because he couldn't pick both up at once. She wouldn't call him graceful, but his movements had a certain fluidity to them, the result of an obviously practiced routine. It reminded her a little of choreography, and as she glanced over at a stereo on a shelf filled with rows and rows of CDs, she wondered if he ever danced his way through making those eggs.

After putting bread in the toaster, Nick placed Hayley's glass of water on a stainless steel cart next to the counter, the sort of thing she'd seen in the Icarus kitchen. She started to stand up, but he wheeled the cart over to her, one hand on the cart and one hand on the walker.

"Figured you might want the water first," he said.

She took the glass off the cart. "What's the deal with this robe?"

He looked a little embarrassed. "I'm a big Rocky fan."

She looked at the name stitched on the front. "So he won a lot of fights?"

Nick seemed to be waiting for the punchline. "Seriously? Rocky. Rocky Balboa." She stared at him, and he pointed at the movie poster hanging over a leather couch. "That's for the movie *Rocky*. Came out in the seventies."

"Yeah, sorry, wasn't around."

His grip tightened on the cart. "Neither was I. I'm thirty-two."

"Oh," she said sweetly. "I didn't know."

Hayley smiled thinly at him until he turned away, jaw clenched. She'd guessed his age correctly, and wasn't that far behind him, but she was enjoying his irritation too much to let him know she was twenty-eight.

Nick was wheeling the cart back to the counter when the toast popped up, and Hayley laughed as he jumped.

"Scared you, huh?"

He kept his back to her. "Not exactly," he said. "I have what's called an exaggerated startle reflex. Came with the leg stuff."

She suddenly hated herself, and then anger welled back up at him for making her seem so mean. "I'm sorry."

"No problem."

He busied himself with the toast, and she decided to take the leap. "So what happened to you?"

"We went through this last night."

"Okay," she pressed. "Why so many stories, then?"

He smirked as he picked up the jelly knife. "Did you do a survey or something?"

"Everybody in that bar knows you, Nick. Everybody thinks you're this fantastic guy, and yet you gave everybody a different story."

"Only the ones who asked."

"You were a gymnast. You got attacked by sharks. You were a skydiver." She counted them off on her fingers. "My personal favorite was that you hit your head ejecting from an airplane. *Top Gun*, right? It's okay to be a pilot, but not a SEAL?"

He chuckled. "It's my tribute to Goose."

She folded her arms. "Why all the bullshit?"

Nick brought her toast to the table, along with his grapefruit and a mug of coffee. "I guess I always figured it mattered to people too much."

"You don't like people caring about you?"

"That's not what they're doing." He sat down, handed her the plate and a napkin. "I can understand asking if I need help. They see the walker and they want to do something to improve the situation. It's a practical question. But asking what happened? That's satisfying your curiosity."

"Maybe I want to get to know you more."

"Sure, because getting to know me involves assessing how broken I am and figuring out how sorry you should be for me."

She was hurt—and afraid he was right. "That's not what—"

"Come on, Hayley. Wouldn't it make a difference?" His blue eyes locked on to hers. "Wouldn't you care if I said I was injured in Afghanistan saving children, or shot while I was robbing a bank? If

I said I was in a drunk driving accident, it'd sure as hell make a difference whether I was the driver or the victim." He dug into his grapefruit. "People have seen too many movies about paralyzed heroes and athletes hit by cars. They're interested in who I was instead of who I am. If they need to fit me into a story to decide what they think of me, I'm going to have fun giving them one."

She watched him. "So you lie to everyone, then."

He shook his head. "Not to kids."

"And you're really not going to tell me."

She saw a hint of a smile—or maybe she just wanted it to be there. "It'd be a shame to cave in after that big speech."

"Come on," she said playfully. "What can I do to earn it? I could swing dance for you again. I know you liked that."

He didn't look up. "By yourself?"

"Or with you."

Nick took a while to answer. "I shouldn't earn something like that by detailing my damage."

Hayley felt a small shock of intuition. Did Nick think he didn't deserve to dance with her?

"I saw the way he looked at you," Alexa had said. And then last night he'd told her she was beautiful. She'd asked if he'd meant it, and he hadn't just said yes—he'd said, *"I think you're full of beauty."* People threw around words all the time, but Nick had been so deliberate, like he'd thought about this. It had meant something to her.

She'd thought he was keeping his distance out of disdain, but what if he was handling her so carefully because she . . . mattered?

She didn't think this was a crush. He wasn't fawning over her. But Hayley had the sinking feeling she'd been reading him completely wrong. It must have shown in her face, because he gave a quick, defensive grin, like using a flashbulb to blind someone.

"You know what?" he said. "Points for persistence. I have cerebral palsy."

Hayley didn't want to tell him she didn't know what that meant, but apparently Nick was feeling merciful.

"That's just another term for brain damage at birth," he continued, "or early childhood. I was born early, so there was bleeding in my brain, so the signals between my brain and my legs got screwed up. Basically I can't walk or stand without something to hang on to."

"And you've got that startle thing." Hayley wanted to avoid screwing up again.

"Yeah." He focused on his coffee. "I mean, there are other things. I'm not that coordinated, and I can't walk very far without getting tired. But everything else is pretty normal."

Hayley digested this, and he took her silence as disappointment. "See?" he said. "I didn't *do* anything. I wasn't someone better before this."

"That doesn't make you any less impressive," she said.

He laughed. "What, because I made breakfast all by myself, like a big boy?"

Hayley shook her head, wishing she hadn't walked into the kitchen carrying so much anger.

"Because you couldn't leave the bar without knowing I was okay," she said softly.

Nick loaded the empty dishes back on the cart. "Yeah, well, should've done better with those clothes."

Hayley watched him walk slowly back to the counter. "Can we be friends, Nick?"

He paused. "Aren't we friends already?"

"Oh, sure, you've been really friendly these past couple weeks. I got more enthusiasm from the cashier at Walmart the other day."

He examined a plate, his grip and his voice tight. "I'm not really sure what you want from me, Hayley."

"How about having a conversation where I don't feel like I've done something wrong?"

That got him to look at her. Hayley felt her throat constrict, like the frustration she had buried was rising up to keep her from speaking.

"I get that." he said. "You tried to be nice, and all I've ever done is make you feel worse. I'm sorry. But if it takes you two or three drinks before you can stand to be around me, why in the world do you want to be my friend?"

His tone was even, his words measured, but she could see pain in his eyes.

"Do you realize you've never even smiled at me?" she asked. "Not a real smile anyway. You're so much warmer with everyone else."

Nick rolled his eyes. "Hayley, you are worth so much more than what I give everyone else."

There it was again, the same resignation that had been in his voice when he'd talked about his "damage." It was like complimenting her went hand in hand with hating himself.

And now, finally, she understood: Nick was keeping her at arm's length because he thought she was better off without him.

And where did he get that idea, Hayley Michelle? Was it when you saw his walker and lost your shit?

"Nick." She tried to keep her voice even. "Ever since we met, you've looked at me like I'm miles away, or behind glass or something. Every word you say sounds like it's gone through a million rehearsals in your head." Her voice cracked a little.

Slow down, girl. Breathe. Don't you dare cry.

"I know I did that," she said. "I killed something in you as soon as I saw the walker. I'm so sorry. And I'm tired, and my head is going to split open, and instead of waking up with Kevin, I'm sitting in your bathrobe, watching you judge me. Help me undo what I did. Please."

Hayley sat still, chest heaving, watching Nick stare into the sink.

"And what about Kevin?" he asked finally. "What's the point of being friends with me if you're with him?"

She frowned. "It's not like I can't do both."

"Really?" he asked. "I mean, there are rules."

"Rules?"

"Things you don't do."

She laughed. "I'm not going to sleep with you, Nick."

He winced, and she wished she could take it back. She'd laughed at the idea of cheating on Kevin, but he'd heard her mocking the idea of sleeping with him. Not that any good could possibly come of trying to clarify.

"Nick," she said carefully, "how many friends do you have? How many close friends?"

He took a second. "Two. Gavin and his wife."

"Well, that's a good enough reason for us to be friends, right there."

"Because I'm a charity case?"

"No," she said patiently. "Come over here."

Nick walked over to the table and stood in front of her.

"Would you want to be friends with me?" she asked. "If it was possible?"

He didn't hesitate. "Yes."

"Then instead of thinking about how this is going to work, maybe just trust me that it will."

He nodded, and she smiled at him as she stood up and headed for the dryer. "You haven't told me why," he said.

She turned. "Why be friends?"

"Yes. You don't owe me this."

She raised an eyebrow. "You know normal people don't need a reason to be friends, right?"

"So I'm abnormal."

She liked the twinkle in his eyes.

"All my friends are in Indiana," she told him. "And I think you're a really good guy, Nick. Definitely the best I've met in Ohio."

"Out of how many?"

She rolled her eyes good-naturedly as he fought to keep a straight face. "I think we could be good for each other," she said. "Want to see if I'm right?"

Finally, she got to see what Nick Freeman's smile looked like with actual light behind it.

9

It was tech week at Vivez Dance.

The company's summer show was premiering Friday night, and that meant every moment from this Monday morning through Friday afternoon would be spent perfecting the technical details of the show on stage, from lighting cues to costume changes, sound levels, prop placement, and everything in between. The cast and crew would be essentially living in the theater from early in the morning until late at night. At the very back of the floor section, sitting behind a long folding table with stacks of VHS tapes and a computer, Nick Freeman was having a blast.

It was the energy of the place. It had been a little weird to be introduced to the company the week before as a new addition to the family, but a family it was. Linda treated every member of the company like she was grateful they'd chosen to be there, and that sort of leadership inspired her employees to be worthy of her gratitude. Even Nick, who still thought of himself as a glorified button pusher, had started bringing in doughnuts every morning. It was a small gesture (and an inexpensive one, since a lot of the dancers were too health conscious for a daily step closer to diabetes), but it allowed him to contribute to the team beyond just helping Linda transfer video. Then there was Nick's ulterior motive: He kept the doughnuts at his table in the back, which meant he could introduce himself to anybody who came looking for a tasty treat. It took him two days to build a fairly comprehensive mental roster of the Vivez Dance team. Just like at the Squeaky Lion, the more Nick knew about the people around him, the easier it was to find where he fit in—and cerebral palsy had trained him to always be aware of people willing to help him. Like the tall Black guy in his mid-twenties who was now approaching Nick's table, with a toothy grin and a mug of hot coffee.

"Happy Monday to the music man!" Calvin Tunney set the mug down next to Nick and came around the table to drum on his shoulders with his hands. "We've gotta keep you loose, brother. Can't have you pulling a muscle changing those tapes."

"How's my favorite person today, Cal?" Nick asked.

"Pretty sure Mimi's in the dressing room."

Nick laughed. "You beat me to the joke."

"I know, I know. I was supposed to say, 'I'm doing fine, Nick!' like I don't know you like her more than me."

Nick tapped the box of doughnuts next to him. "I don't get apple fritters for Mimi."

Cal gave him a fist bump as a young woman with a backpack came jogging up to them. She wore a bright yellow baseball cap, with a daisy on the front, over her long, champagne-blond hair, and there was a look of serene contentment on her face. Nick and Cal waited expectantly.

"Ranier," she said triumphantly.

"Mimi Ranier," Nick said slowly, testing it out. He glanced at Cal.

"I like it," Cal said.

"Me too," Nick decided. "Sounds like you'd be headlining a classy stage show in the 1940s."

Mimi gasped, and brought her hands together in an excited clap. "That's the best answer ever."

"Hear that?" Nick asked Cal. "Best answer ever. Like, better than any answer you could give her."

Cal snorted. "I could give a better one. If I wanted to."

This was their routine: coffee, doughnuts, and banter. He'd quickly become "the music man" to Cal thanks to the same knowledge and recall that dazzled at the bar, and Mimi had involved him in her tireless search for a proper stage name. It was as if they had adopted him or volunteered to be adopted, and either way Nick was fine with it. They reminded him of his students, in all the best ways.

"So, tech week," he said. "How rough is this going to be for you guys?"

Cal shrugged. "We get really good dinners. I'm down with it."

"The hard part's the boredom," Mimi told him. "There's going to be at least one hookup."

"Really?" Nick asked. "Love is in the air?"

She shook her head at him with a smile. It was a look that said he was awfully cute for being so naive, and Mimi made it look adorable. She had grown up in this theater doing summer programs and internships before she was employed full-time, and Nick figured she'd earned the right to remind him she knew more than he did, even if he guessed she was barely old enough to drink.

"Not love, mon chéri," she said patiently. "Put a bunch of beautiful people close together for long enough and at least two of them are going to find a way to pass the time."

Nick mulled that over. "I had no idea." He looked at Cal. "How do you dial back the sexiness? I've never been able to do it."

Cal scoffed. "The ladies can't stay away from this."

"Really?" Nick smiled innocently. "They seem to be doing a really good job of it."

"Uh-huh. Tomorrow's coffee is landing in your lap."

"The eagle has landed," Mimi cut in. "The rooster's in the hen-house. The lion is strolling the wide, desert plain of the Serengeti."

"What?" Nick followed her gaze. "Oh."

"Dreamboat's here," she said.

Kevin Albee had entered the room, and Nick was annoyed.

This wasn't a new feeling. Nick had been annoyed at the sight of Kevin since they'd both started working at Vivez, and he had spent every day of the last two weeks trying to find a defensible reason why. Every morning, Kevin visited Nick's table to collect a couple of cinnamon-sugar doughnuts and cheerfully thank him for breakfast. Then, according to Cal and Mimi, the man filled his days with impressively hard work. Kevin wasn't the class clown, and he'd shown no interest in any of the company gossip, but he was completely and consistently invested in what was going to happen on stage. It was the sort of attitude Nick admired. In fact, the most annoying thing about Kevin was how perfect he was for Hayley—until today. Today Nick could relish how justifi-ably annoying it was that Kevin had failed to answer his phone Friday night, when Hayley had called from the bar.

"Not to brag," Mimi said, "but that man would've been lost without me."

Cal said, "You're not bragging if it's not true."

"You take that back. He never left my side."

"And you never found his phone."

Cal's retort grabbed Nick's interest. "Wait, what?" he asked.

"Mimi was a little too happy to help Kevin find his phone Friday night," Cal explained. "And then she kicked it under the carts in the kitchen so the search wouldn't end."

"I would *never*," Mimi protested.

"Then how come Linda found it Saturday afternoon after you'd already looked in there?"

"A lot of people stampede through that kitchen, you know."

"Shit," Nick muttered.

Mimi was aghast. "I didn't hide his phone, Nick. You think I *hid* his *phone*?"

"No," Nick said. "I think Cal's messing with you."

"Then why do you look so disappointed?"

"Because Kevin lost his phone."

And now Kevin was strolling toward the doughnut table with the affable confidence of a man who knew life would always go his way.

"Hey, man." He nodded at Nick. "Thanks for the doughnuts."

"Of course," Nick said. "Happy to help."

Kevin fished his usual out of the box. "Hayley said I need to thank you for Friday too."

Nick shrugged. "I'm just glad it all worked out."

Kevin held out his hand, and Nick shook it. "Thank you, really. I owe you a beer."

"You don't, but I'll be happy to collect anyway."

Kevin nodded at Cal and Mimi, with a smile, and then they all watched him walk away.

"You're going to tell us everything," Mimi said.

"You know, I don't think I will."

Cal tried next. "At least tell us who Hayley is."

"Hayley's the best dancer you've ever seen," Nick said.

"Hayley was the reason Kevin wanted to find his phone," Mimi countered drily. "What were you doing with his girlfriend?"

Cal's eyes widened. "Oh, this is good."

Nick held up a hand. "You were helping find his phone; I was helping because he lost his phone."

Mimi put on a faux pout. "Why did you get to meet her before we did?"

Nick smiled at her. "Just lucky, I guess."

10

Hayley was absolutely sure now that the waitress at Dom and Tony's 24/7 Diner didn't like her.

The place wasn't packed, and she'd been told to take all the time she needed, but the more Hayley studied the menu, the more she caught some serious side-eye every time this woman passed. She'd only been here once before, just for the few minutes it had taken to retrieve Kevin after their audition, so Hayley didn't see how she could be paying for some past offense. Yet she had obviously done something, and as silly as it was, Hayley wondered if the woman could sense she was supposed to be with her boyfriend.

She'd intended to visit Kevin. She really had. That was the whole reason she'd come into the diner today, to get the burger he'd liked so much and walk it a block or so to Vivez Dance. The company was into their third day of tech week now, and she knew how taxing that could be. But then she started wondering when Kev's lunch break was and how embarrassing it'd be if she arrived too early, and the food got cold—or too late, after he'd eaten something else. She pictured how his castmates might react if Kevin got a burger and they didn't; she worried about what they'd think of her and whether bringing Kevin his lunch made her look like some doormat who existed to serve him. It'd be better for everyone if she stayed here and ordered her own damn burger while she figured out what the hell was wrong with her.

We're not used to being this happy. It had made so much sense when she'd said the words to Nick, and maybe she really was learning to live without stress. She and Kevin used to drink wine at three AM, cross-legged on the living room floor; they used to make love on lunch breaks and rush back to Icarus like giddy kids skipping school. They used to crave more time because there was never enough, and now they'd gained time and lost something else. It reminded her of frustrating choreography: She'd plot out every step of a routine, rehearse it to perfection, and throw her notebook across the room, because she wasn't *saying* anything.

She couldn't mention any of this to Kevin, not when the ache in her heart was something she couldn't even name. Not when they had moved here to fix her. Kevin had wanted to leave; she had needed to.

Bringing Kevin a burger would be a poor apology for taking him away from Icarus.

Hayley was about to cave in and order whatever was at the top of the page when she saw her tormentor glance toward the door. Then the glowering woman smiled so completely and spontaneously that Hayley wondered if the sudden change would strain a muscle in her face. The door opened, a customer walked in, and Hayley started laughing.

Nick Freeman. Of course it was Nick. Who else could get that kind of reaction from the stone-cold diner queen?

"There you are!" the woman exclaimed. "It's so good to have you back these days, kiddo."

Nick grinned. "I love you, Pauline. You always act like I'm returning from war."

"It's been a while since we've seen you every day."

"And I am so very happy to be back."

Someone out of sight bellowed over the sizzle of meat. "Is that the boy?"

Nick looked delighted. "They still let you near the grill, old man?" he called back.

"I've got a new joke for you, boy-o!"

"I'm betting old joke," Nick countered. "And if it's as dirty as the last one, I'll get it from you when all the women and children are gone."

"Hey, rock star," Hayley spoke up. "What's good here?"

She hoped she didn't sound as nervous as she'd felt butting in, but she really wanted to join the party that Nick seemed to bring with him. She wanted that waitress and everyone else to know that the guy with the grin really liked her too. When Nick spotted her, the light that came to his eyes melted all her apprehension.

"Hey!" For the first time, he looked genuinely happy to see her. "Here by yourself?"

She nodded. "Wanna join me for lunch?"

"Absolutely." Nick sat across from her, Pauline standing expectantly nearby, and once he ordered a Coke, she was off to do his bidding.

Hayley leaned in conspiratorially. "She doesn't like me."

Nick scoffed. "Who wouldn't like you?"

"I'm telling you, I've been trying to find a perfect burger, and the woman keeps looking at me like if I eat too much, it'll go straight to *her* ass."

Nick laughed, hard. "You'll be fine."

"What, because I'm sitting with the superstar of Columbus?"

"When Pauline comes back, just tell her all about your search for the perfect burger."

Hayley stared at him, exasperated, and watched him read *don't screw with me* in her eyes.

"Trust me," he said.

Pauline was back with the Coke. "What can I get you?" she asked.

Hayley cleared her throat. "I want a burger I'll have to attack," she told Pauline, "but I don't want the thing to fall apart as soon as I pick it up, because then I'll have to pick through everything like a salad."

To her astonishment, a huge smile bloomed on Pauline's face.

"I'll get you the Dominator," Pauline said. "The bun gives you plenty to hold on to."

"You know what? One for me too," Nick said. "And Hayley's going to need a chocolate shake and some of your cake." He grinned at Hayley. "You're welcome."

By the time Pauline left to put in their order, Hayley could swear there were tears of joy in the waitress's eyes.

"Tell me," she said to Nick.

"She was worried you wouldn't eat." Nick saw she still didn't get it. "You're in good shape," he explained. "When someone like you takes too long with the menu, Pauline sees a picky eater. Pauline doesn't believe in picky eaters."

"Gotcha," she said. "I could tell her I love gluten and I hate hummus."

"I think your aversion to salad did the trick."

Pauline was back in record time, with two hunks of chocolate cake that barely stayed within the boundaries of their plates.

"Oh, wow," Hayley breathed.

"Pauline." Nick imbued her name with grateful apology. "I can't eat this. I just can't."

Pauline's hands went to her hips. "Since when do you not like my cake?"

"I will love your cake until the day I die."

"So why did you think you could get away with not ordering any?" she demanded. "You used to eat a piece of this a day."

"In college," he said gently. "A decade ago. I can't burn off the calories like I used to."

"Calories." The contempt in Pauline's voice made Hayley smile with her mouth full of cake. "You should take a cue from your friend here."

"Probably more than one," Nick agreed. "Just don't gang up on me, okay?"

Pauline winked at Hayley. "I make no promises." Then she was off.

"I like her," Hayley said.

Nick started in on his cake. "Now that she's picking on me, you mean?"

"That helps," she said playfully. "Plus this cake is amazing."

"Just wait until you taste the milkshake."

"So you two go way back, huh?" she asked. "To college?"

He nodded. "This was my home."

"Like the bar is now?"

Nick gave an odd smile at that, almost regretful. "No, the bar is something else," he said. "This place . . . well, I went to OSU, and this whole area is part of Ohio State's campus."

"Seems like the campus takes up the whole city."

"That was the problem. It turns out the diner was closer to a lot of my classes than my dorm room was. I ended up pretty much living here."

"I'm surprised you don't have your own booth."

"I do." He pointed behind her. "I usually sit over there."

She laughed. "The whole world just falls in love with you, don't they? How do you do it?"

Nick went back to concentrating on his cake, and she realized she'd embarrassed him.

"It had nothing to do with me," he said. "Pauline can't resist helping people. She saw this crippled kid coming in every day, and before you know it she's insisting I take her parking space in the back, just to make sure I had one. She never charged me for it. Never told me how much farther she had to walk to work each day either, but I'm sure it was a hike. And if I tell her I'm going to come visit, she still moves her car."

Hayley had welcomed the opportunity to walk off late-night pizzas as an undergrad at Purdue. But it was jarring to reframe the memory of her campus through the lens of someone who couldn't walk very far. And when she considered the size of the campus she was in the middle of now—God, how would you even *do* that, driving everywhere? Nick would've had to pack up his stuff after each class, walk to his car, get in the car, drive to a completely different building, hope for a parking space . . . She was getting overwhelmed just thinking about it, and hoped it didn't show on her face.

"Did the campus give you reserved parking too?" she asked.

"Oh, there were all sorts of perks," he said. "Even so, it was a pain in the ass before Pauline and her husband, Len, stepped in. They let me keep my scooter here overnight."

"You had a scooter?"

"Sure, like a souped-up version of what you see in Walmart. I'd park the car here in the morning, pick up the scooter, come back for lunch, and then plug in the scooter here at night before I drove the car back to the dorm."

"Did you have a helmet?" She reconsidered. "Nah, I bet you just had sunglasses and a leather jacket, like in *Top Gun*." He smiled a little reluctantly, and she gasped. "You did!"

"I looked really cool," he said sheepishly.

She wasn't sure he believed it, but she did. "Is Len the guy at the grill?"

He laughed; this was clearly a more comfortable topic. "No, that's Dom, as in Dom and Tony. Dom and Tony are brothers, and Pauline is Tony's daughter. She runs the place with Len, and the old men work the grill when they feel like it."

She smiled. "And they tell you dirty jokes."

"And they tell me dirty jokes."

Hayley thought about what Nick Freeman must have been like ten years ago, lugging textbooks into the diner, entertaining his friends in the back booth. Had he always been able to gain family everywhere he went?

"Hey," she said, "how'd they make so many *Rocky* movies? Does he just keep punching people?"

He considered this. "First of all, he doesn't punch people. He fights them."

"Fights them by punching them."

"Well, yeah, but it sounded different the way you said it. And there's much more to the movies than just boxing."

Hayley had a reply ready to go, but then Pauline arrived with the food. It only took one sip of a perfect chocolate milkshake to make her forget what she was going to say.

"Oh my God." She closed her eyes, savoring it. "Bless you, Nick Freeman."

He laughed. "What are friends for?"

"I'm getting one of these every day," she decided. "Today is the first day of the rest of my milkshake-filled life."

"You'll be Pauline's favorite person." Nick studied his burger, planning his approach. "So you googled *Rocky*, huh?"

"Oh, I watched it."

That got his attention. "You watched it?"

"Sure," she said. "Kevin was in bed by the time I got home Saturday night, and I figured what the hell."

Nick looked like he didn't quite believe her. "Did you like it?"

Hayley grabbed the Dominator with both hands and bit into a whole lot of grilled goodness. "He's such a shitty boxer. I mean, I thought he was going to just *pound* Apollo . . ."

"He did."

"He just kept getting hit in the face!" She wiped mustard from her mouth. "How's he even alive after that?"

Nick chewed thoughtfully. "Look—"

"Oh my God, you're winding up. Am I about to get a lecture?" She winked at him, and he smiled.

"It's not about whether he wins," he said. "Rocky wants it more. He trains and he gets beat up and he's still standing at the end because he decided he was going to be worth something."

"He wasn't worth something before? Adrian loved him."

"Sure, but he wasn't really doing anything with his life. He had to prove to everyone that he wasn't just a bruiser for a loan shark."

"Prove to himself, you mean."

"Sure."

"By beating someone up."

He took his time. "It's nice to be in a fight with an actual target."

Hayley could see him deciding to be diplomatic, and she didn't want him to hide from her. "If that's the case," she said, "why not watch *Under Siege*?"

Nick looked like he'd just found something rotten in his burger, and she was delighted. "Let me get this straight," he said. "Just so I can tell Gavin exactly why this friendship didn't work."

She said nothing, just watched him with exaggerated, wide-eyed innocence.

He said, "You're saying I'd be better off watching a shitty version of *Die Hard* than the best underdog movie in history."

Hayley shrugged. "There are more fights in that one."

"*Rocky* won *three* Oscars." Nick gestured with a kettle chip. "How many did *Under Siege* win?"

"Not a clue," she said cheerfully. "What'd Rocky win?"

Nick stopped being exasperated long enough to think about it. "Um . . . best picture, best director, and best film editing. And it was nominated for seven others. Best actor, best actress, two supporting actor nominations . . ."

"So it was only good enough to win three out of ten."

"He'll understand," Nick said. "I'll just say, 'Gavin, she prefers Seagal to Stallone.'"

She got a bite full of cheese, onion, and jalapeño and nearly wept with joy. "And film editing," she carried on. "How are you even supposed to judge that?"

Nick slumped forward, burger in both hands, elbows on the table. He only managed to glare for a couple seconds before he started laughing. "I have no idea," he said.

Laughing with him felt at least as good as her milkshake. She said, "You wanted to be Rocky, didn't you? I can just see little Nick Freeman chugging raw eggs and running around Columbus at dawn."

But panic hit when she actually pictured it. *Way to go, Hayley Michelle. He didn't run around Columbus. He can't run to the door. Why don't you remind him of everything else he wishes he could do?*

But Nick's blue eyes were gleaming with mirth, his curved lips smudged with hot sauce.

Screw it. She wasn't going to let this be awkward anymore.

"You would have been better off," she declared, "starting your workout with one of these milkshakes. Raw eggs'll kill you."

His smile grew.

"My mom used to make me French toast," he said. "Never at dawn, though."

God bless him, he was going to let it go. She could have kissed him.

"I've only seen parts of *Under Siege*," she admitted. "Kevin loves that movie."

"Ah," he said, and she wondered what he now thought of Kevin. "He apologized to me the other day. Just like you told him to."

He didn't seem thrilled about it. "What makes you think I told him to?" she asked.

"Because he said, 'Hayley said I need to thank you.'"

"You wouldn't believe what happened with his phone."

"I would, actually," he said. "I heard from an inside source."

"It's not like he was just wandering around," she said. "He used to cook at Icarus, so he was checking the kitchen out, and then he didn't realize he'd dropped anything until much later, and it wasn't like he could call." She sipped on her milkshake until she was convinced she could stop babbling. "Because who memorizes phone numbers anymore, right?"

Nick was suddenly intent on his burger. "Not Kevin."

Hayley took a beat. "You memorize phone numbers, don't you?"

Nick cleared his throat self-consciously, and Hayley stifled a laugh. "They've been working him hard," he said. "This tech week thing is no joke. And I didn't realize how much stuff goes on before the shows each night either. Mimi's working the box office, Cal's serving tables . . ."

"Sure," she said. "It was the same at Icarus. Better to use the people you have than hire twice as many."

He nodded. "It's really impressive."

She was about to tell him it was no big deal, but realized just in time that it absolutely would be with cerebral palsy and a walker. She tried not to blush.

"Have they got you helping with tech?" she asked.

He shook his head, laughing a little. "I bring doughnuts and push a few buttons on a computer."

"Hey, doughnuts are important. There were times during tech I'd kill for a doughnut."

"Just during tech?"

She threw a French fry at him as he laughed. "You I'd kill for much less."

He chuckled. "Coming to see the show?"

She sighed. "Yes."

"You seem awfully excited about it."

She fiddled with her straw. "They'll all meet me as Kev's girlfriend. It'll be, 'Look at Kevin's girlfriend, all alone, watching the show. I guess she doesn't have any friends, or talent.'"

"Hayley." She met his eyes as he gently said her name. "No one at Vivez would ever think of you that way."

She shrugged. "Yeah, well, maybe I think of myself that way."

Nick ate the last bite of his burger, then wiped his hands and mouth with his napkin before he spoke. "So sit with me."

She glanced at him. "What?"

"You won't be alone. Everyone will say, 'Look, our favorite coworker brought a friend. She must be awesome if she's with Nick.'"

She laughed, shaking her head. "Kevin wants me there opening night. You've got karaoke."

He shrugged. "I can skip a week."

Hayley wasn't sure she'd heard correctly. "Don't do that. Alexa told me you've got a three-year streak going."

"And what's the point of being at the bar if I could be having more fun somewhere else?"

She stared at him. "This isn't a rule of our friendship, you know. You don't have to do this for me."

"Look," he said, "this works out better anyway. I was going to go on Saturday, but this way the Becketts can come with me. You already know Gavin, you'll love Mel, and you can throw all sorts of food at me if you want. Just give Alexa a heads-up next time you're in, so they don't think I'm dead when I don't show."

No. This couldn't happen again. She wanted too much, and someone else was about to pay the price. Even if he had volunteered, even if his cheerful sacrifice only amounted to a few karaoke songs, Nick would be giving up his happiness for hers.

"I'm not asking you to give up your karaoke Friday," she said.

"Oh, I won't be going to karaoke on Friday." He smiled. "Actually, I've been meaning to ask: Would you do me a favor and join me at the premiere that night? The Becketts will be thrilled to meet my third friend."

Hayley laughed and felt herself relax. Nick Freeman was being her friend. Exactly what she'd wanted, and this was a chance to be a friend to him, and wasn't this what friends did? Didn't she want him to join her?

Yes. More so with every second.

"Give me your phone," she said.

"What?"

She made a "gimme" motion with her hand. "You can't cancel on me if you don't have my number."

"What makes you think I'd do that?" He seemed a little hurt, but he reached for his phone anyway, and her eyes widened when she saw it. "What?" he asked.

"A flip phone, Nick?" Hayley held up the phone like she was confronting an alcoholic with a hidden bottle. "A *flip phone*?"

"It does what I need it to do."

"But how do you text?" She stared at it. "How do you post online? How do you shop for stuff?"

"It does text," he said, "and I'm not on social media."

"I know you're not on social media."

"Then why did you . . . wait, did you try and find me?"

"I'll bet it takes an hour to write a sentence on this thing."

He leaned across the table, trying to see what she was doing. "You know, a lot of people actually use the phone to talk."

"Uh-huh." She hit the call button and felt her own phone vibrating in her pocket. "Now I've got your number and you've got mine." She held out his phone, and he took it back. "Just . . . don't answer my calls in public, okay? I'd hate for anyone else to know you have that thing."

He grinned. "Still think you can bear to be seen with me Friday night?"

She was already looking forward to it.

11

"Still a long way from nine o'clock," Mel said. "Probably a lot of barflies still looking forward to their evening, thinking they're going to get to see Nick Freeman."

Nick's legs ached as they approached the entrance to Vivez Dance. "Are you going to behave yourself in there?" he said. "Because I'm prepared to disown both of you."

"No, you won't. We make you respectable by association."

Gavin held open the lobby door as Mel announced she was off to find the bathroom. Nick stood and tried to catch his breath—and then he forgot about his breathing entirely.

Hayley was gliding toward him across the parking lot. Her dress was simple and navy blue, with a V-neck and a little pocket over the left breast, almost as if she'd found a T-shirt long enough to end halfway down her thighs. Except this was obviously a dress, tailored for her curves without hugging them, and the color looked great against the tanned skin of her arms and legs. She smiled as she took off her silver mirrored aviator shades.

"Hey, rock star."

"Hey," he said. She slipped into his arms and squeezed him for only a second or so, but he felt stronger afterward, calmer. He could only wrap one arm around Hayley while his other hand gripped the walker, but even so, holding her made him feel like he was home.

He said, "You remember Gavin."

"I do!" Hayley laughed as Gavin tipped his hat to her, and effortlessly crossed one tan sandal behind the other to give a slight curtsy in return. "I have to meet your wife!"

"She's in a hurry to meet you too." Gavin pulled open the door again. "She's in here somewhere."

Nick noticed Hayley was making a point of walking alongside him. "I was thinking," he said. "I'll bet we could request Kevin as our server."

Hayley smiled her thanks. "He's working in the kitchen. But he'll try to pop out and say hi before the show."

Nick tried to hide his relief as they walked up to the box office window, where a delighted Mimi Ranier was on duty.

"Niiiiiick!" she exclaimed, drawing out his name affectionately. "How wonderful of you to elevate the evening with your presence, my darling."

"Mimi, my dear, what little I bring to the party means nothing when all eyes are on you."

"Why Nick, you wouldn't be making fun of my outfit, would you?"

Nick grinned. Mimi was wearing black slacks, but her T-shirt was a shade of yellow normally reserved for a sports car. "I was wondering about it, but we both know you can light up a room in any shirt."

Mimi patted his hand. "That I can, but Linda likes to splash some color 'round the place. How many people are lucky enough to be with you tonight?"

"You've got me down for three, I think, and we'd like to be seated with my friend Hayley Burke."

There was only the slightest flicker of recognition in Mimi's eyes as she made some notations on a list and cheerily announced they could absolutely share a table. Nick could have applauded.

Hayley leaned in as they entered the theater. "A little young for you, isn't she?"

Nick laughed. "Not to worry," he said. "Mimi would tell you I'm not ready for a woman like her."

Cal's shirt was fire-engine red.

"Ladies!" he exclaimed as everyone sat down. "Gentleman! Nick! Welcome to Vivez Dance!"

"See, that's funny," Nick informed the table, "because Calvin is implying I'm not a gentleman."

"He seems to know you well," Mel said, and Hayley laughed.

Cal rewarded Mel with his most dazzling smile. "My name is Cal," he said, "and I volunteered to be your server this evening just so I can make sure the music man doesn't ruin your experience."

Hayley rolled her eyes. "Should've figured he'd find an excuse to sing for you."

"Sing?" Cal looked from her to Nick. "Our boy can sing?"

"Don't," Nick warned him. "Don't you dare."

Cal innocently started listing drink specials, as if the entire Vivez crew wouldn't hear about Nick's talent by the time the show started.

Food was ordered along with the drinks, and it was easy to chat over pizza and chips and salsa and fried pickles and mozzarella sticks. Nick felt obligated to make sure everybody had a good time, but he was soon feeling silly for worrying: It took all of two minutes before Hayley and Mel were laughing like old friends. Hayley had a way of inviting people into her happiness and making them feel valuable because they'd been invited. He'd been the exception to the rule, of course. Nick remembered that first night at the Squeaky Lion and how painful it had been just to have her sit across from him. How damaged was he, to have ever been incapable of enjoying this woman?

"So, how did you two meet?" Hayley was asking the Becketts.

Mel, mouth full of pizza, delegated to Gavin with a look.

"Seventh grade," he said. "Choir practice."

"He showed up to save me from this one," Mel added, nodding toward Nick.

Hayley turned to Nick, feigning shock. "Were you *hitting* on Mel?"

"Of course not." Nick sipped his beer. "I was introducing myself."

"Introducing," Hayley teased. "Right."

"I'll back him up on this one," Gavin said. "I showed up to help Nick carry his books, and there was the new girl in town, all red hair and attitude."

Mel beamed at her husband. "These two could wander the halls whenever they wanted, so long as they said Gav was carrying Nicky's books."

"It was not that bad," Nick objected. "I was allowed to leave a little early to beat the traffic between classes, and the teachers thought it'd be a good idea if Gavin helped me out."

"Okay," Mel pressed, "but how much extra time and help did you actually need?"

Nick and Gavin looked at each other and started laughing. "It's more about the journey than the destination," Gavin said.

Hayley laughed. "Is book carrier something you have to interview for?"

"We've been goofing off since kindergarten," Gavin said. "No one in the world is more qualified to be Nick Freeman's aide-de-camp."

"I don't even know what that means," Nick joked.

"Nicky." Hayley tested out the name. "I like it."

"Nope," he said. "Nicky Freeman stayed in high school."

"Then why can she call you Nicky?"

Nick pointed at Mel with a mozzarella stick. "She's earned it."

Hayley looked at Mel, eyebrows raised. Mel shrugged.

"They're my boys," she said simply.

Nick nudged Hayley. "Looks like the chef wants to say hi."

He recognized the embarrassment that hit him as Kevin approached the table. The same sinking feeling nauseated him when he smiled at a girl at the Squeaky Lion only to watch her boyfriend appear behind her—or worse, when a single girl apologetically turned down his offer to buy her a drink. It was the sudden realization that he was worth less than he thought he was, as if he'd mistakenly taken a seat in first class.

It was what he'd felt when he'd spoken to Vicki for the last time.

He was furious at himself for feeling this way with Hayley. They were friends. The limits of their relationship couldn't possibly be more clearly defined, and that was a good thing, because Nick had no illusions about how much he was worth to her. It didn't matter that Kevin somehow managed to make a black apron and chef's hat look cool as he wove through the tables. It didn't matter that Nick would never be able to fit the walker through the narrow path Kevin had taken from the kitchen, or stand as quickly as Hayley just had as she rushed to kiss her boyfriend. It didn't matter that Nick could never compete with Kevin, because Hayley would never want to replace Kevin. As long as Nick remembered that, he could force an amiable smile on his face and try not to feel like he'd been caught trying to get away with something.

Hayley introduced Kevin to the Becketts. "And you already know Nick," she said.

"Hey, man!" Kevin offered Nick an enthusiastic fist bump. "Good to see you!"

Kevin was different today, more animated than the guy who'd thanked Nick for breakfast during the week. Suddenly, Nick recognized the glint in his eyes: It was the excitement of a performer about to take the stage.

"I still owe you that drink," Kevin was saying. "You going to be around after?"

"Wouldn't miss it," Nick said.

"Awesome. I hear we throw one hell of an after-party." Kevin turned to Hayley and kissed her, hard. "I've got to get back to it."

Hayley beamed. "Light this place up, baby."

Nick heard the love, the affection, the pride all packed into one word: *baby*. What would it feel like if Hayley spoke to him with such gentle intimacy? He wanted it so badly it unnerved him, and he ordered himself never to consider it again. Hayley's friendship was a gift, one that would be taken away as soon as he wanted more than she had to give, so he would give her every possible reason to stay. He'd be the best goddamn friend this woman had ever had, the friend she *deserved*, and he'd kill anything within him that got in the way of that.

Nick was finishing off the salsa when Mimi brought newcomers to their table. "Bill and Joan will be joining you tonight," she announced. "You're going to have a blast."

"I'm sure we will," Nick said. Mimi was still standing behind him after he'd greeted the couple, and he leaned back to look at her. "What's up?"

Mimi put a hand on his shoulder and bent down to murmur in his ear. "Linda wanted me to ask you if we could move your wheels."

Nick glanced over at the walker. "Move it where?"

"Just to the corner over there. She didn't want people tripping over it once the house lights go down."

"Sure. I'm sorry I didn't think to move it sooner, actually."

She scoffed. "Not your job." She watched Nick's smile dim. "What is it, love?"

"Linda wanted you to ask me," he said. "You, specifically."

"Yes."

"Because she figured I'd be more comfortable if the request came from you."

Mimi smiled. "She never said that."

Nick reached back and squeezed her hand. "How lucky am I, to get all my requests through you?"

"Unbelievably so, I think."

"If you ever get a chance to tell her she doesn't have to be nervous around me . . ."

"Say no more, mon petit chou." Mimi straightened up and addressed the table. "If you'll excuse me, I've been ordered to make sure Mr. Freeman doesn't escape."

Bill, their new tablemate, watched with interest as Mimi carried the walker away. He had a silver buzz cut, and judging by the look on his weathered face, Nick could tell he was more interested in the walker than in Mimi.

"That's yours?" Bill asked him.

"Yep," Nick said promptly.

Bill didn't look shocked, but it was obvious he was processing this information. Nick wasn't surprised. His legs were hidden under the table, and his broad shoulders and solid arms spoke of regular trips to the gym. Even with Bill sitting next to him, Nick knew he didn't look remotely like someone who needed a walker.

"Joan's brother's kid was in the Army, ended up with something like that," Bill said.

Joan nodded solemnly. "Got shot in the leg."

What was the appropriate reaction to something like that? Should he look sad? Interested? Nick tried for attentive and felt his shoulders tighten up. Why did people assume all cripples were the same? He'd been born early, for shit's sake—how could he relate to a soldier who'd put himself in harm's way for his country? He was sitting in a room full of people so much more talented than he was, Linda couldn't bring herself to acknowledge his disability in front of him, and now these people thought they knew him because their fucking nephew got shot?

Hayley clasped his hand under the table.

"That must have been horrible," she said. "I'm so grateful for good doctors when I hear stories like that."

Nick forced himself not to look at her. Hayley talked earnestly with Bill and Joan about doctors, about Joan's huge family and her nephew's recovery, and the older couple relaxed under the warmth of the care and sympathy in her eyes. Hayley squeezed Nick's hand in hers, then let it go.

There wasn't a spotlight when Linda Brandazzio took the stage, and the lights in the room didn't dim. In fact, if the house music hadn't abruptly ended, Nick might not have realized Linda was there at all. Her shirt was cyan; the only parts of her wardrobe that set her apart from the Vivez servers were her black high heels and the microphone in her hand.

"Ladies and gentlemen, welcome to Vivez Dance!" The room applauded enthusiastically. "We're thrilled to have a sold-out house tonight for the premiere of our show, Summer Dreams. I'd like to take this time to thank our sponsors, whose kind contributions make it possible for us to share our joy and passion with you."

Nick glanced over at Hayley while Linda ran down the list of contributors. She grinned at him; he grinned back.

"We've got a lot of people behind this curtain who can't wait to spend time with you," Linda was saying, "and tonight it's our pleasure to introduce Mr. Kevin Albee. Please welcome him to the family, and enjoy our summer dreams!"

More applause, and Linda slipped behind the curtain. The lights went out. The curtain went up.

Spotlights hit the stage.

Nick had never seen anything like it.

He'd thought he was prepared since he'd spent the last week literally watching the show come together. But all of the efforts of the cast and crew had coalesced into something that came alive under the bright lights, something more reciprocal and intimate than any play or concert he'd seen. These people loved what they did, and that love was at its peak when an audience got to participate. Not only that, but Nick *knew* these people. He was part of the family, and he was overwhelmed by the pride that welled in him when he watched Calvin do a backflip, or Mimi belt out a song. He was contributing to the energy of the show just by watching.

Kevin took the stage for the first-act finale. They'd brought a sturdy wooden picnic table to the stage, the kind that had bench seats connected to it, the kind Nick struggled with because it wasn't possible to slide his knees under the table from the side. Kevin dominated the damn thing, tap dancing from the floor to the bench to the table and back again. It would have been enough to hit all the right steps, but Kevin Albee knew how to play to a room. His athleticism mixed with his charisma so well that Nick didn't have it in him to be jealous. Here was a dance partner worthy of Hayley Burke.

Nick couldn't think of any use she would have for someone who struggled to sit at a picnic table.

12

Hayley nudged Nick playfully when the house lights went up for intermission.

"What'd you think?" she asked him.

Nick was staring at the lowered curtain. "I thought it was great."

"You look like maybe you found your joy."

Without looking at her, he said, "This is what you did. At your old job."

"Yeah," she said. Then, quieter, "Only they all look like they're having fun."

"You and Kevin." She wasn't sure he'd heard her. Nick seemed to speak more to himself than her, awe in his voice. "I'll bet you brought down the house every night."

She leaned toward him. "Nick . . ."

"How're y'all liking the show?" Calvin had appeared, apparently none the worse for wear after an hour's worth of onstage exercise. "How many times did you have to tell Nick to shut up?"

"Dude." Nick had snapped out of his fog. "That was amazing."

Cal waited. "And?"

"No joke, man. Really, really good."

Cal broke into a grin. "Thank you, brother!" He started gathering up empty bottles from the table. "Normally there's a joke," he explained to the rest of them. "Like, 'Hey, Cal, it was really amazing how you didn't screw up.'"

They all laughed. "Not this time, buddy," Nick said. "You are truly the man."

Hayley could tell he meant it, and it felt good to see Nick Freeman so moved. It was about time the man with the biggest smile in the room got to receive something from someone else.

The second act was at least as good as the first, and when the final curtain call arrived, Hayley was excited to remember her night was far from finished. After Bill and Joan had left, she said, "Everybody headed to the bar?"

"Absolutely." Nick was signing the receipt for his food. "Pretty sure I'm required to be there."

"Actually," Mel said apologetically, "we're going to take off."

Nick looked up in surprise. "What? No."

"It's been a long week, and Rose has the sniffles. We need to be in good shape for the weekend."

Nick gave Mel a small, incredulous smile. "Rosie's fine, Mel. Stay and have a drink with us."

She shook her head. "Next time."

Everybody stood to leave. Nick seemed to struggle getting out of his chair, and Hayley tensed as he nearly stumbled.

"At least let me drive you home," he said.

"Not a chance," Mel said. "You've got a party to go to."

"Can I give you money for the Uber, then?"

"Relax, Nicky. You already got us free tickets."

Nick gave in. Gavin and Mel both hugged Hayley goodbye, and she was surprised and touched to be so readily accepted.

"Thanks for adopting Nicky," Mel told her. "Now we get to spend time with you."

Hayley laughed. "If I knew you guys would be part of the deal, I would have adopted him sooner."

The women watched Gavin and Nick laughing on the far side of the table. "Don't tell him I said this," Mel said, "but you're really good for him."

The compliment made her self-conscious. "I think it's more the other way around," she said. "He found me the world's best chocolate shake the other day."

"Oh, he's a fantastic guy." Mel smiled. "I'm just glad he's got a friend who's seen him be a jerk."

Soon Hayley was left with Nick at an empty table. Patrons filed out of the room as performers expertly navigated around them to wipe down tables and collect trash.

"You really wanted them to stay, didn't you?" she asked him.

"Yeah," he said distractedly. "I thought I could get her to stay out past eleven this time."

He'd said *her*, not *them*. There was some frustration there, and it was with Mel, not Gavin—Hayley had sensed as much when Nick had tried to get them to stay. It was a story she wanted to hear, but not one she felt comfortable digging for. Time to distract him.

"Not everyone can live the life of a free-spirited socialite," she teased.

"Is that what I am?" He turned to her and smiled. "You make it sound classy."

She picked up her purse in one hand and linked her other arm in his. "Would you care to escort me to the bar in the manner of ridiculously classy people so that we may await the festivities, Mr. Freeman?"

"I'd be delighted to, Ms. Burke."

Taking Nick's arm felt natural, even though his hands stayed anchored to the walker. It was a way to give him stability without being obvious about it. She'd watched him fight to stand, and now his stance told her he was definitely tired, if not injured. She kept pace with him as he gingerly walked up the ramp to the back of the room, where Linda Brandazzio was chatting with patrons at the exit.

"How did you two find each other?" Linda asked, delighted. "Did Mimi seat you together? That girl has a knack."

"Nick's a good friend," Hayley said with a smile.

Linda looked at Nick. "And what did you think of your first show?"

"Honestly, Linda," Nick said as he shifted his weight to take one hand off the walker and extend it to her, "I'm very proud to be part of this place. Thank you for roping me in."

Linda beamed as she shook Nick's hand. "We're proud to have you, Nick."

"Thanks for keeping Kevin busy," Hayley joked.

"If he keeps dancing like he did tonight, keeping him busy will not be a problem."

They all laughed, and Hayley and Nick strolled into Vivez Dance's bar and café.

They found a table against the far wall, and Nick eased himself into a chair. Hayley decided getting some water from the bar was more useful than asking if he was okay. Nick accepted a glass gratefully.

"Can I ask you something?" he said as she sat down.

"Sure."

"What does dancing with your heart mean?"

She didn't reply.

"When you introduced me to pickleback shots," he said, "we drank to dancing with your heart."

"I remember," she said. Hayley was surprised at how hesitant she was. This wasn't a secret, but it felt oddly intimate to offer an explanation when the phrase had been on her mind for weeks.

"It was what we drank to at Icarus," she told him.

He nodded. "Like a company motto?"

"God, no." That surprised him. "Our boss didn't really care about our hearts," she explained.

"Sounds like a lovely person."

"I'm not going to ruin the night by talking about Cyd." But Hayley couldn't resist at least one jab. "C-Y-D," she spelled. "She calls herself Cyd Garland. As if swiping your stage name from a couple of actual legends gives you class."

He frowned, thinking. "I know Judy Garland, but . . ."

"Cyd Charisse? From *Singin' in the Rain*?" She watched his face. "Nick Freeman, if you haven't seen—"

"So," he cut in, "not a motto."

She shrugged. "Just something my friend Denise and I used to say. It caught on with some others too, but I don't think it meant as much."

"So what does it mean to you two?"

"It means dancing isn't about what you do with your body."

Hayley grinned. Nick had tried and failed to hide a flash of incredulity that said *the hell it's not*. She'd expected it, and it was kind of adorable how he was trying to be considerate about something so important to her.

"I didn't think dancing was about anything else," he said carefully.

"Dancing is about your relationship to the rest of the world," she said. "How you react. How you interact. Dancing is movement, but that movement isn't always physical. Sometimes it's in a conversation, or a song. You're as good a dancer as I am."

He laughed. "Okay."

"Really," she protested. "I've seen it."

He nodded, sipped his water. Again, she could see him selecting his reply.

"I appreciate that," he said. "But my heart won't let me move like you do."

It was sweet how he was trying to steer the conversation away from rough waters, and she bit back the urge to tell him to stop being polite. Anger wasn't any fun either, but at least when he was angry he was right here, up close, dancing with her. Polite was cold, distant, deliberate.

"Anyway," she said, "Cyd put a lot of emphasis on the technical part of dancing. Step this way, hit this mark, and so on."

"That's not important?"

"It's very important. But unless you start by focusing on what you feel, what you want to say to your audience, then the best dancing in the world can feel empty."

Nick took another approach. "So you and Denise, when you'd say, 'To dancing with your heart,' what you'd actually be saying was . . ."

"Dance well," she finished, "but remember why you're dancing."

Hayley expected more questions, but Nick let it go. "I've been wondering what you meant ever since you said it," he told her. "And tonight I thought I could see it on stage."

"With Kevin?"

"I thought Kevin danced very well."

Polite again, and Nick's kindness made it worse, because she knew he was going out of his way to give a compliment. Kevin danced because of how it made him feel, but it was the crowd that lit him up, the applause, the reminder of what people thought of him. He loved to dance, but he never absolutely *had* to. Sometimes Hayley admired him for that, because needing to dance and expressing so much of herself on a stage left her vulnerable in a way he never was.

"Hey, there hasn't really been a good time to mention it, but you look great tonight," Nick said.

She chuckled. "Do you have a schedule written out or something?"

He flushed a little, which was very cute. "No."

"I'll bet you do. I'll bet it says, 'Tell Hayley she looks nice' in between 'Get out of car' and 'Flirt with Mimi,' but then I was a few seconds late and threw off the whole routine."

Nick went from embarrassed to cocky in no time at all, leaning toward her with his arms folded across the table. Shit. She liked keeping him off-balance, but she'd made a misstep somewhere, and now she was going to pay for it. Their dance was speeding up.

This was fun.

"Are you *jealous* of Mimi?" he asked, delighted.

She snorted. "Shut up."

"Because it sounded just then like you were jealous of Mimi."

"If you want to go after girls the same age as your students, that's fine with me."

He grinned slowly, and now she was the one feeling flushed. "You know that's just our patter. Mimi wishes she was born at a cocktail party in a black and white movie."

"Sure, Freeman."

"I think this is you trying to avoid acknowledging that you look great tonight."

Bam. He'd hit the nail on the head, and she wasn't ready, because she'd ignored his compliment without even thinking about it. Why was she always so completely lost when someone said she was pretty? That had been the goal tonight, after all—she'd picked her clothes and done her hair and expertly applied her makeup so she could look hot for the premiere of Kev's show, and now Nick was saying she'd succeeded, and it still felt like a surprise.

"And if you must know, smartass," Nick went on, "I didn't want to say it around a bunch of people and look like I was hitting on you."

She was definitely blushing now, and she covered by fishing in her purse for some lip gloss. "Got it," she said. "So you'll only be saying nice things about me in private."

"If you're lucky."

She couldn't help but grin back at him. "Thank you, Nick. You look great too." She had noticed before—he filled out his black shirt very nicely—but Nick had a point. Some things would come out sounding too weird.

"I'm surprised you didn't wear your shoes," he said.

"My shoes?"

"You're always wearing those shoes. Black and white, with the pink stripe on the back."

"My Chucks? What's wrong with my Chucks?"

"Nothing," he reassured her. "I just think they're cool, is all."

"They *are* cool." She scooted her chair back and frowned at her feet. "You know what? I should've worn them tonight."

He started laughing. "I didn't mean to bring you down."

"No, it's just that I wanted to, but I had it in my head that the sandals looked better with the dress, and now . . ." She sighed. "You should've said something. This is your fault."

He held up his hands, still chuckling. "Won't happen again."

"It better not." She was laughing too, because after Nick tried so hard to properly deliver a compliment, letting her know he'd noticed her favorite shoes was the sweetest thing he'd done all night.

They sat, and they talked, and it was easy. Hayley taught Nick more about dancing, what it was like to put on a show like the one they'd just seen, but she didn't mention how much she liked dancing with him. She knew he could dance well with just about anyone, in the same way she or Kevin used to pull sheepish members of the Icarus audience up on stage for the Christmas shows: You made someone look good by playing to their strengths, even if they had precious few to choose from. But when it was just the two of them, Nick seemed to dance without even realizing it. Hayley knew she couldn't talk about the energy that flowed between them, or the give-and-take that was getting easier by the day—Nick would be embarrassed and self-conscious, and he would pull away. For now, she was content to try to feel their rhythm, spot their steps.

Nick was obviously tired, but everything from his posture to his steady gaze told her he'd decided she was the most important person in the room. After a while, she wanted to say she was grateful, but she wasn't sure Nick would see anything special about someone who actually listened when she spoke—which just made him more remarkable.

They were talking about Nick's video project when the Vivez crew arrived. "Looks like they're done cleaning the theater," Hayley told him.

Nick lit up when he spotted Mimi. "Can I leave you for a second?"

Hayley laughed. "Go, Nick."

But Nick didn't need to go anywhere; Mimi arrived at their table before he was done stepping into the walker.

"You are *not* getting up for the likes of me!" she said.

Nick wrapped Mimi in an enthusiastic hug. "I am so proud of you," he said. "You are so very good at what you do."

Mimi beamed, and Hayley knew Nick had just given her a precious gift. "And you, sir, are thoroughly lovely."

Hayley was about to add her compliments to Nick's when her heart sped up—Kevin was striding toward her in his faded red Icarus T-shirt and tight jeans. His hair was wet and slicked back; she knew he'd dunked his head in ice water after the show. He'd given his all on the stage, and now this man of extraordinary talent and purpose would want her by his side, sharing the rush of what had happened and dreams of what could happen next. She was relieved to recognize this feeling; they hadn't left everything in Indiana.

"Hey, babe," he said after they'd kissed.

"Hey." She smiled up at him. "Great show, Kev."

"Did I light the place up?"

"You were a supernova."

Hayley loved the light in his eyes when he knew he could conquer the world. She fueled the fire inside of him, helped him ward off the merciless doubts in his mind, and Kevin was never sexier than when he was fearless. He was about to kiss her again when they caught sight of a crowd gathering in a semicircle around an empty stool by the bar.

"Gotta go," he said. "Stay right there."

"What's going on?" Hayley asked him.

Kevin grinned. "Just stay right there."

Kevin jogged over to the bar, and then Calvin was speeding toward the stool with a guitar case. Hayley saw Linda Brandazzio quietly join the crowd as Cal's voice rang out across the room. "Nick Freeman!"

Nick stopped chatting with Mimi as the room went quiet. He took in the grinning crowd.

"Am I being challenged to a duel?" he asked.

Cal gave him a stony stare. "How dare you, sir."

"What offense have I committed?"

"You can sing." Cal looked dramatically around him at his brethren. "And you didn't tell us."

The semicircle let out a collective gasp, and Hayley snickered.

Nick took a step forward, looked at the ceiling, and heaved a huge sigh. He was thoroughly chewing the scenery as a man under the weighty burden of accusation.

"I do not deny it." He glanced at Hayley. "Though I did not anticipate the betrayal of certain loose-lipped witnesses."

Hayley took an elaborate bow while the crowd laughed. Cal bent down and opened the guitar case.

"Hang on," Nick said. "I'm being punished, but it's okay for you to hide that you can play guitar?"

"Everybody knows I play guitar," Cal said. The crowd nodded solemnly. "Except for you. And you're the new guy."

"I see." Nick watched Cal perch on the stool. "And what does the new guy have to do?"

"You will sing," Cal said. "Now. With me."

"Do I get to pick what we're singing?"

"Nope." Cal grinned cheerfully. "But I'll take the first verse."

"So you want me to sing, right now, in front of all these people, without knowing what song we're doing?"

"He can sing *anything*," Hayley offered cheerfully.

Nick pretended to be shocked speechless, but she knew she was making this sweeter for him. "Well, okay then," he said.

The room cheered as Nick joined Cal by the bar. Nick started laughing at the opening chords from the guitar, and Hayley got the joke as soon as Cal started singing. Nick had been "forced" into being Paul McCartney to Cal's Michael Jackson, and they were about to sing their way through a fight over a woman as they covered "The Girl is Mine."

They nailed it.

It was a simple, lighthearted song, and Cal strummed the guitar like it was second nature. Hayley could tell Nick felt the change in the room's energy as he started to sing, but he didn't slip into rock-star mode. Instead, Nick and Cal traded the melody in an effortless conversation. Hayley would have assumed this was all a setup, the product of at least one secret rehearsal, but she knew playing dirty would've taken the fun out of it—and these two were having a blast.

Cal launched into Mr. Big's "To Be With You" for an encore, and everybody waved their smartphone flashlights in the air as they joined in for the chorus.

Here, in this room—this was how she wanted to feel all the time.

13

Nick eased himself onto a bench in front of Vivez Dance and tried not to groan. The bench was damp, his view was a dark parking lot, and he was too happy about getting off his feet to want anything better. Kevin handed him a beer, and Nick tipped the bottle toward him in gratitude. Kevin fished in his pockets for a lighter and a pack of cigarettes.

"Want one?" Kevin asked, lighting up.

"I'm good, thanks."

"Hal hates these things."

It took Nick a puzzled second to realize Hal was short for Hayley. Hal and Kev. Of course. Because they shared a life and a bed, and he refused to be irritated by the reminder.

"So I've gotta know," Kevin said. "You really didn't set that up?"

Nick glanced at him. "With Cal? No. Didn't see that one coming."

"Wow." Kevin gave him a loose salute. "You don't screw around, man. Where's your stage?"

"Sorry?"

"Where do they pay you to do that?"

"Um, they don't." Nick felt his legs start to tense. "I teach high school math."

"Bullshit. You love this stuff too much to be a teacher."

He hated the embarrassment tightening his muscles. "Music isn't the most stable profession."

"Because you wouldn't want to be a music teacher or a choir director," Kevin said. "You'd want to be the front man."

He was right. Nick was a performer, just like Kevin, but he was proud to be a teacher too, and it was time to do a better job defending himself. Nick turned to look Kevin in the eye.

"You know that thing people say about artists?" he said. "Only do this if you can't imagine doing anything else? I found something else."

"You're telling me you're good just doing math." Kevin didn't sound convinced.

"Professionally?" Nick asked. "Absolutely. I get to talk about stuff I like and get the kids to like it too. It's a different kind of thing."

Kevin ambled over and sat down next to Nick. "So you get your fix at the bar, then. Hayley told me you're a big deal there."

Nick watched him. "I think you're more of a junkie than I am."

"Sure. Which is why I do it for a living instead of at parties."

Nick didn't reply.

"Hey, more power to you, man." Kevin took a drag on his cigarette. "Needing to be up there, being made for it . . . that'll eat at you. Take Hal, for instance."

The old joke flashed in Nick's head: *Take my wife. Please.* Instead of *sure,* he said, "She's looking forward to joining you up there."

"Absolutely. And the thing is . . ." Kevin paused. "Look, I don't expect you to understand, but Hal and I share a path. A vision, you know? And I think she's hit a rough patch."

"It's good you're there for her, then."

Kevin exhaled smoke. "Actually, I was hoping you could be."

Nick forced himself to stare at the parking lot as a jolt ran through him. "I thought that was your job," he said carefully.

"Sure, sure." Kevin stood up, started to pace. "You know that movie *Heat?*"

Nick went from uncomfortable to baffled. "Sure," he said.

"You know that part where De Niro's telling his crew they can either rob the bank or walk away? Sizemore says, 'For me, the action is the juice.'"

"Doesn't Sizemore get shot in the head?"

"I'm saying we need this like Sizemore needs the heist. She needs to be up there, and when she's not . . ." Kevin stared intently at him. "Look, I know you can't do what we can do, and I know you want to, and I'm sorry about that. But this could be a way to help."

Nick gripped the rail of the bench to stave off the tension in his legs. Sometimes strong emotion made his spastic muscles tighten until both legs were straight out in front of him, and he didn't want his anger to make him look silly.

"I already help the theater," Nick said. "I work here. And I know exactly what I can and can't do, but I have no idea what you want."

Kevin shrugged, confused. "Just be her friend, man."

Nick blinked, sat back. His legs relaxed. "Be her friend," he repeated.

"Yeah." Kevin sat down next to him. "Did I say something wrong?"

Nick struggled to pick an answer. "I'm not a babysitter, is all," he said. "And she sure as hell doesn't need one."

"Of course not." Kevin chuckled ruefully. "Shit, you thought I was insulting her. How's that for irony?"

Nick had a feeling the situation was more ironic than Kevin knew.

"Hey, I know you have a life," Kevin said. "I'm just saying she likes you. And she doesn't have anyone to hang out with when I'm here." He stood up and stubbed out his cigarette in the concrete ashtray nearby. "Don't tell her I asked or anything. But I would really appreciate it."

So Kevin wanted him to be Hayley's friend. Hayley wanted the same thing. And granting a reasonable request from a caring boyfriend was as close as Nick was going to get to what he wanted.

"She has my number," he said.

14

Hayley stepped out of the noise of the party into the night air. She closed her eyes, savoring the scent of rain that had come and gone.

"Taking a break?" Nick asked.

Hayley opened her eyes. "Looking for you. But it's too nice out here to go back in."

"Do they need me inside?"

She strolled over to him. "No one's forgotten about you, and I'm sure they'd all love to chat." She sat next to him and crossed her legs. "But you could stay here for another hour and not feel guilty."

Hayley loved the look on Nick's face—disconcerted, amazed, relieved she'd known how to give him the answer he wanted instead of what he'd asked for.

"That was impressive," he said.

"You're not the only one with superpowers."

He chuckled. "Cal could've picked a different song."

"I know. And you would've still found a way to entertain."

"What makes you so sure?"

"Because you get better under pressure. Performing in front of a bunch of people wouldn't be any fun if you couldn't fail."

He blinked; she'd brought him up short again, and he was considering his response. She liked surprising him into being genuine.

"You're right," he said finally. "Wow. I hadn't thought of it that way, but you're absolutely right."

"You don't have to act so surprised." She laughed, waving off any apology. "You and Kevin, you both have this 'come at me' thing going on. You know how good you are, but you have to test it."

"Right again."

She watched him. "He's really impressed with you, you know. That doesn't happen a lot."

He shrugged. "We found a movie we both like."

"And there's room enough for both of you."

Nick laughed. "Yeah, we talked about that."

She didn't see anything funny, and she wasn't sure Nick did either.

"Is it that you're so similar?" she said. "I can see how that'd be annoying."

"Kevin's a great guy."

"Try again." He looked at her. "You didn't mean that. Try again."

"He doesn't annoy me."

"Still not what you want to say."

He sighed. "Fine. Right *again*. We're both very good at what we do, and we want everybody to know it, and we'd probably both work here if I could dance. But I can't, so I wouldn't count on me and your boyfriend becoming best buddies."

She smiled. "Lead with that next time."

He studied her. "It's like you actually want me to be mean to you."

"I don't," she said. "And that wasn't. I just don't want you to censor yourself."

"That may end our friendship pretty quickly."

"I'll risk it."

"You say that now, but . . ."

"Come on, Nick. Neither of us wants you to put on a show for me."

They were quiet for a long time.

"Anyway, you do work here," she said. "No 'probably' about it."

He waved a hand. "You know what I meant."

"No, I don't."

"Come on." She heard good-natured sadness, like he was thanking her for playing dumb. "It's true. I can't do what you can do, and I want to."

"You can sing," she offered.

"I could never handle a show, though," he said. "Even if I wasn't dancing."

"Because of your legs."

"Because of everything." He ran a hand over his face. "Costume changes would take me way too long, and I'd have to steer the walker through those sets . . . Hayley, I can't even walk quickly across the stage without sweating and losing my breath."

"Those are all things they could work around," she tried gently.

"I don't want to be something they have to work around."

Hayley felt the breeze pick up. She'd wanted Nick to take off his armor for her, but now she felt responsible for the pain of the exposed wounds underneath.

"I went to the mall earlier," Nick said. "I don't do something like that before an evening like this, but my sister came through town and surprised me today. And when Kendall comes to town, we like to go to the mall."

"Didn't think you were the shopping type," she said.

"More just looking through the stores and people-watching. Plus they've got those soft pretzels with the cinnamon sugar."

"I'm more of a Cinnabon girl myself."

"They don't have a chocolate one, do they?"

She shook her head sadly. "I'd boycott in protest, but then I'd have to stop eating them."

His smile was faint and tired, and it still warmed her.

"I guess we could have driven to my parents' house to get my wheelchair," he said, "but I didn't want to put Kendall through that. Didn't want to spend a couple extra hours in the car just so I could wheel around at crotch level while we got our soft pretzels. So I made the choice to walk through the mall all day and pay for it later."

Nick turned and looked straight at her with a laser-beam focus that gave her butterflies in her stomach. What was she feeling now? Fear?

"I can bring doughnuts and sing and make everybody happy for a little while," he said. "But I'm never going to really be a part of what happens in there, because none of you have to worry about walking through a goddamn mall."

Hayley felt as if she were perched at the edge of a cliff, breathless, like Nick's eyes were pools of clear blue water miles below her. She'd invited him to dance, and he'd accepted—he'd taken the first steps beyond safety, and now it was up to her to meet him where he stood. This was fear, absolutely; he was exposing a fervently protected part of himself that would be so easy to shatter. But there was a thrill here too, one that terrified her, a connection to an electric current between them. She wanted more.

Back away, Hayley Michelle. You'll do more damage than you can fix.

She dove in.

"You're right," she said. "They've got different worries. There are people in there who worry about eating a cinnamon sugar pretzel. Girls and guys. They are watching everything they eat and every pound they gain. And instead of enjoying the party tonight, some of them are obsessing about a misstep they made onstage that we didn't even notice. Not to mention all of the insanely talented people in there who wish they were you."

Nick's laugh was hollow. "Because I'm such an inspiration?" He slumped against the bench. "That's why I work here, ya know. Any idiot can put tapes into a VCR, but I can walk into a room and make everyone feel better. Why? Because they're all so damn glad they're not me."

Something clicked. "That's why you were so pissed," she said. "At the bar, when I asked you how you got the job. You think you're a charity case."

"I *know* it," he said. "She said it right to my face."

Hayley frowned. "She said it?"

"I mean, nobody says 'charity case,'" he said. "But yeah, she said it, and I took the job anyway, and now I get to be exactly what everybody wants." His voice rose as he gesticulated at the empty parking lot. "If you're depressed, at least you're not the cripple. Or maybe you can help the cripple and feel like a good person. I can be a plus one, I can do party tricks, I can be on call twenty-four hours a day. Just as long as I make somebody's life easier."

"Nick, shut the hell up."

He turned, surprised. Hayley stared at him stonily.

"If you call yourself a cripple one more time, I will smack you in the face."

Nick smiled weakly. "You wouldn't dare."

She was not amused. "I don't know about Linda," she said. "And you can shit on your friends in there if you want to. But don't insult me like that again."

Nick drew back a little. "I wasn't . . ."

She moved with him, denying him the space. "I wanted you to join me tonight because I *like* you, Nick. Those people in there like you too, and you just reduced that entire room to a bunch of idiots so hard up for self-esteem that they invited some . . . I don't know, some sort of *mascot* to their opening night. And even if they did, what does that make me? Do you honestly think I use you as a party trick? You think I wanted you at my table so I could show everybody how fucking open-minded I am?"

She leaned closer.

"I'd be surprised if half the dancers in there are as sure of themselves as you are." Her voice was soft and steady. "You have confidence, and you have talent, and you are the only person here who makes me feel more like myself. None of that has anything to do with your legs." She sat back. "So don't be an asshole."

Nick stared at her for so long she wondered if she really would need to slap him to bring him back.

He finally said, "I am so sorry."

"I know."

"I never . . . that wasn't . . ." He collected himself. "I didn't realize what I was doing. I don't hurt my friends. I don't ever want to hurt you."

"I know that," she said gently. "That's why I stopped you."

He smiled. "Thank you."

"Of course."

Hayley felt lighter, relaxed, maybe even a little giddy. They'd opened the door to anger and pain and danced right through it to the other side.

Nick stood up from the bench, and she stood with him. "That's enough of me moping out here," he said.

"Hey, Nick?"

He raised his eyebrows in a silent question.

"Thank you for coming tonight," she said. "I'm sorry your legs hurt."

He grinned. "Totally worth it."

"Is there anything I can do to help?"

He shook his head. "Calling me an asshole did the trick, I think."

They laughed. "Seriously," she said, "I know it's been a long night. Can I grab you a chair or a drink, or something? Round up your adoring fans for you?" She watched him. "I feel like you're afraid to ask."

"Nah." He was definitely embarrassed, and it was definitely cute. "No, I'm good."

Hayley suddenly knew exactly what he needed. She impulsively wrapped him in the hug he couldn't ask for, and her breath caught in her throat as his arms enfolded her.

15

"Ask her about Tom Cruise!" Mel yelled over the noise of the margarita blender she was using in the kitchen. "She's got to know *Rock of Ages*."

"Why can't there be a trivia game just about Rocky?" Nick was texting from the recliner in the Beckett family room. "Or soundtrack albums," he said to Gavin. "I could handle movie soundtracks."

Gavin was loading a movie trivia game into the DVD player. "Sure," he said. "But then you might beat her, and I'd have to handle *that*."

"I heard that." Mel carried a couple of margaritas into the room and handed one to Nick. "What'd Hayley say?"

Nick looked at his new smartphone and laughed. "She knew about Tom Cruise."

"And what's so funny?"

"I told her there was no way I could beat you without her help, and she said I should refuse to acknowledge the filmography of anyone who's played fewer than three disabled people."

Mel laughed. "Pretty brave of her, going for the disabled joke."

"Come on." Nick was a little hurt. "I know things didn't start well, but it's not like she has to be afraid of me now."

"I didn't mean it that way."

"Then what did you mean?"

Gavin stepped in. "You don't exactly encourage those kinds of jokes, buddy."

Mel nodded emphatically. "That's what I mean."

"Oh." Nick sat back. "Well, she's funny, for one thing. And I'd rather she joke than worry about saying the wrong thing." Nick stopped. "Huh."

Mel said, "What?"

"Nothing," he said. "I just realized she doesn't want me worrying either."

Mel's smile seemed just a bit smug.

Nick narrowed his eyes. "What?" he asked.

"Just glad to hear it's going so well."

Nick spent the next couple hours wondering exactly what Mel meant.

There'd been pride in Mel's voice, as if he'd finally learned how to tie his shoes, and that was a little insulting. Nick had no trouble making friends. He just kept most of them at a distance. Granted, his friendship with Hayley was complicated by how attracted he was to her, but that wasn't going to be an issue. After all, he'd survived the woman walking into his kitchen wearing his bathrobe, hadn't he?

What he'd done was freeze and stare. He'd caught sight of Hayley's bare feet, then the smooth skin of her legs. He'd tried to understand how his bathrobe was now draping her curves, struck dumb by the way her hair spilled across her shoulders in coffee-brown contrast to the red fabric. Hayley had been in his home, his space, yet she radiated more self-assurance than he'd ever felt in his life.

He'd spent the week after the Vivez party debating whether he should get in touch or wait for her cue. By the time Hayley texted on Thursday afternoon to complain about her washing machine, he'd been seriously considering deleting her number, just to take the decision out of his hands. They'd been texting for a month now, sharing weekly lunches at the diner and karaoke Fridays at the bar, and Nick always felt like a fireman on call: There had to be a cost to enjoying her this much. One day Hayley would need a ride, or Kevin would need a favor—Nick would be jarred from a deep sleep by a phone call at three AM, all because he loved putting his arm around her to climb the steps of the karaoke stage.

This was another reason he knew his feelings for Hayley wouldn't be a problem: He was far too nervous to be in love with her. He'd been in love once, with Victoria Hall, from middle school through his freshman year of college, and he'd already experienced more stress over Hayley than he had during his entire relationship with Vicki. Love didn't fit his current symptoms.

"And that's the game, guys." Mel beamed as her virtual trophy filled the television screen. "You'll get me next time."

Gavin got up from the couch. "Thanks for your never-ending faith in us, my darling."

Nick said, "You know you can play your keyboard much better than this game."

"Don't start," Mel warned.

"What?" Nick followed her into the kitchen. "It wouldn't have to be a regular thing. You could play the bar at Vivez."

"It's generally not a good idea to leave a two-year-old at home alone, Nicky."

"So you get a sitter to watch TV while she sleeps." Nick kept a smile on his face and his tone light. "C'mon, Mel."

She shook her head with a smile of her own as she washed out the margarita glasses. "You just want a bigger spotlight."

"I want you to have some fun."

"And one day, when you have a kid and I spoil her rotten, you'll see how your definition of 'fun' changes." She dried her hands and gave him a hug. "It's always great having you over, Nicky."

"It's always great being here, Mel."

The night had gone as it always did, and they continued to honor tradition as Gavin walked Nick out to his car.

"Hey, man," Gavin said. "Thanks for coming out tonight."

Nick shook his friend's hand. "Thanks for the free alcohol."

"And as far as this thing with Hayley goes . . ."

Nick sighed. "Mel knows I would tell her if there actually was a thing, right? I feel like the more I tell her, the more she wants to know."

"She knows," Gavin said calmly. "And she wants to know everything, but she really doesn't expect you to tell her. It's just fun for her to try. Much like how you keep trying to get the band back together."

Nick held up a hand. "I hear you."

"Put us down for the next show at Vivez, though. That was a good time."

"Will do."

Gavin clapped him on the shoulder. "Drive safe, brother."

The route home from the Becketts' had become second nature: He drove out of the suburbs, past strip malls and fast-food restaurants, to the freeway. Sometimes he'd listen to the radio, or sing along with a CD. Tonight, it seemed wrong to intrude on the silence.

Until he realized he might not have to be alone.

16

Hayley smiled as she lifted her phone to her ear.

"Don't tell me," she said. "You won."

She heard him laughing. "Of course not," Nick said. "I'm headed home in disgrace."

"What, right now?" She took the book she'd been reading off her lap and placed it on the table next to her. "You're not driving while you're on the phone, are you?"

"That's exactly what I'm doing."

"Nick. That's not safe."

"Sure it is. Just as long as I don't have to use the brake."

"You'd better be screwing with me."

More laughter. "I'm not holding the phone. There's a hands-free system in the car."

She relaxed. "How do you drive, anyway?"

"I'll show you sometime."

"You can't just tell me?"

"It'll make more sense if I show you."

"Sure." She stood up from her chair. "You just like being mysterious."

"Exactly. Otherwise you'll find out how boring I am."

How *did* he drive? She assumed his feet weren't involved, but she couldn't swear to it, and it bothered her that she hadn't taken the time to find out. Or maybe it was good she hadn't thought about it. That meant she focused on him, not his disability.

But what was she focusing on now?

"What're you up to?" he asked her.

"Just reading," she said.

"Yeah? Reading what?"

She glanced at the cover. "It's called *Before I Fall*."

"Tell me about it."

She liked how he didn't hesitate. No flattery, no pretense, just four words that told her what she was doing was worth his time.

"It's about this high school girl who keeps dying," she said.

Silence for a beat. "Keeps . . ."

"Dying," she repeated. "She dies in a car accident and then relives the last day of her life over and over."

"So it's a horror story?"

"Nope. It's kind of a love story, actually. Like *A Christmas Carol* or *It's a Wonderful Life*. She's learning what's important."

"God, I hate those movies."

"You take that back."

"Seriously. You get, like, five minutes of happiness after watching people's lives go to hell for an hour and a half."

"Oh, Nick." She scolded him playfully. "You've got to earn the ending, rock star. All the bad stuff makes the good stuff sweeter."

"That doesn't mean I have to suffer through Scrooge being such a dick."

She laughed. "That's fair. But I think George Bailey and Rocky have a lot in common."

"If you say so."

Hayley realized she'd been pacing the porch. Phone conversations tended to get her moving; she needed an outlet for her energy when she wasn't interacting with somebody in person. She'd been so focused on Nick that she couldn't remember getting here from her chair. It would be impossible for him to find himself on the opposite side of a porch without thinking about it.

"So," she said, willing that thought to go away, "how can I be of service, Mr. Freeman?"

"Oh." He sounded embarrassed. "I can let you go if you're busy."

"No, no," she said quickly. "I just assumed . . ."

"Since I've never actually called you before."

"Well, yeah." She grinned. "Which is weird, considering that flip phone of yours can't do much else."

"I don't know how to break this to you, but the flip phone is no more."

Her eyes widened, and then she was grinning from ear to ear. "No way."

"Yes way. I upgraded, so you'll have to find something else to make fun of me for."

"You broke it, didn't you?" She leaned on a porch rail. "You know those things only have so many flips in them."

"Nope," he said. "Just been doing a lot more texting lately."

"Sounds like a pain in the ass."

"Yeah, some woman won't leave me alone."

She laughed. "Nice of you to call her anyway."

"Nice of you to listen."

Something in his voice triggered an echo of an emotion. Hayley slowed her steps, then stopped completely as she tried to bring a pang of recognition into focus.

She remembered the last month or two at Icarus. Rushing into the building with coffee in one hand and her purse in the other as her castmates asked how it was going. Standing at the theater doors after a show, smiling wide for patrons who wanted to know how fun it must be to work there. Eating quick lunches with Kevin in between rehearsals, the two of them scarfing down sandwiches as he asked, "How's the day looking, babe?" Over and over again, she'd wanted, then ached, then needed to say three words.

Ask me more.

Don't let me get away. I can't ask you for help, because I don't know what I need. I can't say I'm scared, because I can't explain my fear. I can't tell you about the dread I carry around like a weight settling in my chest, because I don't know how to make it go away— but maybe if you dig deeper, I'll be able to attach words to whatever's wrong with me. Then the two of us can see it and name it and map its shape. But I can't drag it into the light myself, so ask me again. Beg me to tell you more.

Nick wanted her to ask. Maybe he didn't know it, or maybe he survived his pain by not giving it a second glance, but she felt it now, the same way she used to walk into her house after school and know instinctively when her parents were home. For the first time, Hayley had a chance to give something she so badly wanted to receive.

"My friend Denise told me about the book," she said.

"About the high school girl."

"Yep. We used to make a game out of finding cheap paperbacks at the used book store, and we'd trade them."

"Did she send you this one?"

"Nope, just texted the title."

A pause. "Do you miss her?"

"Every day."

She wondered if this was a mistake, showing him her pain so he could see they had the same scars. It didn't feel like a mistake.

"She's my best friend," she said. "We should talk more. I should call her more, but . . ." She scraped the toe of her sneaker against the wood of the porch. "Sometimes we're busy, but the truth is I feel like I should be happier. I left her in Indiana to come here, and I'm afraid the more we talk, the more she'll know I didn't have a good enough reason."

Nick didn't answer immediately; she knew he was chewing it over. "Do you want to go back?" he asked.

"I can't," she said. "Kevin's got a job, I'll be getting a job—"

"If it was just about you," he said. "If everybody in your life would be happy with you doing exactly what you wanted to do, would you go back to Icarus?"

Hayley thought of how much she'd cried—and worse, how often she'd cried alone.

"No," she said quietly.

"So you know you left for a good reason."

"Yes. Maybe."

A pause. "I don't know if I'm making things better or worse."

She smiled. "Better. Always better, rock star."

"Not *always* better."

Hayley sighed. "You had a spotless record before me, didn't you?" She sat down. "You honestly don't know how to handle people not liking you."

"I wouldn't say *spotless*."

"What would you say?"

He spoke carefully. "The more I get to know you, the more it bothers me that I ever gave you a reason not to like me."

"Nick." She was gentle. "All the bad stuff makes the good stuff sweeter."

She barely heard him chuckle over the ambient noise of the car.

"Weirdest thing," he said after a moment. "I was jealous of Gavin earlier."

"How come?"

"I was backing out of the driveway, and I'm watching him kind of jog up the front steps of their house, and then I'm thinking he probably didn't even notice the steps. I would've needed a couple extra minutes and someone to lean on."

"Sure."

"It's not a big . . . I mean, that's as it *should* be, right? Because he shouldn't be thinking of me all the time or how those steps are harder for me, or . . . I'm saying the Becketts have a life."

"Sure," she said again. "I hear you."

"It's just that every time I drive away from their place, it's like I can feel the distance growing. Like their life goes on in their house while I'm living my life driving home, and we'll always be on separate tracks. Even if I lived with them, we'd still be separate." He sounded frustrated. "Does that make sense?"

More than he knew.

"There's this movie where these ghosts are bound to this kid," she said. "They have to follow him around, but they can't hug him. I used to feel like that a lot, like I was some special kind of ghost. Like even though I could hug people, it wasn't the same as what other people did. I was in the same room, but I wasn't sharing the same space somehow."

"*Yes.* Exactly," Nick said. "What'd you do about it?"

"I held on to Kevin and left Indiana."

Silence.

Shit. Had she really just told him to get a girlfriend and get out of town?

"I'm glad you found him," Nick said. "I'm glad you found him, and I'm glad you're here."

"So am I," she said. "Hey, Nick?"

"Yeah?"

"I'm always here," she said. "Now, tomorrow, in the middle of the night—whenever. You don't have to have a reason to call."

"Thanks, Hayley. Same goes for you."

Damn it. He'd gone polite on her. Cheerful but polite, and some of the life had gone out of his voice. She tried teasing him. "You say that now, but when I call at three AM . . ."

"Diner's open all night. We'll go get milkshakes."

She'd failed. Nick had reached out, and if anything she'd made things worse. Hayley ran a hand through her hair and tried to think of how to reassure him. *You'll find someone. You're a great guy. I really will answer the phone when you call.*

Except they both knew he might not find someone, even if she could get him to believe he was a great guy. And Nick would have to be hurt and bleeding before he'd even think about bothering her at three AM. He'd taken a chance with this call, and what had it gotten him? A reminder that she had a boyfriend and he was driving home to an empty apartment.

"I'm parking the car," he said. "I'll let you get back to your book."

"Okay," she said. "Lunch Wednesday?"

"Lunch Wednesday. Hey, do me a favor?"

"Anything." She tried not to sound too eager.

"Call Denise," he said. "She misses you."

"How do you know?"

He said, "I would."

17

"Want to stay for lunch?" Kevin was rummaging in his refrigerator. "Plenty of burgers here."

"Sure," Nick said. He gripped the arm of the couch and felt the ache of stiff muscles as he heaved himself to his feet. Sitting through the movie *Heat* had been nearly a three-hour commitment.

"Who were you rooting for?" Kevin asked him. "De Niro or Pacino?"

"Pacino. You?"

"De Niro," Kevin said. "True commitment."

"To what? Himself?"

"His craft. He takes down scores, he looks out for himself, and he doesn't let anything distract from that."

Nick walked slowly toward the kitchen. "Kind of a shitty life philosophy."

"Nah, man. Works for me."

Nick laughed. "No, it doesn't. You didn't leave Hayley behind like Neil left . . . what was her name?"

"Eady." Kevin was piling patties and cheese on a plate. "And it's different. Hal's my partner in crime."

"So what's up with you two, then?"

Kevin paused with one hand on the refrigerator door, and Nick regretted his approach. He'd planned on asking the question today, but he now realized he couldn't betray Hayley by mentioning what she'd said the night she'd gotten drunk: Sometimes it was easier for her to miss Kevin than to spend time with him.

"I don't mean to pry," he went on. "I just know you mentioned a rough patch. I thought maybe I could help."

Kevin stood still a moment longer, his face hidden by the door, and then he stepped back. "I started working at Icarus as soon as I graduated from high school," he told Nick. "Then I went to a homecoming game the next year, and it felt different. Like the place was the same, but I didn't belong there anymore."

Nick took this in. "You're saying you don't belong together?"

"Sure we do." Kevin shut the refrigerator. "Life is great, sex is great, whole nine yards."

"Then what's with the homecoming story?"

"We belong on stage, as headliners," Kevin said.

Nick thought about this as Kevin headed out the back door. Apparently, Hayley and Kevin agreed: They needed to be able to dance together on stage. Nick didn't quite understand why that was so important, but how could he? He would never be able to dance like they did. His job was to be supportive. But as he stood at the top of the back steps and watched Kevin start the grill, he realized he needed to ask one question—and he wasn't sure what he wanted the answer to be.

"Do you love her?" he asked.

"Sure I do," Kevin said. "And she loves me."

No hesitation. He hadn't even looked away from the grill when he'd said it. Nick ignored the flicker of disappointment inside him and said, "You'll be dancing together soon. September's not that far away."

"It's not." Kevin scooped patties from plate to grill. "Problem is, I don't think Linda's a big fan of the headliner mentality."

He had a point: Linda hardly mentioned her cast without calling them a family, and Vivez didn't highlight performers in their advertising. Kevin and Hayley would absolutely earn a featured number or two, but not the sort of fame Kevin seemed to be talking about.

"Wouldn't it be enough to be on stage together?" Nick asked. "Hayley's never mentioned being a headliner."

Kevin's smile seemed a little condescending. "Trust me. She's too modest to say she wants her name in lights."

Nick heard the front door open at the other end of the house. "Babe?" Hayley called. "Is Nick here?"

Kevin said, "Out back!"

Before Nick could cross the room, Hayley was striding into the kitchen and beaming. It was a relief to know he was welcome, especially when two people walked in behind her.

"We saw your car!" She hugged him. "What're you doing here?"

"Had to have Nick over to watch *Heat*," Kevin volunteered. "Is it cool if he stays for lunch?"

Nick tightened his grip on the walker. He should've wondered why Kevin wanted to watch a movie at ten in the morning, but he'd wanted to try his best at a friendship with the guy. He should have asked where Hayley was, but he hadn't wanted to show too much interest in her. It couldn't be a coincidence that he just happened to be here now. Kevin had made sure of it, probably to use Nick as a buffer, probably because the older couple standing behind Hayley were related to her. Nick felt anger building in him—and yet Hayley was still able to blunt the edge of it by looking at him with the sort of teasing reproach he'd grown to love.

"Nick," she said, "when would it ever *not* be okay for you to stay for lunch?"

He managed a smile. "Doesn't hurt to ask."

"Meet my parents." She stepped to the side. "Nick Freeman, this is Tom and Carolyn Burke."

Tom Burke offered a handshake and a broad, open smile. He was a big man, heavy in a way that fit his frame, the sort of guy who looked like he ate huge meals because he needed the fuel. He wore a dark blue polo shirt with khaki shorts, and Nick was willing to bet he sold cars or played golf, or sold cars while playing golf.

"Firm grip," Mr. Burke said approvingly.

"Lots of practice," Nick told him. Mr. Burke's grip went beyond firm, and Nick wondered if he'd ever broken the fingers of weaker men.

Hayley's mother merely looked Nick in the eyes. Her smile wasn't as warm as her husband's, but Carolyn Burke didn't seem mean. She just made it abundantly clear that Nick hadn't earned much of her interest in the three seconds they'd known each other.

"Are you a friend of Kevin's?" Mrs. Burke asked him.

"Yep." Nick hoped he sounded cheerful, and turned up the wattage on his smile. "I'm a big fan of your daughter's too."

"A fan?" Mrs. Burke raised an eyebrow. "I thought she hadn't started dancing here yet."

Nick laughed. "Oh no, I didn't mean . . ." Mrs. Burke's expression didn't change. "I meant I admire her personally. Although she's an incredible dancer."

"We all met at a bar," Hayley jumped in. "Kevin and I were dancing at a bar."

Mrs. Burke considered this. "You must have made quite an impression," she told Nick.

Nick shrugged and immediately wished he'd chosen a better response. Everything about Carolyn Burke demanded a higher standard of behavior, from her pressed gray slacks and dark green blouse to her posture and her piercing gaze.

"They've certainly made an impression on me," he said.

The four of them sat in the living room as Kevin manned the grill, and Hayley told her parents the story of how they'd found a friend in Nick Freeman. She and Kevin had discovered the Squeaky Lion the night they moved to Columbus, and they were so happy with their new home that they couldn't help but dance. That dance caught Nick's attention—and Nick, by the way, was a *phenomenal* singer who brought the house down every Friday. After chatting that night, the three of them just knew they were going to be friends. And wouldn't you know it, Hayley had gotten a job at the Squeaky Lion around the same time Nick got a summer gig at Vivez. So it was a rare day when they didn't spend time with Nick Freeman, who had done so much to make them feel welcome in Columbus—including introducing them to the best chocolate milkshake known to humankind.

Nick was impressed, even as he realized Hayley was using him too. He was a character in a story for Mr. and Mrs. Burke, a tale of how he, Hayley, and Kevin got along famously, with no rivalry or deception or inconvenient attraction.

Soon it was time to eat, and Nick tried not to look too happy when Hayley sat to his right at the kitchen table, or disappointed when Mrs. Burke took the seat to his left. It was easiest just to focus on the food. Nick had to grudgingly admit that Kevin could put together a fantastic lunch.

"Nick, I've got to thank you for helping these two get settled." This from Mr. Burke, as he took a break from his burger. "Makes me feel better about dropping the ball this time around."

"Daddy," Hayley chided. "You were out of town!"

"Could've come back," he said.

She sighed. "Mom and Dad were on vacation in Colorado when we moved."

Nick said, "That sounds wonderful."

"Oh, it was," Mrs. Burke said. "Then we got back from two weeks in the mountains to find out our daughter lives in a different state."

"Mom, it wasn't like we . . ."

"Hayley Michelle." Her mother stopped her. "You could have called us."

Hayley stared back for a beat, then looked at her plate.

"I could still call the guys if you need anything fixed." Hayley's dad had a twinkle in his eyes. "Phil's been roaming the streets for weeks, just looking for an excuse to use his new circular saw."

Hayley laughed. "And how is Phil going to fix anything with a saw?"

"Easy. He'll saw the couch in half, and then he'll use his nail gun to put it back together."

Hayley tried to look annoyed, but she couldn't keep from giggling. "Dad's the leader of a bunch of degenerates," she told Nick.

"Men," Mr. Burke corrected. "You meant to say I equip men of extraordinary skill."

"Most of them are retired," Hayley went on, "so they have all this time and money to play with power tools. Honestly, Dad, you're like a drug dealer."

"Sure, except drug dealers make tons of money."

"You sell power tools?" Nick asked.

"Power tools and so much more, my friend," Mr. Burke said cheerfully. "I run the biggest hardware store in West Lafayette."

Hayley grinned. "He's very proud."

"Definitely could've used you for the move, Tom," Kevin spoke up. "You think you know what you're getting when you hire professionals, but . . ."

Mr. Burke shook his head sadly while Hayley shot Kevin a look. "A lot of 'em don't care as much as they should," he said.

"My uncle got me this huge toolbox when I graduated from college," Nick said, sipping his lemonade. "He said it'd come in handy when I had my own place."

"Your uncle's a genius," Mr. Burke said.

Nick grinned. "That may be, but I've got more tools in that thing than I've bothered to count, and I only know what five of them do. If something breaks in the apartment, I just call maintenance."

Mrs. Burke dabbed at her mouth with her napkin. "Do you sing professionally, Nick?"

Nick shook his head. "I teach high school math."

"Ah," she said. "If only you'd chosen a better subject."

Nick took a few valuable moments to finish chewing. "What should I have chosen?"

"English," she said promptly.

"Mom is the head of the English department at Purdue," Hayley explained.

"I guess I'd be surprised if you *didn't* prefer English, then." Nick's smile didn't seem to have much effect on Carolyn Burke. "I've got a buddy who could chat with you for hours. I tell him I'll start reading more as soon as he learns how to split a bar tab in his head."

"You don't read," she said drily.

"Not as much as English teachers would like me to, no."

"I guess you have those word problems," she said. "Jack has to buy fifty feet of carpet, but the carpet comes in twenty-foot rolls. I always end up thinking, 'Who's Jack, and why does he need that carpet, and what color is it?'"

"And after you answer all those questions, Jack's still going to have to figure out how to buy his carpet."

There was no reply. Hayley's mother had probably told the story of Jack and his carpet dozens of times; her words had the well-polished feel of a line that earned polite laughter at parties.

Nick was quickly getting tired of being polite—he'd been used as a buffer, a convenient friend, and now a punchline.

Mrs. Burke said, "Now I know where my freshmen get their attitude from."

Nick dropped his fork and turned to face the woman. "What are you doing to retaliate?" he asked her.

"Excuse me?"

"In your freshman English class, what are you doing to retaliate against all the high school math teachers who've turned your students against you?"

She leaned back just a bit, as if to regard him from a better angle, and Nick saw Mrs. Burke's daughter in the smile that played at the corners of the older woman's mouth.

"I get some attitude from my kids too," he said, "but it's because they think math is hard or because they think it's not worth their time. So I try to make it easier for the ones who struggle, and then I try to show everybody how paying attention in my class is going to help them in the long run, when they have to buy carpet one day. And in spite of my best efforts, a lot of the kids I teach would rather be down the hall in my pal Gavin's class for his unit on *Romeo and Juliet*. I hear he does a really good job."

It was hard to tell, but he thought he saw her smile grow a bit as she turned away to reach across the table for an Oreo. "*Romeo and Juliet* must've been hard on you," she said.

"Oh God, yes," Nick said. "I still have flashbacks."

Kevin said, "Shakespeare's kind of a big deal, buddy."

"I never really cared for him much," Mrs. Burke said, and Nick barely concealed a smirk. "Give me Hemingway or Steinbeck or Fitzgerald. But if anyone asks," she told Nick, "I love Shakespeare."

"And I love all those word problems," Nick replied. "Though just between us, I've never had to buy carpet."

Nick's eyes met Hayley's as he reached for his lemonade; she was looking at him with the sort of mildly stunned wonder he assumed superheroes and mass murderers got when they revealed their secret identities. He had surprised her, and he wasn't completely sure she was happy about it.

At the moment, he wasn't completely sure he cared.

"I'm glad you stayed for lunch," Hayley said later. His arm was around her shoulders, and he was gingerly working his way down the front steps of her house.

"Yeah," he said. The steps were uneven; the day had gotten hot and humid, and he needed to be in his car, in the air-conditioning, alone.

"My parents really like you," she said. "I mean, wow."

"Yeah, well, I'm a pretty likable guy."

They got to the bottom of the steps, and he hung on to the rail as she jogged back up and retrieved his walker. He eased the front wheels over the curb into the street, stepped down carefully, and then walked to his SUV. He hated how slowly Hayley had to move to keep pace beside him. He opened the car's back door and let it swing upward.

"You want me to put that in for you?" she asked him.

"Nah, I've got it." He put his left hand flat against a taillight and heaved the walker up and into the back of the car with his right hand. He reached up, grabbed the door, and slammed it down, still leaning against the taillight. Then he worked his way across the side of the car, keeping his palms flat against it for support. The car burned against his hands.

"So," she said as he yanked open the driver's door, "can you show me how you drive?"

Nick turned to face her, braced one hand against the seat and the other against the dashboard, and lifted himself into his seat. "Aren't you staying here?"

She looked confused. "Well, yeah."

"Can't really show you how I drive then, can I?"

He wanted to show her. He wanted to do anything she asked of him, even as he couldn't bear another second of working to make everybody happy. No matter what he did, he'd eventually have to drive away without her.

She shifted her weight from one foot to the other. "Did I do something to upset you?"

"You did not."

"Because you're monumentally pissed."

For a moment he was overwhelmed with the urge to beg her to get in the car and leave with him.

"Have fun with your folks," he said, and shut the door.

18

Everything around her was in motion.

Hayley saw the waitstaff slipping nimbly between the tables; she heard dozens of conversations blend together into something with its own momentum, like the sound of water rushing through rapids. Even without her eyes or her ears, she knew she would still be able to feel the life in the room—and instead of being part of it, she felt like she was sitting in an invisible cage, watching the world through walls she could sense but not see. This feeling had been firmly in the past when she'd talked about it with Nick; how had it found her again?

"You're kidding." Dad was deep in conversation with Cal. "A macaroni and cheese sandwich?"

"Macaroni and cheese on top of the regular grilled cheese," Cal told him. "You've got to try it, Tom."

Dad nudged her elbow. "Can we check out this Melt place tomorrow for lunch, sweetie?"

Hayley managed a smile and a nod. "Of course."

Only Dad could get someone to stop in the middle of serving a Saturday-night audience to talk about food that wasn't even on the Vivez Dance menu. It was sweet of him to ask her permission to go to Cal's favorite restaurant, as if he and Mom couldn't easily find the place on the way out of town tomorrow. She knew it would never occur to her parents to eat without her while they were visiting, just as it went without saying that they would spend their Saturday night watching their daughter's boyfriend perform. They loved her, and she loved them, and why wasn't that enough to stop whatever was slowly going wrong? Something was shifting—she was sure of it—and the peace she had embraced here in Columbus was slipping from her grasp.

"This is impressive." Mom leaned over to speak into her ear. "These kids are dedicated."

"Sure are," Hayley said. "It's a lot like Icarus."

"Well. In a way."

This was how it went with her. Mom could have found a way to compliment this place and her daughter at the same time. Something like, *"Wow, sweetie, these kids are just as dedicated as you were at Icarus, and have I told you how impressed I am by all the time you gave to that place?"* Instead, she'd just made it very clear that the theater where Hayley had failed to get a job was more impressive than the theater where she'd worked for years. There wasn't any point in arguing, especially since Hayley was pretty sure she agreed with her mother—but was it too much to ask such an intelligent, capable woman to find a way to be comforting and right at the same time?

"We could see if Nick wants to meet us after the show," Dad said.

Hayley chuckled wearily. "Dad."

"I'm just saying, there's a bar right out there. Least we could do is get him a drink, since he couldn't join us for the show."

"And *I'm* just saying the show is sold out tonight." This conversation had been going on all afternoon. "I know you don't believe me, but Nick isn't taking it personally that you couldn't get him a seat with less than a day's notice, I promise. He was here opening night."

"I'm sure he'd appreciate the invitation," Mom said. "You should call."

Hayley tried hard to stay expressionless, but she knew her shock had to be showing. It had taken Mom years to warm to Kevin, and when she had, it was like she'd decided she might as well be civil to the guy who didn't seem to be going anywhere. Dad was the sort to invite just about anyone home for dinner, but Hayley couldn't remember both of her parents actively trying to spend time with one of her friends. Of course, the one time it happened had to be with Nick and had to be tonight.

"You want to get a drink with Nick," Hayley said to her mother. "You want to stay out late so we can drink with a friend of mine."

"And Kevin's," Mom said.

"What?"

"I thought he was a friend of yours and Kevin's."

"Kevin's, yes," Hayley said quickly. "You want him to come out here at ten o'clock for a drink."

"He can always say no."

"I don't think he will."

Mom smiled wryly. "You can tell him I won't lose any sleep if he does."

"I might," Dad deadpanned.

Mom scoffed. "You don't lose sleep."

"It could happen." Dad was teasing her now. "You know how fragile I am."

"Go ahead," Mom told him. "Get this all out of your system before other people join the table."

Did Mom actually like Nick, or was she pushing Hayley to call because Hayley didn't want to? It really didn't matter. The more Hayley fought this, the more her parents were going to wonder why she didn't want to hang out with her friend, who was also supposed to be Kevin's friend.

God, she needed to move. Needed to dance.

"I'm going to call him," she announced. "We ought to give him plenty of notice."

Without waiting for a reply, Hayley strode all the way out to the parking lot, then kept pacing as she got out her phone. Her call went straight to voicemail: *Hi, this is Nick Freeman, and if you leave a message, I promise I won't make you wait too long for a reply.* She smiled in spite of herself as she pictured Nick diligently responding to each of his messages in the order in which they arrived.

"Nick," she said. "It's Hayley. We're at the show at Vivez, and my parents won't stop bugging me about inviting you for a drink after. Not that I don't want you to come. Because I do. I just meant that they . . ." She sighed. "Look, we all want you to come, but I don't want you thinking you have to come if you don't want to. My mom said she wouldn't lose sleep over it. Which I'm realizing sounds meaner than she meant it. Just call me if you want to join. Call me either way, actually. I want to make sure you're okay. Bye."

Hayley realized she was furious.

She had asked. She had stood in front of him and asked if she had done anything to upset him, and she hadn't even needed to do that, because she wasn't in charge of Nick Freeman's mood. This wasn't her fault.

Come on, Hayley Michelle. You want it to be your fault.

Every step Nick had taken from her porch to the car had been stiff, his body rigid, every facial expression and word tightly controlled and leaving no doubt that he wanted to be far away from her. If she'd made some mistake, then fixing everything would just be a matter of working hard enough. But she hadn't done anything wrong, and he was drifting away anyway. She was already worried about Kevin—the more she fought to hang on, the harder it was to connect with him. It was supposed to be different with Nick. They weren't in love; they weren't working toward something or working to preserve something. Hayley didn't need to carry the weight of whether or not he was okay, and yet she could feel, deep down, that she needed him to be. She needed too much from Mom, from Icarus, from Kevin, and now from Nick, and she hated that she was keeping herself from being happy. From feeling normal.

Hayley didn't cry. She kept the struggle from rising up and out of her, willed it down until the weight settled on her chest, and kept the desperation out of her voice when she pulled Mimi aside to ask if it was okay to use a rehearsal room after the show.

19

Nick had turned off his phone just before walking into Vivez Dance that night, hours before the Burke family arrived for the sold-out seven thirty show. The place was largely deserted, and Mimi was reading a paperback in the box office.

"Do you think the kid sister did it?" Her eyes never left the page as she spoke. "Or was it the tennis instructor?"

"The tennis instructor," he said promptly. "It's a sport full of murder weapons."

"Fair point. But I'm really very done with the kid sister."

"How do you feel about an evil twin?"

"Now *that's* exciting." She put down the book and grinned happily at him, but something she saw changed her smile a bit. "What've you been doing to yourself, darling?"

He could still feel Hayley studying him, caution in her eyes, like she was planning to retreat for her own safety. *Did I do something to upset you?*

"Isn't it obvious?" he said. "I've been spending entirely too much time away from you."

Mimi nodded gravely. "A lesser man wouldn't have lasted this long."

"Hey." Nick leaned his arms on the ledge of the box office window. "Do you think it'd be possible for me to hang out in the green room tonight?"

"You're family," she said. "You can hang out wherever the hell you want."

"You sure? I wasn't sure if that was crossing a line. And I wouldn't want people tripping over me."

"Of course," she said. "We here at Vivez are starved for attention, love. We'd be delighted to show you what goes on behind the scenes."

"Really?"

She watched his eyes. "You're having quite the rough time of it, aren't you?"

Nick considered telling Mimi what had happened that day, but he didn't know how to explain the anger that had filled him as he won over the crowd at Hayley's kitchen table. Tension and guilt had built in him all afternoon until he'd thought of dropping in on the gang at Vivez. If he could focus on them, maybe he could forget about himself.

"I thought it would be nice to be around you guys tonight," he said.

Mimi studied him for a moment more, then patted his arm, hopping off her stool. "Come with me."

"Where are we going?"

She came out of the box office and closed the door behind her. "To the kitchen, then the green room."

"Don't you need to be out here?"

"I'll snag somebody to cover for me."

"That's sweet, but I don't want to take you away from anything."

She shook her head firmly. "You, sir, are in dire need of nachos, alcohol, and good company, and I'm going to get it for you."

He was too grateful to argue the point. "Thanks, Mimi."

"Of course, love."

He followed her down the hall to the kitchen. "Hey, one thing."

"And what would that be, Nick dear?"

"You knew it was me coming through the door, didn't you? You heard the walker?"

Mimi grinned over her shoulder. "You want to know if I ask everybody how my mysteries turn out."

He laughed. "That's exactly it."

"And that will stay a little mystery of my own."

The green room was not, in fact, green, and Nick had yet to find anyone who could tell him where the name originally came from. Instead, the walls were painted gray, which was a good deal less depressing than it sounded, because they were covered by a few full-length mirrors, along with notes from cast and crew scribbled in fluorescent marker. The room was empty at the moment, but it wouldn't be for long.

"Okay." Mimi placed a very large, very full plastic cup on a table in the corner. "I invite you to have your run of the place."

"That's very sweet, Mimi. Thank you."

"Sweet nothing," she said. "You belong here."

He looked at her. "You mean that."

"Nick, my love," she said patiently, "belonging here has nothing to do with working here, but you, my dear, dear friend, happen to do both. We're going to have all the fun tonight, I promise."

Nick was trying to find a reply when Cal came speeding through the far door with a huge plate of nachos in his hands. "There I was," Cal said, "walking through the kitchen, and turns out Roman's making nachos for Nick in the green room. Couldn't believe it. Had to snatch these up so they actually made it *out* of the kitchen, ya know?"

Nick grinned. "Thanks, man."

"You bet." Cal spotted the drink when he put the nachos on the table. "That's a Brigadoon."

"Uh-huh," Mimi said.

"Our boy's in Brigadoon territory?"

"Well, look at him."

The two of them did just that, and Nick got uncomfortable. "Am I really that bad?" he asked.

Cal clapped him on the shoulder. "Take a seat, man. You'll love it back here."

Nick hesitantly did as he was told. "What's with the Brigadoon stuff?"

"Mimi came up with it," Cal said. "That drink only shows up when you really need it to."

Hanging out during a show in what was essentially the performers' lounge meant Nick knew whom to expect, so he wasn't surprised at all when Hayley's boyfriend arrived. Kevin, however, did a double take when he spotted Nick at the table.

"Hey, man!" Kevin grinned. "I'm glad I ran into you."

"Really." Nick wiped his mouth. "Why's that?"

"Because you're a lifesaver! Hal's mom *hates* me. No idea why."

"Who knows?" Nick said. "You certainly charmed me."

Kevin blinked. "What?"

"You didn't ask me if I'd want to be at that lunch, Kevin."

"Sure I did."

"I stand corrected." He thought briefly about actually standing. "You *did* ask me to stay for lunch, and then you said 'plenty of burgers.' You could have used another three words. Like—oh, I don't know, 'Parents are coming.'"

"But it went great."

"Because I'm very good at what I do."

"Then I don't—"

"And if you thought it was going to go great," Nick said, "you had all the time in the world to say, 'Nick! The Burkes are coming! It'll be great!' But you didn't."

Kevin looked down at his shoes.

"Here's what I think," Nick said. "I think you knew there was a chance I'd say no. You knew that if Carolyn hated you, there was a chance she'd hate me too. So you thought it'd be better for you if you took your chances and made the whole thing look accidental."

After a moment, Kevin brought his eyes up to meet his. "You're right," he said.

"I know."

"But it all worked out, didn't it?"

This time Nick did stand, carefully leaning on the table and momentarily regretting the Brigadoon.

"I am your friend," he said, "and I am her friend. I'm sure I'll end up going to idiotic lengths to make life easier for both of you. But you need to start making life easier for me. You need to start goddamn asking."

"Okay," Kevin said, nodding. "I will."

Nick was proud of the fear he saw on Kevin's face as he sat down, until he realized Kevin was probably afraid he'd miss his chair. Once Nick was safely seated, Kevin headed for the hallway to the dressing rooms.

"Thank you," Nick forced himself to call after him. "You do make a really good lunch."

Kevin stopped in the doorway. "You know Hal and her folks are out front," he said.

"I'd rather they not know I'm here."

"Sure," Kevin said. "I just figured you might want to chat, since we'll be moving soon."

Nick looked up. "Moving?"

"Yeah. It'll be better for everybody when we're back at Icarus."

One after another, the cast and crew hurried into the green room in street clothes—jeans or shorts, sunglasses, and ball caps—and acknowledged him with a quick smile or wave. Then it was through the opposite door and into the dressing rooms, and the same person who had seemed almost disheveled on the way in would reappear less than twenty minutes later, hair combed, makeup perfect, clad in the black slacks and colorful shirt of a Vivez server. Nick envied the speed of it, since changing so quickly was impossible for him, but more than that, he liked the energy the cast had in costume. They seemed both relaxed and focused, as if putting on the trappings of this place reminded them of their purpose here. Nick feigned reluctance when Linda insisted on including him in the customary preshow huddle, but he liked standing shoulder to shoulder with his coworkers as they formed a circle around the room—and he made sure to stand next to Mimi so he could ask her for another favor.

The Brigadoon was tart and strong, and Mimi managed to rush a new cup to his table after the huddle. He opened his mouth to thank her, but she waved him off and jogged toward the dressing rooms. He understood: The show was starting in minutes.

God, how did it feel to move that quickly?

He was still dreaming of running when Mimi came back through the door, dressed in her first costume of the evening: sparkly black pants, black shoes, white dress shirt, and loose red tie. "How are we?" she asked.

He looked her up and down and shook his head. "Too classy. I can't be in the same room with this kind of class."

She grinned and straddled a nearby chair. "I asked around for you. There's been no news of a certain tap dancer leaving for greener pastures."

"Ah," Nick said. "Doesn't mean it's not true."

"No, but it'd be poor form to leave during the run of a show he's featured in."

"I doubt that matters."

Mimi lowered her voice. "I can't imagine you'd be upset if he left."

"Not even a little bit."

"Which means you're drowning your sorrows in Brigadoons and melted cheese because Hayley would be leaving with him."

Nick just looked at her.

"I'm sure you've already thought of this, being a math guy and all." Mimi got up from her chair. "But if two people are leaving, one of them might not be happy about it."

Nick had time to smile his thanks before the stage door opened. Showtime.

He'd assumed he was just going to watch the chaos, but the cast immediately made him a part of it. He was an insider, which meant he could be trusted, but he was new to the green room, which meant he was a fresh pair of ears for all inside jokes and complaints about annoying audience members. The cast left to tend to their patrons at intermission, so Nick was surprised when Cal came in with a fresh drink.

"Don't you have tables to cover?" he asked.

"Nah. People owe me some favors." Cal handed him the Brigadoon. "You ever try the Mighty Macaroni?"

"At Melt?" Nick's eyes widened. "Did you bring one?"

Cal laughed, striding toward the mirror on the far wall. "No way I'd let you eat one of those when I couldn't have one."

Nick realized he was holding two cups, and drained the one so he could start the other. "That's just cruel, man. After all those apple fritters . . ."

"You just plowed through a plate of nachos bigger than your head." Cal reached the wall and turned to face him. "You know, Hayley's just as messed up as you are."

"Really?" Nick tried to picture it. "You mean she's out there with her parents, looking like . . ." Nick gestured with both cups. "No way she's as messed up out there as I am in here."

"She's holding it together, but I can tell."

"Yeah, sure—because you can read women like a book."

"You think I can't spot a woman putting on a good show on a bad day?"

Nick remembered where he was. "Oh," he said. "Sorry." He watched Cal reach his table and turn around to pace back to the mirror. "Cal?"

"Yeah?"

"What the hell are you doing?"

"Got to stay moving during a show," Cal said. "Keeps me limber."

"It's kind of freaking me out."

"Hey, I can go." Cal strolled toward him again. "But if you want to tell somebody what happened . . ."

Nick sighed. "Like that'll help."

"You never know," Cal pointed out. "And I'm a *vault*, man. A bona fide, natural-born keeper of secrets."

"Bona fide," Nick said skeptically. "Natural-born."

"Yessir. And a card-carrying friend of the music man."

Cal grinned at him, and Nick raised a cup in a salute.

After a moment, Nick said, "You ever see *Free Willy*?"

Cal stopped walking. "You two got emotional over that whale movie?"

Nick scoffed. "Nah, man. Had a girlfriend who *loved* it, though." He thought back. "This was middle school, so *Free Willy*, *The Little Mermaid* . . . anything to do with the ocean. She loved the ocean."

"Do you?"

"I like to *watch* the ocean," Nick said. "But, ya know, I figured she'd work at an aquarium and I'd teach or something. We'd make it work." He sipped from his cup. "It didn't."

Cal regarded the empty plate that had once held an epic amount of nachos. "Well, that sure explains a lot."

Nick rolled his eyes. "She broke up with me in college," he said. "From San Diego. 'It's over, Nicky. We're moving in different directions.' Didn't know where we were moving, but I sure as hell knew we didn't *have* to be moving, because I could move where she was moving. I was gonna do that anyway. But no. 'I won't make you live a life on the ocean, hon.'"

Cal was strolling again, and looked from Nick to the walker. "Would that be a possibility?"

"Of course not." Nick threw his empty cup; it bounced off the table and clattered to the floor. "Can't spend your life scuba diving with a boyfriend who can barely stand on dry land." He rubbed his eyes. "That hurt, man. Hurt a lot. The only good thing about Vicki breaking up with me was that I never had to get on a goddamn boat."

"I've thought about dancing on a cruise ship," Cal offered, bending to retrieve Nick's cup. "But what if it sinks?"

Nick nodded emphatically and felt the room swim. "I'd do it for Hayley, though."

Calvin paused mid-crouch. "Sink?"

"I'm not even saying, like, if she was a diver or whatever," Nick barreled on. "If she said, 'Nick, I'd be happy if you lived on a boat,' I think I'd do it. I'd be loading up on Dramamine, and she'd be here, and I'd—I don't know—send her pictures of pur-poses or whatever . . ." He realized his mistake. "Porpoises. Porpoises?"

Cal stood slowly as he put it all together. "You're in love with her," he said.

Nick forgot about porpoises. "No." He shook his head and started to laugh. "Not a chance. I've done that. Love is easy."

"Says who?" Cal took aim and sent Nick's empty cup on an easy arc into a nearby trash can. "Love's only easy when it's convenient."

"I just had to take my cues," Nick said. "I'm *really good* at that, man. I could see everything at lunch, what they all wanted from me. Kevin wants an emotional stunt double or something, and her folks like me better than him, so why not? And Hayley . . ." Nick gritted his teeth. "Hayley wants to show her parents this perfect picture of her life. And that's fine. I can be what she wants. Except today." He slumped. "Couldn't do it today."

Cal dropped into the seat next to him. "Of course not," he said. "You want something better."

Nick pointed at him. "You'd think so, wouldn't you? But that's not why I left her on the . . ." He waved a hand in front of him at the imaginary sidewalk. "I left because I realized I will do *anything* to keep her around," he said. "You know how scary that is? All afternoon, I've been imagining all the lunches I'm going to suffer through, and all the pain that's going to come with being nothing more than her friend. And I'm going to do it anyway."

The pair stared at each other.

"It's awfully interesting," Cal said carefully, "how she's as upset as you are."

Nick blinked. "No," he said. "She's . . . look, she probably thinks she did something wrong."

"Did she?"

"No. Come on." Nick was floundering. "It doesn't matter. They're moving away."

"Probably not much of a downside to telling her how you feel, then."

"I'm not going to tell her I'm pissed at her."

"Not what I meant." Cal got up and reached for Nick's plate. "Want some more nachos?"

Nick wasn't ready for the subject change. "Is there enough time?"

"I can make it happen," Cal said. "Though you should know people are going to panic if we ask for two Nacho Days in one night."

"Nacho . . ." Nick started to laugh. "Not Your Day. I knew the plate was larger than normal."

"The emergency menu is top secret," Cal cautioned. "Vivez family only."

"No nachos required," Nick said. "Maybe another Brigadoon. And some water." He paused. "Is there some sort of cookie situation on the emergency menu?"

"Anything for the music man."

Nick was comfortably spent when the show ended, light-headed from laughter and booze when Mimi found him after the curtain call.

"Nick," she said, "how drunk are you right now, would you say?"

Nick gave that some serious thought. "Let's find out." He stood up carefully. "Oh yeah. We're golden."

"And what does that mean?"

"Means the room's not spinning when I stand up, so I am good to go."

"Fantastic. Have you seen our rehearsal rooms?"

He was still working on her first question. "I mean, there are *degrees* of drunk. But I'm not sick drunk. Not *unstable*."

"That's wonderful, darling. So, if you were to, say, talk to Hayley in this condition . . ."

Nick whipped his head around and immediately regretted it. "Where is she?"

"She's upstairs," Mimi said patiently. "In a rehearsal room."

It took a second to land, and then Nick was nodding. "Ahhhh."

"So, if you wanted to talk to her without anyone else around . . ."

Now that he was really thinking about it, panic was setting in. "Maybe not the greatest idea."

"Maybe not," Mimi said. "But I wanted to give you the chance."

They looked at each other for a few long moments.

"I think I'll go upstairs," he said finally. "Check out the rehearsal rooms."

"I think you'll like them."

An unpleasant tingle started in Nick's hands as he left the green room, and by the time he stepped onto the elevator, he wished he could leave his body until everything calmed down. He hated this part of drinking, the space between drunk and sober where he could recognize horrible ideas and know he might follow through with them anyway. He was never entirely sure what he'd do around Hayley, but he could barely control his breathing now, let alone the words that came out of his mouth. Nick was terrified he'd reveal something. Anything. Too much. He had to see her anyway.

The elevator doors opened. Nick walked down a hardwood corridor toward the light streaming through the rectangular pane of glass set in a door to his left. He peered into the room. There she was.

Nick had thought he'd seen Hayley dance before, but giving the same label to what he'd seen at the bar and what she was doing now would've been an insult. To Nick, dancing meant wedding receptions, or the school dances where he'd held Vicki close. Even Hayley's swing dance with Kevin had been something familiar to him. But now, Hayley was moving like something inside of her needed to get out.

He couldn't see nearly enough through the glass window, so he opened the door and slipped through. Loud music filled the soundproofed room, but he doubted Hayley would have noticed him even if the rattle of his walker had broken total silence. Her movements spoke of a primal pulse, and every bit of the physical grace he'd ever noticed in her was on display under bright lights. She moved barefoot across the floor, leaping and spinning and launching into handsprings, commanding her arms and legs according to some design he couldn't predict and couldn't stop watching. At first he thought she was responding to an invisible force, like she was being buffeted by spiritual winds, but the closer he looked, the more each choice in her whirlwind of movement seemed to be executed with fluid, exacting precision. Hayley danced like she had to, threw herself around the room like she couldn't help it, but she was in complete control. He could see the passion surging through her, and he was convinced every moment she spent walking or standing or sitting like normal people was a moment she might as well have been chained to the earth. She was a force of nature, her body in total obedience to her mind as she moved in perfect expression of her soul, and Nick had never seen anything more beautiful.

This longing, this awe, this physical yearning, so all-consuming it stopped his breath and got his eyes stinging with the approach of tears—was Cal right? Was this love?

Nick was still staring at Hayley as the song ended and she stopped moving. He saw the gleam of sweat on her skin as she brushed the hair out of her face, and then his whole body seized up when he realized where he was. He shouldn't be a part of something so private, so perfect—and there was no way for him to get out of this room unnoticed.

It seemed like an eternity before she glanced up, and she jumped when their eyes finally met across the empty room. The sudden movement startled him—of course it did. Everything did. He was disabled, defective—and he was so tense that leg spasms nearly made him fall over. Her hand went to her chest, and the other one shot out involuntarily, as if she could stop him from tripping over himself.

"Nick!" Hayley started laughing. "God, I'm sorry. I didn't see you."

"It's okay," he assured her. "I didn't mean to sneak up on you."

"Hey, it's about time you made me jump for a change, right?" She grabbed a towel from on top of a duffel bag and wiped her face. "What're you doing here?"

"Mimi said I should check out the rehearsal rooms."

"Seriously?"

He watched her swig from a bottle of water. "Yeah."

"So you had no idea I'd be up here."

Her olive-green T-shirt was damp with sweat and cropped at her midriff, her thin gray sweatpants ending halfway down her calves. He watched her walk toward him and thought of the raw power in her legs. He saw her flat, bare stomach and realized he'd never been quite so aware of her body before, soft curves over toned muscle.

"Well," he said.

Hayley smiled, biting her lower lip. She didn't do that often, which was good, because it melted him every single time. There was a mysterious shyness to it, like she knew something he didn't but was willing to invite him in and spill her secrets.

"I'm sorry," he blurted. "I wasn't ready. For lunch, I mean. There was a lot going on, and I didn't know they would be . . . I mean, they were great, of course, even though your mom is, well . . . but you've gotta understand, that movie was *dark*, and then Kevin was saying—"

"Nick?"

Hayley was still smiling, her voice soft.

He swallowed. "Yes?"

"It's okay," she said. "I'm glad you're here."

Sure. Because she was moving away. So he'd better not waste time.

"When you . . ." He cleared his throat. "That thing you say, about me finding my joy. Do you remember when that happened for you?"

Hayley nodded, grinning. "'Rhythm Nation.' The Janet Jackson video."

"You saw that and just knew."

"My whole body knew," she said. "All of me. I was begging for lessons the same day."

He nodded, forced himself to look at her. "So imagine you watched that video," he said slowly. "And maybe there was always a hole in your heart, maybe the need was always there, but you didn't know that until you saw the one thing that could fill it. Now your heart is screaming at you to do something, to grab on to what you need so badly, but you can't follow through. Ever. You can't fix it, and you can't go back, so you have to find a way to manage the pain."

Hayley stared at him.

"Don't do it," he warned her. "Don't you dare cry."

"Okay." She nodded to herself. "I'm teaching you to dance."

"What?" His mouth went dry. "No."

"Yep!" Hayley walked to the back wall, where her phone was plugged into a speaker system. With the tap of a couple buttons, the infectious beat of a joyful Justin Timberlake hit was coming through the speakers. "I'm teaching you to dance right now."

"Hayley . . ."

"You have no idea," she said. "You work here every day, and you find your joy on that stage, and you have *no idea* what you can do." She grinned. "I can fix this."

"Fix what?"

"Just shift your weight. One foot to the other. I know you've got rhythm."

Nick tried to rock back and forth a little as she danced her way over to him. Hayley kept it simple, little more than walking to the beat with a spring in each step, but she did it like she was designed for it.

He felt like he was standing on a boat.

"Good!" She was delighted, standing in front of him now. "That's good!"

Nick had never felt more self-conscious in his life. He had gotten in the elevator expecting a difficult conversation. Instead, he had seen talent that surpassed anything he knew. No, talent wasn't the correct word. He felt like he'd truly seen *her* for the first time. Every moment of knowing her had just been a glimpse of what had been revealed in this room minutes ago, and now Hayley was asking him to respond by doing the one thing he could never truly join her in. With every awkward shift back and forth, he wanted to cry or yell or collapse.

But he wasn't going to cry, yell, or collapse. He was going to make the very best of this, if it fucking killed him, because this unbelievable woman wanted him here with her. This could be the last time they had together.

"Hayley." He tried to smile and move at the same time. "I don't mean to disagree, but . . ."

"Okay. Stop moving." He did, gratefully, but then things got worse. "Just feel the music," she said.

"What?"

"Don't decide anything. Don't plan anything, don't add to the Nick Freeman rulebook. Just feel the music and react to it."

His feet stayed planted to the floor. His hands were gripping his walker so hard that cords of muscle were standing out in his arms.

"I'm trying," he said weakly.

"I know," she said softly. She smiled, and he felt himself relax, just a little.

"I'm sorry." The words were spilling out into the silence where a song used to be. "I really wish I could dance with you."

"Nick." Her eyes sparkled. "We've been dancing for weeks."

He struggled for words. "That's not . . . I know what you're saying, but . . ."

"You know more than that."

He looked at her blankly. "What?"

"I think you can feel it. Our rhythm."

His mind raced back through the last few months. She couldn't be talking about what he'd felt when he'd fallen into her arms at the bar or when he saw her walk into his kitchen in his robe. He replayed their karaoke Fridays, their texts, their lunches at the diner.

"You mean our sparring?" he said.

"Sparring?"

"Yeah." Damn it. She'd been thinking of something else. "Fake boxing. Like when Rocky was training, he'd spar with someone in the ring. Not to beat the other person, but to make him better."

"And I make you better."

"Yeah." She was biting her lip again, and he was flustered. "You surprise me. Knock me off-balance. It's good, though. You keep me paying attention. I throw something your way, you throw it right back."

"Give and take," she said. "Reacting to me."

"Yeah."

"That's dancing."

"Okay."

She was going for her phone again. "Did you know Sylvester Stallone wrote out the entire fight with Apollo in *Rocky*?"

"What?"

"He wrote out every punch, like a screenplay. He choreographed it, Nick. Called it a violent ballet."

"He did not."

"He did." She smiled. "I watched a documentary."

For an instant, he forgot to be terrified and smiled back. "You did that because of me?"

Hayley put down her phone. A much slower song started playing, one he recognized from junior high. Savage Garden's "Truly Madly Deeply." She walked along the wall until she was standing across from him.

"Come here," she said. Then, when he managed to obey her, "Turn around so your back is against the wall."

He did. Hayley stepped toward him, swaying with the rhythm, until there were mere inches between them.

She said, "You know how to dance to this, don't you?"

He coughed a nervous laugh. "This is not a good idea."

"C'mon. I bet you were the king of the slow dance." She picked up his right hand and guided it to the bare skin just above her hip. "That hand goes here."

His heart was pounding. His mouth was dry. *She's got a boyfriend, she's got a boyfriend, she's got that asshole boyfriend . . .*

"Can I have your other hand?" she asked.

He looked down at his fingers gripping the walker. "Um, I don't . . ."

"Please?"

Was there anything he wouldn't give her if she asked?

Very slowly, he took his trembling hand off the walker and lost a little height when his legs braced for balance. She put his left hand on her right shoulder and brought her left hand around behind him, tightening her arm against his lower back to support him. Her right hand found its way behind his neck.

"Okay?"

He nodded.

"Don't worry about the right steps. They'll come to you. Just trust your partner."

Very slowly, they swayed back and forth.

"Dancing is reacting," she said. "Dancing is being so in tune with the world around you that your movement is a response. A contribution."

All he could do was cling to the warmth of her body, the warmth in her eyes.

"I'm going to take a step back," she said softly, "and you'll step forward. Keep your eyes on mine, okay? I've got you."

She stepped and he followed, certain he would fall.

"Perfect." Her smile almost made him cry. "We're going to go to your right, and then I'll step forward and you'll step back. Eyes on me."

He followed, heart lurching with every step, eyes locked on hers.

"You know you're one of the best dancers I've ever seen?" she said.

He swallowed the lump in his throat. "I can't do what you do."

"Really?" She held his gaze. "Because we're dancing now. Without the walker."

He chanced a startled gaze to his left, where the walker stood empty. When he looked back at her, he had tears in his eyes.

She said, "You make me better too, Nick. Thank you for dancing with me."

He was suffused with warmth, speechless. He needed to tell her, but the words wouldn't come, weren't there. He needed to make her understand what she'd just done, what it meant, and he was running out of time, because she was leaving, and oh God, this was a goodbye dance, a parting gift, and he would never get to stand in her arms and feel her warmth again.

He kissed her.

He didn't remember deciding to do it, didn't remember moving his hands to pull her in, only knew it when their lips met and he tasted sweet lip gloss. Her mouth opened in a surprised gasp under his, and her fingers tightened against his neck. She wasn't kissing him back, but she wasn't pulling away either, and the soft touch of her lips both charged him and calmed him—he felt like he could conquer the world, but he didn't need to anymore. He had just enough time to want to taste her forever before he leaned into her, lost his balance, and overcorrected. His back hit the wall.

Hayley looked dazed. "Nick . . ."

Oh God. Oh no. He reached for the walker and pivoted. "Sorry. I'm so sorry."

"It's okay."

He couldn't look at her. "Sorry. I'm drunk."

"Hey." He felt her hand on his shoulder as he stepped into his personal cage. "Nick, sweetie, it's really okay."

"Don't call me that," he said hoarsely. "I'm not your sweetheart or your baby. I'm nothing."

He swung around, and the pity in her eyes broke him. She was going to be nice about this, just like all the other girls who didn't want anything to do with him.

He said, "You know I would've asked you out, right? If you didn't have Kevin, I would have asked you out."

She shook her head.

"Really?" He choked out a laugh. "Great. Well, I would've. And I'm not talking about trying to get you to come home with me from the bar. I mean I would've dressed up and been classy about it, and I would've asked you to dinner or lunch or coffee, or whatever the hell you would've agreed to, because spending time with you is a gift I don't deserve."

Hayley hadn't moved. After all this time, they were back where they'd started that first night, and once again she was blindsided by a part of him he wished she'd never had to see.

"But hey," he said, "I managed to win the jackpot anyway. I'm a jerk to you, and you still want to spend time with me. You want to share with me and listen to me, and I don't even know where I am half the time, because you smile at me and I can think of absolutely nothing else. You're incredible."

Some part of him pictured shutting up, walking out the door while he could still protect himself, but the words flowed from him with a horrible sort of relief. At least it'd be out. At least he could be done.

"I can't do it," he said. "You invite me for lunch, and I can't stop looking at Kevin and knowing I'll always come in second. I was awful today, and you teach me to dance. You did the nicest . . ."

His throat closed up, and he stared at the floor.

"Nothing gives me the right to try and take what you never gave me," he said. "I failed you."

"No."

He looked up. Hayley stared at him in shock, her eyes glistening. "No," she said again, her voice stronger. "You've never failed me."

Of course she would say that. It was the sort of thing a good person did.

"I found my joy in you, Hayley. I ache to dance on that stage, yes, but I was talking about you, and for the life of me I can't find a way to be your friend. That's a failure."

She shook her head. "It was just a kiss. It doesn't matter."

"What you just did was the nicest thing anyone's ever done for me. I need you to know that."

He made himself walk past her to the door. There would be time for the pain later, alone, in the dark.

"Nick."

He turned back to look at her.

"I would have said yes." She smiled, tears streaming down her face. "If you had asked me out."

He could see she believed that, and he wished he could too.

"Goodbye, Hayley."

20

Six days later, Hayley was climbing the stairs to her bedroom. "Just act like nothing happened," she said into her cell phone.

"Nothing happened," said Denise. "Tonight's just a typical Friday night."

"Right. He's taking this too seriously."

"So *you* shouldn't feel guilty about it either. A slow dance isn't code for 'jump me.'"

"I know."

"Unless it's that boner song. You can't dance to a pop song about getting an erection and not—"

"Yes, yes, yes, just stop." Hayley said, grinning. Her best friend was trying to get her to laugh. "Don't worry. I went with 'Truly Madly Deeply.'"

Silence. "You what?"

Hayley stopped moving. "You know. Savage Garden."

"I do know. You danced with him to your wedding song?"

Heat rushed to her face. "I was in fourth grade, Denise."

"Still."

She had called the radio station and taped the song with her boombox. She had worn out the cassette dancing in her bedroom and thinking of the boy who'd dance with her one day. And none of that had crossed her mind when she'd played "Truly Madly Deeply" for Nick Freeman.

"I didn't think about it," she said weakly.

"I'm sure you didn't." Denise paused. "But I'm going to be obnoxious now."

"I'll pretend you weren't before."

"Did you like the kiss?"

His hand had gone from her shoulder to the back of her neck in an instant; there was the sweet shock of being pulled toward him. His lips found hers and she lost herself as everything went warm and tingly. She'd tightened her grip on him as he leaned in. Then, as he fell away from her, she'd tried very hard not to kiss him again.

"He's good at it," Hayley said.

Denise let out a breath. "Hey, maybe I could come visit."

"We'll probably move back before you get a chance."

"You're going to let Kevin make that choice?"

She started pacing. "What do I have here, D? Not a stage. Not Nick. And if I stay, I won't have Kevin either."

"Honey, Cyd isn't taking Kevin's calls. At least you have jobs in Columbus."

Hayley frowned as a door slammed downstairs. "Hey, I've got to go. I think Kevin's home."

"Sure. Love you."

"Love you too."

Kevin was on his way up the steps. "What's going on?" she said.

"Packing a bag," he said. "I'm going to talk to Cyd."

"Did she call?"

He pulled a duffel bag down from the closet and threw it on their bed. "She can't ignore me in person."

"Don't you have shows tonight?"

"Told them I was sick."

Her eyes narrowed. "That's obviously not true."

"They'll live with it."

She watched him yank clothes from the dresser, fueled by anger and panic.

"Kevin, stop," she said. "It's not worth going back."

"Yeah?" he said over his shoulder. "Even if it fixes us?"

She suddenly felt cold. "What do you mean?"

"It's like we're in a play or something. You're playing your part, I'm playing mine."

She wished she didn't understand what he meant.

"Okay," she said, moving to the bed. "Yes. It's different. But we're not going to fix it by moving backward."

"Why not?"

"I was dying at Icarus, Kev."

"I wasn't!"

He'd whirled on her, the words leaving him in a guttural yell. She stumbled backward and saw regret soften his anger. Kevin took a deep breath. Then another. Then a third.

"Don't you want to dance with me?" His voice was quiet. "That's why we're together?"

She was confused. "You want a list of reasons?"

"All those nights sitting on your couch, we talked about our future, where we were going. Remember?"

"Of course," she said. "But we don't need Icarus for that."

He laughed bitterly. "Well, we could try Broadway, but if you couldn't handle Icarus . . ."

Her eyes filled with tears. "That's not fair."

"Not fair." He went back to packing. "Not fair is taking that last show off, Hal."

"You danced in that show!" She stared at him, incredulous.

"That last show ran for three months. Three months when you

didn't have to leave the stage at all, and I was mixing drinks. Do you know how hard it was to stand behind the bar and hear the music from the theater? You were literally dancing in the next room, and I couldn't join you." She threw up her hands. "Sorry— I didn't want to have panic attacks on stage."

"I shouldn't have been in the ensemble," he muttered.

"Yeah, well, blame Cyd."

"Cyd only put me in the ensemble because of you," he shot back. "Because we're a pair. Tickets sell when we dance *together*."

Hayley felt sick. "She told you this."

"She sure did."

"So you asked for more stage time, she said no, and you said, 'I'm out.'"

"You think I fucked up."

She shook her head. "Why didn't you tell me?"

"Because when I told you I wanted to leave Indianapolis, you acted like we'd won the lottery!" he said. "Why should I have told you? What would that have fixed?"

She shrugged, defeated. "I don't know."

"Doesn't matter," he said. "Linda will never let us headline here."

"Who cares about headlining?"

Kevin stopped packing. Very slowly, he turned to face her.

"Who *cares*?" He was incredulous. "What the hell have we been doing this for, Hal?"

Hayley stopped breathing. "I thought you were doing it for me," she whispered. "I thought we were building a life."

The fight went out of him, and he sat down on the bed.

"Well . . ." He started to speak, changed his mind, started again. "What does that life look like?"

"I don't care," she said. "As long as it's with you." But the words sounded childish now, after ringing true for years. She'd been with him for a long time, and this life wasn't enough.

Another humorless laugh. "You want a life with me, but not at Icarus and not here."

"You're the one who's leaving!"

"You want to stay here?" He gestured at the room around them. "We're making it work because we've been doing it for years, Hal. It's habit. That's all."

"And you don't want to fix it."

"I'm *going* to fix it." He sprang up, energized again. "I'm going to get us our old jobs, and we're going back to where this *worked*."

She believed him. Kevin would get things back to the way they were, and she wouldn't need to do a thing. But she would lose herself, little by little, until her fear took all she had to give.

"No," she whispered.

He barely glanced at her. "What?"

"No," she said again. "I won't survive going back."

"That's a little dramatic."

She saw it then, the way he dismissed her. Kevin had always told her everything would be okay, and she'd thought he believed in her strength. But Kevin assumed she'd get better because he'd never thought anything was truly wrong. He hadn't wanted to.

"What if I couldn't dance?" she asked softly.

He paused. "What, like Nick?"

"What if I get hurt?" she pressed on. "What happens when we get old? One day they're going to stop putting us on posters, Kevin. What's your plan then?"

"Those are hypotheticals."

"You left your girlfriend for me, Kevin," she said. "You broke up with Carrie, and you told me you loved me, and you watched *Dirty Dancing* and brought home chicken soup for two weeks when I had the flu, and don't you dare tell me that was all for what I could get you on that fucking stage, because I would give every bit of my life to you even if you *were* in a walker."

Kevin watched her catch her breath.

"Again with Nick," he said bitterly.

"What the hell?" She followed him into the bathroom. "This isn't about him."

"I already told him we were leaving."

She stopped. "When? Today?"

"When you were with your folks."

Her reflection gaped at her in the mirror. "A week ago," she said. "Oh God, he thought that was the last time he'd see me."

Kevin zipped his toiletry bag and pushed past her. "He'll survive."

"He matters to me, Kevin!"

"So stay here with him."

She didn't say a word.

Kevin's eyes widened. "Are you fucking kidding me?" he said.

"I don't want to go back," she said, her voice raw, "and you don't want to stay here."

He took a deep breath, clasped his hands. "All I ever wanted was to dance with you. I'm making that happen, Hal. That's the only move I have."

"Do you love me?" she asked.

"Of course."

"Then trust me. Stay here and we'll work this out. Show me I'm enough."

She saw confusion in his eyes. Then, slowly, they hardened with resolve.

Hayley started to cry.

"Don't do that." He hefted his duffel. "Not when I'm trying to fix this. I . . . just get in the car, Hayley."

She shook her head.

"If you don't come with me, there's not much point in coming back."

"I know," she whispered. The worst kind of calm had settled on her because she knew she couldn't hold on to anything anymore.

He waited expectantly, and then his shoulders slumped. For the first time since she'd met him, Kevin Albee looked utterly lost.

"Well then," he said. "I guess we're done."

21

Nick was hunched in his seat at the Squeaky Lion, his phone pressed hard to his ear. "Tell Rosie a cotton candy hurricane couldn't keep me from her party tomorrow. Will that work?"

"Cotton candy." Gavin was impressed. "Nice."

"You know, massive, but not scary." He told himself to breathe, to calm down. "How badly do you think I hurt her?"

"Hayley?" Gavin asked. "I think she understood."

"Uh-huh." Kevin had been at work every day that week and had showed no sign of leaving the company. If the move to Indiana had been postponed, then Hayley could be working here tonight—and Nick had no idea what to do about that.

"Just take your cue from her," Gavin reassured him. "If she doesn't want to talk to you, she won't."

"But what if *she's* taking her cue from *me?*" Nick peered through the sea of people by his booth; the bar was packed tonight. "What if she wants to talk, but she assumes I don't want to?"

Gavin took a beat. "What's your goal here?"

"I don't want to make things worse."

"Then tell her that," Gavin said gently. "She'll help you figure out the rest."

Nick hung up without saying goodbye, because Hayley was headed straight toward him. He froze, but her eyes were trained on the ground in front of her, and she hadn't spotted him yet. Instead of gliding past patrons, she was shrinking back, like she was afraid she would get hit. She flashed wide smiles as people said hello, but those smiles slid away as quickly as they came.

Then she was looking directly at him.

In that instant, all the dread Nick felt in anticipation of seeing her tonight turned into full-blown alarm. He wasn't just looking at a harried waitress. Hayley was smiling at him, but her eyes were dull. She wasn't moving, and he felt sick when he realized why. Hayley didn't know whether she was welcome.

The superstar grin wouldn't work here; she'd think he was faking it. Nick stood up in the booth, looked pointedly at the walker, then raised his eyebrows in a question. Her eyes flooded with relief.

"Hi!" She rushed forward, and he put his arm around her shoulders to step down into the walker. "Let me help you."

"Thanks." He pulled her in for a hug. "You okay?"

"Me? Fantastic! Can you believe this crowd?"

"It's insane. Are you sure you're—"

She noisily planted her lips on his cheek in a cartoon kiss. "Couldn't be better, rock star. Be back soon!"

Nick almost flinched as she fled into the crowd. Hayley was too loud tonight, too manic. He wondered when she'd stop moving. He wondered if she could.

He had worn that same wide smile over dull eyes; he'd seen it in the mirror on his worst nights at this bar. He'd convinced himself that the solution was to dazzle and distract, to charm as many people as possible so they'd never know how worthless he felt. He never stopped moving on those nights because he'd been afraid of what would happen when he did.

Now he was afraid for Hayley.

22

Hayley spun in a neat pirouette before swooping up a tray of drinks from the bar, and applause nearly drowned out the ringing in her ears. The clapping seemed to grow louder as the light in the room grew brighter, harsher—she locked her grin in place so she wouldn't wince.

"Thank you, thank you all," she called out. "I'll be here all night."

Nick had seemed happy to see her. Maybe they could get a milkshake at the diner after her shift. Just sitting with him would be enough.

Hayley Michelle. You know he's just being nice to you because these are his people. He made you feel good, so you never considered what you were doing to him. Hope it was worth it, because now he wants nothing to do with you.

It was happening again. Her heart was in high gear, panic tingled through her like malicious white noise, and certainty seeped in at a steady, terrifying pace until she was convinced that the very worst had happened and would always happen. She had overstepped, or she hadn't done enough, or she'd wanted too much—she was always wanting too much because there was something unforgivably wrong with her.

"Hello, friends!" She swept up to a table and started handing out glasses. "How're we doing tonight?"

"Great, now that you're here!" This from some guy who was drunk off his ass. "I love you, Hayley."

"I know you do, baby."

Sure, guys love you when they've got alcohol in them. Why do you think Kevin stays out drinking?

Suddenly she couldn't move. All these people laughing and flirting, and some guy on stage ruining a Radiohead song—they all had momentum, and she had stopped. She was marooned in the midst of people who didn't care, anchored to this spot by the violent, relentless pulsing in her temples.

What are you doing, girl? You couldn't handle your dream job, you couldn't satisfy the man you love, and you couldn't keep the one friend you made in this town. You got all you wanted, and it still wasn't enough for you. How many failures will it take before you stop making a mess?

When will you stop chasing what you don't deserve?

"Hey there," Nick said.

His face came into focus, and she started breathing again.

"I was wondering," he said cheerfully, "if I could get another hug."

He slipped his arm around her, and Hayley closed her eyes. For an instant, the rest of the world went away.

"Do you need to get out of here?"

She tensed at the murmur in her ear.

"I've got you," Nick said. "Do you need to leave?"

Sobs welled up in her; she couldn't tell if she was ashamed or relieved.

"I can't," she whispered.

"I'll help you."

"It's too busy. They know I'm not sick."

She felt him release her and wanted to scream for him to stay. He grinned at her, and she told herself to grin back, like they were just joking around.

"You're in pain," he murmured.

"It doesn't matter," she said.

"What if it did?"

She couldn't answer.

"Stay close," he said.

Hayley was left to watch in confusion as Nick walked up to a high-top table in the center of the crowd, between the bar and the stage. She saw him flip through the pages of a karaoke songbook, then look up in a double take as if he recognized someone. He'd been turning pages with one hand while he leaned on the walker with the other, and now his left hand left the walker and came up in a wave while his right hand slid slowly off the songbook.

Nick disappeared.

It was the crowd that tipped her off, the gasps and the murmurs of concern as people backed away from where Nick had been standing. She dropped her tray and was halfway to the table before she even realized she was moving.

Once she'd finally battled her way through the crowd, she saw Nick lying on the ground, holding his knee. Alexa was already crouched by his side; Hayley knelt next to them so quickly she nearly lost her balance.

"What happened, baby?" she asked. "Are you hurt?"

She went cold with fear as confusion flitted in Nick's eyes. Had he hit his head? But then he was wincing. "It's probably just bruised," he said. He tried to get up, and Alexa stopped him with a hand on his shoulder.

"Hold on," she told him. Stephanie appeared out of the fray with a chair. "We're gonna pick you up, okay?"

Nick let the women put his arms on their shoulders, and Alexa and Hayley carefully stood in unison and lowered him into the chair.

"What happened?" Alexa asked. "Did someone push you?"

Nick shook his head. "Nothing like that. Just clumsy, I guess. Wasn't paying attention."

"What can we do?"

He touched his knee gingerly. "I hate to say this, but I may have to call it a night."

"Can we get you a cab?"

"It's fine. I drove here."

Alexa's voice turned gently reproachful. "You don't look in great shape to drive."

"It's fine, really." Nick started to get up, gritted his teeth, sat down again. "The problem is getting to the car."

"I'm sure we could have somebody get it. Theo could carry you out there."

"Yeah, maybe."

Nick beckoned both women closer, and Hayley took his hand.

"What is it?" she asked.

"Look," Nick muttered, "I really don't want to make a big deal of this, but I'm not sure I'll be able to get into my apartment by myself, and I don't have anyone to call. Could one of you . . ." He hesitated. "I know it's busy, but I could pay you or something. I wouldn't ask, but . . ."

Hayley watched him sitting there, eyes on his hands, the picture of reluctance. Then, as she realized what he was asking, the penny dropped.

Son of a bitch. She had to work to keep from gaping at him.

Alexa, thank God, was focused only on Nick. "Anything you need," she said, patting his leg.

He smiled weakly. "Anybody up for a road trip?"

"I've got you," Hayley said, and the irony smacked her in the face. She looked at Alexa. "Are you good if I get him home? I can come back."

"Make sure he's okay," Alexa said firmly. "I'll keep you on the clock. You're helping a customer."

"What? Alexa, you don't have to—"

"Go. We've got this."

Hayley nodded. "I'll get my things."

Alexa was back at the bar when Hayley returned with her bag. She got an arm around Nick to help him transfer out of the chair to the walker. "How bad is it?" she murmured. "Really?"

Nick grunted as he tried to keep most of his weight on one leg. "I'll be okay."

Following Nick to the front door was like being first in line as the Red Sea was parted: People nearly leaped out of the way once they saw Nick was both disabled and injured. Theo, however, actually blocked the door.

"Fireman's carry," he asked, "or piggyback?"

Nick tried to laugh it off. "Theo."

"Pick one, boss."

Nick rode piggyback on Theo as Hayley trailed them down the sidewalk, her bag in one hand and Nick's walker in the other. Theo watched vigilantly as Hayley loaded up the back of Nick's SUV and Nick lifted himself into the driver's seat.

"You're driving?" he asked.

Nick nodded. "Hand controls."

"Okay." Theo backed away cautiously, as if something could still go wrong at any moment. "Be safe."

"Will do."

Both of them shut their doors and watched Theo walk away.

"Wow," Hayley said. "Wow."

Nick said, "I think that went pretty well."

She didn't reply, and when Nick started the car, she knew the instrument lights revealed the tears running down her cheeks. Her breath was coming in short gasps.

"What can I do?" Nick asked. His concern tore at her. He couldn't fix this. He shouldn't even have to *see* this.

"Shut up." Her hands clamped onto her knees and she doubled over, eyes squeezed shut. "Shut up."

"Hayley." She heard the twinge of fear in his voice. "I'm going to take your hand, okay?"

She barely nodded, and he very slowly reached over and took her hand from her knee. He grasped it in his own, and gently tapped a rhythm against it with his index finger.

"Feel that?" he said.

She nodded, still doubled over.

"That's a waltz." He counted out the rhythm of the taps. "One, two, three, one, two, three, one, two, three, one, two, three . . ."

Even with her head down, she could feel his electric blue eyes on her as he kept counting.

"Can you breathe with me?" he asked. "In for six, out for six."

Keeping the rhythm with his finger, Nick tried a six-count inhale, then a six-count exhale. On his third repetition, she started to match him.

"There you go." He kept tapping. "I'm here, Hayley."

She put her free hand on top of his tapping finger, a wordless *stop*, and he took his hand from hers.

She looked up. "You scared me, Nick."

"Sorry," he said, subdued. "I didn't mean—"

"I know what you meant to do. You didn't have to. Did you think about what that would do to me?" she snapped.

"No." Then, almost to himself, "I didn't think you'd be so upset."

"Well, gee, Nick, I'm sorry if I didn't react the right way to you falling down in the middle of a crowd of people."

Nick shook his head. "No, I . . ." He sighed. "I meant it never occurred to me that you would care so much. That I could make it worse."

"Yeah, well, you're an idiot."

"I'm sorry." He stared at the steering wheel. "It wasn't one of my better plans."

"No shit," she said. "Fucking up your own knee, Nick? Really?"

"I actually landed on my hands, mostly. But my knee does hurt."

"Good."

"And I had to ride on Theo."

"Fantastic."

But the memory of Nick being lugged helplessly to the car as a victim of his own plan made her grin a little.

"Okay," Nick said. "We need to call Kevin."

Her chest tightened. "No."

"I know he's busy, but it's not a good idea to—"

"Kevin's gone."

She watched Nick trying not to react, and almost felt sorry for him.

"Gone," he repeated.

"He broke up with me. Best news you've heard all day, right?"

He stared out the windshield, and she regretted taking the shot at him.

"You can go back to work if you want," he said. "I'll call the bar when I get home and tell Alexa I insisted on taking care of myself."

"Don't do that," she said. "You'll look like an idiot, and I'll look like one for letting you go."

And she'd have to spend the rest of the night without him.

Nick started the car. "Your place, then?"

"Too many steps at my place."

He glanced at her. "I don't have to stick around."

Her eyes came up to meet his. "I'd like it if you did."

23

Nick stole a few glances at Hayley as he drove through the city, but she only stared blankly at the dashboard. She was huddled as if she'd been thrown into the seat, like she would have fallen out of the car had her door not been closed. Nick resisted the urge to take her hand when they stopped at a traffic light.

He'd known something like this was going to happen. If he'd taken his cues, stayed in his lane, then he never would've hurt her. He would never have tried to tell her how he felt, because he would've killed those feelings. The key to being loved was being exactly what people wanted—no more, no less. Get comfortable, lose focus, take chances, and those people would leave. He'd braced for her to leave.

Now Hayley was right here, crumpled in the passenger seat, and it felt like he was losing her all over again.

He hadn't known anything at all, had he? Nothing about the breakup, nothing about how she'd react to him falling, and not a damn thing about how to save her from whatever was going on behind her eyes. Hayley looked like her brain was flooding her body with the toll of every wound she'd ever endured, and Nick couldn't make a shred of difference.

"Can you sing?" she murmured.

Nick was relieved to hear her voice. "Now?"

"Yes. You didn't get a chance to sing tonight."

"That doesn't matter."

"Sure it does." Hayley closed her eyes. "I didn't get to hear you."

She wanted him to sing. Hayley Burke was asking him to bring her back to life doing the one thing he knew he couldn't ruin.

Nick smiled.

24

Hayley was afraid to move. Nick sang the entire way to his apartment, and she stayed exactly as she was, hoping the peace inside this car would find its way inside her if she didn't disrupt it. When he took the key from the ignition, she slid out of the car to get the walker before he could object.

"Thank you," he said.

"You're welcome."

She told herself not to reach for him. He got from the seat to the ground, shut the door, hit the lock button on his keys, and still she waited patiently, her duffel bag slung over one shoulder. She finally slipped her arm around his waist when he started toward his building.

"I'm fine," he said.

"Let me."

Two or three steps led directly to his door from the sidewalk, and she'd left that way the morning they'd agreed to be friends. But tonight they took the ramp next to Nick's parking space, walking the width of the building and around the corner to reach his front door. It suddenly seemed unacceptable that Nick had to travel this extra distance every day. He had to work harder than everyone just to go home, he was limping now because of her, and none of that seemed to bother him. If he wasn't going to be angry, Hayley wanted to do it for him, wanted to scream to the world that this man shouldn't have to put up with steps and shopping malls and people like her. She wasn't reaching for Nick because he needed her help. She had her arm around his waist because *she* needed to help *him*.

Nick headed for the kitchen as soon as they were inside, and Hayley dropped her bag on the floor.

"You want something to drink?" he asked.

"I'm good," she said.

"Okay."

He kept moving, but not to find a glass. She watched him as he added items to the top of his silver food cart: first a stack of Hershey's bars, then a giant bag of M&Ms, then a container of chocolate ice cream from the freezer. When he was done, he looked at her and nodded toward the cart.

"What . . .?" She trailed off.

"Chocolate. Candy bars, M&Ms. I wasn't sure about the ice cream, but it seemed like a safe bet." He looked apologetic. "I thought—hoped you might come back."

Hayley shifted her incredulous gaze from the cart to the man behind it. Then, suddenly and completely, she burst into tears.

She was dimly aware of him sidestepping the cart and rushing toward her, reaching out with the hand that wasn't on his walker and enveloping her where she stood. Her hair brushed his face; tears landed on his shoulder as she grabbed a fistful of his shirt.

"I've got you," he murmured in her ear. "I've got you."

"I'm sorry," she sobbed. "Why would you even . . . I'm *so sorry* . . ."

"Hey." Her body heaved against his. "You have nothing to be sorry for."

"I ruined it," she insisted. "I ruined everything."

"I'm still here." He soothed her. "Everything else is on the other side of that door. All those expectations are out there in the dark, okay? It's just you and me in here, and you don't have to do anything or give anything or be anything for anybody. I've got you, Hayley. I've got you."

He held her close until her crying slowed, then stopped. The room announced itself around her—the whir of the air-conditioning, the metal of his walker as she brushed against it with her hip—and she realized where she was and what she'd just done. She swiped at her tears and smoothed his shirt at the shoulders.

"God." She sniffled. "Wow, sorry. That was . . . you didn't need to see that."

"Seems to me it was a long time coming."

Would he understand if she told him everything? Would he even want to listen?

"What can I do for you, Hayley?" Nick asked.

She didn't even know what to ask for.

"I'm gonna go wash my face," she said.

Her eyes were red and her face was too damn pale, and there wasn't much she could do about that in Nick Freeman's guest bathroom, but she pulled herself together enough to feel okay about walking back into the same room with him.

"We're watching a movie." If she said it with enough cheerful confidence, maybe cheerful confidence would actually show up.

"Okay," Nick bent down to grab the remote control from the seat of his recliner. "We can stream one of your musicals if you want. How's *An American in Texas*?"

She sighed. "Paris, Freeman. *An American in Paris*. Texas is nothing but Americans." She saw the sly grin on his face. "Oh, okay. You think you're being funny."

"How could it be Paris?" he asked innocently. "No American would ever be caught dead in Paris."

She threw a chocolate bar at his head as he chortled. "See, you think just because your legs don't work, I won't knock them out from under you for being so uncultured, but I'm much more enlightened than that."

"Uncultured?" Nick feigned indignation as they faced each other across the cart. "I've got all sorts of culture."

"Oh yeah?" She lunged for the M&Ms, and he got there first. "Prove it."

He had to think about it. "I've seen all the *Star Wars* movies, for starters."

She grabbed the ice cream. "If you think aliens shooting at each other is better than a seventeen-minute ballet—"

"Hang on." Nick watched her heft the container in one hand. "There's a seventeen-minute ballet in that movie?"

She nodded. "At the end. It's beautiful."

"Well," he said carefully, "since you're armed, I'm going to say that doesn't sound boring at all."

She sighed. "Why do I hang out with you?"

"Because you can put it on your résumé as special-needs care."

Hayley lowered her arm. "Since when do you make handicapped jokes?"

"I think my people prefer 'joke about a person with a disability.'"

"That takes too long to say."

"True." Nick tossed the M&Ms back onto the cart. "As ambassador to the able-bodied, I'm giving you permission to say 'crip joke.'"

"But Nick Freeman doesn't make crip jokes."

"You haven't heard?" He smiled. "My new stage name is Gimpy the Clown."

Hayley surprised herself with her own laughter. "Something's very wrong with you," she told him through her giggles.

"Maybe I'm trying something new," he said. "Or maybe I just like making you laugh."

She very nearly said *I love you*. It wasn't a choice, but a reaction, the same way her laughter had just been, a response that didn't need any thought. It had been too long since her heart had asserted itself like that, and she didn't want to think about what it might mean. All that was on the other side of the door.

"I know." Nick looked pleased with himself. "We can watch *Dirty Dancing*."

Something stabbed at her. "Let's skip that one."

"Really?" He was surprised. "I thought for sure that'd be a Hayley Burke favorite."

"It is," she said. "I went through two copies of that thing on video tape when I was a kid."

He waited, then smiled and nodded when she didn't keep going. "Got it," he said. "And no Americans in Texas."

"It reminds me of Kevin."

She didn't know why she said it. Kevin had no place here, not when Nick was letting her pretend the world didn't exist, not when he was being far too nice to admit his feelings mattered. But maybe as long as Nick was looking at her with such kindness in his eyes, pain could lose some of its power in this room.

"When Baby sees Johnny for the first time," she said, "before he notices her. You can tell she's hooked. Even if she doesn't want to be, even if she doesn't understand what she's feeling, she's hooked, and I knew I was going to feel that someday. I walked into Icarus that first day, I saw him dance, and I was hooked. I just knew. We'd always see the best in each other, just like Johnny and Baby."

Nick didn't laugh, and he didn't roll his eyes. "Happens to the best of us," he said.

"To you?"

"Sure." He walked to the TV and opened a cabinet underneath. "Can't say I have a lot of movies about that, though."

"Let's watch the next *Rocky* movie," she said.

He stared at her over his shoulder, eyebrows raised. "Seriously?"

"Hell yes."

He waited for the other shoe to drop. "You know it's more of the same, right?"

"Don't try and talk me out of this, Freeman."

Nick found the movie while Hayley put the ice cream back in the freezer and wheeled the cart over to the couch, being sure to pick up her thrown chocolate bar.

"Do you have a blanket?" she asked him.

"Yeah, sorry. I'll turn down the AC."

"That's not what I asked."

He turned to look at her.

"You run pretty hot, don't you?" she continued patiently. "From working harder to get around?"

"Yes," he admitted.

"Then show me where to find a blanket, and I'll use that instead of making you roast."

She waited for him to realize there was no point in arguing.

"The closet in the study," he said finally.

When Hayley returned with a navy-blue fleece blanket in tow, Nick had turned on the TV and loaded the movie.

"Lots of pictures in there," she said.

"Yep."

"You were a cute kid."

He smiled. "Yeah, I don't know what happened."

"Did I see Gavin in a few shots?"

"Yep, you did."

"He was a cuter kid."

He laughed. "Hey now."

She settled in on the couch and watched him walk toward the recliner. "What are you doing?" she asked.

He stopped. "Um . . . sitting down?"

Hayley patted the empty space next to her, praying she wouldn't have to ask. After a moment, Nick crossed to the front door, turned off the lights, and joined Hayley on the couch.

"All good?" he asked.

"Ready to rock."

He hit "Play" and tossed the remote to the side. She kept her eyes on the TV, tried to busy her hands by popping M&Ms in her mouth, but she didn't last more than ten seconds before her hand reached out to grasp his. He gave her hand a quick squeeze, and she squeezed back.

Two hours later, *Rocky II* was over, and Nick was looking for the remote control. Neither of them had moved except to deplete the bag of M&Ms. He pressed "Pause," and Hayley kept staring at the screen.

"He won!" she said.

Nick laughed. "You bet he did."

"I was hoping he'd win. If this was just a series about how he keeps getting beat up . . ."

"Yeah, I don't think I'd be into that."

She squeezed his hand. "Can I get a glass of water?"

"Of course."

She hopped up from the couch and headed for the kitchen. "Is it possible those guys were just a little too into boxing?"

"What do you mean?"

"I mean their wives were pleading with both of them to stay out of that ring, and it's like they couldn't be happy unless they were beating the shit out of each other."

"That's what they do," he said. "It's who they are. Like if somebody told you not to dance."

She filled a glass. "Dancing doesn't require beating someone else, in any sense of the word."

"You're wondering why I like Rocky so much."

"Not even a little bit. He makes a decision, and gives it his all, and sticks to it even when it hurts." She grinned at the look on his face. "Superpowers, remember? I'll bet you and Gavin sat in your basement and watched the whole set over and over in high school."

"Nope," Nick said triumphantly. "We did not."

"His basement, then."

"Wrong again." He watched her return to the couch. "I watched them with my dad a lot when I was really young."

"Aw, that's even more adorable." She folded her legs under her. "Baby Nick boxing with Daddy."

"There may have been occasional matches, sure."

"And you were always Rocky."

"Absolutely." Nick smiled. "I'd sit on the couch, and he'd box from his knees."

Hayley put her glass on the cart. "I still don't think Rocky had anything to prove to anyone."

"Maybe not. But he wanted to be better."

Hayley looked from Nick to the battered, triumphant boxer on the television screen and wondered what either of them felt he had to fight.

She stretched to hide her nervousness. "Is it okay if I stay here tonight?"

"Sure," he said. "The bed's all yours."

"No way. I'm not putting you on the couch again."

"Yes, you are." He grinned. "Though it's nice of you to give me a choice this time."

She could let herself fall into his arms, right now, and kiss him until morning.

"Damn it, Freeman." Hayley jumped off the couch, grabbed her bag, trusted her momentum to put some space between them. "You need to stop being so considerate."

"Yeah, it's one of my many failings." He stood up. "You good? I threw away your toothbrush—"

"There you go. Less considerate."

"But I'm sure there's a new one in there."

"You keep those for all your lady friends?"

He flushed a bit. *Come on, girl. Don't be a bitch.*

"I'm good," she said, a little softer. "I've even got clothes, so you don't have to run a laundry service."

"Way to be prepared." He grinned. "Was this all just a plot to use me for my chocolate?"

She narrowed her eyes. "I was planning on using the rehearsal room, dumbass, so I've got . . . You know what? It's not even worth explaining."

"You're going to sleep in your dance stuff?"

"Maybe."

"You're welcome to go through the dresser."

She raised an eyebrow. "I'm not going to find anything weird in there, am I?"

"Of course not. That's all in my closet."

She rolled her eyes, dropped the bag, and hugged him. "You really are a monumental pain in the ass."

"I know." He wrapped an arm around her and held on tight. She tingled at the pressure of his fingers and realized that Nick wasn't clinging to her—he was steadying her.

"And thank you." She lightly pressed her lips to his cheek. "I mean it."

She'd never heard such tenderness in his voice. "You're welcome, Hayley."

She resisted the urge to look over her shoulder as she walked down the hallway. She hoped he was still watching her. Hoped she was still seen.

25

After he heard the bedroom door shut, Nick wandered over to the television, turned it off, and put *Rocky II* back where it belonged. He ambled to the cart, limping slightly, and pushed it back to the kitchen. He very deliberately put the chocolate back where he'd found it.

Because as long as he was still awake, the evening wasn't over.

Hayley was not okay. He'd known as soon as he'd seen her in the bar tonight that she was losing the kind of fight he understood very well. It was time to protect her. Time to be the person he wished had been there for him during too many nights and too many losses.

But.

She'd called him *baby*. It was just one word, and she'd been hanging on by a thin thread, one he'd very nearly cut when he'd decided to be a genius and hurt himself for her sake. But to see her fight through the crowd to get to him; to see her drop to the ground, to his level, without a second thought; to see nothing but concern in her eyes and then to hear her say that one word with all of the intimacy he'd barely allowed himself to want. Hayley hadn't acted like she was concerned for a customer or a disabled person or a friend. Hayley had responded to his little con game as if even the possibility of his injury was the single worst thing that could happen to her. She had responded the same way he would have if she'd gotten hurt.

She'd called him *baby*, and for the first time, he was considering the possibility that she might feel for him what he felt for her.

After their kiss, she'd been supposed to move away with Kevin, and he'd been supposed to have all the time in the world to recover from this mess. Instead, Nick was standing at his kitchen counter, breaking a chocolate bar into tiny pieces while the newly single Hayley Burke took off her clothes in his bedroom. She was the one who'd wanted to come back to his apartment. What was stopping him from opening the bedroom door and seeing what happened next?

Nick didn't even make it halfway down the hallway before he turned around.

What was *stopping* him? Seriously? As if he deserved a reward for scaring her half to death. For all he knew, after what'd happened in that rehearsal room, the breakup could've been because of him. Hayley would've made it clear who kissed whom, but maybe she'd defended Nick. Maybe she'd realized she liked their kiss. Maybe she wanted to do it again.

Sure. As long as he was dreaming, maybe his cerebral palsy would disappear tomorrow. Hayley was a mess, and this was not the time, and even if she wanted to give him her body, accepting him and his damaged legs and everything that came with his condition, Nick had to know it wasn't just because she was too vulnerable to resist. He wanted Hayley to choose him when she could've chosen anyone else.

But she wouldn't be choosing him at all, of course. There would be someone else for her to dance with. The bedroom door would stay closed tonight, she would leave tomorrow, and he would be alone with nothing but a bruised knee to show for his attempt at being a hero. Nick dropped onto the couch and tried to get a look at the damage, but the leg of his jeans bunched up too readily. He'd have to take off his shoes, then his pants.

"What's that?" Hayley said.

Nick jumped. Hayley was standing in front of him, barefoot, the cuffs of his cotton pajama pants rolled up at her ankles. Her hair obscured the lettering on the back of his show choir T-shirt from high school.

"What?" she said. "You said I could wear whatever."

He cleared his throat. "I remember."

"You're looking at me like I'm wearing that robe again."

"Do you honestly not know why?"

To his surprise, Hayley blushed a little before her gaze dropped back to his leg. "So, what is that?" she asked again.

Nick looked down, even though he knew what she was asking. His leg was encased in a sort of plastic boot, ending at the top of his calf and held in place by Velcro. The top of a sock was visible past the edge of the plastic, and the bottom of the whole thing was hidden by the sneaker he was wearing over it.

"It's a leg brace," he said. "They stabilize my ankles, I think. Gives me more support when I walk."

"I've never seen them before."

"I don't show them to people."

She studied it. "That's why you never wear shorts, isn't it?"

What was happening right now? He'd told himself not to go into the bedroom, he'd braced himself for a lonely night on the couch, and now, out of nowhere, she'd come back? What was he supposed to do with that?

"Did you need something?" he managed.

Hayley looked up, startled. "No. Just didn't want to hold your toothbrush hostage."

His toothbrush. Of course. He hadn't realized he'd been hoping for something else until all that hope turned to embarrassment. "Sure," he said. "Thanks."

Moments later, he was spitting toothpaste into the sink.

"You're going to sleep in that?" Hayley was perched on the side of the bed as he walked out of the bathroom.

"That was the plan," he said.

"Do you normally sleep in that?"

"Well . . ."

She rolled her eyes. "Get dressed, Freeman."

"It'd be easier just to—"

"I'm not going to keep you from being comfortable. Get dressed. I'm going to go find the M&Ms."

Hayley headed for the hall, muttering to herself. Nick was taking off his shoes when she yelled loud enough to be heard through the closed door of the bedroom.

"Why the hell did you put them away?"

Nick smiled.

It wasn't long before he was dressed in pajama pants and a T-shirt. Hayley knocked on the door, and he stood up as he told her to come in.

"Is there anything else you think I need to do?" he teased.

She shifted her weight from foot to foot in the doorway. "Actually," she said, "I was thinking we could share the bed."

He blinked. "Share the bed."

"Uh-huh."

Something was off. Hayley was tentative, not seductive, and there was a slight tremble in her hand as it hung by her side.

He said, "You're going to have to be more specific."

"No sex," she blurted.

He raised his eyebrows. "No sex."

"No kissing, no sex. Just sleeping together."

"And when you say sleeping together, you literally mean—"

"I thought you wouldn't want to be alone."

He squinted at her. "What?"

Hayley looked like she wanted to strangle him. "You hurt your knee. And the bed is big enough for both of us and more comfortable than the couch, and I just thought . . . You know what? Forget it. Horrible idea."

She tried to walk past him, and he gently grabbed her shoulder. "Hey, hold on."

She stopped. His pulse was racing. Was she doing this for him? What did she actually want? How could he help?

Come on, Nick. Neither of us wants you to put on a show for me.

"You're right," he said. "I don't want to be alone."

Soon they were lying in bed, shoulder to shoulder, under the covers and in the dark.

"See?" Hayley said. "Better for your knee."

"Sure."

Nick focused on the tiny light on the room's smoke detector, narrowing his world to that one pinpoint on the ceiling so he could stop thinking about her warmth beside him, or how soft her skin must feel. He didn't want her to go, and he didn't trust himself enough for her to stay.

"You okay?" she asked.

"Sure," he said again. "Just . . . if I suddenly jump out of bed and run for the door, don't take it personally."

"If you jump out of bed and run for the door, I'll consider it a miracle."

He turned his head and saw her propped up on an elbow, grinning at him. They burst out laughing.

"This'll help," Hayley said, falling back against a pillow. "Don't freak out."

"What?"

Hayley slid her arm under him, and her other hand went across him to rest on his shoulder as she pressed her cheek to his chest.

26

Hayley had expected Nick to tense when she put her arms around him, but the opposite was happening. Nick's breathing slowed, and his body seemed to sink into the mattress.

"See?" she said. "Worked like a charm."

"Yeah." He paused. "You're not doing this just for me, are you?"

She almost laughed, but she knew he'd take it the wrong way. Only Nick would think she was doing him a favor here. Holding him was the best and most selfish thing she'd done all night.

"I never said we couldn't cuddle," she said.

He laughed. "Well, okay then."

His arms encircled her, drew her in—God, the strength in those arms!—and it felt so good she groaned. His fingers trailed across her shoulder blades and started to play with her hair a little.

"Mmm." She snuggled closer. "You're *good* at this."

"Just like riding a bike," he said. "Or so I've heard, anyway."

She giggled. "Been a while, huh?"

"Longer than that. I haven't been near a bike since I was seven."

"Shut up," she teased. "I meant holding someone like this. Being held like this."

She listened to him breathe. "It's been a very long time."

Hayley couldn't remember the last time Kevin had held her. "Me too," she whispered.

His fingers kept moving as they lay there, up to her shoulders, through her hair, down to the small of her back. Eventually he started moving his fingertips back and forth in a light scratching motion, making her tingle just a little.

She said, "How do you do it, Nick?"

"Do what?" he asked.

"How do you hold everything together?" she murmured drowsily. "Not with the . . . I'm not just talking about your legs."

"It's okay. We can talk about my legs."

"You're always *you*, I mean. Doesn't matter if the world's going your way or not. You know who you are and what you're going to do."

"I just make choices," he said. "They're not always the best ones."

"You make choices and people love you. I make choices and things get worse."

"That's not true."

"It is." Tears filled her eyes and strained her voice. "You don't know."

"Hey." He pressed his lips to her forehead. "I know you chose to meet me."

She shook her head. "Stop it. I insulted you. You have so much to deal with every day, and I was an idiot."

"Hayley," he said gently, "you saw me."

Hayley lifted her head to look at him, and he smiled at her.

"Remember what you said?" he asked. "You saw my heart in my eyes. You saw something nobody else did, something I didn't even know was there, and you were so happy that night that you had to make me happy too. I've never seen anyone do that for a stranger. You didn't even know about the walker."

Even in the dark, she could swear she saw his eyes sparkle.

"Why can't I ever get it right?" she whispered.

"Did you see the picture of the beach on the wall by the bedroom door?"

"Yeah." She remembered a sandy path through brush, a glimpse of the ocean under the clouds, the colors in a gorgeous sky.

"My mom took that on vacation. The first time I was there, I was eight, and that path was impossible. The walker wheels sunk into the sand. Dad said he'd carry me, but I wanted to walk it. Insisted on it." He chuckled. "I don't even remember why now."

"So you made it?"

"I did, and it was awful, and I was fine with Dad carrying me after that. Turns out they make a special wheelchair for the sand, but we didn't know."

"See? You're so much stronger than me."

"Hang on," he said playfully. "Don't you want to know why I put that picture there?"

She smiled. "I *guess* so."

"If I look at the path," he said, "I think about all of the hard work I have to put myself through for something you could do as easily as breathing. But if I look past the path, there's a glimpse of this amazing, endless ocean. If I look up, I can see the sky and it takes my breath away. I can always choose where to look. I don't always look in the right place, but there's always beauty and there's always pain, and it's always up to me."

"Okay." She tried not to sound disappointed. "Okay, sure. Make better choices."

"No," he said gently. "I put that picture there because sometimes the path's going to be hard no matter what I do."

"Because stupid people make things hard for you."

"Hayley, I'm saying you *always* get it right." His fingertips teased the nape of her neck. "You choose the sky all the time. I have to remind myself to do it every day, and you walked up to some sad guy you'd never met and tried to get me to see beauty. It's not your fault I was a jerk. Just because I couldn't see what you were trying to show me doesn't mean you didn't do the right thing."

"Do you see it now?" she asked softly. "How much you deserve to be happy?"

Nick didn't say anything for a long moment.

"Whenever I look back on that night," he said, "all I see is how grateful I am that you found me."

27

Nick lay absolutely motionless, eyes closed, breathing steady. If he focused, his body might just decide to obey him tonight. He would not allow a spastic muscle or startle reflex to wake the woman sleeping in his arms.

He'd been terrified of doing the wrong thing—and then Hayley had wrapped herself around him.

He had wasted so much effort seducing women so he could believe he was worth their attention, but Hayley had led *him* here.

He had stood in the Squeaky Lion tonight wanting only for her to be okay, and now she was giving him something beautiful.

Nick wanted to kiss her now more than ever, wanted to touch every inch of her, wanted to look into her eyes as he made love to her. But there was no sign of the emptiness he so often felt, no compulsion to prove anything to her or demand that she prove anything to him. Hayley was here, and that was so much more than enough.

She stirred, and his eyes filled with tears when his startle-prone body kept still. He loved the way she burrowed against him, like she was trying to find their perfect fit.

"Do I help?" she mumbled sleepily.

He rubbed her back. "Help with what, sweetheart?"

"Do I help you look at the sky?"

Nick remembered falling into her arms, getting lost in her smile for the first time. *We've got this, rock star.*

"You are the sky," he said.

28

Hayley woke up slowly, feeling foggy and loose with the fatigue in her muscles. Her cheek was still on Nick's chest, her arms around him, his arms encircling her. She felt his chest rise and fall under her.

Okay. So all of that had actually happened.

She slid carefully out from under his arms and slipped out of bed. Nick was still fast asleep, legs tangled in the sheet that covered him to his torso.

Come on, girl. Go brush your teeth. Wash your face. Find a chocolate bar.

She couldn't look away from him.

Because she didn't want to leave. What she wanted to do was reach forward and brush back the hair that had fallen over his forehead. She wanted to climb back into bed, pull the covers over them both, and be in his arms when he woke up. She wanted to take care of him.

It reminded her of her first night with Kevin.

There had been something delicious about the inevitability of Kevin. How he'd waited outside her dressing room before the late show that night, just so she'd know she was on his radar. How he was the only thing she could think about for the rest of the night, until she was standing in the dimly lit Menagerie bar, and he'd appeared at her side with two words: *Carrie's over.* He had chosen her.

She'd awoken before him the next morning, crept to the bathroom, returned to watch him sleep. Elation had quietly pulsed through her: She'd gotten exactly what she wanted. And under that pulse, barely asserting itself, a hollowness, a question—whether everything she wanted should have been more.

It hadn't been enough, and now Hayley was standing in another bedroom, with another man.

Was it possible to be embarrassed about what they'd done and still glad they'd done it? She shouldn't have collapsed in the car or cried in his arms; she really shouldn't have talked him into bed like it was for his sake. She was unquestionably a train wreck. And yet—it all *felt* okay. She felt comfortable with him, and she didn't often feel comfortable at all any more.

But of course she felt comfortable with Nick. Nick didn't require anything of her. She'd wanted to be friends, and he decided to follow through. She'd wanted a listening ear, and he decided to be there. She'd nearly lost her mind at the bar, and he decided to save her. Fall for her, literally, which was clumsy, idiotic, and adorable all at the same time. Why the hell hadn't she caught on sooner? If Nick Freeman had actually hurt himself, he would've smiled, insisted everything was fine, and hobbled to his car without another word.

Hayley caught sight of his leg braces where he'd discarded them by the bed. For Nick, just wearing shorts would reveal too much weakness—and he had done so much more than that for her.

Shit.

She had to leave. Now. She'd done nothing but take from him, cheerfully oblivious until he'd literally injured himself for her. Why deal with actual relationship problems when you can run off in the middle of the night and slow-dance to goddamn Savage Garden? She hadn't wanted Nick to have feelings for her, so she hadn't seen them. She hadn't wanted to have feelings for him, so she'd told herself they weren't there.

You're a liar, Hayley Michelle. You wanted it all. You knew the whole time, and you played dumb so you could keep your karaoke star on a leash.

You wanted too much, and someone got hurt.

Hayley spun toward the bedroom door so quickly she nearly tripped over his walker—and there was the beach photo on the wall. She'd dreamed last night that she was on that beach with him. She'd asked him a question, half-awake.

"You're the sky," he'd said.

No. She wasn't a liar. She had made the right choice. She had tried her best. She had helped him.

And she hadn't run away. Kevin had, right out the front door, so there wasn't anything wrong with being here with Nick. She liked their dance, and she liked the dancer she was with him. She could choose the beauty here and worry about the pain later.

Like any second now, when Nick woke up and wondered why the hell he'd destroyed his closely guarded dignity in his favorite bar for a crazy woman, and what the hell had possessed him to allow her to spend a sexless night in his bed. What would she say when he asked what they were, what she wanted? That she wanted to feel safe? That she wanted to hold him? That she had no idea what they were, but she knew she wanted to take care of him? It had nothing to do with his disability, but how could she explain that?

"I'll have to get you a copy of that," Nick said.

She turned around to see him grinning lazily at her. "That'd be great," she said, finding a shy smile. "And good morning."

"Good morning to you." He propped himself up on an elbow. "Did you sleep well?"

"Yeah." Then, more softly, "I really did."

His smile broadened. "Me too."

Okay, so he wasn't freaking out. Did he expect her to get back in bed? Would he be offended if she didn't?

And for the love of God, why was she acting like a teenager on her first date?

"Did you bring a change of clothes?" She was relieved he was talking again. "Other than your dancing stuff, I mean."

She remembered her bag at the foot of the bed. "Um, yeah," she said. "Why?" She looked down at the T-shirt she was wearing. "These are yours. I'll give them back. Or, um . . . I'll do that later, because you're here. Not that . . . it's your bedroom, so why wouldn't you be here, but I just meant . . ." She saw the laughter in his eyes. "I should shut up. I'll shut up."

He scratched at the stubble on his cheek. "I could be way off base here, but it seems like you're nervous."

"No." She gave a quick laugh. "Why would I be nervous?"

"No reason," he said, then: "Thing is, I've spent enough time being nervous around you that I know what it feels like."

"Well. It's not . . . I'm not . . . It's just that I don't . . ."

"I asked about the clothes because I figured you'd want to wear clean ones after you showered." He rolled to his stomach, slid off the side of the bed until his feet hit the floor, and pushed against the mattress to stand up. "You don't have to shower, of course, but the guest bathroom has a tub. We could have breakfast afterward."

She nodded, got more comfortable with her own smile. "Sounds great."

Nick lunged easily from the mattress to the wall, then stood with one hand on the doorframe of the bathroom.

"Still no expectations," he said gently. "I'm good. I promise."

"Okay." It came out much too fast, and she tried again. "Okay."

"I know last night wasn't an invitation."

Slowly, the tension in her evaporated. How did he do that, just by looking at her?

Hayley said, "You're pretty great, you know that?"

Nick Freeman grinned at her, unguarded and unrehearsed. "I'm starting to."

Hayley was dressed and drying her hair when she heard music coming from the living room. She dropped the towel and hurried quietly down the hallway.

Sure enough, there was Nick Freeman, dancing to David Bowie on the stereo.

He was doing little more than stepping back and forth in rhythm, both hands on the counter in front of him for balance. She didn't care. Nick was dancing, arms flexing in his T-shirt as he boogied to the right, to grab a glass from a cabinet, then stepped back toward the sink and drummed on the counter. Then he saw her, and gave her the biggest smile she'd ever seen.

"Hey!" He raised his voice over the music. "Want a bagel?"

Hayley was so happy she could have tackled him, but she settled for crossing her arms and leaning against the wall. "Nick Freeman. You've been holding out on me."

To her delight, he got a little shy. "Just trying out some things."

"Teach me," she said.

"Teach *you*?"

"Sure." She pushed off the wall and came toward him.

"It's not like I have a signature move or anything."

She ducked under his arm and stood between him and the sink, facing away from him, his arms now on either side of her. "One of the best parts of dancing is sharing it with someone."

Nick's breathing quickened, and she leaned back against his chest. "What?" she said playfully.

His mouth was next to her ear; she thought about how it would feel if he kissed her neck. "You smell amazing," he said.

Butterflies fluttered in her stomach. "It's just your shampoo."

"Really? I think I smell M&Ms."

She laughed, smacked his arm. "Come on. Let's dance."

He played along, stepping to the right and counting off the steps. "Right . . . two, left . . . two."

"Get your shoulders into it," she said.

"What?"

"Here." She took his hand and guided it across her so his arm rested below her breasts, his fingers against her ribs. "You don't have to move your legs. Just plant your feet and lean from your waist." She put her hand over his and moved with him. "See? Left . . . right . . . left, right . . ."

His stubble tickled her neck. "I like this."

"Now we combine the two." She was flushed, grinning, pressing his arm firmly against her to give him more stability. "Right . . . two . . . right-lean-left-lean-left . . . two . . . left-lean-right-lean. There ya go! You're a natural."

"I have a great teacher."

She spun neatly to face him. "Ready for the finale?"

His eyes sparkled. "Absolutely."

She walked him backward toward the oven, his hands on her shoulders, her hands on his hips.

"Okay. Put this hand on the counter behind you." He did as he was told, and she stood with her back to him again. Then she brought her hand across her body to grasp his and spun out to his left, unfurling their arms until only their fingertips touched and then spinning back into his embrace.

"Ta-da!" she said, and fell against him as they laughed. "Who says you can't dance with me?"

"Guess I just needed to trust my partner," he said.

Nick had never looked more comfortable as he leaned against the counter in his T-shirt and blue jeans. He was relaxed, thoroughly content, and the butterflies were back in her stomach when she realized she had something to do with the light in his eyes. He had hardly been able to take two steps in the rehearsal room, and now he was looking at her like he wasn't afraid of anything.

"Can we keep dancing?" she murmured.

Nick reached for the remote control on the counter, and then David Bowie was replaced by a much slower song: "Truly Madly Deeply."

She laughed softly. "You set this up."

His smile turned bashful. "I was hoping you'd ask."

Hayley slipped into his arms as easily as she had a week ago. She leaned into him, held him tight, hoped the closeness would speak for her when she couldn't find the words she needed.

"I didn't know," she whispered. "In the rehearsal room, I didn't . . . Kevin hadn't told me we were leaving." Her lips brushed his cheek. "You thought I was saying goodbye."

His breath quickened. "What did you mean to say?"

She couldn't reply because her mouth had found his.

Hayley felt Nick shudder as he breathed her in, and then the current that passed through them made all of her ignite at once. Some part of her was screaming that she was making the worst possible choice—but this didn't feel like a choice. This kiss was the natural progression of their dance, the consequence of their rhythm and their magic and all of the choices that had preceded it. The sensation was almost too much; she was falling from a great height, hurtling into deep water. She needed it to stop, knew it would overwhelm her, and ached for it to continue.

"Thank you," Hayley managed as she pulled away. "I meant to say thank you."

Nick gave a breathless chuckle. "Am I allowed to say you're welcome?"

"No." She was proud of how sure she sounded, shaking her head with a palm against his chest as she stepped away, but then she pulled him back to her so quickly she stretched the collar of his T-shirt. Nick lurched forward with the momentum, and he managed to grab the edge of the sink behind her as he fell forward and pinned her against the counter.

"God, sorry!" she managed in between kisses. "You okay?"

"Of course not," he said against her mouth. "I'm *appalled*."

She laughed. "We should stop."

"Absolutely." His tongue teased hers. "I'm more than just a piece of meat."

"Seriously," she gasped. "It's not fair to you."

"I know!" He nipped at her ear. "I feel so used."

"That's not . . ." Nick's lips were making their way from her neck to her throat now, and her eyes closed involuntarily. "I meant what I . . . I'm still not . . . oh my God . . ."

Nick slowed, then stopped; she felt a hint of stubble brush against her collarbone as he caught his breath.

"You're not with him," he said finally. "But you're not with me yet."

"I want to be sure," she said. "And I don't want to hurt you."

"Apart from yanking me around my own kitchen, you mean."

"I'm such a bitch."

"No, no." He shook his head, straightened up. "You don't want me getting my hopes up."

"Don't be mad," she pleaded. "Please?"

He smiled. "I'm not mad."

"You're not." She looked at him skeptically. "Because I'd be mad."

"How could I be mad about you kissing me?"

"Well, don't say stuff like that, or I'll do it again." His eyes lit up, and she put a hand over his mouth. "Breakfast, Freeman."

He chuckled as she headed for the toaster. "You've got to work on your threats."

She toasted the bagels and he made the coffee, and they were sitting down at the table to eat when she asked, "Are you about done with your video project?"

"For Vivez? Yep." He reached for the cream cheese. "I want to make a database using all those old programs Linda has. All that footage isn't going to do her much good if there isn't an easy way to search through it."

"Was that part of the deal?"

He shrugged. "She's already paying me too much."

"School's gotta be starting soon, isn't it?"

"Tuesday."

She bit into her bagel. "I bet they'd still let you hang around even if you weren't working on something."

"Yeah, well." He sounded overly casual, and she knew she'd read him correctly. "I wouldn't want to just be wandering the halls."

"Is that all?"

"I mean . . ." He cleared his throat. "It'd be fun if we worked there at the same time." He glanced at her. "Oh, don't look at me like that. I'm not a baby puppy."

"Then stop being so sweet," she teased. "Don't stick around on my account, though. I might not be working there."

"You will," he assured her. "I know you've got your doubts, but Linda's putting you on stage."

"But I might not want to work there."

"Oh." He busied himself with the food. "Headed back to Icarus?"

"It's not that," she said. "I just don't know if I'm up for that kind of work again."

"Okay."

She watched his eyes. "Try again."

He held up his hands in surrender. "I don't know how you can love dancing so much, be so good at it, and not want to do it for a living."

There was a familiar tightness in her chest. "Loving it and being good at it aren't enough."

"I'm sorry."

She believed him. She knew he wouldn't ask any questions, no matter how badly he wanted to know, no matter how much he deserved to have those questions answered after last night.

"My mom calls me by my full name when she's pissed," she told him. "When I auditioned for Icarus, it was, 'Hayley Michelle. Dancing is not a stable profession.'"

"Has she seen you dance?"

"Oh, she and Dad were at Icarus at least once a month. She knows I'm good. She just minds me trying to make a living at it."

"What about your dad?"

"Dad worries too," she said. "He figures if he can't change my mind, he'll try to protect me along the way."

Nick smiled. "Especially if protection involves a power tool."

Hayley nodded, laughing. "More than one."

Her eyes lingered absently on her coffee. "I never had a choice, ya know? She never understood that."

He nodded. "Not everybody has that kind of passion."

"Why not, though?" Hayley leaned forward. "You know how in *Singin' in the*—" She stopped. "I forgot. You don't know who Cyd Charisse is."

"I've seen *Singin' in the Rain*." He laughed at the look on her face. "And now you're going to kill me."

"Were you just screwing with me?" She sighed. "And I'd almost forgiven you for that *American in Texas* bullshit."

"I don't know all of the actors or anything," he said. "I had this girlfriend in high school, and musicals were her thing. I watched a few back then, is all."

"Do you remember when Don takes Kathy onto a sound-stage to sing and dance with her? He doesn't know another way to tell her how he feels."

He nodded.

She shrugged. "It's like that."

"Dancing is your native language."

"Exactly!" She beamed. "It's how I communicate, Nick. It's how I touch the world around me and how I stay aware of myself and how I *breathe*, really. Doesn't everybody have something like that?" She paused. "You think I'm crazy."

"Not at all." He grinned. "Tell me what it's like."

She grabbed his arm, eyes shining. "So my feet are moving across the floor, and I'm jumping through the air, and all my muscles are working together with my breathing and my heart and my pulse. I'm existing the way I'm supposed to. I can cry and laugh and yell, but I'm not truly *responding* to something unless I dance." She watched him. "You have that, right? When you sing?"

"Sometimes." He thought about it. "You have to give up a lot for something like that."

"What do you mean?"

"Well, you're plugging straight into your heart. That means whatever's feeding you can break you too. You might not be as happy without it, but at least you have some control."

Hayley thought about losing control. "You think it's worth it?" she asked.

"I think you're much better at it than I am."

She wanted to plead with him not to think so highly of her.

"Icarus was perfect at the beginning," she said. "Like my whole life was revolving around the thing I couldn't live without. Especially once I had Kevin."

Nick didn't prompt her, and she was grateful. The choice to move closer had to be hers.

"You get another family when you join a dance company like that," she said. "I still love them. All those crazy people who love what you love—they become your life, and they have your back. Because the job takes all of you. You don't make any money, and you don't have free time, and you pretty much wave goodbye to anybody outside of Icarus. I thought that was the least I could give to something I loved so much."

"Sure," he said. "You had to do your best."

She rubbed her eyes. "So first I thought I was just tired, you know? There was always something to be rehearsing or thinking about or taking care of, and for a long time I just tried to be good enough. I had to learn to rehearse for a new show all day and then go on stage to do the current one that night. I had to listen to some girl in the kitchen call me a bitch because I could dance better than her and then smile my way out to serve tables. I always had to be on."

"You think that's going on at Vivez?" he asked. "I know they're always moving, but I don't see the stress."

She shook her head. "I can't say for sure, but I haven't gotten that vibe. I think everybody probably treats one another better, for starters."

Nick got up from the table and transferred their dishes onto his cart. "Still," he said, "if they're wigging out, I want to help."

"You help plenty already." She grabbed the cart. "Here. Let me clean up."

"Are you sure?" he asked. "Using that toaster can take a lot out of a person."

"Sit your smart ass down, Freeman."

His compromise was to give her free rein of the kitchen as he stood nearby. "It's good that everybody helps with everything," she continued. "At Icarus, being stressed even starts to feel good, because you finally figure out how to do a dozen things without screwing up, and then Cyd says congratulations and adds something else. You feel like you're earning the work. So I go from dancing in a group to dancing by myself or with Kevin, and then dancing and choreographing, which is awesome. Plus I find out I'm really good at bartending."

"Sounds like you're more of a rock star than I am."

"That'd depend on who you ask."

"Nah," he said. "You kick ass, and you know it."

The excuses started running through her head, the lines she'd give to patrons, lines she told herself when she tried to be grounded and sensible. *Thanks, I had a lot of fun. Thanks, but it's really a team effort.* And always in her head, but never out loud: *Thanks, but you don't know me.*

She didn't want to make excuses anymore.

"Yes." She grinned. "I kick ass."

Nick grinned back, reflecting her glow. "And what's it like, having millions of adoring fans?" he asked.

She rolled her eyes at him, but she was still smiling. "Fans are good, but at Icarus most of them wanted something. Which is fine, I guess, except that's all in addition to actually doing my job."

"You couldn't just tell them no?"

"Sure, but it never seemed to happen. I mean, nobody got my phone number. But I felt bad if I said no to a picture or a hug, let alone telling Cyd I couldn't handle a dance number or needed a day off."

"Icarus was doing all of this before you got there," he pointed out. "They'd have to understand if you said you wanted a break."

"It was complicated." She wiped down the counter. "Everyone would bitch at the bar after work, but the job was our choice. If I wasn't happy, I could always throw myself into the next show. Leaving would mean I couldn't cut it. And then I'd have to hear 'I told you so' in a million ways from Mom."

He nodded. "Not an option—I get it."

"So at first I was just tired, but everybody was tired. Then I was tense, like I was always about to cry or kill somebody. But we all fought like a family, right, so there was always somebody I could blame for feeling shitty. No matter what happened the rest of the time, I could get on stage with my man and feel it all melt away for a couple shows a night. Then one Friday night I felt worse after the curtain call than I had at the opening number. I just stared at a wall backstage, thinking, 'My God, I have to do all this again in an hour.'"

"I can't imagine doing it all once," Nick said. "That's not a crip joke," he added. "Just saying I don't have the energy."

"Honestly, I think you find what you need," she said. "But it is crazy. We were never not tired. Just exhausted on a good day and destroyed on a bad one."

"I'm guessing the bad days started coming more often?" he said gently.

She nodded. "I started carrying it with me, you know?" She tapped her chest. "Like everything that wasn't okay was collecting right here. If I didn't keep it under control, I couldn't breathe."

He stepped closer, eyes warm and on hers. "I'm sorry."

She smiled weakly. "So we finish the late show one night, and Kevin heads to the bar, right? But I go home to work on some staging. Except I can't find the notebook I've been using to put together the new show. And when Kevin comes home I'm curled up on our living room floor, just sobbing. I've gone through the entire house, and I can't find that goddamn notebook anywhere, but Kevin can't convince me to stop looking and go to bed. I fell asleep right there on the floor that night."

"Did you talk to anybody about it?" he asked.

"Sure. Kev knew. And Denise."

"And?"

Hayley sighed. "They said get some rest, but it didn't work. There wasn't much else to do. Time off meant no money, and it's not like Kevin could've supported both of us."

"Still, it seems like—"

"It wasn't worth killing myself?" she snapped. "I should've gotten the hell out of there?"

Nick stood there in silence, and Hayley's glare faded.

"People have been working at Icarus for a lot longer than I did." She ran her hands through her hair, swept it off her shoulders. "They don't need someone to hold their hand. They get through it."

"Hayley," he said softly.

"Every day, I would . . ." She sniffled, cleared her throat. "I'd stand in front of the bathroom mirror, and I'd go through every hour of the day and where my breaks would be and exactly how long I'd have to keep everything under control. I was drinking all the time and hanging onto Kevin like he was a life raft . . ." She sniffled again, forced herself to keep her head up. "But I kept dancing, and I kept smiling, and then I couldn't dance or smile anymore. It was like the closer I got to that stage, the more my entire body would scream at me to stay away. So I tended the bar for the run of the next show. I could handle that most days." She shook her head. "Do you know what it's like to have your mind go a million miles an hour all the time? My body was exhausted, but my brain was just *churning*, you know, and it was all I could do to make a mojito and hand it to a customer."

He was next to her now, standing at the counter, their shoulders almost touching. "It scares me to not be in control," he murmured. "My body fails me when I want it to do more, and my mind . . . it'd be easier if my mind could do *less* and stop with all the second-guessing."

She stared at the wet paper towel clenched in her hand. "Kevin got fucked over at Icarus because of me," she whispered.

"He's brilliant on his own, but Cyd only wanted him with me, so when I broke down, she put him in the ensemble. The background. We're here because of me, and he's gone because of me, and you've gone through so much shit because of me."

Nick's fingers closed over her hand where it gripped the sink. Hayley wrapped him in her arms and held on tight.

"You don't want me," she whispered.

"I do," he said. "I swear to God I do."

She shook her head. "I'm using you, Nick. That's not fair."

"No, you're not," he said. "You're leaning on me. Like I lean on you to get up those steps at karaoke." She wasn't convinced. "You're done with Kevin, aren't you?"

She nodded easily; Kevin was behind her now. Nick pulled back to look her in the eyes.

"I've tried so hard to be worthy of someone like you," he said. "And then yesterday, when you really needed someone, I wasn't ready. I didn't have a plan or a charming story. I was just me." He smiled. "And it turns out when I stop trying to be someone else, being there for you is easier than breathing. So as long as I'm not taking someone else's job, you can lean on me all you want."

Hayley had seen his showman's grin at the bar and heard the easy laughter he shared with his friends. The smile Nick gave her now was different, tender. Her heart told her this smile was for her alone.

"Your heart is in your eyes again," she said.

He said, "I sure hope so."

29

"It'll be great, I promise." Nick checked his side mirror and changed lanes. "A birthday party means birthday cake."

"I don't know." Hayley rummaged through her purse in the passenger seat. "I wouldn't want strangers at my birthday party."

"Mel's thrilled," he said. "And I know you trust Mel more than me."

"Hey, do I finally get a demonstration?"

He glanced at her. "What?"

"How do you drive this thing?"

"Hand controls." Nick nodded toward his right hand, which was gripping a spinner knob mounted to the steering wheel. "That lets me steer one-handed."

"What about the gas and the brake?"

"See this handle over here?" It jutted out to the left of the wheel. "It's connected to the pedals."

Hayley was using the mirror on the sun visor to carefully apply pink lipstick. She caught him looking and winked.

God. Just knowing this woman was in the world made him feel better.

"So the handle moves the pedals," she prompted.

"Yep," he said. "If I push the handle toward the dashboard"— he showed her—"it moves the brake pedal. But if I release it"— he brought the handle back toward himself—"and then press it down toward my knee, like this, it hits the gas."

"Is it harder to drive that way?"

He shrugged. "I learned this way."

"Oh. Of course." She looked out the window, embarrassed.

"Don't feel bad. Everybody asks."

But she did feel bad, he could tell. Nick was eager to answer Hayley's questions, just so cerebral palsy could seem less like some foreign country to her. But he was willing to bet Hayley's heart was big enough for her to equate not knowing about his hand controls with not caring about him enough.

"You know one thing you've never done?" he asked her.

Hayley glanced at him cautiously. "What?"

"You've never told me I should put snow tires on the walker."

She waited for the punchline. "In August?"

"It'll snow," he said, "and somebody'll always say, 'You need snow tires on that thing!' There's something funny about comparing it to a car, I guess."

She frowned, puzzled. "It's not a great joke."

"I know," he said. "If they really wanted to show me they understood, they'd notice when life was a little too much, like at Vivez when Bill was staring at my walker like it was a spaceship. They would reach under the table and grab my hand, and I would know everything was okay." He looked over at her. "But only one person has ever done that."

Hayley's smile started in her eyes, and Nick knew they were dancing.

30

If the cars lining the street hadn't tipped her off, Hayley could've spotted the balloons tied to the house's mailbox. Nick pulled into the vacant driveway.

"Preferred parking," he said.

He had his hand on the door handle when Hayley caught him by the elbow.

"I know you think this is a good idea," she said, "but Rose doesn't know me."

"You won't have to put on a show for anybody," he assured her. "If you're not glad we've come after five minutes, I'll drive you out of here as quickly as possible."

He was getting really good at making her smile.

"Safely," she said.

"I promise I'll stop at every third red light."

"Then lead on, rock star."

Hayley smiled at the sight of children enthusiastically splashing in an inflatable pool as she walked arm in arm with Nick into the Becketts' backyard. Gavin waved and jogged toward them with a lawn chair.

"Hey, big man." He shook Nick's hand and gave Hayley a hug. "Welcome to the party."

"Thanks!" Hayley watched Nick lower himself into the chair. "Kind of far away from the crowd, aren't we?"

"Just thinking ahead." Nick winked at her before he yelled. "Hey, Rosie Bear!"

A little blond girl radiated pure delight as she scrambled to get out of the pool and run toward them. Watching this little bundle of energy in the hot-pink swim suit was enough to make Hayley melt inside, but it was Nick's face, and the joy in his eyes, that brought a lump to her throat.

"Uncle Nick!" the little girl squealed. "Uncle Nick!"

"Rosie Bear!" Nick hauled her into his lap as she flung her arms around his neck. "Are you having a fantabulous birthday?"

"Yep!"

"I brought somebody super cool to meet you." Nick perched her on his knee. "Rosie, this is Hayley. Hayley, this is Rose."

"We're best friends," Rose explained.

"That's wonderful, Rose." Hayley crouched down to the girl's eye level. "Can you and I be friends too?"

Rose seriously deliberated for all of a second before giving Hayley a toothy, open-mouthed grin. "Yeah!" She shot out her arms, and Hayley scooped her up without thinking. "You can be my super-cool big-girl friend."

"I would love that so much, Rose."

"Rose, you want to show Hayley the pool?" Gavin asked.

"Yep!" said Rose. "Uncle Nick, I'm showin' Hayley the pool and my friends and the special tree and Mommy's bench, and then we're gonna talk about big-girl stuff."

"Okay!" Nick waved goodbye. "See you soon!"

Hayley shot a wide-eyed look at Nick as the elated ladies headed across the lawn, and soon she was kneeling by the pool with a bottle of bubbles, dipping the wand and holding it so Rose could blow.

"How many bubbles do you think we'll get this time, honey?" she asked.

The little girl deliberated. "Three."

"You sure? I think we can get more if we work together."

Rose grinned, eyes wide. "Three hundred!"

Hayley gasped. "Wow! Are we going to fill the whole pool with bubbles?"

"Yeah!"

Asking the little girl to be her roommate was sounding like a perfectly reasonable idea by the time Mel Beckett walked up beside them.

"Did you make a new friend, Rose?" Mel asked.

"She's my super-cool big-girl friend, Mommy!"

Hayley rose to her feet. "You've got a perfect little girl."

"And she really likes you." Mel hugged her. "I'm glad you're here."

"Me too."

There must have been something in her voice. Hayley had already noticed an intensity in Mel that seemed to infuse everything from her amber eyes to her bright red hair, and Hayley could tell that energy was currently focused on diagnosing what Mel had just heard.

Mel asked, "Everything okay?"

"Sure," Hayley said. Then, as Mel waited, "Actually, not really."

Mel squeezed her shoulder. "Talk later?"

"I'd really like that."

Mel smiled and gave a decisive nod, and Hayley knew she would not be leaving the Becketts' house without having a conversation.

31

Nick leaned back in his lawn chair and caught a glimpse of Hayley walking across the lawn. Her strides were loose and easy. She was gliding again.

Nick smiled.

"I keep meaning to tell you I'm pissed at you," Gavin said.

Nick glanced at his friend in the chair next to him. "You can't be all that pissed if you keep forgetting to tell me."

"I finally remembered when we saw *G.I. Jane*."

"Good."

"And I started laughing, right there, so I had to explain to Mel what was so funny."

Nick grinned. "You were pretty pleased with yourself at the time."

"Double entendres are an art form, my friend." Gavin sipped his beer. "Most people would watch *Striptease* after *G.I. Jane* and say, 'Oh, great, a Demi Moore double feature!'"

"I'm sure Mel was blown away by your idea to call it Double D Night."

"I told her we were in high school. Before she had a chance to fully refine me."

"Uh-huh."

"Also that it was your fault."

"Screw you."

Nick and Gavin were enjoying the party from the lawn chairs that Gavin had carefully placed just off the patio. The key was to sit in the heart of the action, so they could socialize with anyone who happened to pass, rather than feeling obligated to move any farther than was necessary to drink their beers.

"Did they break up?" Gavin said. He didn't have to specify who he meant.

Nick shifted in his chair. "Yeah."

"So what does that mean for you two?"

Nick watched Hayley over by the fence. It looked like she was trying to console the neighbors' yapping terrier. "Well," he said, "as long as Kevin doesn't come back, and no one in Columbus ever hits on her, I might have a shot."

Gavin shot him a look. "Don't make me say nice things about you."

"You think I want you to blow smoke up my ass?"

"I think she's here. With you. And you absolutely looked like a couple walking in here."

Nick lowered his voice. "Vicki and I looked like a couple for years."

"You were," Gavin countered. "Just because something eventually stops doesn't mean it wasn't real."

"So you think Hayley and I won't last," Nick concluded.

"Honestly?" Gavin said. "I think you're made for each other."

Nick sighed. "You haven't seen her dance."

"And that wouldn't change a thing."

They watched party guests mingle on the lawn. Hayley was back at the pool now, chatting with one of the parents.

"It feels like that," Nick admitted. "Like we were made for each other. Except my legs got busted in shipping."

"She doesn't care about that."

"I know she doesn't. But one day she's going to find someone who can give her more."

Rosie dunked her head into the pool and vigorously emerged a second later. Nick saw Hayley notice the commotion and smile.

Gavin said, "Part of you doesn't believe that. Focus on that part."

"How do you—"

"You brought her here. That's how I know."

Nick led the room in singing "Happy Birthday" when the party moved to the kitchen for cake and ice cream, and then the birthday girl had a request. "Sing the Rosie song!" she told Nick.

He made his way to her high chair. "Absolutely, baby girl!"

"You sing too!" This was directed with much delight to Hayley.

"Sweetie," Nick said, "I promised Hayley she didn't—"

"I didn't know what a super-cool little girl you were," Hayley said, joining them. "Can you teach me, honey?"

"Uncle Nick knows all the words."

Which brought everyone's focus to Nick. "I make up the words," he said. "And the melody's kind of negotiable too. Except for the end."

"Just sing it with her, and then I'll give it a shot." Hayley had laughter in her eyes. "I'm a professional."

Nick pretended not to hear Mel snicker.

"Here we go, baby girl!" He started to sing. "Oh, this is Rosie's birthday song, but it will not be very long, 'cause I would sing with her all day, but then we'd have no time to play!" A deep breath for the ending: "No matter what, it's plain to see . . ."

"I love Uncle Nick, and Uncle Nick loves me!"

Their audience started clapping, Rosie started clapping, and Nick looked apologetically at Hayley as she started clapping. Rosie prompted Hayley gleefully. "Now your turn!"

Without a moment's hesitation, Hayley stepped forward and started to sing. "Rose is my new birthday friend, and I don't want this day to end, 'cause Rose is awfully nice to me, and I'm so glad she's turning three!" Rosie joined in: "No matter what, it's plain to see . . ."

"I love Hayley, and Hayley loves me!"

Nick was staring at Hayley, delighted and shaking his head in amazement, and Rosie had to wave her hand in front of his face to get his attention. He and Hayley gave high fives to the birthday girl before working their way back across the room. "Nicky," Mel told him as they passed, "Rose definitely likes her better."

"Don't I know it," Nick said wryly.

Gavin was handing out plates at the kitchen table. "Should've figured you'd prep a ringer," he told Nick.

"Hey, I'm as surprised as you are," Nick said. "She's been holding out on us."

"It's not exactly a complicated song," Hayley pointed out. She watched Nick beam at her. "What?"

Nick shrugged happily. "You can sing," he said. "I didn't know you could sing."

32

The guests started leaving after they'd had their fill of food, and it wasn't long before only Hayley and Nick were left with the Becketts in the kitchen. Rose stood in front of her high chair, covered in the remnants of her birthday treats.

"All right, little girl," Mel said. "Time to get you washed up and into some clean clothes."

"I can do that." Gavin picked up his daughter. "Mommy ran the party, after all."

"Thanks, Gav." Mel looked at Nick. "While he's doing bath time, maybe you can see what you can do with the box I saw my husband take upstairs from your car."

Nick brightened. "That is an excellent idea." His eyes narrowed. "And an excellent ploy to separate me from Hayley so you can turn her against me while I'm gone."

Hayley shrugged. "She can't make me like you less than I already do."

"Uh-huh," he said. "I knew it. You were in it for the cake."

"From the very beginning. Now go." Hayley waved to Rose. "See you when you come back down, honey!"

"See ya, Hayley!" The women could hear her talking to Nick as Gavin carried her down the front hallway. "What are you gonna do upstairs?"

"Me?" Nick said. "I've got a top-secret birthday mission."

"What is it?"

"It wouldn't be a secret if I told you!"

"Daddy, do you know?"

"Of course I do," Gavin replied. "I know everything."

Hayley laughed as their voices trailed off up the steps. "Nicky got her a tent that looks like a princess castle," Mel said. "I'm sure you'll be invited in."

"I hope so." She turned away from the hall. "Is there anything I can do to help you clean up?"

"Nah, don't worry about it. Right now I just want to sit down."

"I'll bet."

Hayley took the recliner in the family room while Mel dropped onto the couch. They surveyed the birthday presents in front of them.

"Rose will never use all this stuff," Mel said.

"That's what happens when you have lots of friends."

Mel looked around. "I mean, she'll love that doll, and she'll wear the clothes. But all she really wanted for her birthday was to play with her friends."

"I'm so glad I got to be one of them."

"We all are. Which will be a pain because Nicky will be full of himself for thinking of it."

Hayley laughed. "I love that you call him Nicky."

"Everybody did, once upon a time," Mel said. "I like remembering him before he was Nick."

Hayley remembered searching for a blanket the night before. "He has some really great pictures of you all from back then."

"In his study? Absolutely. His mom's got a good eye." Mel watched her. "Did you see the graduation picture?"

"With you three and a blond girl."

"That'd be Vicki," Mel said. "His girlfriend."

"Oh," Hayley said. Mentioning Vicki by name brought Nick's ex out of the past, made her too real. "Okay."

"He told you about Vicki?"

"Um, he mentioned a high school girlfriend." Details suddenly seemed like a betrayal. "I didn't know her name."

"They were Nicky and Vicki since middle school. King and queen of the senior prom."

Hayley smiled. "I'll bet he rocked a tux."

"Oh, he did. They always looked gorgeous together, but I think it was because they were always having so much *fun*. She was in everything—cheerleader, show choir, student council, theater—you name it. And Nicky was her ambassador to the commoners."

"Really?" Hayley leaned forward, surprised. "That was a good thing?"

Mel laughed. "Sure. That was just something Gavin used to say. Vicki was so popular that people would assume she didn't want to associate with the kids who were just trying to get through the day. It was like she'd say hi to you in the hallway and you'd look around for whoever she must've been talking to. But Nicky—people *loved* Nicky. He'd invite someone different to their lunch table every day, just because he liked making their day. I know that sounds like they were royalty or something, but you have to understand: Having lunch with those two was pretty much the highlight of high school. Nicky would listen to you, and he'd remember every conversation he'd ever had, and before long people would see Vicki was just as nice as he was. Everybody'd be laughing, and it wouldn't matter that the quarterback was sitting across the table from the math geek."

She could picture the scene, almost feel the warmth of Nick's attention and see the glint of his blue eyes, and she suddenly missed somewhere she'd never been. "It must have been great to be a part of that."

"My favorite part of senior year," Mel said. "Gavin and I shared a lunch period with them, and sometimes I'd just sit back and watch him go back and forth with Nicky."

Hayley grinned. "I've seen that."

"Not like that, though. Nicky didn't worry about a thing back then." Mel glanced toward the front hall. "He broke a little without Vicki."

"Oh." Something shifted in her then. Hayley was seeing the pain in him again, the ache in his eyes when they'd met hers for the first time.

Mel turned back to her. "He still knows how to make people feel special, but I don't think it's the same thing anymore. Now he does it without letting anyone in. Like he's put all of the work back into working a room."

"Uh-huh."

"You don't know what to say. I'm sorry."

"No, it's okay." Hayley weighed her options. "I know what you're talking about. It's just that he's barely mentioned Vicki, and I have to wonder how much he wants me to know."

"He'd appreciate you saying so." Mel let the silence settle, kindness in her eyes. Gently, she asked, "What's been going on, Hayley?"

Hayley sat hunched over in the recliner, hands pressed together in front of her. "Kevin walked out yesterday," she said.

"Oh, Hayley, I'm so sorry."

"Yeah, well, I don't even know if I am." She looked up. "I was so messed up I had to Uber to work, but I didn't want to stay in an empty house, you know? And maybe I wanted to see Nick, even if he didn't want to see me, because . . ." She sighed. "Because

I know he likes me. And then he just . . ." She threw up her hands. "Did you see how he's limping? You wouldn't believe what he did."

Mel smiled. "I think I might."

"And this is the point where normal people would've walked away, right, because Kevin hadn't been gone six hours, and suddenly I was looking down at this whip-smart rock star who didn't hesitate to throw himself *on the ground* just because I was having a shitty day. I hadn't talked to him in a week. I thought he was going to run the other way. But as soon as he saw me, all of our issues? Gone." Hayley snapped her fingers. "Just like that. He didn't even know we'd broken up."

Mel was unfazed, so much so that Hayley wondered if the story was coming out accurately. "You were in trouble," she said simply.

"And *I'm* the one driving this bus." It felt good to get revved up. "He should've just dropped me off at my place, but I told him to go to his. And he listened, and there was chocolate . . ." Hayley shook her head, laughing in disbelief. "And then I was talking my way into his bed. I knew he wanted to sleep with me, I knew he felt shitty about it, and I decided to climb in and say, 'Nah, we're just gonna cuddle.' Who does that?"

"Couldn't've been a disaster," Mel offered. "I mean, you're both here."

Hayley looked helplessly at her. "He was perfect. And then this morning . . ." She thought of dancing with him. "He tries so hard to be charming, but honest to God, all he has to do is be himself."

Mel waited. "And the problem is . . ."

"Mel, the last thing I need is someone who'll do anything for me. I'm just going to hurt him."

Mel sat with this for a moment.

"You know, Nick and Rose really are best friends," she said. "Rose loves her mom and she loves her dad, but I think she's fearless because of her Uncle Nick. She knows he'd do anything for her."

"I believe it."

"I think he'd actually cut his arm off if it would keep her from hurting," Mel said. "Just because he decided to."

Hayley nodded, smiling. "He decided to be my friend too. Like, there was an actual conversation, with an agreement."

"Uh-huh. Even though normal people don't operate that way."

"That's what I told him."

Mel laughed. She got up and busied herself with arranging Rose's gifts.

"We had two miscarriages before Rose," she said, "and she was three weeks early, so things were scary. We drove to the hospital at one in the morning, and Nicky was there in an hour. I told Gav not to call him—I mean, there was nothing he could do. But he was there with us until I went into the delivery room, and he stayed until we told him Rose was okay."

Mel kept her head bent over the gifts, but Hayley could see tears.

"The whole time, he was so sure," she said. "I mean from the moment we told him I was pregnant again. 'This one will be okay,' he said. 'I'm gonna be Uncle Nick.' We were terrified, of course, but he had us believing too. So when Rose took her first steps, we decided to surprise Uncle Nick. I made him dinner, he sat in that chair, and Rose walked to him. It was just a few steps, but he . . ." She took a breath. "He hugged her so hard, and he was crying. First time I ever saw Nicky cry, and I realized he'd been terrified too, the whole time, because he was a preemie. Much earlier than Rose, but still. He was afraid she wouldn't be able to walk. I wish you could have seen his face when he realized she wouldn't have to handle what he deals with every day. He finds a way, but he'd never wish it on anyone else."

"He looks at it like a fight," Hayley said softly.

Mel nodded. "He was going to be Uncle Nick regardless, though. He was set on that from day one. Didn't matter if Rose couldn't walk or speak or see—he was going to do every single thing he could for that little girl. He'll try to brush it off if you ask him, like it's just something friends do for one another."

"They don't."

"No, they don't. But Nicky's not like most people."

Mel wiped her eyes as she returned to the couch. She looked straight at Hayley. "He wouldn't love this conversation," she said. "And maybe it's not my place to tell you about Vicki or Rose. But Nicky doesn't really date. I've only met a few of the girls he's liked, and he's never brought anyone to our house. And I have never heard him even suggest anyone was good enough to meet his Rosie Bear, let alone play with her or sing the Rosie song."

Hayley didn't have to ask what that meant. "What do I do?" she asked.

"If you don't want him," Mel said gently, "you're going to have to cut and run. Say goodbye as soon as he drops you off, because he is way past the point where he can just be friends with you."

Hayley nodded.

"But I think you do want him," Mel said. "And if fear is the only thing keeping you from seeing where that leads, you should know that I have known that man since before I really knew myself, and there has not been a single moment of my life since seventh grade when he hasn't been there for me when I needed him."

Hayley smiled weakly. "He's one of your boys."

"Hayley," Mel said, "Nick is decent to everyone he knows. But he will go to hell and back for the people he loves."

33

Tours of the princess tent had to end sometime, and eventually they were back in the car, waving to Rosie and her parents on the front porch. Nick figured it would take about five seconds after they started driving away.

Five, four, three, two . . .

"Oh my God, Nick. That girl."

He smiled. "I know."

"Did you see the way she runs? It's like her body has to catch up with her legs."

"Yep."

"And her friends," Hayley said. "Nick, that girl loves everybody. They were all in the pool, but they were playing *together*, you know? Totally getting along. She introduced me to each one of them like they were family. Have you ever seen an adult love so many people like that?"

"Nope, can't say I have."

She stopped. "Mel was right. You're completely full of yourself right now."

"Am not."

"You are! You're practically preening."

"I'm sure I don't know what you're talking about," Nick said airily, "but if you're suggesting I might be feeling some very justified satisfaction for introducing you to the sweetest little girl on the planet, then yes, I am."

"Okay, rock star." She smiled. "Maybe you deserve to feel a little cocky for this one."

"Thank you. You're back on the VIP list."

"What's that mean?"

"Rosie's obviously going to be the next Taylor Swift," he said. "She'll have her dad's knack for lyrics and her mom's musical talent, and her Uncle Nick is going to be her manager. You'll want to go to those concerts, believe me."

"Does Rosie know about this?"

"I wouldn't want to burden her with her destiny at such an early age."

Hayley laughed, settling into her seat. "I didn't know Mel could sing."

"She can do more than that. You know the song "Uninvited" by Alanis Morissette?" Hayley nodded. "Talent show, senior year, she forbids us to try and find out what she's doing. That curtain went up, and there was Mel, at the piano, with half the show choir on stage. She's got percussion, guitars, a couple of violins, and Vicki's covering the high harmonies . . ." Nick got chills as he pictured it. "To this day, best musical performance I've ever seen on stage. We brought it back for the band years later, just her and the piano, and she still brought down the house."

"Of course you had a band," Hayley said. "That makes perfect sense."

"Nothing big," Nick said. "We never got around to recording or anything. Then Mel had Rosie, and you can't play shows until one in the morning with a baby."

She hesitated. "Was Vicki in the band too?"

A sick ache ran through him, like she'd just tapped a bruise. Mel had told her, obviously. Not Mel's business, but that was okay. Hadn't he been sitting in this seat a few hours ago, thinking of all the things he wanted to share?

This hadn't been on the list, though.

"No." He tried to sound casual. "Vicki was gone by then."

"Mel and I were talking about the pictures in your study." Hayley sounded apologetic; apparently he hadn't been casual enough. "She mentioned her name."

"Yeah, we ended up at different colleges."

She turned playful. "Mel also said you looked great in a tux."

"Oh, I looked amazing." He happily changed the subject. "And let me tell you something: Tuxedos are not built for the electric slide. I don't see how anyone can wear the shirt and the vest and the coat and not sweat all over the place."

"I see how it is." Nick turned to see Hayley smugly cross her arms. "You've been dancing for years, and you never told me."

"That barely qualifies," he said. "And you never told me you could sing."

She started laughing. "It's not a big deal."

"The hell it's not."

"Come on," she said. "I can't sing like you."

"But you sang for Icarus."

"Yeah, but I was a singer the same way our guitar player could swing dance. Not a headliner that way."

"And to think of all the karaoke Fridays," Nick said sadly. "The microphone was right there."

"I was busy bringing you drinks, genius. Besides, with karaoke you never know what key it'll be in, or whether the words'll show up. Not everyone loves a microphone like you do."

"Well, be brave," he said, "because you're going to sing now." He smiled at her. "This is my native language."

Hayley played reluctant, but he knew she understood. "Okay," she said. "You're singing with me, though."

"Of course."

"And I get to pick the song."

"Sure."

"And you've got to tell me how you knew what to say to me last night."

Nick stared blankly at the road. Somehow they'd strolled right up to another door he didn't want to open.

"You held on to me," Hayley said softly, "and you knew exactly what to say to make it better. How'd you do that?"

After a while, he said, "I just said what I'd want to hear."

"Don't," she said. "Don't sell yourself short."

"I'm not," he said. "I wish someone had said those things to me."

She waited.

"My mom makes really good lemon chicken," he said. "I wanted to learn to make it on my own after I got the apartment, so I could have my favorite food at my own place. So I followed Mom's instructions, and I figured out how to use the oven without burning myself, and it turned out really well."

"I can't cook at all," she offered.

"You can toast bagels."

"Only if I don't get distracted."

He gave her a wan smile. "So I'm sitting in my apartment, eating my own food, listening to Ben Folds on my stereo," he said. "And I'm maybe five bites in when I can't breathe. Because none of it mattered. It wouldn't make any difference to anyone if I choked on that damn chicken and died. I'd worked so hard at *becoming* someone, you know? Getting a job and an apartment and being as functional as everyone else, and then I come up for air and I'm completely empty."

Hayley touched his arm. "I get it," she said softly. "I really do."

He glanced at her. "Yeah?"

"Nick, I can't even tell you how many times I've cried alone this last year."

The ache to hold her was so strong that he nearly pulled the car over. "So that's why," he said. "I walked into the bar and you were drowning, just like when I wake up in the dark and feel like screaming. I tried to help."

She smiled. "Thank you."

"Happy to do it."

Hayley got her phone out of her purse. "What do you want, Nick?" she asked.

"To sing with you."

"We'll get there," she said patiently. "But I mean when you feel empty. What do you really want?"

He wanted years of car rides and birthday parties, late nights and lazy mornings and playful fights. He wanted to kiss her as the sun was rising above the ocean.

"I want to take you on a date," he said. The panic came immediately. She was only in this car because he hadn't asked for anything, and now he'd blown it.

"Okay," she said.

It took him a solid five seconds to realize she wasn't rejecting him. "Okay?"

"Okay," she repeated calmly. "*Singin' in the Rain* is playing at the Ohio Theatre Thursday night, and I very much want you to take me."

He was suddenly afraid he was imagining this entire conversation, but there she was, in his passenger seat, smiling at him.

"Okay," he said, a little calmer this time.

"You'll have to dress up." She started searching the compartment between their seats. "Is there a way I can hook my phone to your stereo?"

"There's a white cord in there," he said distractedly. "You're not doing this because of what I just said, are you?"

She shook her head. "I decided before I even got in Rose's tent."

He had to make sure. "And you want this too."

She was biting her lip. "I want *you*."

"Oh." He switched lanes in a happy daze. Then he groaned as a familiar guitar intro came through the speakers. "Backstreet Boys? Really?"

"What?" Hayley teased. "I get to pick."

"I knew it," he said, shaking his head. "I knew something like this would happen."

"Like you don't know this song."

"Of course I know this song. Vicki had me learn this entire album."

"Okay, then," she said. "I'm going to start this over, and we're going to sing."

Then they were belting "I Want It That Way" at the top of their lungs.

34

Exactly on schedule, Hayley heard a car pull up in front of the house. She heard a door open and shut. She waited another minute and a half before she stepped out the door.

It was totally worth it.

Nick was standing between the car and the curb, one hand on the handle of the passenger door and the other casually in his pocket. He'd gone for classic and formal: crisp white shirt, bright blue tie, black slacks, black shoes, and not a hair out of place. He looked polished and confident and comfortable, and she took a moment to savor the excitement, the hunger, that rushed through her. Nick Freeman was *hot*.

"Wow," Hayley said, smiling. "It's my very own rock star."

"At your service," he said.

The look on Nick's face as she walked down the steps was worth every second she'd spent preparing for tonight.

There were too many men who looked at her like something they wanted. She was no movie star, no willowy supermodel, but because she had boobs and did enough cardio to stay slim, because people paid money to see her on stage, men thought it was okay to show her the hunger in their eyes. But not Nick Freeman. He was definitely interested; she saw him take in the neckline of her purple dress and how the fabric hugged her hips and celebrated her curves. But there was only happy recognition in his eyes when they returned to hers, like she was every single wonderful thing he remembered her to be.

"You wore a tie!" she said.

"You said dress up," he said. "I don't think I can compete with that dress, though."

Hayley put a hand on her hip, posing for him. "You like it?"

"It's stunning." He grinned. "And you're wearing your Chucks."

She glowed. "You, sir, will be perfect arm candy." She moved in and fiddled with his tie. "Are there math equations on this thing?"

"It was a gift from my kids last year," he said. "I could've sworn it was perfect when I left the apartment."

The tie was perfect. She just wanted the excuse to tingle with the easy closeness of him. "You're lucky I'm here for the finishing touches," she said.

"These are the finishing touches?" He was a little breathless. "I was hoping there'd be more."

Hayley leaned a fraction closer. "So stay hopeful."

She could just kiss him now. To hell with the rest of the night.

"Well!" The voice came out of nowhere. "Don't you look lovely!"

Nick reacted as if someone had just fired a gun inches from his ear. His body jerked, his knees buckled, and he started sliding sideways against the car. Hayley shot out her hand and pressed a palm against the car so his shoulder rested against her arm.

"Hi, Mrs. Hennessy!" Hayley called cheerily to the silver-haired woman briskly walking a large brown-and-white dog across the street toward them. She eased Nick back into a safe standing position with one hand while she used the other to sur-reptitiously grab his wrist and put his free hand on her hip. She gave a tiny shake of her head in response to the embarrassed apology on his face and ran her hand softly up his arm.

"Did Charlie tell you it was time for a walk?" she asked Mrs. Hennessy.

"We've actually been walking more since . . ." Mrs. Hennessy noticed Nick as Charlie the dog reached the sidewalk. "Since you!"

Hayley had to hand it to him: Nick's top-of-the-line, take-no-prisoners smile immediately hid the flash of bewilderment in his eyes. "Me?"

"Charlie was barking hello when you came to visit a couple weeks ago," the woman said. "I saw you climb those steps all by yourself, and I thought, 'Bernice, if that young man can do that, there's no reason you can't get yourself out of the house and give Charlie some more fresh air.' You're just so inspiring."

"Well, thank you, Mrs. Hennessy. I'm Nick."

"And I'm Bernice." The dog strained at his leash. "Looks like Charlie wants to say hi. He's got some hound dog in him, you know. Charlie, I can't let you shed all over the gentleman's slacks!"

Charlie had other ideas, and while Mrs. Hennessy tried to talk sense into him, Hayley stepped closer to Nick to block his shaking legs from view. She moved her hand from his arm to his ribs, trying to silently reassure him. *Hang in there, rock star. Soon the nice lady will go away and it'll just be you and me. And please, God, don't let the dog bark.*

"Are you taking Hayley out this evening?" Mrs. Hennessy asked.

Nick nodded, smiling for all he was worth. "I do have that privilege, yes, ma'am."

"It doesn't sound like you're taking it for granted either. Good!" She pulled Charlie along. "Keep doing what you're doing," she told him. "Don't let anything get you down."

"I'll try my hardest, Bernice," Nick called after her. "Have a great night!"

They watched Charlie lead Bernice away, and then Nick's smile vanished in a sigh of relief. His knees buckled, and Hayley held him tighter. "I've got you," she said soothingly. "Let's get you in the car before Bernice remembers I haven't returned her cookie dish, huh?"

35

It was cooler than normal for a Thursday night in August, but after the ordeal with Mrs. Hennessy, Nick didn't waste a moment cranking up the car's air-conditioning.

"I'm sorry," Hayley said. "I know you hated every minute of that."

"Not your fault," he said easily. "Not her fault, really."

"But hey, at least you've inspired a senior citizen to walk her dog, right?"

Nick sighed. "Why is that inspirational?"

"Because it's harder for you. And I cannot believe, by the way, that Kevin didn't help—"

"Kevin didn't know." There was no way he would ever let that guy help him. "So what was the alternative?" he asked her. "Not going up the steps?"

"Well, yeah," she said. "A lot of people wouldn't."

"Doesn't that make those people lazy, though?" He shook his head. "I could've been trying to rob you or something."

Hayley stared at him, incredulous. "I'm sorry, *what*?"

"I'm saying I'm not a better person just because I have to work harder. I could've been coming up the steps to rob you."

She started laughing. "What exactly would your getaway plan be, Slick?"

"I could be a thief if I wanted to be."

She mimicked a phone with her hand. "Hello, Officer? I'd like to report a robbery. Yes, he's still here. Climbing down the front steps, actually. Such an inspiration, that one."

Nick tried to keep a straight face, but she had him. "It's all about commitment," he insisted. "I could be the world's greatest thief if I committed to it."

"Uh-huh. I'm not bailing you out when you get caught."

After a moment, he said, "It's weird, you know? I'm just try-ing to live my life, and people want to give me awards or some-thing. And if I *didn't* do anything, they'd be saying I needed to get out of the house."

"So you don't want people telling you you're awesome."

"Honestly? I don't think I deserve it. And no matter how many people are inspired watching me climb a flight of steps, I'm still the one who has to do the hard work."

Like trying not to fall over on a first date because he got scared by an old lady.

"Okay," Hayley said. "I had to give out flyers at Icarus after our shows. So everyone had to walk past me, and a lot of them would tell me how great the show was, you know? How great I was."

"That doesn't surprise me at all."

"Point is, all they saw was how good they thought I was. Meanwhile, one time I was throwing up in the dressing room during intermission. I'd disagree with some people's praise, but that didn't make them wrong. Just because I didn't see what they got out of the show doesn't mean it didn't happen."

"So I'm inspirational whether I like it or not."

"Yes," she said. "You're strong and you're decent and you're sexy and you're inspirational, even if you think you know better. Even if you think you're a shitty dancer. Sometimes it's about how other people interpret your dance."

He thought it over. "What'd you call me?"

She rolled her eyes. "You heard me."

"I don't know," he said slowly. "See, I'm disabled, and . . ."

"Asshat," she said. "I called you an asshat."

"Did not."

"I meant to."

36

"So you're telling me you don't even *like* musicals," Hayley said.

Nick shook his head as they walked. "I'm just wondering whose idea it was. Who decided logic shouldn't get in the way of singing and dancing?"

"You can't tell me people don't like singing and dancing."

"It'd be one thing if the movie was *about* singing and dancing." He stopped to give a passing jogger a wide berth. "I get why *Dirty Dancing* has dancing in it. But can you honestly watch *Guys and Dolls* or *West Side Story* and tell me it makes sense for all those gangsters to burst into song?"

"Look at you, getting all the titles right."

The heat of the day had faded to give Hayley a comfortable summer evening, and she was on a date with plenty of electricity and zero anxiety. She *knew* him—it was like they'd gone through all the hard stuff before anybody started keeping score, and now she could just be here in the moment with him. She was surrounded by movement: the give and take of their conversation, the rush of the cars and the people around them, and even the light breeze that toyed with her hair. Then a new sound joined the rhythm of their walk: Nick was breathing heavily.

Really, Hayley Michelle? You know him? The theater's still two blocks away. He's arguing with you because he doesn't want you to notice him suffering.

"Hey, rock star," she said. "Are you trying to get rid of me?"

She saw sweat on his forehead when he glanced at her. "What?"

"Seems like you're in a big hurry. We've got time."

He shook his head and went back to concentrating on the sidewalk. "I'm good."

Nick didn't seem good. Even at a slow pace, it seemed to take a lot of effort for him to keep moving. He dragged his feet across the concrete, one doggedly after the other, stumbling when his walker wheel caught the edge of an uneven sidewalk square.

"You'd think they'd have handicapped spaces nearby," she said.

He shook his head again. "Where would they put them? Everything's crammed together down here."

"You knew that ahead of time."

"I had a pretty good idea, yeah."

Hayley put her arm around him. "I could have dropped you off," she said gently.

"Nope. You'd steal my car."

"I know how you feel about wheelchairs, but I wouldn't—"

"We'd be stuck with crummy seats." His tone turned apologetic when she didn't reply. "I know you wouldn't care," he said. "But I wanted to walk with you."

She stopped. "So walk with me."

"Isn't that what we're doing?"

"Nope," she said. "You're just walking next to me. Take a breath. Look around."

He sighed. "You're just trying to slow me down."

"You bet your cute little ass." She leaned closer. "Wanna know a secret?"

Nick nodded, and she kissed his cheek.

"I'm having a really good time," she whispered. "And I want to make it last."

He slowed down for her then, and she still had her arm around him when they walked into the theater's lobby.

"Look at this place," Hayley said. "This is amazing."

Nick grinned. "Do they not have theaters in Indianapolis?"

"Of course they do, but that doesn't take anything away from this one." Hayley caught sight of a woman who'd just entered the theater.

A royal-blue dress was slit all the way up the woman's long legs, and she sized Hayley up with a smile that never reached her eyes. Then, as Nick nodded to her amiably, her gaze flitted over him like he didn't exist.

"How often do you get that look?" Hayley asked him.

"Her?" Nick looked surprised, then a little embarrassed. "More often than you'd think."

"That bitch."

He laughed. "At least wait to attack her until after the movie, okay?"

Hayley seethed. "She didn't even *see* you!"

"Who cares? I'm with you."

Hayley stopped staring at her new nemesis as his words sunk in. "Aww," she said. "You wouldn't rather be with Miss Legs over there?"

"Come on," he scoffed. "Too young, too mean, too tall, and probably not all that bright."

She laughed. "Good answer."

"I know you want to make out during the movie," he said once they'd gotten seats, "but I'd really like to watch the film, if you don't mind."

Hayley kept reading her program. "Idiot."

"I'm just saying, it's not every day you get to see a cinematic gem in this sort of setting, so if you absolutely must suck face, we should do it now."

Hayley bit back a laugh. "Suck face. Wow." She slapped down her program. "Am I not worth your best material, Freeman?"

He grinned. "Well, if the easy stuff works . . ."

"Go on," she demanded. "Lay it on me. Now."

"You want my best stuff."

"Unless I'm about to be disappointed." Nick got a faraway look in his eyes. "What?" she said. "What is it?"

"Hmm?" He blinked, came back to her. "Nothing. It's silly."

"Sillier than sucking face?" He looked a little sheepish, and her smile turned tender. "C'mon," she said gently. "You can tell me."

Nick glanced around them, then beckoned her closer. "I was just thinking about my legs."

"Nick." She thought about Charlie the dog, the walk from the car, the girl in the lobby. "I never should've . . ."

"Seeing you come down those steps," he said. "You were breathtaking. The way the sun glinted in your hair and off your skin . . ." He trailed his fingers across her shoulder, brushing her hair away from her neck. "You sounded so happy to see me, and I just wanted to touch you."

She swallowed. "Yeah?"

He nodded. "I loved having you so close, messing with my tie, smelling so good. And then you ran your tongue along your lip while you concentrated on the knot, and all I could think of was how those lips were going to taste." He smiled. "I have all five senses, and I know you fit perfectly in my arms. So what the hell do I even need my legs for?"

Hayley forgot to breathe. "You don't."

"Wanna know a secret?"

She nodded, and bit her lip to stop a gasp as he kissed her neck.

"My best material," he whispered, "only works when it's true."

Hayley's mouth dropped open.

Nick sat back and calmly opened his program. "Disappointed?"

"I hate you," she said.

He smiled. "I don't think you do."

When they were almost to her place, she asked, "So, did you like it?"

"Absolutely," he said cheerfully.

"What was your favorite part?"

"Watching you enjoy it."

He parked the car, and she stopped him from opening his door.

"I'll come to you," she said.

Nick was standing with one hand firmly on the inner handle of the open door by the time she circled the car to stand in front of him.

"So," she said.

He looked into her eyes. "So."

"This was fun."

"Absolutely."

She bit her lip. "So you knew what you were getting into, huh?"

"More or less."

"The parking, the walking, Miss Legs . . ."

"You're worth it, Hayley."

She felt impossibly strong and utterly helpless in front of him.

"Nick," she said. "That girl tonight . . ."

"Was nowhere near as beautiful as you."

"She was, Nick." Hayley took a breath. "And I'm worried too many pretty girls have looked at you just like she did and made you think I'm the best you can get. You're seeing what you want to see in me. There are prettier girls out there. Better dancers. Better *people*, Nick."

Hayley saw disbelief in his eyes. She saw sadness.

"I don't know who's been lying to you," Nick said, his voice raw, "but I'm going to kick his ass."

"Please," she pleaded. "Listen to me."

"Here's what I see in you," he said. "I look in your eyes and I see how deeply you feel things. When you smile, I see so much joy that I'll do anything to be a part of it. You move and I see you using your talent to express who you are. I'm not fooling myself, Hayley. You make it impossible for me *not* to see you."

He reached out his free hand for hers, and she took it. "People don't . . ." She tried again. "I'm used to a lot of comparison."

He smiled. "Me too."

She'd never thought of it that way. Hayley had spent so much time trying to be enough, trying to meet the Icarus standard for beauty and talent, trying to heed the incessant critics in her head without letting any of them take over—but Nick had to know that struggle too. He was trying to dance in a world that wasn't built for him. How often had he stepped into the ring against his own insecurity and shame? She ached for him to believe his legs didn't matter, to trust that she wanted him and no one else. Maybe she could trust him too.

"In that case," she said, putting her arms around his neck, "now you can see me up close."

He brushed back her hair to better see the thin line under her eye. "You even have a sexy scar."

She laughed softly. "I fell off the monkey bars."

"Thank you for letting me close enough to see it."

Then, as Hayley hoped he'd do, Nick leaned forward, pulled her in, and kissed her.

Her mouth opened under his with an almost overwhelming thrill of relief. She'd been resisting him for all the right reasons, trying to fight the rhythm of their dance, first for Kevin's sake and then for Nick's. But now, as what was gentle became urgent and she pressed herself against him and thrilled at the broad, solid muscles of his shoulders and back, the undeniable truth of a man who was here for her and not going away—Hayley gave herself completely to their dance and thought of nothing else.

She had no idea how they managed to slow things down, but eventually their kiss ended and life started again as they looked at each other, wild-eyed and breathless.

"Do you want to come inside?" Hayley asked.

"Oh God, yes." Nick winced. "Um." He looked like he wanted to kick something. "I can't. It's a school night."

Shit. She'd completely forgotten he'd gone back to his actual job.

"I'd call in sick," he said apologetically, "but tomorrow's only their third day back."

"I'm such an idiot," she said. "I'll stay over at your place."

"No."

She stepped back. "No?"

She was hurt and confused, and Nick suddenly looked like a man who had to defuse a bomb.

"Just to be clear," he said, "I really want to come inside."

She smiled. "Okay."

"I mean it. I'm willing to crawl."

"Mrs. Hennessy would be very inspired."

He laughed.

"When we do this, I don't want to be exhausted," he said. "I don't want to rush it, and I don't want to wake up tomorrow morning and hurry out the door. I know you want to jump my bones, Ms. Burke, but I absolutely refuse to treat you like anything less than the best thing that's ever happened to me."

This was actually happening. A man was standing in front of her on a perfect summer night and saying these words. Hayley blinked back tears.

"Well, gee," she said. "I never thought a rejection could be sexy." She kissed him, gently. "Karaoke tomorrow?"

"Mm-hmm."

Hayley kissed his lips again, and his jaw and his neck.

"I'm coming home with you tomorrow night," she murmured. "And we're going to take our time."

37

When Nick stepped into the Squeaky Lion, his adrenaline spiked like he was catching sight of his first crush.

"Hey there, rock star." Hayley slung a towel over her shoulder. "They've got me behind the bar tonight."

He got the same hug as he did every Friday, the same smile. His frantic heartbeat was the only indication that they'd made out in front of his car less than twenty-four hours before.

Interesting.

"How're things?" he asked.

"Fantastic," she said. "I had a date last night."

"Uh-huh."

She stepped behind the bar and started organizing bottles. "Have you ever had a really good kiss, Nick? Like so good your legs go out from under you?"

"I don't know if you've noticed, but the thing about my legs—"

"Sometimes it just clicks. Like there's this switch that flips deep inside me and I'm *gone*. Totally his as long as he doesn't stop."

He fought a grin. "And that happened on your date?"

"God, no," she said. "He was better."

His mouth went dry. Hayley kept doing her job, looking for all the world as if she were bored.

"Better," he said.

She nodded. "He even tasted good."

He knew exactly what she was doing. Hayley was paying him back for his best material at the theater, except she was making it a hell of a lot sexier by making sure only the two of them were in on the secret. He'd spent the entire day trying to anticipate how things would go when he walked into the bar tonight, and this was better than he'd imagined.

"Can I get you some water?" Hayley asked innocently. "You look a little flushed."

"Maybe later," he managed. "I'm going to turn in some song slips." And find a way to retaliate.

"Sure thing," she said. "I'm here when you need me, baby."

38

Hayley snatched up the receiver when the phone rang behind the bar.

"Squeaky Lion!"

"Hal? Baby, I'm coming back."

It was Kevin. Her stomach clenched.

"No." She kept her voice low and scanned the room for Nick. "I'm at work."

He laughed. "That's why I called the bar, babe. I'm coming to get you."

"Kevin, you can't just come back. You can't do this at my job."

"It's all going to be okay. Talk soon. Love you!"

"Kevin!"

But he was gone. Hayley rooted around under the bar for a bucket, sure she was going to be sick.

He was coming back. He was coming here. But he wasn't coming home. Kevin had said he was coming to get her, not his stuff, and that meant he would be walking into the bar any minute now, expecting her to be okay because he was okay. Expecting her to leave with him. It would be a problem for her, for Nick, probably for the whole bar. She would be a problem, and why had she ever thought she could move on from Kevin so quickly and everything would be okay?

The bar was frustratingly bucket-free, and when she stood back up, Nick was returning to her.

"You okay?" he asked.

"Yeah." She swallowed, grinned. She *was* okay because he was here, and why get him worried about Kevin ahead of time?

Nick put his arms on the bar. "I forgot to tell you. I had a date last night too."

"Wow." She feigned nonchalance. "What're the odds?"

"Actually, I'm a pretty popular guy."

"I hadn't heard that."

He was unfazed. "It's been a little too long since I kissed her, though."

Hayley put a cup of water in front of him. "That's all I can do for you, champ. Patience is a virtue."

"Oh, I'll be fine," he said cheerfully. "I'm actually worried about her—she's probably pining for me right now."

Hayley smirked. "How good do you think you are?"

He shrugged. "It's just that our date got cut short last night."

"That's too bad."

"And singing isn't the most impressive thing I can do with my mouth."

Hayley's imagination clicked into high gear, and warmth built inside her as Nick grinned like the Cheshire cat.

"That was good." She drained the cup of water and nearly choked on it as she started laughing. "Didn't see that one coming."

He winked at her. "I'm here all night."

She flicked her towel at him. "Go greet your fans, Freeman."

Hayley felt like she was floating as she watched Nick walk away. Who cared if Kevin came back? Kevin had gone, and Nick was here, and she could do whatever she goddamn well wanted with her life, because she hadn't done anything wrong.

And what she wanted was her rock star.

39

Nick had been hanging on to the bar with both hands as he chatted with a regular, so he was only surprised, and not injured, when someone jostled him from behind.

"Oh!" One hand came over his shoulder while the other stayed near his hip. "I'm so sorry, Nick. Are you okay?"

He swallowed back his laughter and turned around. Hayley seemed genuinely concerned. "I guess I lost my balance," she said.

"It's okay," he said. "Sometimes I have that effect on women."

"Such big arms too! Do you work out?"

"Here, let me just . . ." Nick reached past her to grab the walker and roll it forward. "Oops."

He'd neatly nudged the back metal bar against her, trapping her between it and him.

"Gee, I'm sorry." Nick leaned into her. "What do we do now?"

She bit her lip. "Looks like you got me."

"Maybe if I . . ." He put a hand on her hip as if to move around her. "Nope, not enough room."

She countered with a step forward and to the side, so her mouth nearly touched his ear. "Take me out to your car."

Nick hurried to follow Hayley through the kitchen, trying to look like all of this was completely normal and expected. He was so focused on getting out of the building that he nearly ran into her when she stopped at the back door. Hayley peered cautiously into the parking lot.

"Okay," she said, "we're good. Hurry."

This was good. Best not to be seen. Nick hurried to his car, unlocked it, then stopped.

"What . . ." He was at a bit of a loss. "I mean, how do you want to . . ."

"Get in the back." Hayley was hushed and giddy. Nick climbed into the back seat, shutting the door after him, and then he listened to Hayley open the back and load the walker in. Also good. Wouldn't want anyone seeing an empty walker in the parking lot. He wouldn't have thought of that.

This was impressive on so many levels.

The door across from him flew open, and Hayley hopped in and slammed it behind her. She grinned at him, breathless, eyes bright.

Nick dove for her.

She twisted as he moved across the seat and met him halfway, kissing him hard. Nick kept his hand behind her head, thinking she would hit it on the window, but she neatly scooted forward and underneath him. Her legs locked around his waist.

"Holy shit," he breathed.

Hayley was radiating every bit of joy he'd seen the night he'd first caught sight of her, and now it was enveloping him too. He wasn't watching from a distance anymore.

She said, "C'mere, baby."

He moved in again. Her hands were everywhere, through his hair, down his back, past his belt to the seat of his jeans, slipping under his shirt and running upward. The feel of skin on skin drove him wild, but he didn't want to stop exploring her mouth, feeling her tongue greet his, letting her bite his lip for a change. Then his lips seemed to move on their own, finding her collarbone, her neck. His hand slipped under her T-shirt, brushed her stomach, caressed her breast. She moaned, rocked against him, and he almost couldn't take it. He reached around her and neatly unclasped her bra.

Hayley laughed, and he could feel her breath on his skin as she nibbled at his neck. "Very good!"

"Practice," he gasped, laughing along, because it wasn't a skill gained in the back of cars. It'd been one rainy Saturday afternoon in ninth grade, while Vicki's parents were gone for the day. They'd watched trashy TV movies, and he'd kept at it, working the clasp one-handed, and they'd whooped and cheered like he'd just won the Super Bowl when it finally came free. Then she'd fasten it again, and he'd work on it again. The funniest part was that Vicki never took off her sweater. He could barely believe it now, but for that afternoon, learning the trick was more important.

So many years later, this was the first time he'd thought of Vicki without a twinge of pain.

"Let's get out of here." He breathed in the scent of her skin.

Hayley ran her fingers through his hair. "What'll I tell them this time?" she teased. "Are you going to go play stuntman again?"

"Shit," he said, and she laughed. "Can't pull that two weeks in a row." He thought about it. "Can we?"

Hayley sat up, smiling as she shook her head. "How about we go back in and play rock star and waitress a little more, huh? We'll make it fun."

"You're amazing." He kissed her. "I'll get the walker. You're the one they need in there."

"I don't know." She winked at him as she fastened her bra. "They'll probably riot if you don't sing soon. Hurry back."

Hayley blew him a kiss as she went out the door, and in that moment, nothing in the world mattered to him but her.

He took his time stepping out of the car, working his way around to the back, unloading the walker. This was a night to be savored, after all. The first of many. There was so much of his life that would be better with her in it. He'd show her his classroom, and she'd join game night at the Becketts', no question. Maybe Mel would let Uncle Nick and Aunt Hayley take Rosie on adventures.

Nick heard footsteps behind him, and he turned to offer the newcomer a broad smile. Kevin smiled back.

Nick's stomach dropped so quickly he nearly doubled over. He'd known this would happen. Kevin Albee was here to ruin everything, and Nick wasn't going to let him.

"Hey, man." Kevin fished out a pack of cigarettes. "How're things?"

"Hey, Kevin." Nick kept his friendly grin as he shut the back door of the car. "What brings you to the Squeaky Lion?"

"I'm picking up Hal."

Nick's pulse was thudding in his ears. "In the middle of her shift? Is something wrong?"

"Not at all," Kevin said cheerfully, flicking his lighter. "I'm getting her back."

For as much as Nick wanted to stick Kevin's cigarette deep into his eye, Hayley's ex hadn't really done much to him personally, beyond being kind of a shitty friend. There was more to be gained here from staying civil.

Nick said, "She told me you left her."

"And now I'm back."

"You think the world stopped in the meantime?"

Kevin laughed, confused. "Of course not."

"I didn't get the impression she was waiting for you, Kev."

"Look, just because I said . . ." Kevin waved it off. "It doesn't matter. We had a problem. I fixed it."

"Except she's moved on."

Kevin looked like Nick had just said Hayley had left the planet, but Nick thought he saw some fear too. "Bullshit," Kevin said.

"You honestly think you fixed everything, don't you?" Nick shook his head. "It never occurred to you that she'd have a different opinion."

"It's barely been a week," Kevin said. "No way she moved on in seven days."

"I can't believe you let her go for seven minutes."

They glared at each other.

"Wasn't she hanging out with you?" Kevin found some footing. "She couldn't be with someone else if she was with you."

"Yep," Nick said. "And now she's with me."

He couldn't help but feel triumphant when he said it. At last he had something Kevin wanted.

Kevin laughed.

"With you," he said. "You really had me going, buddy. Well done."

Nick wanted to feel angry; his face burned with shame instead. "What's funny?"

Kevin shook his head, chuckling. "Look, man, I'm sure there are plenty of girls who'd be interested . . ."

"But nobody who can walk would ever want to be with me."

Kevin almost looked apologetic. "Nobody who can dance like her," he said.

Nick tried to shake it off, but Kevin's words felt true. Nick had said as much to himself.

"So you told me to hang out with her," Nick said dully, "because you knew she would never sleep with someone whose legs were all fucked up."

"I was at Vivez most nights." Kevin threw down his cigarette and ground it out. "And she was here. You know how many douchebags there are in bars like this."

"Because it's not like you could actually trust the woman who moved here with you. Or, ya know, spend more time with her."

"Enough, okay?" Kevin started for the back door. "I meant what I said. You were her friend, and I appreciate it."

"I'm more than that," he shot back.

Kevin glanced at him with pity in his eyes. "No, you're not."

"We were in the back of my car tonight." It was the only ammunition Nick had left, and it got Kevin to stop.

"You didn't," he said. "She wouldn't."

"So if you were to go in there and ask her whether it was her idea to climb into my backseat just before you got here, what do you think she'd say?"

Kevin stood stock-still, and Nick watched incredulity turn to rage.

"I've been out there," Kevin was shaking, "trying to make it all *work* again." He reached for the door. "And if that *bitch* thinks she can just—"

The breath he needed to finish got knocked right out of him. Nick had rushed forward and driven the palm of his hand into the center of Kevin's chest. Kevin was too surprised to brace himself, and Nick was propelled by anger. The force of the shove threw Kevin up against the side of a van.

"She's mine, you piece of shit!" Nick was yelling now, almost screaming. "She was in my bed the day you left, she'll be in my bed tonight, and there's nothing you can do about it!"

Kevin stared at him, mouth gaping, and then something else got his attention.

Nick's stomach dropped. He turned toward the building, already sure of what he'd see.

40

Hayley had decided to go back to the parking lot ten minutes after returning to the bar. Nick was taking too long to come back, and she didn't want him running into Kevin without her.

She had not expected to open the kitchen door and see her rock star shoving her ex into the side of a van.

Nick's words sent her stumbling against the door. Kevin looked angry when he noticed her standing there. Nick looked half dead.

"Is it true?" Kevin asked.

"It . . . I . . ." She was stammering.

"In his backseat," he said, disgusted. "Wow."

Kevin pushed off the van, and she wasn't sure who she was afraid for. Judging by the look on Nick's face, if Kevin decided to hit back, he wouldn't be making it out of the parking lot alive. Kevin settled for spitting at Nick's feet and walking away.

Hayley stepped into the lot. "What did you do?" she asked, dazed.

"I couldn't take it anymore." Nick's eyes were dull. "I couldn't."

"You *hit* him," she said absently. "You hit him, and then you told him I'd been cheating on him."

"I never said that."

She watched Kevin's car peel out of the parking lot. "What the fuck did you do?"

"He called you a bitch."

"Well, sure," she said. "I'd think I was one too."

"He wouldn't believe we were together."

"And you wanted credit," Hayley said. "Six years. Six years, and *not once* did I even *think* of cheating on him."

"I didn't—"

"What do you think he thinks now?" she demanded. "*I* barely believe we didn't fuck the night he left."

"He laughed!" Nick was shouting. "He only wanted me near you because he thought I was the one man you'd never want!"

"What difference does it make?" she said. "You and I weren't together! I wasn't supposed to want you."

Nick stared at her, stunned. "Hayley, he used me to keep you in line."

"And you were never going to be happy," she said, "until I *belonged* to you."

"Yes!" he exploded. "Better me than him!"

Hayley threw up her hands. "Well that's just great, Nick. Doesn't matter what happens to me or my reputation, as long as you screw him over."

"That son of a bitch has never done *anything* for you!"

"This from the son of a bitch who tried so hard to *win* me," she shot back. "You were terrified our breakup wouldn't stick, weren't you? You had to make absolutely goddamn sure."

Nick laughed. "I could have broken you up months ago," he said. "I'm the only reason you're still together."

"Don't." Her voice got dangerously low. "You don't know anything about us."

"The hell I don't," he said. "You're barely a couple. You live in the same house and you sleep in the same bed, and you're both thrilled I'm here because I keep you from noticing you barely like each other. He doesn't have to spend time with you or listen to you or tell you everything's going to be okay. I do that. And you're working so hard to believe you're still in love with him that you're the only one of the three of us who hasn't noticed you're getting your love and your sex from two different guys. But that's fine. It'll all be okay, because good old Nick will settle for whatever he can get, right?"

Hayley's entire body hurt, as if the pain were trapped and boiling inside her. Nick didn't care about her. He just wanted her body. Worse than that, he wanted to be able to claim her. Hayley was still reeling from her failures, but she had tried. She had fought. And she would not be reduced to someone else's accomplishment.

"No expectations, right?" Her voice was guttural, her hands clenched. "I'm the best thing that's ever happened to you, because Nicky Freeman's prom queen ran away, and now he'll say whatever he needs to if it means he can fuck me. You have no idea what it means to love somebody. No idea what it means to build a life with someone instead of whining about what you think you deserve."

Nick's eyes were ice-cold, his body rigid. The wall was up between them again.

He said, "Using a cripple was never going to fix you."

Hayley slapped him in the face, hard.

She said, "Fucking me was never going to make you less of a cripple."

41

Mel came out of the house as soon as Nick rolled into the Beckett driveway the following night. She was moving quickly, and he did not take that as a good sign.

As soon as he rolled down the window, she said, "What did you do?"

"What do you mean?" he asked.

"What did you do to Hayley?"

Nick had been looking forward to starting the evening on the moral high ground, and he was more than a little annoyed. "Who told you I did anything to Hayley?"

Mel's face told him she was not in the mood. "Nicky, you will get out of this car and tell us what happened."

Gavin was waiting by the foot of the stairs as Nick came through the front door. "She handed off Rose when we saw you coming," he explained.

"Rose wanted to talk to Hayley before bedtime." Mel kept talking as the men followed her to the kitchen. "I thought it might be better to text, in case she was busy."

"Mel, I don't know what she told you, but—"

"Please tell Rose I love her." Mel cut Nick off with her recitation. "Nick and I are over."

They faced off, with the sink at her back. Nick registered Gavin moving behind him toward the refrigerator.

"That's all it took?" Nick was indignant. "One text and you drag me out of my car?"

"I can see it on your face!" Mel retorted. "You were going to sneak Gavin out of here so you'd never have to tell me what you did."

She was absolutely right, and he didn't care. "Maybe talking to him is easier than talking to you," Nick said. "You think that might be a possibility, Mel? Or do you think I look forward to these interrogations of yours?"

He'd slowed her down a bit, but Mel was used to being able to read people. "I know you," she said.

"Really? Did you know she called me a cripple?"

"Okay." Gavin stepped between them. "I have beer. Sit down."

Mel didn't argue, and Nick welcomed the distraction. Gavin sat at the head of the table so that his wife and best friend were facing each other, on either side of him.

"Obviously, we don't know what happened," Gavin said. "I would appreciate you telling us. Both of us."

Nick stared across the table. "Interrupt me and I'm out, Mel. Swear to God."

She nodded, and then Nick had to decide what to say.

Lying to his friends had never really been an option, certainly not while he was looking them in the eyes. So he told them the truth. All of it—which meant he didn't have much of an excuse when he realized he wasn't painting a very flattering picture of himself.

"So then I left," he said finally. "There wasn't anything else to say."

Gavin and Mel were quiet. Nick didn't sense much sympathy, but he didn't see anger either. It might have been sadness.

"You can speak now." Nick tried to make it a joke.

Gavin went first. "I'm really sorry, buddy."

"Do you at least understand, though? I wasn't using her."

Gavin glanced at his wife. "You talk to him," Mel said. "I'm good."

"Come on," Nick said. "Kevin was being a dick."

"I get why you said what you said," Gavin told him.

"But?"

"But that doesn't mean you didn't hurt her."

Nick relaxed a bit. "I wish I hadn't. I wish we'd stayed in the bar."

"Why?" Mel asked. "Because then you'd have had an audience for your little pissing match?"

Nick looked at her coolly. "I didn't want him there at all."

"But since he was there, you wanted to make it crystal clear that you were better than him," she said. "God, Nicky, you're only fooling yourself."

It had been years of this. Years of her thinking she knew better than him, and it was going to stop right now. "Should I have called you?" he said, voice rising. "Asked your advice?"

"You should have kept your mouth shut and trusted Hayley to take care of it."

Nick pressed on the table so hard he half stood out of his chair. "She's been in a shitty relationship with this guy for six years. A guy who thinks cerebral palsy is code for 'can't get laid.'"

"Because that's what matters, isn't it? How many women want to have sex with you?" Mel shook her head sadly. "What happened to you?"

"Mel." Gavin was cautioning her, but it was too late.

Nick looked at both of them in disbelief. "I didn't find my soulmate in the choir room, Mel. Life happened to me while you were building your safe little family, and it turns out life sucks when you don't get married at twenty-one. Especially when women have better options than a guy with shitty legs. So yeah, it'd be nice to know that either one of them took me seriously."

"And if she took her clothes off, that would mean you were worth something."

Nick stood up. "Tell you what. I'll go out and find some other loser to take your advice, and maybe if he needs you desperately enough, he won't be such a disappointment."

Gavin moved to stop him. "Nick, don't."

"I'm done, man." Nick headed for the door.

"You had her, Nicky."

Nick turned around when Mel spoke.

"You had her," she said, "and you lost her because you hate yourself."

It didn't hurt. He couldn't feel a thing.

"You don't care about what I had at all," he said. "You want to sit here and take all the credit for Nicky Freeman's fairy-tale ending because then you can pretend we never left high school."

"I care," she insisted. "I've always cared. I care because the Nicky I know would never hurt somebody for the sake of his ego."

"The Nicky you know drops by to make you feel better about yourself."

Mel stepped back. "To make *me* feel better."

"Sure," he said. "You forget you gave up music, and I get to be there for a little girl who doesn't look at me like I'm damaged."

He'd seen Mel shocked and hurt. This was stunned.

"Rosie is three years old, Mel. She'll be okay. But you can't look away from her for a second because something might happen to her. You can't stop trying to control my life because you don't want to admit I'm not Nicky Freeman anymore. I can be Nicky for you, Mel. I'll make jokes and talk about the old days and pretend

I'm still the guy I was with Vicki. But then I have to go home. I have to be what everybody wants and try not to notice that nobody ever wants *me*. So you're not allowed to give me my part and then get mad about what I do when I'm not here playing it."

Mel watched him, speechless. "Vicki wanted you," she said.

"Vicki got tired of dating a cripple."

"You really think that."

"I can't believe you don't."

Mel looked past him, around him, and Nick wondered what she was searching for. Someone she used to know, maybe.

"Vicki left you because she was in California and you were here," she said finally. "She left because sometimes people leave, Nick. And you can keep trying to replace her with whoever you find in that bar, but those girls are never going to want you. Not really."

"Because I'm a cripple."

"Because the girls you bring home for the night don't want to find out who you are. And you're trying to show them someone else."

Nick was too angry to back down, but there wasn't anything to attack in what she said.

"Hayley sees what I see," Mel continued softly. "But if you truly believe I'm wrong, maybe you should leave."

So he did.

Nick could hear them talking in the hallway as he made his way down the front steps.

"You're not going out with him," Mel said. "Not after that."

"I'm going to sit with him in the driveway," Gavin said, "and then he's going home."

"Did you know about this?"

"No, Mel. But I do know he's still our friend."

For a while, Nick and Gavin just sipped their beers.

Eventually Nick said, "These lawn chairs are so much nicer than the ones your parents had."

"It's true," Gavin said. "I've really made something of myself."

The neighborhood was quiet, and they were running out of daylight. The view wasn't exactly scenic—just the cars in other people's driveways, really—but sitting like this felt like it had in high school, when they were surveying the world of possibilities before them.

"I should go back in there."

"No," Gavin said.

"I really pissed her off this time. That's not me."

"Actually, you hurt her. You made her feel like you spend time with her out of pity." Gavin idly tapped his bottle against his knee. "Go back in there now and you'll just make it worse."

Nick studied his friend, who appeared to be tracking a cyclist returning home across the street.

"How are you not furious with me?" he asked.

Gavin thought about it. "I'm not exactly happy," he said, "but I think most of that needed to be said. By both of you."

Nick didn't have a reply.

"You know what's funny?" Gavin continued. "You both get each other really well. Better than you realize, I think. This would've happened sooner, except you both thought you were being nice by not pushing each other's buttons."

"So she really thinks I'm horrible?"

"Of course not. She just thinks you're an idiot."

"And what do you think?"

Gavin took his time. "I think we're all a little more scared than we let on."

Nick felt the humidity in the air and wondered if a rainstorm was on the way. It would be a fitting end to the day.

"You have to understand how much she looked up to you," Gavin said.

Nick wasn't sure he'd heard correctly. "Who? Mel?"

"Absolutely. We both did."

"You *both* did?" Nick laughed. "Come on."

"I'm telling you, man, I've never seen you in a room where you didn't know what to say. Plus that Rain Man recall of yours. Do you remember when Cassie Ellis came to town?"

"Sure." Nick stared at the sky as he thought back. "It was a month or two into sophomore year, maybe? I think she used a calculator just to make the rest of us feel better about ourselves."

Gavin nodded. "Do you remember how Mel wanted to ask her for tutoring? She waited for you to introduce her, because you'd been palling around with Cassie for a solid week."

"I was trying to make her laugh. Cassie would've talked to Mel."

"Mel thought Cassie would think she was stupid."

"Not a chance," Nick said. "Cassie was a sweetheart. She just didn't do well with people."

"See? That's what I'm talking about. You could connect with people like that. I had to double-check whether Mel still liked me half the time, but you could remember the favorite song of every kid in the special ed class. We'd just stand back and watch you move."

"You mean that time I let Jeremy Dolan push the walker?"

Gavin laughed. "Definitely that. But I mean the way you worked a room. It was like you were Apollo floating through the ring."

"Or dancing."

"Yeah. Or dancing."

Hayley had said dancing was reacting. Being in tune with the world.

"Guess I don't do that so well anymore," Nick said.

"Oh, you've still got it," Gavin said. "But I think you need it more now than you used to."

"Things changed."

"I know they did. I'm sorry I wasn't there for you."

"What?" Nick turned toward his friend. "You've always been there, Gavin."

"Yeah," Gavin said, "but I got distracted. You were down for the count after Vicki, and I thought it'd be enough to be there if you asked. *I* should've asked, man."

"No. You had your own stuff."

They watched the neighbors' terrier sprint out of his house and test the limits of his leash. "You know you were you before you met her, right?" Gavin asked him. "Vicki wasn't the reason people loved you."

"Maybe not, but she was the reason I was happy, you know?" Nick let out a long breath. "And then she calls, and she says we're moving in different directions, and I can't fix it, because she knew we were done before she picked up the phone."

Gavin sighed. "I wish you'd told me you thought it was because of the walker."

"Of course it was. She wouldn't let me live on a boat."

"That's not what you told me she said."

"And trying to find dates after that, man . . ." Nick laughed ruefully, then sat up straighter. "What do you mean, that's not what she said?"

"You told me Vicki said she wouldn't make you live a life on the ocean."

"Exactly. Same thing."

Gavin shook his head. "Not at all."

"Okay." Nick put his bottle on the ground. "I know you love your word games, but could we not?"

"Let's say you weren't disabled," Gavin persisted. "How would you feel about living on a boat?"

"Could be fun."

"Bullshit. You'd hate every second of it."

"I mean, if Vicki had asked me . . ."

Gavin pointed at him. "And that's exactly what she meant. You like to be rooted, Nick. You pick a place and you make it yours. Your classroom, the bar, Vivez . . . hell, this house. My family. You invest yourself in places and people, and you take pride in being the guy people can count on to be there. It was never about Vicki letting you bring the walker on a boat. She knew she could make you commit to a life on the ocean, where you'd never get to be who you are."

Nick blinked. "Huh."

Gavin leaned back in his chair. "Funny thing happens when you're actually treated normally," he said. "Sometimes people hurt you for normal reasons."

Nick nodded slowly, remembering his last conversation with Vicki. He could hear the emotion in her voice, the pain of having to hurt him.

"We'd been together for so long," he said. "I just thought marriage was what happened next, like with you guys."

"Let me tell you something about marrying your high school sweetheart," Gavin said. "All those mistakes you make in your twenties, all that time figuring yourself out? You're doing that together. Things actually get harder when you're husband and wife."

"Really?" Nick said. "I always thought . . ." He trailed off. "I guess I thought it'd be great not to have to worry about her leaving," he said sheepishly. "Since you take vows and everything. Sounds stupid."

Gavin smiled. "Hey, you know I was all about the vows."

"How could I forget? If Mel had let you read what you wrote, the ceremony would've been six hours long."

Gavin chuckled as he took a drink. "As great as it is hearing her promise not to leave, it might be even better when you realize you can't leave either."

"Don't tell me you've considered it."

"Not for a second. I'd marry her again today," Gavin said. "Best decision I've ever made. I've never considered leaving because I'd never want to. But if she can't leave, and I can't leave, that means we've got to get through the hard stuff together. So sometimes you end up patrolling the front yard after *Breaking Bad* and thinking life would be easier if you didn't have to be in your bathrobe in the dark."

Nick laughed. "I wouldn't have recommended the show if I knew she'd send you searching for drug dealers."

"Sure you would've." Gavin got quiet. "Sometimes it's much worse than that."

Nick stared at the darkening sky. He knew what Gavin meant, but he couldn't say the words. Couldn't say the babies' names.

"You were right," Gavin said. "We leaned on you a lot. We'd laugh with you, and then we'd go to bed, and she'd just sob. Nothing I could do. Doesn't matter if a miscarriage is nobody's fault. I wanted it to be mine just so she wouldn't blame herself."

The Beckett house had felt submerged in sadness back then. Nick felt tendrils of it returning now.

"You were never a burden," he said softly. "It's just that I had no one to come home to after."

His friends had dealt with real pain. Hayley had dealt with real pain. They had chosen not to leave. All he had chosen was rage.

Nick said, "I should've just kept my mouth shut."

"I don't know," Gavin said with a smirk. "I'd have been disappointed if you hadn't at least shoved him into that van."

"You're just bummed you didn't see it happen."

"Absolutely. He deserved it."

"Hell yes." Vindication felt good. "So why is Mel so pissed?"

"Mel doesn't think you need to prove anything to Kevin."

Nick studied the dim outlines of Rosie's chalk artwork on the driveway. "I really wanted him to know," he said. "He needed to know that Hayley wanted me. He insulted her, he treated me like less than a person, and all Hayley's upset about is what *I* did?"

"Maybe she didn't understand."

"What's not to understand?"

"Well, sex isn't really the important part, is it?" Gavin asked. "It didn't matter if he thought you'd actually slept with her. It was just insulting that he thought she'd never give you a second look."

Nick nodded. "Yeah," he said, after a moment. "Usually the sex is *all* that matters, you know? But . . . it's weird, but it felt like she'd already given me more than that. I just wanted things to go well, and then this dickhead shows up and says I'm not worthy of her. He decides to break her heart and walk away, but I'm not worthy of her because my legs don't work."

"So would it be safe to assume," Gavin said, "that Hayley, having just been accused of cheating immediately after hearing you declare that she belongs to you, might not have been in the best place to truly understand what it's like for you to be told you're not a man?"

Nick started laughing. "That was your teacher voice," he said. "If this is how you lead class discussions, I should come by more often."

Gavin smiled. "I just call it as I see it."

Maybe he could call her, explain things. He could apologize for what he'd said to Kevin. But could he apologize for what he'd said to her? He'd been mean, but he wasn't sure he'd been wrong.

He wasn't sure Hayley and Kevin hadn't been using him, consciously or not, and he wasn't going to be used again.

"Using a cripple was never going to fix you."

"Fucking me was never going to make you less of a cripple."

Nick said, "What's so great about knowing you can't leave?"

Gavin neatly flicked his bottle cap upward, then snatched it out of the air with the same hand. "Getting through the hard stuff makes you stronger," he said. "Not just individually. If you do it right, it fuses you together."

What was it Hayley had said?

"All the bad stuff makes the good stuff sweeter."

42

Hayley was lying on the couch when her phone started vibrating. It had been a bad idea to keep the stupid thing on at all; there was no reason to interrupt a perfectly good evening of staring at the ceiling after yesterday's disaster in the parking lot. But she knew too many people who might eventually show up in person if their calls went unanswered, so she dug the phone out of the couch cushions. She groaned when she saw who was calling.

"Hello," she mumbled.

"Hayley." Her mother always sounded so commanding on the phone, as if she'd just finished teaching a motivational seminar. "Did I wake you?"

"No."

"Good. We were hoping we could come see the show again next weekend. Your father says we need to invite Nick."

She could say Nick was sick. No, that wouldn't work—he could get better by next weekend. Nick was out of town next weekend, and *Kevin* was sick, so it'd be better if they stayed away from Columbus for the next decade, maybe. Until she felt like getting off this couch.

But maintaining lies took energy, and at the moment she really didn't give a shit. "They're gone, Mom. There's no point."

"What? Who's gone?"

"Kevin and Nick. So you really can't invite one to a show that the other's not in, because I fucked everything up."

"Hayley Michelle."

"Shit." Her mother didn't like it when she cursed. "I will call you," Hayley said. "I will call you and answer all your questions, and we will both agree on all the things I should've done so you could be proud of me, but right now I'm very busy not doing any of that, so it'd be wonderful if we could postpone."

There was a long pause. "Your father and I are coming to see you."

43

"Nick Freeman." Linda Brandazzio leaned against the doorframe of the tiny room. "Just the man I wanted to see."

Nick turned from the shelf of binders. "You wanted to see me?"

"Absolutely," she said. "Which doesn't mean you need to be rooting through here on a Sunday morning."

Nick didn't really need to be doing anything, but last night with the Becketts had left him unsettled, and being at Vivez Dance was oddly soothing. And if Hayley Burke was going to be anywhere near Vivez, it didn't seem likely to happen at ten in the morning on a Sunday.

"I want to do something with these binders," he said.

"For free," Linda said. "During the weekend."

He smiled. "The door was unlocked."

"Yeah, but I'm *always* here," she said. "How's your real job going?"

"Still getting to know the new kids. Hoping I've got a few like your son."

She chuckled. "Ben's hoping all of his professors are like you."

Because he was such an inspirational person, no doubt. Because doing a decent job teaching kids meant more if he had a disability. But there was no way he'd be able to convince this woman that there was anything wrong with that point of view, and Nick was a little surprised to find he didn't particularly want to. Linda had made his life better, and her son had been hungry to learn, and if he made the Brandazzios happy just by existing, so be it. Sometimes it was about how other people interpreted his dance.

"Been taking a lot out of you?" Linda asked him.

"Hmm?"

"You look tired," she said. "Must take a lot to get the classroom up and running every year."

"Nah." Nick shrugged it off. "It's work, but it's worth the effort."

"Wouldn't want to do any work that wasn't."

"Sure."

She was working up to something, he could see it. Maybe a little afraid, maybe a little unsure, but definitely choosing an approach.

"Can you do me a favor?" Linda finally said. "I want to ask you a question, and I think it's important, but I don't want to insult you."

Great. This was not the day for this, but he was an ambassador to the able-bodied, after all. If he didn't let her ask now, she might be awkward around him forever.

"Ask away," he said. "I won't take it personally."

Linda nodded. "We all took to you from the start," she said, "and you always seem happy to be here. But I've been thinking a lot about your perspective this summer, and there's something I'd really like to know."

"Go on," he prompted. "It's okay."

"Is it difficult for you to be in such a physical environment?" she asked. "Has anyone at Vivez given you reason to believe you don't belong here?"

"Well . . ." He tried not to hesitate. "Those are two different questions."

"It's just that so much of what goes on here is a celebration of the body," she went on. "There's a lot more to it, of course, but that's how our joy manifests itself. I want to invite absolutely everybody into that, and I think I've got some good ideas, but I've got to wonder if it's . . . I don't know, cruel? Is it insulting to think you would get a lot out of what we do here?"

"You mean because I can't participate the way others can," Nick said gently.

Linda managed to look both relieved and guilty. "Yes."

All of a sudden he was back in that booth across from Kacey with a K, watching Hayley dance for the first time. Watching Cal and Mimi on stage. Watching Hayley in the rehearsal room.

"It can be hard," Nick said. "But I love it here. I love the people and I love what you do, because of the music and the energy and the dance—all of it. And I'm beginning to think I'm uniquely suited to appreciate dance, actually. I can't do it like you all can, so I don't take it for granted. So, no, I don't think it's insulting or cruel to invite anyone here, even if sometimes it does hurt to want to be more like you guys."

Linda relaxed. "What about my other question?"

Nick stalled. "Has anyone ever given me reason to believe I don't belong here."

"Yes."

"What would make you think that?"

"I hear things," Linda said. "Like maybe someone who no longer works here told you that you can't do what we can."

"If he's not here anymore, I don't see how it matters."

Linda was calm but firm. "It matters," she said, "because that's not the sort of attitude that belongs here. So I would want to make that abundantly clear, and think very hard if ever that person wanted to come back. Or anyone associated with that person."

Nick tried to hide his surprise. This was an unexpected opportunity. If he didn't want Hayley at Vivez, then this was how to keep her out. If she really was using him, he could make sure she paid for it. It was time to think hard and speak up. It was time to voice his anger.

His anger was gone.

It was like returning to an animal's cage and finding it empty. Nick had been so angry at Hayley's reaction, her preference for Kevin, her fear for her reputation. But now all he could see was someone who was quick to forgive a man she'd loved for six years, a man she probably still loved. Nick Freeman had a lifetime of experience studying people, and as hard as he tried, he couldn't make himself believe someone who held him and kissed him and smiled at him like Hayley Burke could ever think he was anything less than a man worthy of love.

"Kevin and I didn't always get along," Nick said, "but that wasn't entirely because of his perspective."

Linda nodded. "Maybe it had to do with a mutual friend?"

"It might have," Nick said carefully. "If you're concerned, I can tell you Kevin was the only one here who ever came close to treating me poorly, so I don't think you need to talk to anybody. I wouldn't rehire him if I were you, but I really don't think he's coming back. And as far as Kevin's girlfriend is concerned, I think she would be a perfect fit here."

Linda smiled. "I think so too. Thanks, Nick."

"Thank *you*," he assured her. "It's really been a pleasure working here."

"Oh, the pleasure's mine," she said. "Especially since I can tell Ben I've made up for making a fool of myself last time."

Nick looked at her quizzically. "You never did that with me."

To his astonishment, Linda looked thoroughly embarrassed. "Okay," she said. "I've been arguing with myself about whether to even tell you this, but I was so excited to meet you at the senior awards ceremony. Ben prepped me, you know—found pictures of all of his teachers in his yearbook and showed them to me, and I just could not wait. So we get there, and I just *descend* on this poor man at the reception. I tell him I wanted to thank him for getting Ben so excited about learning and for showing my son how math could help him understand the world around him. I tell this guy he's so incredibly inspirational for dedicating his life to helping kids like my son, and if I could ever do anything for him, anything at all, then I would be personally insulted if he didn't ask. And of course this poor man is getting more and more confused, and it turns out I've been pretty much bowing at the feet of the *women's basketball coach*. I was so intent on getting it all out that I guess I just went up to the guy who looked most like a math teacher!"

Nick was so mystified by her story that he'd started to unconsciously lean against the shelf behind him, and now he had to catch himself before he toppled the thing.

"You thought Tony Snyder was me?" he asked.

"I couldn't tell you," she said. "I'd just given this whole speech to the coach, and I was too embarrassed to do it again and claim that I thought so highly of you when I obviously didn't even know who you were."

Nick's smile started slowly and grew until he was grinning from ear to ear. Linda had considered him inspirational before she'd ever known about his cerebral palsy. And if Ben hadn't even thought to mention CP, Mr. Freeman must've been an excellent teacher.

Nick had been profoundly wrong, and it felt fantastic. "Don't worry about it," he told Linda.

"Oh, don't be nice."

"No, really," he said. "Mixing me up with Coach Snyder was probably the nicest thing you could have done for me. That story is a gift."

Linda smiled, still a little reluctant. "You're going to have to explain that one to me," she said. "And after you do that, I've got some easier questions for you."

44

Her dad had texted to say he would be arriving with Mom at eleven Sunday morning, which meant their car would be in front of Hayley's house by eleven at the absolute latest. Hayley was not going to keep them waiting, even just for the time it took her to answer the door. She couldn't afford to start this visit off on the wrong foot.

The milkshakes threw her off a little, though.

"That diner had mint chocolate chip." Mom was very pleased as she climbed the front steps. "Not everybody has mint chocolate chip."

"Or blueberry." Dad handed Hayley a giant Styrofoam cup and kept one for himself. "I got blueberry for the antioxidants."

Mom gave him a look. "You don't even know what antioxidants are."

"I don't have to know what they are. I know they're good for me."

"Not when they're buried under all that sugar."

"You don't know that. They could counteract the sugar."

Thirty-three years together, and they still wanted to tease each other after a four-hour car ride. This was the kind of love she wanted. This was the love she could never seem to get for herself.

Hayley started to cry.

Mom embraced her from one side and Dad from the other. "It'll all be okay," Mom said.

"Sure it will," Dad agreed. "We'll go back and get some anti-oxidants for you too."

Hayley giggled through her sobs, and then she was laughing in her parents' arms for the first time in far too long.

"And then I went back to work," she said later. "That's it."

They were on the couch now, and the Styrofoam cups had been drained as Hayley told her parents everything. It was like cleaning out a wound. Mom and Dad already knew the worst part: Both Kevin and Nick were out of her life. There wasn't any point in lying about why. Better to get it all out so nothing festered.

"Is there anything we can do?" Dad asked.

Hayley shrugged. "I'll be fine."

"Okay." He clapped his hands on his thighs and stood up. "I'm going to tackle the laundry."

"Dad, you don't need to do that."

"I don't?" he said amiably. "So everything's squeaky clean upstairs, huh?"

He winked at her, and she waved him on. They both knew her room was a mess on a good day.

"He needs something to do," Mom said as Dad climbed the steps.

"Uh-huh." Hayley braced herself. "And you wanted him to go so you could talk to me."

Mom shifted on the cushion, brushing her legs with her hands, as if wrinkles or crumbs would ever dare to mar her slacks.

"I wanted to talk to you about your father and me," she said. Here it came. "Mom," Hayley pleaded. "Can we skip this?"

"No, I don't think we can."

"Grandma Marjorie let you do whatever you wanted," Hayley recited wearily, "and you wish every day that you'd had more boundaries growing up, so I should be happy you care enough to give them to me. If it weren't for Dad showing up, you'd be a mess now. I could tattoo the story on my arm at this point. Doesn't mean I'm ever going to find someone to love me like Dad loves you."

"I haven't explained it well enough."

"You've explained it, Mom." Hayley slumped. "You're smarter than me, and I need to find a good man."

"No," Mom said quietly. "I'm not. And falling in love with your father wasn't what saved me."

Hayley's head shot up. Carolyn Burke had never said these words—not to her daughter, at least.

"You know I met your father in a bar," she continued. "You know he was there with his friends; you know we went to different schools. But you don't know that he came to my table because I was crying into a margarita pitcher that I had emptied all by myself."

Hayley stared. "Mom, what—"

"I honestly don't remember all the courses I took that year," she said. "All of the different subjects—flailing around, trying to find what I wanted to do, and somehow in the midst of that mess a very nice young man had become very interested in me. He'd asked me to marry him that night, but I couldn't give him an answer because I was also seeing someone else at the same time. And then I met your dad."

Mom was holding her gaze, articulating each word clearly. At first Hayley was amazed at how calm she was, until she realized Mom was forcing out one word at a time.

"You know your father could have a conversation with a lamppost," she said. "He came over and asked me what was wrong, and I told him. I told him about the classes and the proposal. I told him how utterly lost I was, because for some reason it was easy to talk to this complete stranger."

Hayley smiled. "Only Dad."

"Only Dad." Mom smiled too. "He listened, like he always does, and then he said, 'What makes you happy?' I tried to dive back into it all and explain what I liked and didn't like, what I couldn't decide, but he held up his hand. He said, 'In life, what makes you happy?'"

Hayley held her breath. "What did you say?"

"Stories." There was a gleam in Mom's eyes. "That was all I could think of. I told him I liked to get lost in stories. Can you guess what he said?"

Hayley thought about it, then tried her best imitation of his voice. "Let's make that happen."

Mom nodded. "Exactly. So we made a plan. I started my English lit major, which I'd dipped my toes in before, except this time when things got boring or difficult, I'd call your dad. He'd remind me why I was working so hard, and he celebrated with me when I knew I wanted to teach. But we weren't dating then, Hayley. He was just a really good friend who helped me understand what I wanted and how to get it."

"Mom." Hayley didn't know what to say. "Why didn't you tell me?"

After a moment, Mom said, "I didn't think you'd listen to my advice if you knew all the mistakes I made. I thought it was enough to tell you what I'd learned. Otherwise you might decide you wanted to make all my mistakes for yourself."

"You thought I'd have *less* respect for you because of the mistakes you made? Mom, look at who you became." Hayley realized what she was saying, then hung her head. "God. I am totally your daughter."

"You are," Mom said. "You are creative, and you're passionate. But you get your resolve from your dad. That's a real strength."

Hayley snorted. "Why? So I can keep making the same mistakes? You moved forward. You got stronger."

"Hayley Michelle," her mother said gently, "you have never done a bad job at anything you've cared about. Ever."

Hayley sat back, shocked.

"It reminds me of Dad's projects," Mom said. "How you used to laugh?"

Hayley grinned and imitated her father's bellowing, "Oh, for Pete's sake!"

Mom nodded. "You'd run in, and he'd be holding the wrong nail or the wrong board, and he'd explain to you why he needed the right one, and you'd think it was the funniest thing."

"He acted like the world had tricked him!" Hayley laughed. "Like he'd brought the right thing home, and it'd magically changed."

"So you'd go to the store with him and get the right part."

"And we'd always go for ice cream after."

Mom paused. "Your dad is the best craftsman I know," she said, "but if he tries to put the wrong nail into the wrong board, he's going to fail every time."

The words hurt, but Hayley knew she had to pay attention now. She had to really listen to her mother if she was ever going to change.

"That's a pretty good analogy," she said gamely. "Am I the board or the nail?"

"Hayley," Mom said, "when your dad came up with the wrong nail or board, it wasn't because they were broken. There wasn't anything wrong with the nail or the board. They were just made to fit somewhere else."

Not at Icarus, though. Not with Kevin. Not with Nick.

"Persistence comes so much easier to you than it does to me," Mom said. "You press on. You work so hard at your job and your relationships, and you'd keep going even if it meant walking through a hurricane, if you thought it was the right thing to do. It never occurred to me that you would press on because you thought we wouldn't be proud of you if you didn't. We've always been proud of you, Hayley. Always."

It was too much. Hayley was used to navigating conversations with Mom by picking a reaction she'd approve of, but now she was too overwhelmed to react at all.

"You always seemed so disappointed," she said.

Mom reached out and took Hayley's hand. "I wasn't disappointed," she said. "Not with you. When I pushed—really pushed—it wasn't because I thought you'd make a mess of things or that you wouldn't survive. I was worried that you'd get hurt or that you were already hurting, and I hated that I couldn't change anything. It didn't matter if I tried not to say anything, because you'd always see it. I'm capable of many things, but I've never been able to turn away when someone I love is hurting. Especially not you."

Hayley looked at her mother. She'd studied her own face in the mirror countless times, trying to see how much had been passed down from this woman who always seemed so confident, never sensing the similarities she couldn't see.

"Do you ever wish you could turn away?" she asked. "Not care?"

"Of course," Mom said. "But I have a daughter who wouldn't dare do such a thing. I get my courage from her."

"Me?" Hayley could barely get the word out.

Mom nodded. "Everybody fails, Hayley. But it's never been because you didn't try hard enough. You're not capable of that."

It took a moment to really hear her, to understand and believe, and then Hayley was crying. "I always want too much," she said. "I want too much, and then I'm the problem, and people get hurt."

"A job you love and a man who loves you? You deserve at *least* that much." Tears came to her mother's eyes. "You're worth that and so much more."

Hayley wrapped her mother in a hug. She whispered, "I love you so much."

"I love you too, sweet girl."

Hayley heard her father clump back down the steps, and the two women took a hurried moment to dry their eyes.

"The thing is," he said, "there's no way to tell what's clean and dirty up there, and I didn't really want to try too hard." He took in the sniffling Burke women. "I can get more milkshakes."

"Not yet," his wife said. "I was about to ask our daughter what makes her happy."

45

Nick had never rung the Becketts' doorbell in his life, so when he did, Mel opened the door with the same sort of guarded surprise she'd show a magazine salesman.

"Nicky." Not altogether icy, but cool.

"You were right, Mel. I lost her." He started to crumble. "I had her and I lost her."

Before he could do anything to stop it, Nick was sobbing uncontrollably.

"Oh, Nicky." Mel flew out the front door and wrapped him up.

"I'm sorry, Mel. I'm so sorry."

"I'm sorry too," she said.

Nick took a seat at the kitchen table, and Mel brought him tissues.

"I would do anything for you guys," he said. "And Rosie. I never want you to think—"

"You don't need to prove it, Nicky," she said. "I know you were upset."

"That's no excuse."

"I'm telling you I don't need one."

Nick wiped his eyes. "I don't deserve that, Mel."

"Can we forget about who deserves what?"

He looked at her for a long moment, then nodded.

"There have been times when I depended on you too much," she said. "Everything would go crazy, but I knew Gavin would always be here, and you'd always be Nicky Freeman. I wanted you to be the same, even when things changed. That wasn't fair."

"I'll be that guy again."

"Don't," she said.

"But you said—"

"I like you better now." Mel had never lied to him, not even when it probably would've been better for both of them, and he could tell she wasn't starting now.

"I was talking to Linda Brandazzio this morning, and it turns out I'm a pretty good teacher."

Mel smiled. "I'm glad you heard it when she told you."

"It's like everybody gives me glimpses of who I am," he said. "And that should be good news. All I'd have to do is just believe you or the Vivez crew, and then people like Kevin wouldn't matter, because I would know I was better than he thought I was. But it's Kevin's opinion that sticks with me. I've known you for years, I trust you with my life, but somehow it's easier to see myself as he sees me."

"If you expect the worst," Mel said, "at least you can be ready for it."

"Fortune cookie?"

"That's a Mel Beckett original." She stood up and headed for the refrigerator. "You'd think it'd be the other way around, wouldn't you? Like we'd be so eager to believe we're great that we'd ignore anyone who didn't confirm it. But if you start expecting good things, you can be disappointed."

"Like if you care about it too much, it might not happen."

"Exactly." Mel brought milk to the table. "Rose has me bargaining for each day. I'll start thinking about her prom or her wedding, and I'll cut it off. I'll remind myself she may not be around then, so I should be grateful for today."

The thought of Rosie dying nearly undid him. "If I had known . . ."

"What?" she asked. "You'd pull your punches? I can't write or try to book a gig without feeling like I'm betraying her by loving something else. It feels like I'm not grateful enough for her." She got three glasses from a cabinet. "But what am I teaching Rose if I'm too afraid to live *my* life?"

"Rose will always know you love her more than music."

"I know." Mel grinned. "So I should show her how much I love music."

Nick took a shaky breath. "Mel, I'm really scared I'm going to keep hurting people."

"People hurt each other all the time."

"Mel."

Mel set down the glasses. "You're not mad at Hayley anymore, and you're not mad at me, so now you think you have to punish yourself."

"I can't just—"

"Yes, you can." She set a cookie jar on the table. "Make your apologies, but if you're really worried about doing more damage, you need to forgive yourself and move the hell on." She sat next to him. "Your problem," she said, "is that you're too smart."

Nick laughed. "Is that it?"

"You know people," she said. "And you're right about people often enough that you expect to be right about them all the time. If Vicki didn't love you, you figured no one could, so you thought you'd turn yourself into someone people would like. Except you might hate lying more than anything in the world, Nicky. So you don't trust the people who *do* like you, because you think you've tricked them, and you hate yourself for pretending. You're never more miserable than when you're bringing home those poor girls you think you want."

You're clearly miserable. What're you doing here?

"I can't just stop being nice to people."

"What would change?" Mel asked. "If you stopped being the star of the Nick Freeman show, what would change? Are you going to start throwing everybody into vans now?" She saw his embarrassment. "I'm sorry."

"No." He chuckled. "That's fair."

"I don't know where you got this idea that some horrible person is going to come out if you stop pretending," she said. "I've never met that guy."

"He was here last night."

"Oh, please." Mel waved a hand. "You were pissed last night exactly *because* no one was letting you be yourself. It's ridiculous, by the way, that it took a fight for us to be honest with each other. I'm not letting that happen again."

This was why he loved her so much. Melanie Beckett, protecting her friendships through sheer force of will.

"Why do you like me?" he asked her.

Mel narrowed her eyes. "That is just about the dumbest question ever."

"Seriously," he persisted. "Why do you like me? I screw up my chance with someone who actually matters. I come in here like you're the reason my life is so hard. I act like I know better than you when it comes to raising your own child. And now you're telling me you like me better than the kid you grew up with in high school. That kid was happy, Mel. That kid liked people."

Mel plucked four napkins from a nearby holder. "I *loved* high school," she said. "I needed someone to make me smile, and I ended up with one guy who loved me and another who was better than anyone I'd ever seen at making people happy. But you didn't have to make a choice then, Nicky. You loved your life, so why not make someone's day? It's different when you decide to be here for us even when you don't have the energy. It's different when you're there for Hayley even when it hurts you. The Nick Freeman I know now does the right thing when he doesn't have to, or even want to. That's why I like you better. And you absolutely like people, Nicky. You just don't want to admit you're human enough to not like all of them."

Nick watched Mel position the napkins in front of four seats. "So maybe we can start hoping for better things."

"I will if you will," she said.

He exhaled. "So how do I get her back?"

"You don't need my help with that."

"You're actually passing on an opportunity to advise me on my love life?"

Mel sat down. "If you get her back, it's going to be because you listened to nobody but yourself."

"Because that's worked beautifully so far."

"Look at the stuff that really matters to you," she said. "Rose. Your students. Those kids at Vivez. You're not putting on a show for them."

He hadn't put on a show for Hayley either.

"Here's the thing, Nicky," Mel said. "No one's really that good at hiding. People can already see you. We love the real you, I promise. You just have to trust that you're worth it."

After a moment, Nick said, "You got it wrong back there."

"What?"

"You ended up with two guys who love you."

Nick thought he saw tears in her eyes, but Mel snatched up a tissue and turned away quickly. "Don't think this gets you early cookies," she said.

"What?" Nick looked incredulously around the table. "Then what's all this stuff for?"

"This is me getting ready," she said. "Once Gavin and Rose are home with the pizza, then we can all have the cookies my daughter baked for her Uncle Nick."

46

Hayley called Kevin at two o'clock Thursday morning.

He picked up on the second ring. "Shouldn't you be with Nick?"

"I never asked if you cheated on me," she said.

"I'm not the one who cheated."

"It wasn't like I didn't want to know," she said. "I just never thought of it. Which is crazy."

"Instead of trying to make this my fault, why don't you—"

"Take responsibility for my own mistakes?" Hayley said calmly. "I'm trying to. But maybe that's not what you were going to say. Go ahead. Tell me what to do."

She rubbed one bare foot against her leg under the covers to warm it up. She'd confused him. There wasn't any challenge in her voice, but it must've seemed like a trick question.

After a while, Kevin said, "You can't expect me not to be angry about this."

"I should expect you to be angry with me anytime somebody tells you I've cheated?"

"I saw it on your face."

"Saw what? That I had sex with Nick?"

"Yes."

"Well, I haven't," she said. "And now this is about whether you believe me."

Silence.

"I was so pissed," she said. "I hated him because I thought he'd ruined what you thought of me. But how could Nick possibly do that, Kev? How could some guy you made small talk with for three months make you so sure I cheated?"

"You're taking his side now."

"I think you'd actually like that," she said. "It'd keep things simple."

"It's either him or me."

She shut her eyes and took a breath. Had Kevin always thought he'd been competing for her? "How about neither?" she asked. "How about I stay away from anybody who thinks I'm not responsible for my own decisions?"

She wished she'd put glow-in-the-dark stars on the ceiling, like she had done when she was a kid. Probably not something common when adults shared a bed, but now that he was gone, it'd be nice to think of an unknown universe extending light years beyond her bedroom.

"When did you know you loved me?" she asked him.

"Hal . . ."

"Look, if we're already done, we can talk, right? Where's the worst place this can go?"

"I don't know when I knew," he said eventually. "After we moved in, I guess."

"I knew as soon as I saw you dance," she said. "I decided." Hayley slid down the mattress until the blankets came up to her chin. "The thing about deciding," she said, "is I never had to think about leaving. Because when you love somebody, you don't leave over one thing, you know? I couldn't just march out the door because I'd had a bad day. That's ridiculous."

She wished she had that picture of the beach.

"And we were *headed* somewhere," she said. "But what's the point if it only works if you're headed somewhere? Shouldn't it work when you're sitting still? When you're stuck?"

He sounded cautious. "Are you okay?"

"Ya know, I am." She stretched. "Had a couple hot toddies."

"Stop there, Hal. You'll feel like shit tomorrow."

"Thank you," she said. "I mean it. Thank you for caring like that."

"I didn't want this," he said. "You there and me here."

"I know," she said. "Did you want me?"

"Always."

She realized she needed to rephrase. "Did you want me when I didn't want what you wanted?"

He didn't answer.

"Deciding is different from knowing," she said to him—and to herself. "I'm sorry."

"But I was happy with you," Kevin said. Hayley wondered where he was. Whose floor he was crashing on. Maybe he was on a couch.

"You were sometimes," she said. "But not in Columbus. Now that you're home and I'm here, aren't you a little relieved?"

Again, he didn't reply. She imagined the stars.

"So we're over?" he finally asked.

"Yes." There was power in allowing herself to let go. She was crafting her universe.

"Because of him?"

Hayley thought for a long moment. Would she be here if she hadn't met Nick? Would she be happier? "Would you take me back if I asked?" she asked Kevin. "Right now?"

He hesitated. "If—"

"That's why we're over," she said simply. "Too many ifs."

47

Nick told himself there was nothing particularly fancy about the lobby of the Icarus Showcase, but he still felt awkward as he walked up to the front desk. Maybe the statuesque blonde behind the counter was throwing him off. She glanced up as he came in, then took another look and held it.

"You're Nick," she said. "Or else I'm a bitch."

Nick gave that some thought. "So if I wasn't Nick . . ."

"That'd be bitchy, wouldn't it? Assuming the disabled guy who walks through the door is the disabled guy I know?"

He smiled; Hayley had told her best friend about him. "Hi, Denise."

"Hi, Nick." She looked him up and down.

"Deciding whether to kick my ass?" he asked.

"Well," she said, "you haven't called her."

"Had to do this first."

She crossed her arms. "It took you a week to get here?"

"Aren't all the stars of Icarus here on Friday night?"

Her expression had an irritated intensity, like she was working on getting food out of her teeth. "What the hell are you
doing here, Nick?"

"I want to talk to Kevin."

She raised her eyebrows. "You do."

"And I've got all weekend to make it happen."

Without looking away, Denise picked up the phone behind
the counter and pressed a button.

"I've got Nick Freeman out here for Kevin," she said. "Yeah.
Yeah, I know. I'll see."

She hung up. "You've got about five minutes until the preshow meeting," she said. "And he's not coming out here."

Nick smiled. "Care to lead the way?" he asked.

Denise led him into the theater, her high heels clicking on
the polished marble floor. The whole place was a little too sleek,
but the theater itself wasn't a huge departure from where he'd
spent the summer in Columbus. Sturdy chairs, big tables, bigger
stage.

Denise reached the entryway to the floor seats and stood
aside. Kevin was leaning with one arm on the edge of the stage,
watching him approach.

Once he'd reached him, Nick said, "Can we talk?"

Kevin shrugged. "Go ahead."

Nick glanced around. There were at least a dozen people in
the room.

"Talk now," Kevin said, "or not at all."

Nick cleared his throat. "Hayley didn't cheat on you," he
said. "I kissed her once when you were still together. I was drunk,
she was trying to help me, and I responded by disrespecting you
both. I'm sorry I did that, and I'm sorry I led you to believe she
ever did anything inappropriate. She never even looked at me
that way before you left."

Satisfied that he'd said what he needed to, Nick turned around and started back toward the hallway.

"You came all this way," Kevin called, "and you're not going to apologize for hitting me?"

Nick kept walking. "You called her a bitch, Kevin."

"You just came here to be a dick, then."

Nick turned back. "I came here because I needed to talk to you in person. I'm not going to be the reason you two don't work out."

Kevin shook his head, started toward him. "You know she's not coming back," he said. "You just wanted to rub my face in it in front of everybody."

"You wanted the audience, not me." Nick kept his voice level.

"And *you're* the reason she's not here."

They were standing nearly toe to toe now.

"Tell you what, Kev." There was ice in Nick's voice. "If you tell me what I did, I'll let you deck me."

"You know I can't hit you," Kevin muttered.

"Sure you can. I'm giving him permission," Nick told their spectators. "He can punch me in the face if he can tell me what I did to keep Hayley Burke from being in this room right now, because I honestly don't have a clue."

The room got very quiet, and Kevin stopped glaring at Nick long enough to take in the crowd. His castmates obviously had no idea what was coming next, but they sure as hell weren't going to miss it.

"You had her talking like she didn't want to dance," Kevin said.

"Bullshit," Nick said. "How the hell could I do that?"

"Same way you got her to leave me for you."

"*What?*" Nick was speechless. "How could I . . . She's not . . ."
He wished he could shake Kevin by the shoulders. "She was with *you*, Kevin. She was with you for years, right here, and you were

the only thing she took with her when she left." He looked around him. "I mean, my God, she must've poured *all* of herself into this place."

Nick caught sight of the empty stage and imagined Kevin and Hayley under a Saturday-night spotlight before the glow had started to fade for her.

"I could get on stage with my man and feel it all melt away for a couple shows a night."

"All she wanted was you," Nick said, "and you couldn't see it. After all those dances . . ." Nick trailed off.

"Damn it, Freeman, raise your glass. To dancing with your heart."

"It's how I communicate, Nick. It's how I touch the world around me."

He had danced with Hayley too. For a brief moment, all she'd wanted was him. And he hadn't seen it any more than Kevin had.

"I think you can feel it. Our rhythm."

Dancing was give and take. Reacting, sparring, movement . . . But Nick had missed something.

"Just trust your partner."

Dancing was surrender.

Hayley had given all of herself. She'd trusted herself to Icarus, to Kevin, even to Nick, because dancing with true, unfettered joy meant leaping into the air and believing her partner was going to catch her. How many times had she fallen to the ground? How many times had she nursed bruises from people who just wanted to take from her? Nick had been so obsessed with helping her, protecting her, keeping her—but he'd never trusted her with the decision to stay. He'd never believed she'd catch him if he leaped.

"Oh my God," Nick said softly. "And she thinks it's her fault."

Kevin stared, uncomprehending. "It's not *my* fault."

Nick was barely listening. "Don't you get it? We want the spotlight, and she just wants to dance."

He locked eyes with Kevin, who seemed to be getting more uncomfortable by the second.

"We want the spotlight," Nick repeated. "You and I want someone to tell us we're amazing twenty-four hours a day because otherwise we don't believe it. Hayley wants the *connection*. We want to take from the crowd, she wants to share with them. She just wants to know she matters. She wants to be seen." He stared at Kevin intently. "Did you honestly think I could take her away from you? Did you think anyone could?"

Kevin didn't look too sure of anything at all. "You did."

"Oh, for shit's sake!" Nick exploded. "You didn't actually think she'd leave with the first guy who smiled at her. You were just afraid she'd figure out she could do better than you."

Nick looked around at this place Hayley had called home. Somehow he couldn't imagine her warmth here.

"Don't you get it?" he said. "She's so good at seeing what's good in other people that she actually thinks it's *her* fault when things go wrong. I told her she was beautiful, and she looked at me like she never knew. It doesn't matter how much you *tell* her, Kevin. She needs someone to *choose* her. She had to leave here because she was giving her all to this place, and all it gave back was a spotlight."

Nick remembered where he was and quieted a little.

"Look," he said. "Nobody makes Hayley do anything, Kevin. The best part of dancing with her is knowing she wants to. You have to believe she wants to."

Kevin wasn't angry anymore. If anything, as he watched Nick catch his breath, he looked a little sad. "You should go," he said.

"The show. Right," Nick said. "Are you going to call her?"

"I don't know."

"Well, if she calls you, don't hang on too tight. Let her lead."

Kevin hesitated. "Why are you helping me?"

"Because it's her choice," Nick said. "And I want her to be happy."

Nick was nearly at the lobby before he realized Denise was following him. "Can I hitch a ride?" she asked.

"Aren't you in the show?" he said.

"Nope," she said. "Just a choreographer this time around."

"So you want a ride to Columbus," he said, just to be sure. "With me."

"I'll chip in for gas if we swing by my place and you give me ten minutes to pack." Denise turned sheepish. "I don't have a car," she said. "And she needs a hug."

48

Hayley hated that she was happy to see Nick's car. It was a reflex, a calming as she spotted him coming down the street from her seat on the porch, as if he were about to pick her up for milkshakes. This was not the time to be sentimental. If he was here, he wanted something. She would not, must not, make any decisions based on what Nick Freeman wanted. She needed to shut down whatever he had planned before he got out of his car.

Hayley's determination lasted halfway down the front steps, and then she stood in disbelief and watched her best friend open Nick's passenger door.

"Sorry!" Denise rushed to get her bag from the backseat. "I should have just taken the bus, but you know how buses creep me out." She jogged up and hugged Hayley hard. "Sorry, girl. I love you."

"Love you too." Hayley looked over Denise's shoulder at the car and tried to put the two together. "How . . ."

"He came to me," Denise said. "He's not boring, that one."

Nick, still in the driver's seat, raised his hand in a tentative wave.

"He came to get you?" Hayley said in disbelief.

"Not even close. You should go say hi."

Hayley looked at her reproachfully. "I don't know what he told you, but I'm not ready to say hi."

"Then go tell him that. He'll go away, and we can talk about how much we hate him."

She was fine until about three steps from the car, when her heart started pounding. Nick took off his sunglasses and rolled down the window. "Hey," he said.

"I don't want to talk to you," she said.

"Okay," he said. "Can *I* say something? Three things, actually?"

Hayley had practiced refusing him dozens of times, but she hadn't anticipated him being so calm.

"Three things," Nick said. "Then I'm gone. Forever if you want."

She didn't want him to be gone forever. She wanted him to be here, with her, always, but letting him in now would be just another decision made for the wrong reasons. "Go ahead."

"One," Nick said. "I'm sorry. I should've just trusted you, but all I could see was what Kevin thought of me. I was afraid you saw me that way too. You never gave me any reason to think that, but I guess I'd spent so long expecting to get hurt that it was easier to focus on the pain. I should have believed in you. You don't deserve anything less than that."

"I'm sorry I called you a cripple," Hayley blurted out.

He shrugged. "I deserved it."

"No," she said firmly. "Never. Kevin was wrong to treat you that way."

"And I was wrong to treat you like a prize," he said. "It was hard for me to believe you'd choose me, and when I thought you wouldn't . . . I tried to hold on too tight. But it'll always be your choice, Hayley."

She crossed her arms. "Two."

"You're not a failure," he said. "I don't know what you're blaming yourself for, but I really don't think Icarus or Kevin was your fault. Certainly what happened between us wasn't your fault. Sometimes your dance partners aren't worthy of you."

She gripped her arm to stop her hand from trembling. "Are you?" she asked.

Nick looked down at the steering wheel, thinking. After a moment, he said, "I wasn't ready for you."

Was he ready now? How could she be sure?

How could she know she was ready for him?

"Three," she said.

He held her gaze. "I love you," he said. "I didn't recognize it, and I couldn't say it, but I love you, and I've loved you for a while. I don't expect that to change things or affect your decisions. But I wanted you to know. You asked me if I'd ever been hooked, and I have. Just once, when you smiled at me."

Joy flooded her, sweeping away the tension in her chest, and she very nearly said *I love you too*. It wasn't a choice, but a reaction, a response that didn't need any thought. But thinking about it had never been more important.

"Thank you," she said instead.

He nodded once. "You're welcome." He put on his glasses and reached to roll up the window.

She took a shaky breath. "Nick?"

He looked at her. "Yes?"

"What do you want?"

"You." No ifs, no hesitation. "I want to keep dancing with you."

Hayley knew she should head back into the house after he drove away, but her legs didn't get the message.

"How'd that go?" Denise walked up beside her.

"You said he didn't come to get you," Hayley said. "Why was he there?"

"Kevin."

Her eyes widened. "What? Tell me."

"I don't have to," Denise said. "The video's on my phone."

49

There was no contest, Nick decided. Not even close. Vivez Dance was better than Icarus.

Even if Vivez hadn't had cake.

"It's good that she feeds us," Cal said, putting a plate on the table in front of him.

"Uh-huh." Nick lifted a fork. "I'm so surprised you think so."

"I'm saying I have a theory," Cal said. "Feeding us gives us more calories to work off, which makes us dance harder."

"What am I supposed to do, then?"

"You just keep running your mouth."

It was Labor Day, a week or so since Nick's trip to Indiana, and in accordance with tradition, Vivez Dance was having an end-of-season party. It was time to give the seasonal help a proper send-off, and that time was ten in the morning, because tech week started after lunch for a show that opened Friday night. Nick had been told his attendance was absolutely required, but he would've come regardless. He was even a little disappointed he wouldn't be around for tech.

Nick asked, "How's my favorite person today, Cal?"

"Mimi is retrieving potential musical talent," Cal said.

Nick squinted at him in mid-bite. "She's what?"

"Uncle Nick!"

It was a sneak attack. Rosie must have crept across the room before yelling at the top of her lungs, because Nick only had a second to drop his fork before she took a running jump at him. Fortunately, he was no stranger to sneak attacks.

"Rosie Bear?" He swept her off her feet. "What a fantabulous surprise, baby girl! You came to our party!"

"Mommy and Daddy came too," she said, pointing.

"I see!" Mel and Gavin were standing a couple tables away with a grinning Mimi by their side. "Rosie, this guy here is my very good friend Calvin. Calvin, this is my best friend, Rose."

"Well, hello, Rose!" Calvin crouched down. "You can call me Cal if you want. My buddies all call me Cal."

Nick watched expectantly, but he saw something completely new: Rosie beamed at Cal and gave a shy little wave. "Okay."

Cal grinned. "Would you like to come with me to get some cake?"

Rosie nodded. Cal picked her up, and she hugged him around the neck.

Nick started to chuckle. "Oh, wow."

"Don't start," Cal warned him.

"Whatever you say, lady-killer." Nick walked over to the Becketts while Cal and his admirer went in search of cake. "Rosie has a crush!" he informed Gavin.

"I'm not worried," his friend said. "She can't date until she's old enough to rent an RV."

Nick laughed, turning to Mimi. "Not that I'm not happy to see the Becketts, but . . ." Something clicked, and he grinned at Mel. "Please tell me I'm looking at potential musical talent. *Please.*"

"Don't get too excited, Nicky." Mel tried to look annoyed, but she couldn't completely hide a smile. "You'll be up there with me."

"Mel called me, wondering if we needed some entertainment in our little café." Linda Brandazzio strolled up to them. "And I told her to come to the party. Now I'm telling you there is no way we're *not* having you play in Adagio."

Mel smiled politely. "I appreciate it, but I'd want to audition."

"You already did," Linda said. "I used to catch your solo set at Carmany's downtown. Have you seen her do 'Uninvited'?" she asked Nick. "Hot damn!"

Nick laughed. "Couldn't have put it better myself."

"Come with me," Linda said. "We need you up front."

Nick knew better than to object, and soon he was standing in front of the Vivez crew.

"Attention!" Linda called. "Attention, my darlings!" There were chuckles as everyone settled obediently. "As you know, this is the time when we say goodbye to one season and hello to another. We had many a returning star join us for the summer, but we only had one addition to our family." She highlighted him with a grand sweep of her hand. "Mr. Nick Freeman!"

Everyone from Linda to Rosie applauded, and Nick was overwhelmed. He hadn't set out to gain so many friends, but here they all were, smiling at him.

Linda continued, "Today Nick will be playing my favorite game, which is . . ."

Nick jumped as the crowd roared back at her. *"Five things we love!"*

"We here at Vivez are very enthusiastic about singing one another's praises," Linda told him, "so at some point we had to limit the count to five. I'll start. Nick is one of the best teachers I've ever had the pleasure to know." The compliment almost brought Nick to tears now that he understood how deeply Linda meant it and the difference he'd made to her son.

"Nick brings us doughnuts!" someone yelled from the back. Nick tipped an imaginary cap amid more laughter and applause.

"The man can duet," Cal said. "Not everybody likes singing with someone else, but my boy knows how to take a duo up a notch."

"Nick listens," Mimi spoke up. "Doesn't matter if it's serious or ridiculous, as long as it matters to you."

"Uncle Nick is my best friend!" Everyone laughed as Rosie hollered, and Nick blew her a kiss. She grinned as she caught it, then looked up the ramp to the back of the room and went wide-eyed. Nick couldn't see what had her so excited, but Cal could, and he set her down to run off at full speed. Mel or Gavin must have circled around with some cake.

Linda said, "That makes five. And normally we'd get all teary-eyed about Nick leaving, but today we will not, because he is not." A murmur went through the room; not even Cal or Mimi knew about this. "Mr. Freeman will be staying on as Vivez's official archivist, filming each of our shows and maintaining our digital database. He'll still have free run of the place, so everybody behave in the green room." She turned to Nick. "And it is an understatement to say we'll be happy to have you."

The crowd started clapping again, and Nick wanted to respond with more than a smile. These people had given more to him than he ever could to them.

"Could I say a few words?" he asked Linda.

Linda smiled. "Of course!"

The room quieted expectantly.

"This wasn't a job I applied for," Nick said. "I didn't even think it was a job I was suited for. I'm embarrassed to say it now, but I thought Linda was throwing me work because of my condition."

"You mean that great hair?"

Cal got some laughs, Gavin among them, and Nick shook his head with a grin. "I have something called cerebral palsy," he said. "I don't know how many of you know, or care, but telling you now and showing off these"—he gestured to the leg braces that were visible thanks to his new khaki shorts—"is my way of saying, if it doesn't matter to you, it shouldn't matter to me."

A lump in his throat surprised him; he paused.

"It took me too long to realize it really doesn't matter to you guys," he said. "You welcomed me and you included me and you loved me." He pointed at Mimi and Cal, who were now standing together. "Especially you two. And you know I will always love you back. Linda's asked me to help Vivez figure out how we can better involve artists and patrons with disabilities here, and I'll give it my best shot, but the truth is we're all different. We all have different capabilities and passions and preferences, and as long as you guys are as kindhearted and generous and attentive with everybody who walks through that door as you were with me, I can't see how anyone could possibly have a problem belonging at Vivez. This job, this place, is one of the best things to ever happen to me, and I can't thank you enough."

Nick was looking at Cal and Mimi during the applause that came next, and because the three of them were busy trying not to cry, he barely registered movement as someone made her way down the ramp from the back of the room. Eventually, the clapping stopped, and Nick took a seat at the nearest table.

"Can I say what I love about Nick?" a new voice asked.

Nick turned around so fast he wrenched his back. Hayley Burke was quickly weaving her way through the tables to the front. She was gliding, even with Rosie on her hip. And she was wearing her Chucks.

"Absolutely," said Linda. "All, this is Hayley Burke, our newest member."

Hayley stopped in front of Nick, and he looked up in amazement as his two favorite girls smiled down at him.

"Hi," he said.

"Hi." Hayley handed Rosie to him. "You stay here with her. We can't have you trying to steal my moment."

Nick perched Rosie on his knee as Hayley joined Linda at the front of the room.

"I'm Hayley," she said. "I can't wait to dance with you guys. For a while I thought I was done with the stage, but the truth is I just need the right one. There's nothing I love more than truly dancing with others, and I dream of being in a creative community where people care more about one another than they do about impressing everybody else. I really think I've found that here." She looked at Nick. "I'm hoping I've found a partner too."

Everyone was watching Nick now. It seemed ridiculous somehow, like he should stand up and correct her. *Sorry, guys, there's no way she's talking about me. She can't be looking at me with so much joy.*

"I used to think finding a partner was about magic," Hayley said. "As long as you found that rhythm, that fit, then nothing else mattered. And then I thought it was about work. I thought you could make the magic if you tried hard enough. Now I know it's about both. You have to find a rhythm that's worth the work. You have to *want* to work on it together."

He thought of all the times she'd held him up, put an arm around him, helped him climb and kept him from falling. *"Easy does it. We've got this, rock star."*

"Nick Freeman is the best dance partner I've ever had," Hayley said. "We've got more magic than I know what to do with, but even so, we've stepped on each other's toes more than once. I think we . . ." She paused, met his eyes. "I think we see the light in each other more than we've ever been willing to see it in ourselves. But Nick *fights* for that light, you know? He fights to shine for others so that nobody he meets will ever doubt how important they are. He brings out the absolute best in his partner. That's what I love about Nick. When I dance with him, I'm completely me."

Nick ached to jump out of his chair and wrap her in his arms. He wanted to tell her it was the other way around, that he never felt stronger or lighter than when she was by his side—but of course, she'd anticipated this and put a three-year-old in his lap.

"None of this is really my style," Hayley said, "but last week Nick took a trip to talk to someone who doesn't like him very much, in a room full of people who weren't on his side, and he actually tried to do all that for me without me finding out. So now that he's taken a risk in front of all my friends, I wanted to come here and do the same for him." She walked over to his chair. "Rose, can you help Uncle Nick?"

Rosie jumped off his lap and started tugging his hand. "Come on," she said. "I'll help you."

Nick got to his feet and into the walker, and the little girl stood proudly by his side.

Hayley said, "I'm sorry, Nick. I'm sorry I hurt you, and I'm sorry I didn't listen, and I'm sorry I'm just telling you now. But nothing I've ever cared about this much has turned out right, and I had to be sure I wanted this for me, instead of because I was lonely or because my parents could see how happy you make me. I didn't want your feelings to make a difference."

She was beaming, and he could see her heart in her eyes.

"Did they?" he asked.

Hayley shook her head. "Those three words didn't make a difference," she said. "But when I looked back on everything you've done, everything I know, I realized you never needed to say them."

Then, before a breathless crowd, she held out her hand.

"Wanna dance, rock star?"

Nick reached for her. "More than anything in the world."

Hayley squeezed his hand and spun neatly into his arms. "I love you, baby," she said. Her arms encircled his neck. "You're the sky."

He kissed her, and they danced.

EPILOGUE

Three months later

Mimi Ranier stuck her head into the green room. "A14 is asking for you."

Nick put down Louise Penny's *Still Life*. "This isn't a trap?"

"Yes, Nick," she deadpanned. "The Grinch is waiting at table A14."

Nick sighed, stood up, and followed Mimi out the door. "I hope you experience real terror one day, Mimi."

"It was a *doll*, love."

"It was *life-sized*, Mimi dear. And let me tell you, when you look in the rearview mirror and see that green bastard leering back at you from your own backseat . . ."

"You don't know what size the Grinch is in real life."

Nick and Cal had recently started an escalating war of holiday pranks with Hayley and Mimi, who had become roommates so they could afford to live in a first-floor apartment with doors wide enough for a walker. Having her own space was important to Hayley after living with Kevin for so long, but it was just as important that her new boyfriend be able to visit as easily as possible. Mimi couldn't have been happier: The roommates got along famously, she'd convinced Nick to sample her extensive collection of paperback mysteries, and she had ample time to herself when Hayley was depleting the chocolate supply at Nick's place.

Nick was trailing Mimi through a bustling kitchen as she scooped up a couple trays. "It can't be this busy every night," he said.

"Nonstop until Christmas break." Mimi grinned. "And I love every second of it."

The annual Vivez holiday show wasn't just on the weekends—it sold out every night from just after Thanksgiving to just before Christmas, and the Vivez crew only had Sundays off. Seating was underway for the seven thirty show on the first Saturday in December, and Nick had never seen so many people doing so much at once, or doing it so well. Up until five minutes ago, he'd been in the green room just to stay out of the way.

They emerged out of the swinging kitchen doors and split off as Mimi headed for the higher sections and Nick for the floor seats. He was so focused on navigating the crowd that he nearly collided with a woman standing at the bottom of the ramp.

"Sorry about that," he said, steadying himself.

"My fault." Kacey with a K turned to face him. "I should get out of the way."

They stared at each other, surprised.

Nick cleared his throat. "Can I help you with something, or . . ."

"No," said Kacey, and then blushed a little at how quickly she'd replied. "I was headed back to my table."

Nick looked out at the room. "But you don't want to fight through all these people."

"I'm worried I'll trip someone with some trays or something," she admitted.

"They know what they're doing," Nick assured her. "Come on, I'll block for you."

"Oh, you don't have to . . ."

"Least I can do," he said. "Where're you sitting?"

"A14."

He looked at her, confused. "You didn't . . ."

"No." Kacey smiled this time. "But I'm sitting with people who did."

He grinned back. "Then let's go."

They set off across a sea of people, dodging servers and scooting in chairs, and Nick thought about sitting across a booth from Kacey with a K. Had it really been more than six months ago?

"Hello!" he announced grandly as they approached. "I've been told that . . ." He went wide-eyed as he gaped at the table. "*What?* No way!"

Theo the bouncer grinned and offered him a fist bump. "Happy holidays, man."

"Hi, guys!" Nick took hugs from Stephanie and Alexa. "Who's minding the bar?"

Elliot turned in his seat to shake Nick's hand with a grin. "The Friday night crew isn't the only crew, dude." He put his arm around Kacey as she took the seat next to him. "I heard you've met my girlfriend."

"I have," Nick said promptly. "Did she tell you I was a jackass?"

Elliot laughed. "She left that part out."

"Well, I was, and I'm sorry," Nick said to Kacey. "Date night's on me."

"Seriously?" Elliot said. "Thank you, man."

"My pleasure." Nick felt fingertips trail across his back as someone passed behind him. "Who's your server?"

Stephanie smiled. "Who do you think?"

Nick glanced to his right and saw a glimpse of Hayley's violet T-shirt through the crowd. "Well, when she gets back here," he grinned, "make sure and tell her you two are on my tab. Enjoy the show, okay? I'll come back after."

Kacey put a hand on his wrist as he turned to go. "You look different," she said.

"So do you," he said cheerfully. "I like the haircut."

"No, I mean . . ." She seemed a little sheepish. "You've got a glow, if that makes sense."

Nick grinned. "That makes perfect sense, Kacey, and I'm thrilled you're here."

Of course he had a glow. He was done working a room to dull his pain; now he did it because he was good at it. He still hit the Squeaky Lion once a month with Gavin, but now most of Nick's Friday and Saturday nights were spent here, chatting with the cast and bringing lesson plans to the green room, so his weeknights were as free as Hayley's. He liked sharing this world with her when she was working, and he loved it when she swept by with a fleeting touch, as she had just now in the midst of holiday chaos. Just a whisper of connection, a reminder their dance had never stopped.

He made his way to table A6, and Tom Burke looked like Christmas morning had already arrived. "Should I get the rig?" he asked Nick.

"I think it'd be best for all of us if you did," Carolyn said drily from beside him.

Nick laughed and nodded at Tom, who dashed off to the back of the room. "I'm reading a book," he told Carolyn. "Voluntarily."

"No need to strain yourself on my account," she said. "You're already my ideal son-in-law."

He started to laugh, and then her words sank in. "Carolyn . . ."

"That's not a request," she assured him gently. "But I know you love her, and I know she loves you. So just in case you were worried, I wanted to give you an early Christmas present and say Tom and I would love nothing more."

Nick was overwhelmed. "I'm going to hug you later," he said.

Carolyn laughed. "Go contain Tom."

The Burkes had been to Vivez several times in the last three months to see their daughter dance; they were here tonight because Nick was going to film it. Nick was now standing a safe distance away as Tom Burke wheeled a large platform against the back wall and locked the casters into place.

"It won't move on you," he said. "I promise. And I double-checked the railings earlier."

Nick stepped forward. "Tom, this is awesome."

This was the rig. Once word had gotten out that Nick would be regularly filming Vivez shows, Tom Burke and his merry band of handymen had leaped into action to create this. Three concentric squares were stacked on top of one another, like the first layers of a broad pyramid. Two metal stair rails were mounted in one corner, and a waist-high railing ran around the perimeter of the top level. At the top sat a chair in front of a high-quality digital camera on a swivel mount.

Nick could easily leave the walker on the ground, use the stair rails to climb the steps, walk along the railing to the chair, and operate the camera from his perch above the crowd. He could do all this without assistance, just because Mr. and Mrs. Burke had decided to use their time and money to make it happen.

"Go on," Tom said, delighted. "Climb on up."

Nick obeyed without breaking a sweat, and then he was grinning down at the older man, hands on the railing. "This is perfect," he said. "Seriously. A game changer. I owe you."

"No, you don't," Tom said cheerfully. "There's only one other person in the world we're this happy to help."

Nick was peering through the camera and adjusting settings when he heard someone bound up the stairs behind him. Hayley leaned over his shoulder and kissed his cheek.

"Picture for Rose," she said.

Nick leaned back as both of them beamed into Hayley's phone for a selfie and looked at the result. "Aw," he said. "Send me that one."

Hayley did. Rosie, of course, did not have a phone, but she was permitted to enlist her parents to take one picture a day for Uncle Nick and Hayley, usually at bedtime. They'd made a game out of reciprocating as soon as possible.

"Did she send one just now?" Nick asked. Hayley showed him Rosie's latest, texted to both of them, and he laughed. Rosie was snuggled up in pajamas next to Mel, and both of them were laughing hard.

"Mel told me to remind you about rehearsal tomorrow," Hayley said.

Nick snorted. "Like I have ever once forgotten about rehearsal."

"Probably because she reminds you," Hayley teased. "The show's almost sold out, by the way."

"Really? We're a week and a half away."

"I've already sold half a dozen tickets tonight."

Nick couldn't wait for his return to the Adagio stage. This would be his fourth monthly gig with Mel in the Vivez café, and it had become so popular with patrons and crew alike that the Vivez singers were bummed to have to do the holiday show that Wednesday night instead of joining Nick and Mel on stage to croon a little.

Hayley came around the side of the chair and dropped into Nick's lap. "Hey," she said playfully. "Why'd you do that?"

"Do what?"

"Could've just left that girl alone."

Nick laughed. "I wondered if you recognized her."

"I did." She put her arms around his neck. "And you were very kind."

"You know," he murmured, their noses almost touching, "everyone can still see us up here."

She nodded solemnly. "We'll have to explain that I can't go onstage until you kiss me."

So he did. Nick pulled her close, savored her lips on his, and didn't stop until he was absolutely sure that all of him had said to her, clear as a bell, *I choose you.*

"Wow," Hayley murmured. "I'm coming back for more at intermission."

He grinned. "Love you."

"I love you more than chocolate, baby."

Then she whispered familiar words in his ear, dashed down the steps, and slipped effortlessly into the whirlwind below.

For twenty minutes, Nick Freeman sat above the crowd and watched a woman with olive skin and joyful brown eyes glide from table to table like she was skimming across a lake. Nick saw all she could do and all he would never do; he chose the beauty in each of them, and the beauty in who they were together.

As the house lights went down and the show began, Nick thought of the six words Hayley had whispered in his ear, the words they told each other every day.

Thank you for dancing with me.

AUTHOR'S NOTE

Nick Freeman and his story are products of my imagination, but his disability is mine. Cerebral palsy varies widely in its types and symptoms, and I gave Nick my exact condition so I could write about it as vividly, accurately, and specifically as possible. All of the physical elements of Nick's experience with CP are lifted from my own life, but it's important to note that even those details are informed by personality. For instance, Nick and I have the same hand controls in our cars, and we both live in first-floor apartments, but I had to give some thought to how Nick would navigate a karaoke stage, because I'd be more likely to sing from the floor than go through the trouble of climbing steps without railings. Nick, however, would want to be front and center, above the crowd—and he would climb those steps like a rock star.

ACKNOWLEDGMENTS

First and foremost, thanks to God for this book. It took the better part of a decade for Nick and Hayley's story to reach bookshelves, and this journey from inspiration to publication has divine fingerprints all over it.

Thanks to my wonderful agent, Leslie Zampetti: You saw my potential, you champion my efforts, and you're so good at your job that you're frequently providing assistance I never even know I need. Thank you for teaching me to ask for help!

Thanks to my fantastic editor, Jess Verdi: I'm blown away by how deeply you love this story and how well you understand what makes it special. Thanks for making this book shine and taking such good care of Nick and Hayley—your enthusiasm made this process so much fun!

Thanks to the team at Alcove Press for all they've done to make this book a reality: I treasure every bit of your hard work.

Thank you to Ana Hard for creating a cover so beautiful it literally brought me to tears: You ably captured the mood of the book and gave me a gorgeous picture of the couple I've been writing about all this time.

Thanks to the people who were kind enough to critique the book along the way, these friends from whom I received such valuable feedback and support: Andrea Davis, Megan Hargest, Kim Letso, Emery Lord, Jenelle Miller, Christine Nadalin, Tony Snyder, and Don and Katie Thompson.

Thanks to Mary Shullenberger for reading, for cheering me on, and for Mimi.

Thanks to Kate Johnson: This book is better because of you.

Thanks to Victor Sabelhaus for the Squeaky Lion and for all the years we've spent talking about stories while surrounded by too much junk food.

Thanks to Sonya Huber for encouraging me to write this story, showing me how to improve it, and telling me I had a "real goddamn book" on my hands once she'd finished reading it. Those three words kept me going for years.

Thanks to Joe Mackall, who taught me that good writing and good living require the courage to examine who you are and what truly matters to you.

Thanks to all the metaperformers of Shadowbox Live, past and present: To steal some words from Nick, you welcomed me, you included me, and you loved me—and I will always love you back. This book wouldn't exist without you.

Thanks to my family: I love you for so many reasons and for every single time you asked about the book, listened to my answer, and gave me the gift of your perspective and support. Knowing you're proud of me is the best feeling in the world. Thanks to my sister, Katie, for sharing her publishing knowledge, and to my brother, Thomas, who offhandedly suggested that Nick should share his occupation. Recasting Nick's job changed so much for the better.

And thanks to Philip Gerard, acclaimed novelist and my uncle, who provided treasured encouragement and advice for this book—and my entire writing career—before he passed away in 2022: You were the writer I always wanted to be, and you dedicated your life to showing writers how vital it was to be themselves. I'll love you and miss you always.

For years, I've posted about this book on social media and concluded those posts with the same words: Thank you, as always, for caring. If you ever asked about this book, if you ever cared about this book, if you bought this book or mentioned this book or you're reading this book right now, thank you. I hope Nick and Hayley's story brings as much joy to you as your support has brought to me.